To Jess
your inlaws
Duan Vadlen Evans

I dedicate this story to Kylie my beautiful daughter for her support and encouragement. Her caring heart has touched my work and my life.

Copyright 2020
Ravenword Publicizing
Second Edition

All rights reserved. No part of this publication may be reproduced or transmitted in any form or by any means, electronic or mechanical, including photocopying, recording, or by any information storage and retrieval system, without prior written permission from the Publisher.

-Forward-

In my stories I like to impart some history where I can. There is a heroic spirit in the old west forged by heartbreak and triumph. It calls to us. In our struggles we find strength.

Bad Water is fictional, but behind the story are sepia tones of true events which I hope reveal some of the richness of our past.

As a writer of historical fiction, I have qualms about inserting real people into my stories. Yet truth is never what it seems. It is merely one man's perception colored by his own perceptions. With any given incident, one can find multiple tales, all differing slightly. So what is truth?

Knowing this, I research historical events and the people involved, then take the commonalities and try to find as much truth as possible.

I have my own opinions about the actual participants in the Lincoln County War. It was a sad time in history when evil prevailed. In life, the bad guy sometimes wins. Because of this I am not too kind in my treatment of the real characters I placed in Bad Water. In my opinion, they were despicable men who deserve no respect, and I have no problem painting them with a brush dabbed in the dark hues that stained their souls.

In some cases, I make them an amalgam of several men of the same ilk, while in others I will leave their name unchanged perhaps seeking a small measure of justice postmortem.

As for Billy the Kid, while a killer and a horse thief, he was basically good; a youth who had the misfortune of growing up in a very evil place. He was better than most of the men in power during the time of the Lincoln County wars.

My story however is not about Billy or the dishonest men of power who shaped his life, they are the backdrop for a family torn apart by hate. It, too, is a story of heartbreak and triumph.

Bad Water

By
Duane Vadron Evans

Bad Water
Chapter 1
Dry Ground

Crow Crossing wasn't much more than an unsightly scar carved from a grassy knoll where the desert got a little less greedy allowing a few acres of tillable earth for any down-on-his-luck homesteader fool enough to try a shovel.

Four slat board buildings connected by an uneven boardwalk made it a gathering place though no one would've dared call it a town. The dilapidated structures protruding dark and dismal upon the barren point jutted into the hostile land like an accusing finger warning travelers to beware.

The only reason Crow Crossing existed at all was because two trails going pretty much nowhere happened to cross in the dry wash below the knoll so the word 'Crossing' seemed to fit.

It's said that Jasper Crow followed a deer trail into the country forty odd years back on his way to California, and being a mite drunk and not knowing which direction to take just plum gave up.

The lopsided cabin at the higher end of the boardwalk, Crow built himself, and after his untimely death at the sharp end of an arrow it laid abandoned until it was finally turned into a blacksmith shop.

Ruben Stang who knew Crow at the end of his life, built his house next to him so they could share supper and spirits together. The two cantankerous curmudgeons whose vulgar ways no decent women could abide, consoled themselves in the solace of slovenly bachelorhood with ample amounts of rum.

It was Ruben who named the joining of trails Crow Crossing in honor of his departed friend who he would often lament in tearful tribute with a raised bottle, then punctuate his eulogy by calling Jasper a son-of-a-bitch for up and dying on him.

A number of years later Ruben met a similar fate though by then the Indians were using Winchesters. Ruben might have gone on living, but it was beyond him to part with his beloved brew of which the thirsty renegades also desired.

Martin Hayes came next. Being an enterprising fellow, he built the last two structures and finished off the boardwalk Ruben Stang had started.

Martin's wife, Emma, assumed the responsibility of running the dry goods store on the east end. She also pops into the adjacent structure to serve a meal when called upon; money being what it is.

Ruben's old house in the middle of the row was turned into a saloon befittingly called Rubens. Folks who knew Ruben said if he looked up from hell, he'd be right proud. Spirits once more flow freely in his old home and a sign above the door proclaims; No Injuns allowed. If a patron happens to spill his drink which occurs with great regularity, everyone shouts, "that's for you Ruben," then they all laugh and go back to drinking. Yes sir, that's Crow Crossing, don't spend your time looking for a whole lot more, you won't find it.

With the sun burning the haze from the top of the hills, it was pleasantly warm for a winter morning and not a bad day to sit a horse. Molly Creed slim of figure, brown haired and dark eyes that flash with every emotion, balanced a yellow wicker basket in front of her on Queenie the old plow mare. Jean Marie her pert thirteen-year-old held on behind chattering nonstop while Will, Jean's younger brother by two years, marched quietly in front holding the reins. His worn leather boots made a soft crunching sound as they broke through the thin layer of frost permeating the brittle desert soil. With little snow, their grassy valley laid in muted shades of brown marking the passage of nature's calendar between the bright colors of fall and winter's patchwork blanket of white.

The ride took less than an hour from the Creed farm to Crow Crossing where Molly hoped to sell her eggs to kindly Mrs. Hayes. It was their Saturday morning ritual, and as usual they got a late start. Jean, ever hopeful a Lincoln County boy might happen to be at the crossing, refused to leave the mirror until every curl was in place. This time of day most boys were likely farming or herding cattle, but Jean struggling with the insecurities of youth couldn't risk the off chance a young lad might catch her at anything other than her very best.

Jean craned her slender neck over her mother's shoulder. "Don't know why we can't live in Lincoln or even Silver City; a real town Mama. They've got schools. There is so much a girl needs to know these days. Why I'd have my very own books."

Molly smiled and paid no mind to her daughter's daydream. Young Will however couldn't help muttering. "Only thing you want to know about books is who's going to carry 'em for you."

Scrunching her face, Jean shouted. "Will Creed you shut your mouth. Iffin' a boy wants to carry my books home, well it's none of your concern. Mama tell Will to mind his own business."

Rolling her eyes, Molly admonished her son. "Will, don't get your sister in a lather or we'll have no peace."

"Ma!" Jean Marie protested with her usual effusive indignation. "It's Will who gets me all fired up. I wasn't thinking no such thing about boys, and nothing wrong if I was. William would do well to learn how a proper boy should treat a refined girl, carry her books, opening doors n' such, then maybe he'd wait for me without complainin' and we'd have some peace."

A lengthy silence followed Jean's outburst where she felt she'd made her point and was about to let it drop when her brother somberly queried, "You don't know how to open doors?"

"Ma!"

"Children! It's a beautiful day, can't we just be a happy family for a little while. Least ways not make a scene in front of Mrs. Hayes."

The road while basically straight as the crow flies meandered left and right and up and down as it traversed a succession of small gullies which trickled into the Ruidoso.

Coming to a grassy field where the road stretched out for some length, Molly noticed two men riding towards them through the morning haze. As the distance closed she recognized their faces. It was John Tunstall and Alex McSween. Molly cautioned her children in a strained whisper. "No more bickering. Please don't embarrass me."

Tunstall, an Englishman, and McSween, an easterner, were very prominent men. They along with old John Chisum were the kind of visionaries who brought hope of prosperity to Lincoln County. It was sorely needed with the Murphy Dolan stranglehold that now cast a long shadow over the once peaceful valley.

Molly brought the mare to a stop and smoothed her frayed gray cotton dress as the tall men came along side. Mr. McSween smiled politely. "Morning Mrs. Creed. Nice day for a ride. Sure good weather we are having so early in the year."

Tunstall tipped his hat but said nothing, allowing McSween to lead the conversation though he kept his eyes keenly fixed on the young widow. Like her, he was single, and while she was beneath his station, he couldn't help being drawn by her feminine manners as she tilted her head, hiding a shy smile in a cascade of thick brown curls.

Alex McSween glanced bemused at his tongue-tied friend then turned back to Molly. "Haven't seen you in Lincoln for a while. Susan was asking about you at breakfast this very morning. So few women out here. You must come to dinner while the weather holds." Smiling graciously at his offer, Molly nodded. "Thank you kindly Alex. You tell Susan I said hi, but what with chores and children, I'm not sure when I'll make it."

The men tipped their hats again and rode on. Molly knew a trip to Lincoln was unlikely with only her old plow horse. A petite woman perched on a giant mare plodding down Main Street would surely draw snickers if not outright laughter. The embarrassment would be too much, but she couldn't admit it to such distinguished men. It was her desperate hope there would be day when she wouldn't be shamed by her poverty. For now, pride would keep her home.

As the Creed's dappled mare lumbered up out of the winding ravine, the low winter sun momentarily blinded them. Shading their eyes, the dark outline of irregular rooftops began to take color. Doors and windows appeared like old familiar friends. Several horses already hitched outside Rubens proclaimed that drinking had started early.

A tall freight wagon was being loaded with supplies in front of the Hayes store. Emma would be more inclined to buy their eggs with money in the 'til. Molly's heart quickened.

Leaning forward Jean excitedly pointed. "That's Jimmy Webb's sorrel, and Bobby Maxwell's bay."

Just then the lean boys came out of the store with grain sacks hoisted on their square shoulders. Jean stifled a squeal as they heaved their heavy burdens up into the wagon before stopping to acknowledge her arrival with eager smiles. Pretty girls were a rare sight.

Stepping to the edge of the boardwalk, Jimmy even tipped his hat. He was always the polite one.

With a glance back at her daughter, Molly cajoled. "Looks like ol' Pete got some help loading the judge's wagon, and you've just stopped the work."

"Mama!"

The boys were a few years older than Jean but she didn't care. Boys, too, were a rare sight for a wishful young girl trapped on a farm on the backside of nowhere as Jean put it.

Being sympathetic, Molly took the reins from Will and eased the mare up to the hitching rail alongside the wagon. "Mornin' Pete."

Molly's voice was monotone as she addressed the older man, but she flashed a genuine smile for the boys. "Mind helping us ladies down?"

Blushing, Jean whispered. "Maa..."

While Bobby dutifully took Molly's basket, Jimmy happily reached up and set Jean on her feet. "There you go Miss Jean, light as a feather."

Jean blushed. "Thank you, Jimmy. It's so difficult in a dress."

Young Will tied off the reins mumbling under his breath. "You didn't have any trouble getting up there in a dress."

A menacing sneer darkening her face, Jean swatted at her brother. "You shush Will." Just as quickly she reclaimed her sugary smile and turned back to the boy who was still holding her by the waist. "Jimmy was just being gentlemanly."

"Morning Mrs. Creed." Ol' Pete stood up in the wagon stretching his back as if he'd been doing the lifting. "Still holding on to the farm are ya'? Lotta' work for a woman."

It was false concern and Molly answered with cold silence. Pete spat his chew on the dry earth and prodded a little harder. "The judge has offered you a fair penny."

Molly briefly held her tongue as she stepped onto the boardwalk, but her temper got the better of her. Turning she fired back. "And a penny it was."

She lifted her chin as much from an old wound as from Pete's meddling. "I may be a woman, but I can raise my crops as well as any man and I will not sell my husband's farm to the scoundrel whose shadow hangs over his grave."

The foreman frowned and spit again but this time with unveiled anger. "You aughten' be talkin' that-a-way, what got your husband in trouble. Fences are few n' a man only owns what he can hold onto. You may be able to hoe a pretty row Mrs. Creed, but who's gunna' defend it?"

Molly's knuckles whitened against her basket. "You tell me Mr. Briscolm. Have the Boys stooped to murdering defenseless women? Does the judge now feel a penny is too much to pry from his heavy purse?"

"Mrs. Creed, if you are referrin' to the Boys, them are Jessie Evans doins, not the Judges. You best be showin' him some respect n' not throwing around accusations you can't prove if you know what's good for ya'. These are hard times n' that skirt only protects so much. The Boys, as you call 'em, may well pay you..."

The old man clamped his mouth shut. He'd let his anger get the better of him and had said too much.

Starting again, he softened his tone. "Sorry Mrs. Creed, but you best be real polite to the judge. He's an important man, and you should...well..."

"Remember my place? Good day Pete." With that Molly hurried inside and slammed the door behind her. "Old coot." She muttered to herself.

Leaning against the door she took a needed breath and did her best to put the unpleasant man out of her mind. There was business to take care of.

As she calmed herself her eyes adjusted to the dimly lit room. Amber sunlight filtering in through the east facing window cast a warm glow across the cluttered store. Dust particles drifted lazily in the air settling on everything that stayed in one place too long.

Mingling with the dust a heavy scent of spices permeated the musty room reminding Molly of her mother's kitchen long ago. It made her feel safe.

Regaining her composure, she stepped away from the shadowed entrance with a hopeful smile. "Morning Mrs. Hayes, appears to be a busy day."

The older woman looked up from her ledger. Her hair was pulled back in a bun with arrant strands of flaxen and gray falling gently across her rosy cheeks. Setting down her pencil she scooted from behind the counter with a soft inviting chuckle. "Dear, dear Molly when you call me Missus instead of Emma, I know you are here to do business. It is Saturday, isn't it? How time flies. Well let's see what you got in your basket. I was just going over to cook some breakfast for the men if they are sober enough to eat without emptying the vile contents of their stomachs on the floor. Rubin wouldn't like that.

"Oh good! You baked bread too. Big card game last night. Win or lose morning finds them boys hungry as bears, bragging or making excuses."

With a sigh of relief, Molly set her basket on the counter delighted that Emma was in a buying mood.

As the older woman reached into the till, Molly cast a glance back at the door, her brow wrinkling. "Saw the men hanging outside of Rubens, and... Ol' Pete out front. Everyone appears a mite tense."

Emma's smile faded. "Bob Casey down on the Hondo was killed last night. Seems like every morning we wake to murder and no rain. Poor winter we're having. Guess the good Lord is savin' up for a flood. With all the sinning around here can't say as I'd blame him if he washed Lincoln County clear to the sea."

Outside the store young Will, sour faced, uttered a single word. "Mush."

His sister's sugary discourse with Jimmy Webb turned his stomach. The boy was tempted to yell; 'He can't work if you keep hanging on him,' but if Jimmy could put his sister in a better mood, he'd leave well enough alone.

Looking for something else to do, Will walked the opposite direction. The sharp ringing of the blacksmith hammer in the cool morning air drew his attention to the other end of the boardwalk.

Old Drifter was lying contently in his usual spot to one side of the door. Even at that distance the shaggy hound spied the boy and wagged his tail.

Will glanced back at his sister. "Mush," then bounded down the walk in long loping strides that pounded out an eager cadence on the loose planks. Sisters were okay, but they certainly didn't compare to no dog. Skidding to a halt he knelt by his old friend. "Hey Drifter." Drifter wagged his tail even faster and sniffed Will's pockets. "Are you hungry boy? Shame you don't have no owner; havin' to beg for scraps."

Will pet the dog's gray head. "Sorry I ain't got nothin'. Near as poor as you."

The dog looked up with sad eyes as though he truly understood and perhaps he did.

Young Will scooted closer. "When I grow up you can come live with me. We will go hunting rabbits together. Maybe the two of us could tree a bear..."

Just then a tall stranger in a weather stained canvas slicker ducked out from under the roof sheltering the blacksmith's forge at the west end of the boardwalk. He was leading a dark stallion.

Shiny nails in the horse's hoof explained the ringing hammer. The somber man showing as much wear as his coat, paused and looked down at Will. An honest smile brightened his stubbled face. "Looks like Drifters' found himself a friend."

Will cradled the dog's head in his lap. "He's real hungry. Heard his stomach growl. Poor pup."

With a soulful expression meant to reflect the dog's misfortune, Will stared up at the stranger. "Real hungry."

Peering out from under the brim of his hat, the man's stern eyes softened. He'd been there a time or two himself. Taking a moment to fish under the flap of his saddlebag, he turned and knelt by the pair of street urchins,"here."

In his hand were two strips of dried jerky. "Give him this. Have one for yourself."

"Thanks Mister!" Hanging one strip out the side of his mouth, Will offered the other piece to the dog. "Here fella."

With a cautious nose and an eager mouth, Drifter made quick work of the tasty morsel while the boy compassionately petted him.

Will bit off a piece of his own, chewed for a moment then looked into the sad eyes of the dog. "I guess you need this more than me. There ya' go."

Drifter wagged his tail again, accepting the second act of kindness.

Leaning forward, Will laid his ear on the dog. "Can't hear his stomach anymore." He looked up at the man. "I think he's happy now."

"Life is brighter on a full belly." Reaching out a weathered hand, he stroked the mutt. "Yes, I'd say Drifter has found a good friend."

Will smiled gratefully at the stranger happier himself. "You need a dog Mister?"

With a soft chuckle restrained by some unspoken sadness, the stranger shifted his hand to the boy mussing his hair. "Ol' Drifter wouldn't be able to go where I go. Beside I think he'd miss your company."

From behind the young lad, a woman's terse voice snapped. "I thank you to take your hand off my son."

Stunned, the stranger stared at the woman then turned his startled eyes to the boy. "Will!"

There was a long pause where the air hung heavy and no one breathed. Then rising slowly, the stranger came to his full height and held a moment longer. Sadness flickered in his blue eyes as hatred burned in the woman's. Without a word, the stranger tipped his hat and backed away stealing a final glance at the boy.

He took the reins and threw a leg over his saddle then rode away leaving his story untold.

Coming from behind, Jean caught up with her mother and clutched her arm. "Mama he knew Will's name. Who is he?"

The color drained from Molly's face as she stood rigid watching the man disappear. Jean repeated her question. "Who is he Mama?"

Extending a beckoning hand to her son, Molly answered through clenched teeth. "He's bad water."

Will hurried to his mother's side. Feeling her tremble, he looked up confused. "I don't understand."

Molly pulled the boy close. "Bad water." She spit the words. "He poisons everyone around him."

Bad Water
Chapter 2
Reflections

Holding the small door ajar, Molly stared into her children's room. Jean lay in the lower bunk, her long honey brown hair now in braids. Though thirteen and boy crazy, she still slept with her favorite doll tucked beneath her chin, with the innocence of childhood gracing her delicate face. Morning would find her vocal and defiant, but bathed in silver moonlight she was Molly's precious angel once more.

Will slept in the top bunk. On a wooden peg at hands reach was his single shot rifle, a gift from his father on the day he was born. In spite of his young age, Will managed to keep much needed meat on the table, usually rabbit, squirrel, or grouse. It was a man's size responsibility that he took without complaint. Each morning he'd quietly disappear into the fields or wander down by the creek, and if necessary into the hills, never returning empty handed. Her son was a good shot. When they couldn't afford bullets, he'd bring home fish even in the dead of winter. The boy was growing up strong.

Molly rested her cheek against the wooden doorway. How much he looked like his father. She nearly wept. He was just three years old when John died, and for Molly struggling to raise the children on her own the wound had never healed.

Reluctantly she closed the door and turned away. Her weary eyes trailed apprehensively across the cluttered room seeking assurance their family was safe. Outside the air was calm, no wind to knock menacingly at the door or rattle loose window panes. Tonight it was quiet, too quiet. It was as though she dared not exhale lest her breathing awake some slumbering evil in the dark.

Their small three-room home on forty acres was all Molly owned. It was her little patch of earth, a humble haven for her children, yet increasingly it seemed like an elusive dream that might easily slip away.

Holding the lamp high, Molly walked past the large stone fireplace heading back to her room on the opposite side. Morning comes when the rooster crows at first light, though she doubted she'd get much sleep; too may thoughts.

Dropping down on her soft feather bed, Molly picked up a silver framed picture from the nightstand. It was of her and John on their wedding day. Ever so gently her slender fingers touch the polished glass, lingering. Yes, Will looked so much like his father. She was surprised Cole hadn't recognized him there on the boardwalk.

Her anger flared. Molly set the picture down. It should have been Cole who took that fatal bullet and not his younger brother.

Blowing out the light, Molly hid beneath the covers. She had begged John not to go that night eight years ago, but he worshiped Cole and would follow him through perdition's gate.

The warring parties in Lincoln County were too powerful. There was the Murphy Dolan faction that started it all, the John Kinney Gang, Jess Evans and his rustlers known as the Boys, and the Seven Rivers Warriors; they were too many and too dangerous.

The law was corrupt all the way to the governor or the Santa Fe Ring as they were called. Far removed from the rest of the civilized world, the New Mexico territory had collapsed into total villainy. Even the U.S. Army was involved in murder and mayhem. There was no way to reach beyond the borders for help, no one cared anyway. New Mexico had become a battleground.

Molly believed it was best to lay low and let the wave of hired assassins pass. These murders and cutthroats would ignore the smaller farms if they didn't take sides, but Cole wouldn't be pushed. To him and men like him, the gun was the only answer. And what had he accomplished? Widows were left to weep and fear the night. A score of good men dead, among them his own brother.

Curling into a ball, Molly hugged her pillow. It should have been Cole who died. To her he had. She killed him in her heart.

The last time she saw Cole was at John's funeral. Unable to bear his sight any longer she screamed and cursed him, telling him to never come near her or the children again. He was bad water and she would not let him poison her family with his violence anymore.

The passing years had not eased her grief or lessened her hatred for the infamous Cole Creed. She wanted him to know the loneliness that tore at her heart each night, but men like him have no sympathy for a woman's tears, all they know is death.

As far as Molly was concerned Cole Creed was a killer as lawless as the men he battled. His hands were stained by those he laid low and the blood of his own brother as well, the last of his kin.

After the funeral Cole disappeared, left the territory they said. Tales were told by passing strangers that he'd been killed in Colorado or died battling Mexican soldiers across the border. People seemed to delight in fanciful yarns about Cole Creed, but no matter how many times he was reported slain, his name would pop up time and again in some distant conflict; his fame growing. Now he was back in Lincoln County.

A neighbor said that Cole had bought the old Jaramillo place only a mile away. They say he rounded up a hundred head of wild cattle from Injun country, just him and two Mexican brothers. It was considered nothing short of amazing; taking cattle right under the Apache's watchful eye. Others had tried and died for their efforts.

Molly knew better. There were stories. John had told her about Cole and the Apaches; said they were friendly to him; said he could ride right into their camps unmolested. There were accusations that Cole had secreted rifles and ammo to the Apaches for safe passage, but no one could prove it, or would dare say it to his face. Cole may have been able to dodge the law and his crimes remain unproven, but he was as deadly as any that now set flame to Lincoln County. That was like Cole, seeking out danger, conspiring with savages and shady characters alike. He had known Earp, Holiday, Masterson and other men who lived by the gun. Hell rode on Cole Creed's tail.

Molly pulled the blankets close to her cheek. Why did he have to come back? She had enough trouble dealing with Judge Warren Brewster. She didn't need black sheep kin stirring up trouble and bringing the judge's wrath down on her family. Brewster was powerful, but Cole worried him. Cole didn't care about the law, leastways in Lincoln County. Neither was he impressed by gunmen like Jess Evans, Bob Olinger, or Billy Bonney. Cole lived by his own law, appointing himself judge, jury and executioner as it suited him. And being that his name was Creed, every sin he committed was shared by Molly and her children.

Overcome by worry and fatigue, Molly slowly surrendered to sleep with two words lying bitter on her lips. "Bad water."

"Mama...Mama, wake up."
Rolling over Molly moaned and pulled her long auburn hair from her face. "Is it that late honey?"
She knew it was. The sun was already shining through the dusty window.

Jean's brow wrinkled. It wasn't like her mother to sleep past sunrise. "Don't you remember the O'Donalds' are coming for supper. Do you want me to have Will kill a chicken?"

Rising up on a stiff arm, Molly glanced out the window again. "It's Sunday. I forgot."
"Are you okay Mama?"
Throwing the blanket aside Molly set her bare feet on the cold wooden floor. "Yes. Just didn't sleep much."

Jean plopped down on the bed and leaned her head on her mother's shoulder. "Mama, you been thinking about that man we saw yesterday? Haven't seen you smile since. Who is he?"
Ignoring the question, Molly got to her feet and pulled Jean with her. Let's not talk about him. It's Sunday and we've got a meal to fix."

Jean ducked her eyes. "Mama, Jimmy Webb might stop by..."
"Oh darling." Taking her daughter by the shoulders, Molly gave her a stern parental stare." Did you invite him?"

The young girl blushed. "No Mama, not really. I just told him we were having a meal, bragged about your cooking, and said it would be nice to see him." Her words trail off. "Sorta..."
Molly sighed. "Oh, Jean Marie, if I don't watch you every second, you will be married by the time you are fifteen."
"Mama you were married at fifteen."
Shaking her head, Molly defended. "Fifteen and a half...okay fifteen and two months, but I just want you to slow down. Times were different then."

Jean smiled hopefully. "Then Jimmy can come?"

"Guess he already is." Molly opened a drawer looking for a fresh blouse. "I'm not saying you did right, but folks have to be polite, and we can't very well uninvite him, now can we?"

Turning back to her daughter, Molly's eyes narrowed. "But you know Jimmy works for Judge Brewster. No good can come of it. I just wish you would find a boy more like our own kind."

Jean dropped her hands to her side and stomped. "Mama that's not fair. Jimmy weren't more than seven when Papa died. He had nothing to do with the killings."

Molly shook her head in protest. "Water takes the color of its surroundings. I said he can come, but that boy already wears a gun, and I saw a notch on the handle."

"Mama, that was for a coyote..."

Slipping on her blouse, Molly refused to listen. "I don't care. You tell him to hook his holster over his saddle horn before he comes inside. I won't have the O'Donalds thinking we've taken up with outlaws and rustlers."

"Mama he's not an outlaw. He's just a boy."

"Doesn't mean he won't throw a rope on another man's brand if told too."

Ending the conversation, Molly threw open the door. "Will! Your sister invited a boy. With Tom and Annie, Chad, little Polly, and Grampa Charlie, that makes nine. It would sure help if you could get some nice fat grouse so we don't have to slaughter the hen house." Molly cast an accusing glance at Jean as though one more mouth made all the difference."

Heading back into her room, she scooted Jean out with a swat to the rear. "I got to get dressed. You best get plenty of potatoes from the root cellar. Watch out for snakes."

Outside the bedroom door Jean stood silent for a moment ruffled by being dismissed so abruptly, but she got away with just a mild scolding for inviting Jimmy. That changed her mood. Rather pleased with herself she giggled mischievously tossing her hair from side to side. The rest of the morning would be spent in front of the mirror making sure Jimmy never thought of the meal no matter how tasty it was.

Skipping to the front door she threw it open. Her little brother was already heading thought the gate with his rifle. "Will, before you go Mama wants you to get potatoes from the root cellar, and watch out for snakes."

"Sure's nice you havin' us over Molly."
Tom took a bite of a hot biscuit and wiped the melted butter from his chin. "My little Annie is a good cook, but lately she's had to fix a lot of meals for the church. Seems like Lincoln County is filling up with widows n' orphans. Mighty nice of you to give her a break."

Annie smiled up gratefully, her eyes sparkling. At twenty-four she was younger than her best friend by four years, but age didn't matter. They were two peas in a pod. Besides even after the tragic death of Molly's husband and rearing her children alone, she still looked youthful, often being mistaken for Jean's sister and not her mother. It was something the two young mother's giggled about while trying to recapture their youth. Molly's youth had been snatched away but the hardships drew them closer, and they dearly loved each other.

Grampa Charlie set his drink down with a heavy hand as though the tin cup were a gavel. "If we had an honest governor instead of that Santa Fe mob, we'd get the army down here to clean up this mess right quick. Them Murphy Dolan toughs would be sent packing."

At the opposite end of the table, Jimmy Webb shrunk into his chair. The judge often had him run messages to L. G. Murphy & Co, or the Big Store as the locals called it. He had seen Jess Evans there a time or two, but that didn't mean Mr. Murphy or the judge were doing anything wrong. They were just protecting their interest and cleaning out nesters. Jimmy started to protest, but couldn't quite muster the courage.

He cringed looking miserable. Annie sensed his discomfort and took pity. "Let's not have such unpleasant talk. It's Sunday and we are sharing a delicious meal with neighbors and kin. There's still good in this valley...Jimmy would you like another biscuit to sop up that gravy?"

The boy was happy for her smile. "Thank you ma'am. They sure are temptin'."

Jimmy's eyes darted to Grampa Charlie. Folks around Lincoln County called Charlie O'Donald a colorful fellow, other called him just cantankerous, but today he had a little more bile than usual.

"Saw them Olinger brothers n' Andy Boyle ride down my fence line plain as day, lookin' around, eyein' things as if they had a right too. If ya' got so much as a milk cow ya' better lock the barn. I tell you when them filthy Seven Rivers Warriors come crawling out from under their rock in broad daylight, trouble can't be far behind."

"Now Grampa we are not going to talk about such awful doings. You'll just get indigestion." Annie smiled sweetly but let a subtle reproach sharpen her words.

"Fine meal Molly." Tom leaned in his chair and patted his belly to back his claim. He grinned wide. "Why I'm as stuffed as that ol' turkey."

Reaching to his side he placed a hand on Will's back. "So three bird with two shots. Pretty fancy shooting."

Will shrugged. "Just planned it that way sir. Shot low so I got two side by side, then got the last on a dead run with a steady shot laying down. Nothing fancy."

Mr. O'Donald refused to be dissuaded. "You should take Chad with you next time, most as old as you. He could learn from a dead eye like Will Creed."

Grampa Charlie gave Jean a wink. "I wouldn't mind another piece of that blackberry pie there, Sweetheart."

Eagerly taking the plate from Jean's hand like it was his first piece instead of his third, he turned to her brother. "My son is right young fella. Fancy shooting. Got the Creed blood in ya'. Dead eye and steady hand just like your Uncle Cole..."

"Grampa!"

Annie's terse scolding stopped him in mid-sentence but it was too late. The room fell silent.

Will looked up confused. "My uncle?" His eyes searched the veiled faces of the adults. Jimmy Webb's lips parted as though he would answer, but he clamped his mouth shut and lowered his head.

As the silence grew Annie exhaled. "Never mind son. Grampa is just prattling."

The old man realized his slip-up. "Sorry Molly. No offense. A full belly makes the mind soggy. Especially an old one. Sorry."

Will looked to his mother, but the strained expression on her face told him he'd better not ask any further questions.

Forcing a paper-thin smile, Molly breathed. "It's all right Grampa Charlie. Enjoy your pie." She looked to the others. "Everyone have some pie."

A clattering of plates and forks resumed around the table dismissing all thought of Grampa Charlie's remark. Tom spoke to the boy hoping to break the tension. "Did you shoot the berries too?" Will grinned. "No sir," then glared at his sister. "Had to leave something for Jean to do. I chopped the wood, bucketed the water and got the potatoes."

Feeling not the least bit guilty, Jean scrunched her face at Will. "If it's outside it's boys work. Besides a girl needs time to make herself pretty." With a quick sideways glance at her mother, Jean stabbed her tongue at Will, then quickly conjured a smile for Jimmy while daintily tugging at a curl. "Want some pumpkin pie Jimmy? I add sugar and spice."

Hiding behind his fork, Jimmy grinned knowing full well what she meant.

"More milk to help you with that pie Jimmy?"

"No ma'am. It's delicious pie Mrs. Creed." He wiped the flaky crust from his mouth. "...but two slices are enough for me. We don't eat like this at the bunkhouse, just beef n' beans." The boy set his fork down. "Best meal I et' in the longest time. Iffin' you don't mind I would be obliged to be excused ma'am. Got to get back to work."

"Certainly Jimmy it was nice having you over. You are a polite boy." Molly cast a forgiving glance at her daughter. Jimmy slid his chair back, nodded courteously to everyone and headed for the back door with Jean quietly at his heels.

Noting the concern on Molly's face as the kids scurried away, Annie stood and put a gentle hand on her shoulder. "Come on dear, I'll help you wash the dishes. Everything will be fine in no time. Don't pay Grampa Charlie no mind."

On the back porch Jimmy scanned the surroundings, his young face drawn by fears unspoken. "I best be going Jean before ol' Pete has my hide."

Something told Jean, the boy was more scared of facing her than his ill-tempered boss. Itching with curiosity she hurriedly stepped in front of Jimmy blocking his way.

The glint in her eyes stopped Jimmy in his tracks. He'd seen that look before.

Putting her hands on her hips Jean cocked her head to let him know she meant business. "Jimmy you tell me straight out what Grampa Charlie meant."

She took a step closer. "I saw the look on your face. You know something...tell me, tell me or I'll burst."

Jimmy turned away hiding his eyes in the distance. "Well heck it's okay Jean. Not your fault."

"My fault?" Shocked, Jean reached for the boy's arm. "What's not my fault?"

Fidgeting, Jimmy relented. "Your uncle being a killer n' all. Not your fault. Every family's got skeletons."

"Jimmy Webb what are you talking about? I don't have no unc..." Jean's hand flew to her mouth. She suddenly remembered the man at Crow Crossing. He called Will by name. "My uncle!"

Seeing the expression on Jean's face, Jimmy began to realize that she really didn't know. "Maybe you were too young Jean. Heck I was not yet eight, but I remember the stories. Him n' your pa. The judge said Cole Creed was the bad one. Your pa just followed him."

Jean shook her head in disbelief. "Mama said our father was bushwhacked and nobody knows who done it."

Sympathizing with Jean's distress Jimmy awkwardly took her hand and tried to comfort her. "Maybe that's so. What do I know? Just stories. Like I said I was young, but now that your uncle is back and runnin' cattle on the old Jaramillo place, people are worried."

"My uncle lives down the road?"

"There could be real trouble Jean. Heard the judge talking to Jess..." The boy bit his lip. "Jean I best go. Spoke too much. Pete will have my hide for sure. I'll see you around."

"No Jimmy! Wait! The judge was talkin' with Jessie Evans about...my uncle?"

Wiping his hands on his britches Jimmy kept edging sideways trying to get around the persistent girl. "Well he had too. Jessie is the only one as fast as Cole 'septin maybe Billy Bonney which ain't no good, him being a friend of your uncle, n' not likin' Mr. Dolan. Jean I gotta go."

Scooting around her, Jimmy quickly climbed on his horse. "Like I said, it ain't your fault."

Standing in the shade of the doorway, the crisp air stinging her cheeks, Molly watched with a motherly concern as Will and Chad headed off into the sagebrush carrying their rifles. Tom stepped up beside her and tucked his thumbs in his belt. "Molly I know you don't want to talk about it, but having Cole back could be a good thing. The unsavory element has been shying away, not wanting to cross his path. Even the sheriff has been staying out of Crow Crossing. They don't know if Cole has come back to ranch or settle old scores."

Molly slowly closed the door without looking up and started clearing plates off the table. "The quiet before the storm Tom. They're regrouping, and when they come it will be in force. Next time they won't pass us by."

Setting a stack of dishes in the wash basin, Molly's eyes unconsciously drifted to the window. "Yes, eventually they will come. Their greed will consume our valley like an unquenchable fire. Good grazing land is scarce, and what us farmers got of it nestled in these low hills is precious little, but they want it all. They will clear us out."

She turned and faced Tom. "Cole might be just the excuse they need to come riding in. It's one thing to murder innocent families who weren't doing nobody harm, but to say they were defending themselves against a famous killer and say we were behind him..." Molly couldn't bear the thought. "Damn him."

Coming to her side, Annie put an arm around her. "Now Molly you're just getting yourself all worked up. Sure they've tried to scare us all out, but that's a long way from sending marauders in the dark of night. We still have some law...or something like it."
Molly turned in her arms. "Annie, he's no good."

Struggling up out of the rocking chair where he'd been brooding, Grampa Charlie shuffled into the light and cleared his throat. "I may be old n' talk too much, but I can count. Not but eight small farms left out here when there was double that last fall. Most of them that left were bullied or burnt out. The rest are buried in Boot Hill like your Johnny. No one ever names who done the killin' but we all know just the same. When that twisted pair at the big store ain't holdin' hands, n' makin' eyes at each other, they're plottin' to get our land. Somethin' fishy about how they handed out them deeds. Maybe that's why they want 'em back."

Shocked by the old man's accusations, Annie scolded. "Grampa Charlie, you stop that. Such things shouldn't be spoken of."

Ignoring Annie's outburst, Grampa Charlie turned around and shuffled back to his chair. "If I was thirty years younger I'd be riding with Cole myself."

Tom let his hand trail across his Winchester left leaning against the wall; a reminder it was no longer safe to travel without it. "Grampa's right. They're picking us off one by one. Cole might not be the answer but the judge ain't buying him out, and that's got to make Murphy and Dolan stop and think."

Turning back to the window, Molly shook her head. "All Cole can do is add fuel to the flames. We got to find another way."

The autumn sun was setting low. Anxious to talk with her mother Jean sat on the top rail of the corral moping. It seemed as though the O'Donalds would never leave. Will and Chad had returned long ago and were now locking the chickens in the hen house.

Without a sister or a best friend to talk with she felt very much alone. Wandering to the barn Jean climbed the ladder into the hayloft as she often did when she needed to think.

Heavy with thought, Jean plopped down on her stomach. She had an uncle who her mother never told her about and he was living right down the road. Why had he been kept a secret?

Rolling over she put a straw to her lips and stared at the rafters. An uncle! The thought wouldn't leave her head. Jean tried to recall the face of the stranger she saw on the boardwalk. He was tall with piercing blue eyes. That was all she could remember; those dark piercing blue eyes. He was a killer no less and the sudden turn of events had left her shaken. She didn't like having her world turned upside down.

Over her head, a tiny spider hanging from a single web caught the sun drawing Jean's soft brown eyes upwards. The spider was so small the light passed right through it making it nearly invisible. Stretching out her arm, she pointed a finger at it. "Little spider, I'm just like you, lost in a big world that don't know I exist."

Jean had always felt small. Her family was small. They often had to rely on the charity of men from the surrounding farms to repair fences, shingle their roof and bring in a store of firewood for winter. Without a father of their own to protect them Jean felt helpless, always fearing an ill wind might blow them away like dried leaves that nobody would notice.

It seemed like all the grown-ups talked about anymore was the warring factions. For a young girl who had no say, it scared her. "Little spider we are both hanging by a thread. How do you keep from falling?"

As if answering, the spider crawled up its web and hid in a crack between the timbers leaving Jean alone. "Maybe I should find a hole of my own."

She curled in the hay wrestling with the shame of having a killer for an uncle. It wouldn't have occurred to her to feel shame, but Jimmy's gushing defense of her made it clear she should be embarrassed, as did her mother's silence. But then again, for the first time they weren't so invisible. Important people like the judge who never gave them a second thought now feared and maybe even respected her family. What would become of it all? It was too much for Jean to wrap her mind around. She really needed to talk with her Mama.

Coming out of her trance, she lifted on her elbows; and turned her thoughts to Jimmy. How dare he hide secrets from her. She bit the straw in two. "Jimmy Webb I'll make you tell everything you know..."

In her ever-changing moods, a quick smile brightened Jean's face with the prospect of seeing the handsome boy again. He may rue the day, but she would see him for sure. For good or ill, she was born of Creed blood and as her grandpa used to say, Creeds were stubborn as a tree stump growing out of rock once they made their minds up.

Jumping to her feet, Jean went to the window and stared west towards the setting sun. She leaned her soft cheek on the rough wooden sill wondering if she'd ever get to meet her mysterious uncle. Raised with Creed determination Jean rose to her full height. Yes, she would meet him. She would see to that too.

Bad Water
Chapter 3
Searching for Answers

There was no carved stone, just a painted board sticking up from the dry earth. No green grass to comfort a grieving soul or flowers for remembrance. It simply read, 'John W. Creed' Beloved husband and father.

Molly stood quietly, her folded hands holding a paper rose she had made. In reverence she whispered. "I'm trying hard to forgive John. But no one knows how difficult...or how lonely the years have been without you."

Molly dropped to her knees, a courageous smile at odds with her tears. "Will looks so much like you. You would be proud of him. He's a hard worker and keeps meat on the table. It's a heavy burden for an eleven-year-old boy."

Struggling to quell the anguish welling inside her Molly sat quietly staring at the lonely grave. The only sound to break the silence was the mournful cry of a whippoorwill flitting above the distant meadow.

At length Molly lifted her head, a smile suddenly spreading across her damp face. "You'd laugh at Jean...or me I guess. Your little girl has grown up to be as stubborn as her ma. They say she has your smile and my temper. She is beautiful."

Molly's head dropped back into her hands and she sobbed. "I'm trying to forgive. Really I am. I know you wouldn't want me to hate him, but he took you from me as sure as if he pulled the trigger. I miss you so bad and I need you. The children don't understand there's trouble coming and I can't stop it. I want to run, but there's nowhere to go, and it doesn't seem right that we should be driven off our own land. We had such dreams, and now there's only surviving.

"I love you John. If you have any pull up there. We could sure use a miracle right about now. Send me a guardian angel. If there is any justice between heaven and Crow Crossing, I can't find it."

Wiping her cheek, Molly slowly got to her feet. Her mind was numb, but she felt better. She usually did after her visits with John. Backing away she whispered, "Goodbye my darling."

It was a long walk back and the pale sun was pleasantly warm. Lifting her skirt, she took fast strides almost breaking into a run. She wanted to hide from everything. For her children she had to be strong, but when she was alone fear and grief tormented her. Nights were the worse. She felt so isolated, so small, needing to be held. How she missed Johnny's strong arms.

Perspiration breaking on her forehead Molly ran herself out and returned to a walk. Once again she'd worked herself into a miserable state and felt foolish for it.

In the distance she could see Jean walking towards her. Molly could tell by the young girl's stiff posture that she was worried and had come to find her.

Slowing, Molly checked her face not wanting any trace of tears. She took a deep breath, threw her shoulders back and forced a smile, once more becoming the courageous mother her children needed.

As Molly got closer, Jean stopped and waited, her face a hollow mask betraying her deep concern. "Hi Mama."
Fearing her voice might break; Molly simply took Jean's hand and kept walking. For now, it was enough. Mother and daughter were together. The road was gentle and the monochrome shades of winter fit their mood.

After her heart had calmed Molly flashed Jean a smile letting her know everything was okay. She sidestepped and bumped her daughter's shoulder. "You don't need to come looking for me. I'm the mother."
Jean returned her smile. "Mama it's been almost a week since Grampa Charlie spilled the beans about...well...are you ever going to

tell me anything? People been talking. Seems like everyone knows 'sept me and Will. It ain't fair?"
"Isn't fair."
"Well Mama it isn't. Is he as bad as they say? A killer like Billy the Kid. Will said he was real nice to ol' Drifter. I don't know what to think. Please Mama."

Molly had hoped that her children would never find out about their uncle, but deep down she knew it was inevitable. "Oh Jean honey. There are men who are fathers and there are men who leave widows and orphans in their wake. Cole doesn't see right and wrong the way decent folk do. It's best to forget him."
"Cole. That's the first time you said his name. It makes him seem more real to hear it from your lips."

Jean swung her mother's hand and skipped a step to stay up with her. "Mama, why don't I remember Uncle Cole?"
"Oh Jean..."
"Please Mama."
"Baby, you were only five when your father died. There had been trouble before that and Cole seemed to be in the middle of it, so I told him not to come around. When he did, it was usually late at night after I'd put you to bed. Never saw any point in telling you about him."

Molly looked down at her daughter. "I know what's in that pretty little head of yours Jean. Don't be getting attached to the idea of having an uncle. He's..."
"I know Mama. He's bad water. But if he's a killer like they say then why haven't they hung him?"
"Jean!"
"Well why haven't they Mama?"

Molly quickened her step not wanting to answer. Jean pleaded. "Please Mama."
There was no escaping the girl's curiosity. Molly rolled her eyes. "Darling, a man like Cole takes a lot of killing. If someone wants him dead, they are going to have to want it real bad. I guess no one has yet, leastways no one who's come back to tell about it, but his time is coming. A man, who lives by the gun, falls by the gun. I just don't want you kids in the way when it happens."
"Would he hurt us?"
"No silly he would never hurt us."

Her curiosity partially satisfied, Jean strolled quietly by her mother's side. Behind her eyes danced a myriad of thoughts. She suddenly brightened. "He looked real handsome."

Molly couldn't help but chuckle. "All the Creed men are handsome, like your father. He was the most handsome of all."

"Did Pa like Uncle Cole?"

It was Molly's turn to go silent. They walked past several fence posts and it seemed as if she'd go right on home without answering.

"Mama?"

"Yes Jean, your father adored Cole. It was what got him killed. So don't be putting any stock in that."

"Just asking."

Down the way Molly could see Will in the yard chopping kindling. It was getting near supper time. She knew the boy would have water by the stove and a cord of wood neatly stack without her asking.

Jean tugged her hand, pulling her back. "Mama, if bad men came would Uncle Cole protect us?"

"Jean let's not talk about it."

"But Mama..."

"Yes, I'm sure he would. Now no more. You stay away from him. Is that understood?"

"Yes Mama."

"I mean it Jean."

"Yes Mama."

Lifting high on the long wooden handles, Tom dumped his wheelbarrow load of horse dung at the edge of Annie's garden. "There! That ought to keep you girls out of trouble for a while."

A green cloud of pungent dust settled over the women. Coughing, Annie and Molly's faces soured as they waved their hands in front of their noses. Seeming not to notice, Tom gave the wheelbarrow and extra kick to loosen the remaining dirt, winked at Annie then left without another word.

Annie blew her retreating husband an 'I love you too' kiss', then laughing leaned on Molly's shoulder. "I'm glad you came. Who knows when we'll get to work in the garden again. Silly, planting tulips when there is so much to do, but Tom doesn't seem to mind if I add a few feminine touches to the farm."

Molly placed a peck on Annie's cheek then stood and brushed the dirt off her dress. "If you hadn't invited me I'd be hurt. Jean too, she sure loves babysitting Polly."

The afternoon sun was already sinking beneath the snowcapped western hills. With sunny days few, time spent in the small garden behind Tom and Annie's house were all the more special. It had been a very mild winter, yet spring seemed as though it would never come.

Setting down her spade, Annie stood by Molly brushing off her own clothes and shaking her thick golden hair. "Dirty work and horse dung too. I think Tom did that on purpose."

Her lips suddenly parting in a naughty grin of pearly white teeth that seemed out of place on her dusty face, Annie beamed mischievously. "We could grab Jean, hop in my buggy and take a ride up to the hot springs for a late night skinny-dip."

Molly held up her grimy hands looking disapprovingly at her nails and broke into a smile of her own. "I'm so filthy we'd have to drain the spring when we are done."

The women laughed. Weighing the wisdom of the delightful dip, Molly arched her brow. "What about Tom and the boys?"

Annie, placed her hands on her hips trying her best to look defiant. "Not invited. Girls only."

She tugged on Molly's hand. "Come on it will be fun, and the water is so warm."

Giggling like schoolgirl conspirators, the pair bursting with excitement, hurried into the barn only to pull up short. Tom was kneeling by the buggy with the wheel off.

Annie stepped forward and hesitantly rested her fingers on Tom's broad shoulder. "We want to take the buggy up to the hot springs for a skinny-dip."

Sticking his hand into a can of black grease, he held it up to Annie. "Not in the buggy you ain't. Got to grease the axles. Am I invited?"

Annie slapped his shoulder. "Girls only. I'm not having you drooling over Molly. I can't compete with that figure."

Returning to his work, Tom shrugged. "Eh' I've seen Molly naked. Not much to look at as I recall."

Molly's mouth dropped opened in shock. "Why Thomas Charles O'Donald you have never seen me naked, and if you had you'd have plenty to recall."

Grinning, Tom winked. "Did too see ya' in your little pink birthday suit'...you was skinny-dippin' then too. It was the day that rascal Corey Martin surfaced behind you and threw a bullfrog on your back."

Tom laughed remembering. "You shot out of Conner's pond like you had a snapping turtle attached to your little fanny."

Molly stomped her foot. "Tom I was six years old, and that bullfrog was as big as a wildcat." She blushed. "Think I've changed a mite since then, so you can just stay here and grease your wheels."

Still grinning, Tom motioned out the barn door. "You girls can all fit on Queenie. Countin' Jean, you don't weigh three-hundred pounds soakin' wet. That ol' plow mare can handle you as easily as if you was horseflies. Get going. See if I care, and if a bullfrog lands on your back, don't come running naked to me. I don't want to see it."

With Molly in the middle working the reins, Annie holding her waist from behind, and Jean riding in front, the ladies plodded up the hill laughing and giggling. The tempting hot spring was nestled in a grove of thick trees a little more than an hour from Tom and Annie's farm. It was a merry ride.

Holding on to Molly, Annie leaned out to see Jean. "I can't believe you talked me into letting you bring Polly along. Tom could have taken care of her."

Cuddling the baby in her arms, Jean defended. "You said girls only and Polly is a girl. Besides, she will love the warm water...Won't you sweetheart?" Jean cooed to the bright-eyed child who busied herself tugging at Queenie's mane.

By now the night sky was scattered with stars, and to scare away the dark, the ladies sang The Yellow Rose of Texas over and over punctuating it with laughter when they messed up the tune.

Jean eager to prove she was a knowledgeable young woman with more than silly thoughts in her head, expounded on the legend of the song. She told of Emily West, a mulatto, and the battle of San Jacinto. Even Molly was duly impressed, though rather shocked to hear her own daughter talk about General Santa Anna having sex with Emily while Sam Houston attacked. "Baby where do you read such things?"

The young girl seemed quite proud. "You know Mrs. Hayes lends me books. I like stories about brave women."

Annie interjected. "Well then you should write one about your ma. She's the bravest woman I know."

Molly blushed. "Oh shush Annie."

"Well it's true."

"We're here." Molly pulled the reins bringing the slow moving mare to a stop. Annie, young and nimble, slid off Queenie's rump, then skipping forward took Polly from Jean.

After Jean climbed down, Molly prodded Queenie under a thick shaggy tree budding with new leaves, then dropped to the ground and tied the mare to a branch. Much of the grove was green due to the warm air rising off the spring, making the approaching spring seem already here.

Large smooth rocks at the water's edge provided a place for the girls to sit as they disrobed. With the eagerness of youth, Jean finished first. Taking the blanket off Polly she carefully slipped into the warm water with the baby cradled in her arms. "It's great Mama. Polly likes it."

Jean made her way to the far side of the pool where she could play undisturbed with her young charge.

Still giggling, Molly and Annie held hands for balance as they tiptoed between the rocks and made their way into the steaming mist. The secluded hot spring was oval shaped bordered in lush reeds and tall overhanging trees with a million stars shining overhead.

After a day of digging in the soil the pool was inviting. Annie settled beneath the dark water. "Oh Molly it's dreamy. I feel like a dumpling simmering in chicken broth."

Easing into the water, Molly teased. "Maybe you should have let Tom come. He would have found you delicious."

Annie laughed. "Tom's got a big appetite. I'm not sure he'd be satisfied with just one little dumpling. Seeing you, he'd likely toss in a rock and yell bullfrog."

The laughter died away as the women let the warm mineral spring work its magic on their tired limbs. Crickets along the bank chased away the silence with their soothing chirps, a music unto themselves, never out of tune.

Having floated a distance from her friend, Annie dipped her chin beneath the water and returned to Molly's side. The twinkling stars and a bashful moon hiding behind the clouds lent enough light to read the emotions on the women's faces. They both knew it was more than an evening dip that brought them here. A lot needed to be said. Beneath the water Annie found Molly's hand. "It's been eight years Molly. That's a long time. Aren't you the least bit interested in seeing Cole?"

Lowering her eyes, Molly silently shook her head. "No Annie. He's a killer."

With a quick glance towards Jean, Annie moved closer so they would not be overheard and lowered her voice to a soft whisper. "We were just kids then. Heck I was barely sixteen when Cole...well...when he left, and you weren't quite twenty; just kids."

In the starlight Annie could see Molly's eyes sparkle. Somewhere beneath her friend's anger there were still feelings. Annie lifted her hand from beneath the water and cupped Molly's face. "People change."

Leaning her cheek into Annie's tender touch, Molly nearly cried. "Oh Annie. People do change, but some for the worst. Seems like every stranger who rides through this lonesome valley has a story about the infamous Cole Creed."

Molly sniffed. "If half of them are true, he's killed a score of men." Annie thumbed a warm tear from Molly's cheek. "They're just stories; never saw any wanted posters on Cole. Maybe you should see him, find out the truth."

Turning away, Molly rested her head on a damp rock weary in body and soul. The sulfurous steam off the water was having a hypnotic effect. She closed her eyes and breathed in deeply. Cole had returned. She could never forgive him, but what really angered her was that no matter how hard she tired she couldn't forget him either. His presence was everywhere. Even now, Annie's words brought him closer than Molly could bear. She opened her eyes searching the shadows half expecting to see him sitting on the tall roan beneath the trees, his cold blue eyes watching her, a penetrating stare reading her thoughts, stripping her bare. She couldn't escape him even in her dreams.

Annie floated up behind Molly and slipped her arms around her. "Molly I'm sorry. I didn't mean to hurt you. It's just..."
She pressed her cheek against Molly's. "...I'm sorry."
Molly turned with a forgiving hug. "It's okay. If the day ever comes that we can't talk honestly...I think I'd die, so lonely out here. I don't know what I'd do without you."

An involuntary giggle escaped Annie's throat. She blushed. "They say he's handsome."
"Oh Annie, you are incorrigible."
Leaning closer, Annie teased. "Is he? ...handsome?"
Molly tried to hide her face. "Yes, he's handsome I suppose in a roguish sort of way, but it doesn't change how I feel about him. Wanted posters or not, he's a killer and I'll not have him poisoning my family with his evil."
Rising up out of the water, Annie threw her arms wide to the stars. "Well I want to see him, the notorious Col..."

Molly lunged at her friend and clapped her hand over her mouth. "Listen!"
Keeping her hand in place, Molly turned her head and stared into the trees at the end of the clearing. It came again. They all heard it, the sound of hooves splashing in the stream that spilled from their pool.

Jean, eyes wide with fright, hurriedly waded across the pool with Polly clutched to her breast.

Letting go of Annie, Molly pressed a single finger to her lips telling them to be silent. She motioned to the thick bushes overhanging the water, while pushing Annie and Jean under them.

They huddled together listening intently. A shod hoof scraped on a rock, only this time the sound was closer. Holding their breath, the women snuggled deeper into the shadows moving back as far as they could.

When you spend your whole life in one place you learn what belongs and what doesn't. Molly knew these were strangers on the mountain. The shod hoof told her it wasn't Indians, and local men from the valley didn't come this way, and certainly not at night.

The only reason anyone would take the back trail was to avoid being seen, or because they were tracking someone. Both answers filled Molly with dread.

A horse whinnied just beyond the trees causing Queenie to lift her head. Molly gave a start. If the mare answered, they'd be found for sure. Looking toward the bank, she gasped. Their clothes were piled on the rocks for anyone to see.

She had to do something fast. Hurrying from the safety of the reeds, Molly scrambled out of the water. In a mad dash to the mare she scooped up the pile of dresses without stopping and tossed them behind a rock. In an instant she was beside Queenie. Throwing her arms around the big horse's muzzle, she whispered. "Quiet girl."

Behind the shaggy tree, thick oak brush created an impenetrable wall of darkness. Untying the reins, Molly tugged the mare deeper into the shadows hiding her tall head among the twisting branches.

Queenie's coat was a dappled gray that fortunately blended into the muddled background. As big as the horse was she was all but invisible beneath the tree. The same couldn't be said for Molly. A sliver of moonlight peeking from behind an errant cloud glistened brightly on Molly's damp white skin from her shoulder to her knee. She started to slip deeper into the brush then froze. Two riders suddenly appeared in the clearing less than ten feet away. The men appeared sullen, even bitter. It was something in their posture and the way they crouched in the saddles. Neither of them spoke as they pushed their mounts to the water's edge coming even closer.

The riders took a quick look around as the horses lowered their heads to drink. The man closest to Molly searched the shadows beneath the tree. It was the obvious place to look. The light on Molly's skin caught his eye, but the unlikely curves of a naked woman had not yet registered in his brain when his horse suddenly jerked back from the warm sulfurous water pulling the man's gaze away. His gruff voice broke the silence. "Steady boy."

Thirst overpowering his fear, the horse edged towards the water and sipped gingerly. Patting the animal's neck, the rider looked about nervously. "Everything's a bit jumpy tonight."

His partner turned from searching the other side of the clearing. "Thought I heard voices...woman's voices."

"Wishful thinkin' George. We've been out here too long...way too long. This god forsaken land is hard on men, n' hell on women. Wishful thinkin'."

"Maybe you are right Dex. Sounded soft n' sweet like music, or water bubbling over stones. Probably jes' my mind playin' tricks...still it seemed so real."

Forlornly he shook his head. "Ain't had no woman since...hell, I can't remember."

Slumping deeper into his saddle the man sighed. "Women! Sure would be nice."

Risking a tiny breath, Molly knew their situation was bad. There was just enough light to discern Annie and Jean huddled beneath the overhanging branches, their heads and shoulders well above the water. Worse, their eyes wide with fear, shined bright as candles. Fortunately, the men, only feet away were staring over the water and not downwards.

Molly doubted their predicament could get any more desperate when suddenly the moon peeked out from behind the clouds illuminating the clearing with ghostly light. She could see the girls distinctly now staring at her in near panic. Her stomach knotted fearing for them when it suddenly registered. They were frightened for her. Molly looked down aghast. Her pale skin was bathed in a silver glow completely exposed.

The distance between her and the riders vanished with the shadows. Only feet away, if the men were to turn they'd see her for sure. Standing in her bare feet on dry leaves, she dared not move. Molly shuddered. The strangers might just as easily look down and see Annie and Jean.

Fortunately for the women, it was the men's dark mood and not the night that blinded them.

Her heart pounding, Molly lifted her eyes upwards towards the patchy cloud moving slowly across the moon. She prayed. 'Please hurry.' It would be half an hour before the moon would set, leaving the clouds her only hope.

One of the men cleared his throat. "Ain't lookin' forward to what we got to do. Nasty business."

The man named Dex replied. "Well we ain't getting' paid for our good looks so get use to it."

Distracted by a nagging feeling, his partner paid him no mind. "Sure sounded like women; can almost hear their soft voices."

Leaning forward he sniffed the air. "Maybe it's the steam rising off the water, but it's like I can smell their sweet fragrance...more than one woman."

George moved uneasy in the saddle. "You want ta' look around?"

He backed his horse away from the spring; its hind quarters pushing beneath the tree. Stretching out her hand to the horse's rump, Molly raised on her toes fearing the beast would trample her, but bad luck follows good, and good luck follows bad.

As George turned bring Molly into his peripheral vision, the cloud she'd been desperately praying for passed in front of the moon extinguishing the revealing light like a lamp snuffed out in the nick of time.

At the same moment Dex pulled his reins in the opposite direction. "No. Can't see anything out here anyway n' times a wasting. Let's get out of here. We got blood money to collect."

Turning his horse to follow, the cowboy passed inches from Molly. She pulled her arms to her breasts fearing he might scrape her with his spurs, then at the last second, he gave a kick of his heel, and hurried to catch his partner as the moon suddenly returned.

Stunned, Molly followed him into the clearing watching them go. Water splashed behind her. Annie grabbed Molly's arm and drug her back under the tree frantically whispering. "What are you doing? Are you crazy?"

Molly couldn't pull her eyes away. "He said, 'Blood money', they are up to no good Annie. We need to tell Tom."
Shaking her head, Annie grew adamant. "...and have Tom come riding up here, maybe get shot? Even if he didn't, he'd never let me out of the house again. We will keep quiet about this Molly Creed. Do you hear?"
Annie waited, then took Molly's face in her hands. "...promise me?" Her shoulders slumping, Molly nodded. "I promise, but the law should be told."
Turning away, Annie scoffed. "Maybe they are the law. Who knows now-a-days?"
As Annie reached behind the rock fishing out her dress, Molly was drawn back to the clearing. 'Blood money', it reverberated in her mind. Something evil would happen this night. She could feel it in her bones.

Bad Water
Chapter 4
Dexter Cooly

Pulling the heavy cinch on his saddle, Cole Creed's voice rolled deep and husky on the cold night air as he left instruction for the Mexican standing beside him. "Carlos keep a sharp watch out while I'm gone. No tequila tonight."

"Senor, you think they will come so soon?"

"No, I don't, but they will come. It is better to watch each night than be asleep the night they do."

"Si Senor. Me n' Miguel will keep our eyes peeled. We know what to do."

Carlos patted the pearl handled revolver hanging low on his hip.

Putting his boot into the stirrup Cole threw a leg over Brazo his tall blue roan stallion. Thanks to his recent good fortune, from another man's misfortune, Cole now owned twelve-hundred and eighty acres of rolling grassland with the lower forty bordering the Ruidoso. Old Pas Jaramillo deeded his sprawling Tierra Amarillo ranch to Cole from his deathbed, a parting act of defiance for the bullet in his lung. Pas knew it would take a man like Cole to keep his hard-earned homestead from falling into the murdering paws of Murphy and Dolan. It was an offer Cole couldn't pass.

Sheriff Brady was caught dumbfounded when Cole showed up deed in hand backed by two burly Mexican pistoleros. He ordered the good sheriff to clear Dolan's cattle off his land. There was only a few dozen head that had wandered across the river, but the insult was bitter just the same. You don't buck old army brass like Murphy. Brady told Cole so in veiled threats, then high-tailed it at a dead run knowing you don't buck bad men like Cole Creed either. Cole made a silent promise he'd kill Sheriff Brady one day if someone else didn't beat him to it.

Every night for the last month since Cole and the Siringo brothers settled in, Cole had made an evening patrol of his property.

The moon had dropped beneath the tall hills leaving only stars to guide him but Cole knew his land well. He took a different trail each time. There would be no back shooter lying in wait like they had done with his kid brother or old Pas. Both men had been shot with a 50 caliber slug. It might have just been coincidence but Cole doubted it. The Sharps 50 caliber had been used as a sniper rifle during the Civil War. It could drop a man at 800 yards. Cole figured somebody was getting paid for a special skill, and if his guess was right, they were still on the payroll.

This night Cole was heading to the Ruidoso River. He'd swing wide to the north until he reached its banks then follow it down letting the gurgling stream hide the sound of his approach. Brazo's tracks were not the only one he'd seen on his side of the creek. Somebody was trailing him or trying too. This night they would fail.

Accepting a cautious pace, the slow curving trail was quiet. Cole's mind drifted back to seeing his sister-in-law at Crow Crossing. Molly was volatile with a tongue that scorched flesh like a branding iron when she got angry. It didn't take much to get her blood boiling, just the mention of his name was usually enough.

What was done was done as far as Cole was concerned, and all the tears and hate wouldn't bring his brother back; water down the Ruidoso so to speak.

On that tragic night eight years ago when he'd found Johnny lying on the trial his life slipping away, Cole made his dying brother a promise to protect Molly and the children, but Molly wanted nothing to do with him. She never understood that he was grieving too, or maybe she did and found some perverse satisfaction in it.

Molly and the kids were the only family he had and turning him out was cruel. Alone and in his early twenties, carrying anger of his own, he'd used his gun too freely to ease the pain. As stories about him spread, some of them true, Molly's hatred of him grew blinding her, but she wasn't fair.

Always making up answers when none could be found, Molly kidded herself that by staying clear of the warring factions she was keeping her family safe. And so it seemed she had. If Molly only knew that a parting threat pinned to a dead body dumped on Murphy's doorstep warned all that, if harm was to come to her, there would be hell to pay. It was that oath and fear of his gun that kept the murdering hounds at bay. His reputation was already such that no one would cross his path if they didn't have too. He was gone and good riddance. So until now it had been easier to bypass the Creed farm than spend each day looking over their shoulder.

Cole kept watch from afar, receiving letters when they could find him, from old Paz, the parson and Mrs. Hayes. Now and then he sent money to the kindly storekeeper, making sure Molly had credit if she ever needed it.

Now for whatever reason, events were changing rapidly. He had received word that Murphy and Dolan were grabbing up land around Molly's farm in the Alamo valley either by foreclosing on worthless deeds or by gun if needed.

It was why his old friend Pas Jaramillo was killed. His deed was genuine as was Molly's deed, making the gun the only answer to drive them out. The time had come for him to return home. His old threat could no longer protect her.

Cole smiled to himself knowing Molly would swear he put down his stakes so close to the family farm just to spite her. She was like that, might even think he killed ol' Pas himself merely to ruin her day.

The only thing that mattered to Molly was her children. He couldn't fault her for that, but her problem as Cole saw it was she would never face up to cold hard realities when she had no answer for them. She found it easier to hate him than seek justice against the unassailable forces hiding behind to the law.

Still, Molly was a good woman despite her temper. She was pretty too when she smiled, damn pretty.

There had been a time when Cole had strong feelings about her before Johnny made his intentions known. Two brothers and only one girl; he should have seen it coming, but he moved at his own slow pace, never liking to be rushed. So he couldn't blame Johnny for stepping in. Something about Molly just drew men to her. And Molly apparently got tired of waiting. Cole didn't blame her either.

It was Molly's father who caught her and Johnny lying in a stable. He planned their wedding at the end of his shotgun. Being only fifteen she had no say, still the marriage was a good one, and when

Cole saw how happy they were, he stuffed his feelings. The years passed and he played the part of the happy-go-lucky brother. Marriage was not for him he'd say. Eventually he even convinced himself it was true.

Cole always figured Molly understood he had backed away for his little brother and not for lack of caring. Nothing was ever said, but an occasion twinkle in her eye hinted that she knew of his secret affection for her.

That was long ago, and there was no use in trying to talk with her now. Molly had made up her mind about him. There would be no reconciling with the intractable Molly Creed; more water down the Ruidoso. He would keep his promise to his brother, and somehow find a way to stay close to Molly. Cole clenched his jaw. She wasn't going to like it. Not one bit.

When Cole reached the river his thoughts turned to the task at hand. Caution was needed. The turbulent stream hid the sounds of his approach and the moonless night made him all but invisible to anything on two legs or a saddle.

The years had been hard and lessons learned, an education often paid for in blood, some his own. There were men faster than Cole Creed, but a quick draw is worth only so much. Winning a gunfight takes more than just showing up. It was knowing when to shoot and choosing your ground. Out here there was no second chance or second place. Winner takes all. Yes, there were men faster than Cole but few were deadlier. The desert was littered with unmarked graves to prove it.

If Cole had to kill he made a point of not being seen. He didn't want a reputation. Usually the only evidence against him was somebody bragging about how they were going to best Cole Creed then not coming back. Still, people fear what they can't see and the reputation came anyway.

Taking his time Cole studied the dark horizon. If any movement blotted out so much as a single star, he'd know it. Cole closed his eyes and bent all his will listening to any sound that might not be the river; a hoof on a rock, a man spitting, anything. For now, he was alone. Cole put his heels to his horse and moved on.

Finally, he came to a small rise. Nothing caught his attention, yet on the other side of the rocky slope, flat layers of gray limestone rising up from the river's edge afforded a natural hiding place where someone might get comfortable, hopefully too comfortable. It's where he'd wait if he were spying on himself.

His cattle came here to water at sundown. For several weeks now, Cole had made sure of that until the cows learned to come on their own. If men wanted to hunt him, he'd give them a place to hunt, a place he would know and not some lonely trail in the desert where a man could be back shot.

Cole eased out of the saddle and moved forward on foot. Before he reached the top he was more crawling than standing. Suddenly he froze in his tracks. Hidden by the night he slowly filled his lungs with the cool night air. Tobacco!

Slipping his .44 from its holster, Cole inched the last several yards up the hard rock to the rim. For a moment he waited, searching. In short order he found what he was looking for, the dim red glow of one then two cigarettes.

The faint embers would raise and stop, then grow bright as the unseen men took a drag. At this distance Cole could easily shoot a few inches from the telling light and drill the men through their heads, but for now he would watch. There might be others.

Above the lowing of the cattle voices began to take form. At first it was a word or two then sentences. A man coughed and threw his cigarette down. "Makes no sense bein' out on a night dark as this. Couldn't see 'em if he was holding my hand."

Cole recognized the voice. It was George Grady, a squat bowlegged near-do-well who rode for John Kinney or anyone else who would pay for his kind of work.

In response, a second man spoke. "Well don't shoot me by mistake for hell sake. I plan to live long enough to make a few bucks n' skedaddle."

It was Dexter Cooly. Cole had no use for either of them.

Their conversation carried on for several minutes covering the gauntlet from biting mosquitoes and Spanish gold, to cold nights and warm whores, then back to their reason for being on this dismal trail.

As Cole listened, no one other than the two men spoke nor did Grady or Cooly direct their comments to anyone other than themselves.

Dexter paused and searched the dark around him. He had an uneasy feeling. Turning up the collar of his shaggy buffalo coat he shook it off. "Got to be a better way to make a living George. After we finish this we should head up ta' Colorado. Get real jobs with an honest ranch. No more of this skulking around in the dark lookin' fer' rattlers. Got a brother up that way. He says the women are pretty as...."

George heard a thump on the ground and all went silent. "Dex?"

There was no answer, but George could hear hooves plodding the unseen ground and sense a horse siding up to him. He gave a sigh of relief. "Why'd ya' stop talking? Something a matter?"

A cold voice carried from inches away. "Hello George. You are on the wrong side of the river."

"Drop the strongbox over the side real careful like."
The tall masked man wearing a shaggy buffalo coat and sitting a white footed bay waved his rifle at the stagecoach driver. "...and hurry I ain't got all night."

Doing as he was told, the driver dumped the box on the ground. "Sure you know what you are doing feller? There's a thousand dollars of L. G. Murphy payroll in that box as well as the U.S. Army payments to him for beef contracts. You are going to make some important people mighty angry."

The outlaw didn't seem to care. "They'll get over it." He rode in closer. "Kind of funny running a stagecoach in the middle of the night isn't it?"

Respecting the rifle aimed at him, the driver raised his hands above his head as did the man riding shotgun beside him. "Long way across the desert carrying lots of money...or was. Guess it didn't help much. You found out about it."

Pushing the bay forward, the gunman dropped from the saddle and lifted the strongbox onto the horses back, then he climbed back up. "Loose lips. That's what happens when everyone is stealing from everyone else, can't keep a secret."

The second man named Milo, chimed in. "Guess that applies to you too. Somebody is bound to find out. Wouldn't want to be in your boots when they do."

Tipping his hat, the masked robber backed away. "Well if you are willing to forget a few details about me, I might not kill you next time I rob your stage. You gents enjoy the rest of this starry night, and let's hope Murphy believes you when you say you were robbed. Ya' might want to ride down the road n' put a few bullets in the stage for proof."

The two men looked at each other and swallowed. Murphy would be angry as hell and Jimmy Dolan would go insane. When they looked up again the bandit was gone.

Searching both directions, Milo shook his head. "Jake I'd swear that was Dexter Coolie; a buffalo coat and the white socks on the bay. His voice was muffled by the mask, but if it was Dex, he's a dead man."

Whipping the bay up a side draw, the rider made for the high ridge. It was going to be a busy night. Jake and Milo were right about one thing; some mighty important people were going to be mad as hell. Lincoln County was being bought and sold like a Mexican whore. If L.G. Murphy came up short, there were people in Santa Fe and Fort Stanton who were not going to be too sympathetic.

At the top of the ridge the rider pulled to a halt. Three Apache warriors sitting paints blocked his way. He nodded to them then rode on past. They fell in behind and kept moving.

Far below in a narrow valley Jessie Evans along with four of the Boys were driving twenty head of horses they had just stolen from the Mescalero Apache Reservation. It wasn't the first time they had tried this and it wouldn't be the last. Horses, like land, had a way of being sold multiple times through the network of rustlers that worked for Murphy.

If the information was right, Jesse would be heading to a hideout were the horses would be held until they could resell them to the Clanton gang, the money coming back to L.G. Murphy.

Further down the trail, a young Indian not more than fourteen on a piebald paint appeared from beneath the dark pines. He held the reins of a tall blue roan trailing behind him. The youth looked to the cowboy with respect glistening in his eyes. He knew he'd ride with this man again.

Turning up the collar of the buffalo coat, Cole smiled proudly at the boy and continued on. There was much to do.

Like he had told the stagecoach driver, no honor among thieves. Murphy and Dolan were so sure of themselves they had gotten lax. They figured everybody would play by the law but them. They hadn't counted on Cole. So for a bottle of whiskey and fifty dollars' silver, a disgruntled Mexican ranch-hand with big ears was encouraged to spill all. Yes sir, it was going be a busy night.

The trail ahead of the horse thieves squeezed between two jagged pillars of rocks where the canyon narrowed in a grove of ghostly aspen where shadow and winter haze subdued sight and sound. Man and beast would have to go single file. With Jessie Evans leading the way they started through. The outlaw had come this way before and with dawn fast approaching he hurried into the gap.

Jessie's keen eyes searching the patchwork of shapes where the craggy walls loomed before him, pulled to a sudden stop. From out of nowhere a masked man appeared blocking his way holding a Winchester aimed at Jessie's heart.

It was dark, but Jessie could see the starlight glint on the barrel of the rifle. He could also see the white sock of the horse. Jessie quickly searched the trees and rocks around him, fearing a posse, but that was ridiculous. There wasn't an honest lawman within a hundred miles. He turned back to the lone gunman eyeing him suspiciously. "Dex?"

The masked rider remained silent, letting the rustlers get use to his presence. Jessie tried again. "Dex if that's you, you're a dead man."

The rider laughed. "You may not be too far from right. We might all be."

Jessie frowned, his fingers spreading ready to reach for his gun. "You're not Cooly. Who are you?"

Cole thumbed back the hammer on the rifle. "A man with an offer."

Evans was as fast and deadly as they came but the bold stranger had the drop on him making the killer a little more willing to listen. "Well let's hear it?"

Cole waved his arm and four Apache warriors materialized out of the shadows behind him. "Those horses don't belong to you. Let my friends here take them back?"

Shifting uneasy, Jessie made no attempt to hide his displeasure. "Doesn't sound like much of a deal. No profit in it."

The masked rider chuckled. "You worried Murphy and Dolan might get upset?"

Jessie nodded. "Oh I'm sure of that, n' me too. I like getting paid."

Lowering his rifle, Cole smiled beneath the mask. "Then you are going to love my offer."

Jessie's eyes danced with curiosity. Whoever he was the rider had his attention.

Studying the famed rustler, Cole took his time answering. "Here's my deal. Give the Indians the horses and I'll give you a thousand dollars. You can tell Murphy and his pretty boy Jimmy that the horses were guarded so no luck."

Jessie gave a start. "You are going to pay me a thousand dollars for horses that ain't even mine! What's in it for you?"

Shoving his Winchester into its scabbard, Cole drew his pistol at the same time and kicked the bay forward. "Call it a good deed. Gives me a warm fuzzy feeling."

Reaching into the pocket of the buffalo coat, Cole produced a thick bundle of bills. "Deal?"

A huge grin spread across Jessie's face. "Mister, you got a deal."

He turned in his saddle. "Boys let the ponies loose. We got some celebrating to do tonight, and church tomorrow."

Jessie laughed out-loud then looked back to the masked man. "This better be on the up and up."

Prodding his horse alongside Jessie, Cole dropped the bundle of money into the gunman's hand. "Ain't nothing on the up and up out here, not you, not me, but the money is real."

Cole backed away waving his pistol. "You and the Boys can pass."

Shoving the money into his saddlebag, Jessie eyed his mysterious companion. "Anytime you want to do a good deed, there are plenty of horses I'm willing not to steal."

He rode pass Cole then stopped and looked back. "Dex is dead ain't he?"

Cole shrugged. "Some fools make deals with me. Others make deals with the devil."

Pausing, Cole watched the Apaches herd the horses out the other end of the clearing before continuing. "A lot of people have seen Dexter this night. Was he alive or dead, who knows?"

Turning his head, Cole whistled and a tall blue roan charged through the gap. The great horse leaped over a fallen log and came to a stop by his side. The rustler's eyes flickered with recognition. Cole watched him carefully. "Jessie you may be a lot of things, but you're no fool. Stick to horse rustling, I'll stick to good deeds, and we won't have to worry about each other. That's the deal I came to make."

Bad Water
Chapter 5
Neighbors

"Wait, I'm almost ready." Jean came running out of the house putting the last touches to her hair. Will tugged on the reins before Jean was even able to climb from the porch onto Queenie's back. "Wait Will!"

"Heck Jean, we do this every Saturday. It's not like you don't know we are leaving."

Jean wiggled in behind her mother. "Mama tell Will to be nice."

"Will be nice." Molly mimicked Jean's sentiments without conviction.

Knowing she was being teased, Jean hissed. "Someday a pretty girl is going to steal your heart Will Creed and then you won't mind waiting."

The boy shrugged. "Can she hunt?"

Jean's voice spiked with exasperation. "No she can't hunt, and she won't be lugging no gun or chopping wood. She's pretty."

Will frowned. "...another sister."

"Mama! He's horrible to me."

Molly laughed. "Oh Jean I don't know why you are complaining. He admitted you're pretty."

Not satisfied, Jean challenged her brother. "Just you wait Will, there's gunna' be a girl someday. Would you rather she be sunburned with calloused hands and dirty nails, or sweet smelling in a pretty dress with ribbons in her hair?"

The boy kept walking. "I'd rather have a huntin' dog."

Coming up the last rise, Jean craned her neck and looked over her mother's shoulder searching the hitching posts for horses she'd recognize. If someone had business in Crow Crossing, Saturday was the day for it. After a week of hard work and Sunday being the Sabbath, Saturday was the only occasion to meet friends and neighbors.

This morning seemed particularly busy. Horses were lined from one end of the boardwalk to the other. Molly took in the scene, her face coloring with concern. "Looks like something is going on."

Outside the Hayes store, Annie O'Donald sat stiffly in their buckboard, baby Polly in her arms and Chad sitting by her side. The door to the store kicked open. Tom stormed across the boardwalk. He tossed a sack behind the seat and climbed up beside Annie. Jerking the reins, he gave them a hard snap. It was obvious Tom wanted to be gone in a hurry.

Molly slowed the mare and waited, but it didn't look as though the O'Donalds were going to stop. Shouting with anger Tom laid the whip to the horses. The team picked up speed breaking into a run, but Annie caught Molly's eye and placed a hand on her husband's arm. Red faced and tight jawed, Tom brought his rig to an abrupt halt. He kept his eyes forward ignoring the women.

Her hand sliding from his shoulder, Annie nodded and tried her best to be cordial. "Molly. Not a good day. Best be careful. Sheriff Brady is at Rubens. He's brought the horrible Bob Olinger and two other deputies." She hesitated casting a sympathetic glance at her husband. "They're bullying the men and makin' threats if they don't tell..."

Annie paused, wishing Molly could read her thoughts. She glanced at the kids wishing to hide the truth from them, but it was no use. "Molly they've come to arrest Cole."

Young Chad piped up. "For murder."

"Chad shush!" Annie put her arm around her boy covering his mouth. "Sorry Molly. Best you see Emma, do your business and get home. Ain't nobody safe."

Clutching her throat, Molly gasped. "Good God Annie, I'm so sor..." Tom snapped the reins ending the conversation. Their horse lunged forward and in no time the O'Donalds were gone.

Staring after them Molly had a terrible urge to follow. Sheriff Brady was a man without conscience and Deputy Olinger was a killer with a badge.

Molly looked down at her basket. There was no other way, they needed the money. "Come children. Let's hurry. We will sell our eggs and be gone."

Urging Queenie into a trot Molly glued her eyes to Ruben's door fearing it would open at any second. Every step of the big mare's hoof sounded to Molly like a drum beating her arrival.

Once at the hitching rail Molly quickly dismounted. "Tie her off Will. You kids come inside."
Jean looked up. "But Mama, there's Jimmy's pony."
Molly grabbed Jean's arm. "Inside now!"

Before she could push through the door, Sheriff Brady stepped out of Rubens. His angry glare shot immediately to Molly. She ducked her head and herded the children before her. "Quick! Inside."

Molly slammed the door behind them. From the opposite end of the room Emma looked up from handing change to Mrs. Proctor. Both women stood rigid as fence posts. No words were needed. Being a Creed was about the worse thing a person could be right now.

While Molly composed herself, Jean's eye caught movement in a dimly lit corner. Pressed up against a stack of grain sacks Jimmy Webb tried to go unnoticed. He turned his head too late to hide a black eye and a swollen lip. His shirt sleeve was torn as well. The poor boy looked miserable. It wasn't hard for Jean to guess he had been warned to stay away from her family.

Hurrying around the counter Emma glanced at the door then took Molly's basket and pressed a silver dollar into her hand. "You get home Molly. Go now."
Molly looked gratefully to the older woman. "Thank you Emma."

Her heart pounding, Molly turned to leave when suddenly the door burst open. Scowling, Sheriff Brady strolled in and stood spread legged as though judgment day had come to Crow Crossing. Behind him, Bob Olinger pushed his way in. "You! The Creed 'Widder!" Olinger snapped. "...wanna' talk ta' ya'. Get over here."

Molly came to her full height. "I'm addressed as Mrs. Creed, and if you will kindly get out of my way, I have work to attend too."

Squeezing between the lawmen before they had time to think, Molly ushered her children onto the boardwalk, but she made it no further. In front of her stood the other two deputies sneering down, enjoying their role as badge toting bullies. By the looks of them, they'd spent more time running from the law than enforcing it; a breed who cared nothing for justice, and with no men left to humiliate, Molly Creed would feed their primal hunger.

Storming out of the store, furious at being ignored, Bob Olinger caught Molly roughly by the arm. "Said I wanted to talk ta' ya' woman. Where's that murdering kin of yourn? We're gunna' hang 'em this time for sure."

Molly tried to jerk free but Olinger squeezed harder causing her to wince. The ill-tempered deputy shoved his ugly face into hers burning her nose with his soured breath. "You ain't goin' nowhere, now get your pretty ass back here n' start answering questions."

"Let go of my mom." Shoving between them Will swiftly kicked the deputy in the shin as hard as he could.
Howling, Olinger let out a curse. "Why you little bast..."
The deputy suddenly dropped Molly's arm like it was a hot iron. "Son-of-a..!" He stared over her head as though she no longer existed.

Molly turned with a gasp. Riding bold as day, Cole Creed turned the corner by the blacksmith's shop and came straight at them. Behind him rode two Mexicans rumored to be the notorious Siringo brothers known for mayhem across the border.
Sheriff Brady came to the deputy's side. He uttered one word. "Shit!"

Upon seeing the lawmen, the deadly Siringos' moved their horses alongside Cole for better position and rode up to the boardwalk three abreast. The older Mexican pranced his horse sideways, his hand hanging menacingly by his shiny gun, a clear warning.

Cole's steel blue eyes capturing every detail, never left the deputy as he climbed from the saddle.

Taking advantage of the moment, Molly pulled her children to the side. She stared at Cole wondering if he'd gone mad.

Neither anger nor fear could be discerned in the cold hard lines chiseled into his bronze face. In contrast, the cheery Siringos' sported mischievous grins. Molly knew men like them had no fear. If the thunder of guns suddenly awoke bringing death, they would laugh even if it were their own. She took another step back. Brady and the deputies did the same.

Unhurried, Cole came up the stairs, his spurs ringing ominously with each measured step. The lawmen, unsure if Cole had seen them roughing up Molly, held their breath fearing the next second would bring death.

Scared as rabbits the deputies made not a move as the gunman stepped onto the porch. Cole eyed them keenly but with hardly a pause he walked right through the startled men and into the store as if they were of little matter.

Chuckling, the two brothers casually nodded to the stunned lawmen before stepping inside and slamming the door in their faces.

The sheriff stood speechless. It was an odd scene, like somebody played a piano badly out of tune or laughing at a funeral.

Watching from the windows, the local men cautiously emptied out of Rubens. After being bullied by the lawmen, no one appeared to be too sympathetic to Brady's plight. The sheriff and his henchmen had come hell bent on killing only to find out the devil rode a roan stallion.

Shaking off his disbelief Olinger muttered. "What the hell?" Sheriff Brady just stood staring at the door in dumb silence He had boasted they were going to arrest Cole Creed, only right now they seemed like a pack of toothless hounds baying at a mountain lion.

Hiding his own shame, Olinger goaded. "You just going to let him waltz right past us?"

Jean, seeing her mother rubbing her bruised wrist, quipped. "Yea. Thought you were going to arrest him?"

A blood vessel bulged on Brady's jaw. He wanted to backhand the belligerent girl, but Cole Creed was her uncle and that changed everything. He growled. "Watch your mouth kid."

Molly's eyes flashed. "I presume you and your rude deputy have no further desire to question me on the where abouts' of Cole Creed? However if you'd like, I'd be happy to introduce you to him."

She risked her defiance knowing she was trading on Cole's reputation. With her hatred of Cole, she should have been eager for the posse to hang him and be done with it, but her stomach knotted in fear. Molly hurried to her mare trying to bury the idea that she might actually care what happened to him. "Come children."

The sheriff snarled. "If you know what's good for you, you'll steer clear of your murderin' kin."

Untying Queenie Molly smirked. "That shouldn't be a problem now that you've caught him."

Brady's face flushed crimson. He was in a predicament. Knowing he must do something to save face, Brady turned to the crowd of shabby men, most of them farmers. "I'm going to deputize all of you so raise your right hand."

The men stood dumbfounded. The thought of them arresting Cole Creed or even wanting to was ridiculous. After a long silence, old man Turney tugged his peppered whiskers and scoffed. "Ain'tcha' gunna' ask us which side we is on?"

Emboldened the men began to chuckle. Ray Corey held up his right hand. "I'd help ya' Sheriff only I think your deputy done broke my trigger finger."

The crowd laughed openly. Someone shouted from the back. "Could you pay us first just in case he plugs you?"

Laughter rolled again. Brady would find no help here. Desperate he turned once more to Molly wondering if detaining her might offer some advantage. "Mrs. Creed, maybe you'd better stay in case we need your statement."

Molly sneered at sheriff's plight. "So now it's Mrs. Creed." Turning her back on Brady just like Cole had done, she dismissed him and led Queenie alongside the boardwalk where she could mount the big horse more easily.

Molly reached for the mare's neck when the door suddenly opened. Everyone turned, the lawmen's hands twitched by their guns, but it was only young Jimmy trying hard to be invisible. He quickly zigzagged between the deputies and made his way to Molly all the while keeping his head down. "Mr. Creed said I should come out and help you."

Nodding, Molly reached for the horse's wither. "Thank you Jimmy."

The boy locked his fingers together like a stirrup. Molly took a last glance at the door then placing her foot in Jimmy's hand, climbed on the mare.

Hurrying, Jimmy took Jean by her waist and lifted her up behind Molly. The young girl reached down and trailed a gentle finger alongside the boy's black eye, a sympathetic pout tugging at the corners of her mouth. Jimmy looked up for the briefest second then turned to her brother. "Come on Will. You will ride behind me. Your uncle gave me a dollar to see you home."

As Molly and the kids started to ride away the fateful door opened once more. Only this time the shadow of a tall man beneath a dark Stetson held for a moment in the archway calmly taking in the scene.

Cole stepped out as boldly as he had entered. Everyone stared in disbelief. Molly unconsciously pulled the mare to a stop, her mouth suddenly dry. Killers were supposed to run from the law, but that wasn't Cole's way. She silently cursed him for his arrogance.

The sheriff with his face contorting in physical pain, had made his boast and Cole was leaving him no way out. Uncertain how to handle the mess he'd gotten himself into, Brady took a nervous step back before finding his courage. "Cole Creed. I'm here on official business."
His voice was weak and uncertain, but loud enough to get Cole's attention.

With visible scorn Cole turned and faced the sheriff. He towered over him looking as though he might strike him. Backing away, Brady grunted and started to speak. "There's been..."
The sheriff barely got a word out before Cole stepped right past him and went to the hitching rail completely ignoring the hapless lawman. A mummer of amusement rumbled from the bystanders over Cole's affront. Brady's temper flared. "Wait a minute Cole. I said I got business with you. George Grady and Dexter Cooly were found floating face down in the Ruidoso with their throats cut."
Molly tensed as if she felt the very knife at her own neck. She knew Cole was capable of such deeds, but her stomach sickened to hear it laid so cold.

When Cole made no response, the sheriff continued. "You are known to use that Bowie on your hip as carelessly as you do your gun."

Untying his horse, Cole turned around and moved to a position where he could face all the deputies. "Did they file a complaint?"
There was snickering from the crowd.
Brady burned knowing Cole was making him look like a fool, but Cole Creed was a deadly man and he dared not challenge him openly. "Creed, hoof prints show they were on your property. I'm askin' straight out, did you kill 'em?"

"Ask them."

The crowd started chuckling, then burst into laughter. Somebody hollered. "Yea Sheriff, ya' got any witnesses?"

Trying to ignore the jeering, Brady barked. "Look Cole, they rode out your way after dark. Nobody else out there but you...n' your greasers. What do you got to say?"

Pushing his slicker back, Cole exposed the ebony handle of his black .44. "Now what would two honest law abiding men be doing riding out to my place after dark?"

Brady swallowed. "Creed. I'm asking the questions here."

Unimpressed, Cole pulled on the reins and led the roan away from the post. "Not of me you ain't."

Crowing forward, Bob Olinger, a bitter man unable to contain his hate, growled his contempt. "We're here to arrest you Creed."

The assemblage of men gasped and fell silent. Even Olinger was stunned by his own brashness and clamped his mouth shut.

The silence held for a moment then an evil chuckle erupted behind the deputy. It was Carlos Siringo, the older Mexican brother stepping out of the store carrying a box of cartridges. "This I think I'd like to see."

His brother Miguel joined him. "Si Sheriff. Maybe you should deputize us greasers. I hear this Cole Creed is a most dangerous Hombre."

Laughing, Carlos reached out to the tall deputy standing next to him, and plucked the badge from his shirt as the bewildered man stared in disbelief. "Here Miguel I'll deputize you." He pinned the badge on his brother. "There. You look as handsome as these pretty gringos."

Brady cursed and turned back to Cole. "Look here Creed. This mockery will do you no good. You better cooperate."

Olinger spat, his nerves fraying like old rope as he tried desperately to get the upper hand. "I'll take your gun."

Letting the reins slide through his fingers, Cole's eyes narrowed. "Take it."

The meaning was clear. Olinger shuddered right down to his boots. Fueled by his own bile, he'd spoken without thinking as he often did, only this time it was not a farmer he was facing. Before him stood Cole Creed; a killer of legend and myth.

Olinger's face turned a sickly pallor. He was in it with no way out. Rubbing his mouth with a trembling hand, the ill-tempered lawman nervously looked to the other deputies. "Take his gun men." The two deputies wisely developed a sudden case of deafness. Olinger suffered an awkward silence that ended when Cole's voice rang cold. "No Bob. You take it."

Sheriff Brady stuttered a weak protest. "D-Damnit Creed, we're the law."

Cole ignored him. "I'm waiting Bob."

Bob's leather boots scraped uncertain on the hard wood planks as he backed away. The infamous Cole Creed had called his hand. Sweat beading on his face, he looked to Brady but saw no willingness to help. He was on his own.

The deputy's fist opened and closed several times. He had to back his words or turn tail.

The condemning silence held a moment longer then snorting like a roped bull, Olinger squared his shoulders. "I ain't afraid of you Creed."

Cole's deadly blue eyes glinted. "Yes you are."

The deputy hissed. "Damn you ya' son-of-a-bitch."

Everyone scrambled to get out of the way as the deputy took a step sideways ready to draw.

"Stop it! Stop it!" Screaming, Molly jumped down from the mare and dashed between the two men her voice raw with pain. "You fools! What will this solve? Just more killing. She looked at Cole then Olinger. Are you both so dead that life has no value?"

Turning her anguished face to the throng of men, Molly clutched her hands to her heart. "I could tell you about killing. It's not the dead who suffer."

She whirled around. "Sheriff don't do this. You have no evidence to arrest Cole."

Her eyes pleaded. "Please. It's a beautiful day. No one has to die. Just go. Please go."

Brady was in a bad fix and Molly had just given him a way out. Licking his lips, he faced Cole. "Creed. She's right. I'll be back when I have more evidence."

Cole turned to the deputy. "What about you Bob? You want to play this out?"

Olinger eagerly backed away. "I ride with the sheriff."

Finding courage behind a woman, Brady strutted forward. "Too many men disappear around you Cole. Someday you'll slip up and when you do I'll be there."

Turning to his sister-in-law Cole took Molly by the waist and set her curtly upon the mare while casting a sideways glance at Brady. "Sheriff, I'm counting on you being there."

Gathering his reins Cole swung into his saddle. "Carlos, Miguel." Carlos mounted up. "Si, I think I'd prefer the smell of cattle to chicken."

Taking the badge from his shirt, Miguel tossed it in the dirt and the three desperados rode away.

Bad Water
Chapter 6
Reunion

With Crow Crossing a disquieting blur dissolving behind them, the knot in Molly's stomach began to ease. She took her first deep breath. The immediate danger had passed, but raw emotions left her unsettled. Riding beside her was the notorious Cole Creed guilty of two more murders.

Staring forward she vented. "Don't you ever pick me up like that again. I'm not a child to be placed where you want."

Keeping his eyes on the trail, the gunman turned a deaf ear and kept on riding. It aggravated her. "...and we shan't need your protection so you don't have to ride with us."

Still the grim man made no reply, his piercing eyes intent on what lay before them.

Molly turned towards him ready to burst. "Did you hear me?"

Appearing indifferent Cole studied the terrain before answering. "Not riding with you, just going the same direction."

Peaking over her mother's shoulder Jean stared at her uncle. He was tall and lean with a bold continence that stole her breath. Danger charged the air about him. She could tell he was the kind of man you didn't mess with, and yet her mother was scolding him as if he were a witless child.

His canvas slicker blew back exposing the low hung .44 in a tied down holster. It was the kind of gun that warned trouble-makers and tempted fools. Jean stared at it in awe knowing it was a man-killer.

The sheriff had put names to the men he'd killed; George Grady and Dexter Cooly. She had seen them and heard their names only the night before as she huddled naked beneath the willows in the hot spring with Annie and the baby. They seemed so terrifying at the time, talking of blood money, and now to know this man, her uncle had coldly dispatched them and dumped their bodies in the river. It left her stunned.

She was young when her father died, and save for Will, she'd not seen another Creed male since. 'Killer n' kin.' The thought played over in her mind. She couldn't tear her eyes from the imposing figure.

Turning his head, Cole winked teasingly. Jean quickly retreated behind her mother. He turned his eyes back to the trail, and spoke in a deep melodic voice. "Pretty daughter you got there. All growed' up."

Jean blushed and buried her face against her mother's back. A moment passed, then he added. "Looks like you Molly. Eyes of an angel."

Molly felt her face flush. He had always been a charmer. She used to like it but now it made her so angry a hiss escaped her tightly drawn lips. "My children would be safer without a murderer in their midst. Can't you just ride on?"

The muscles in Cole's face hardened. He started to put the spurs to the roan when Jean peeked over Molly's shoulder. "I'd feel safer if he stayed."

The young girl could feel her mother tense, but she desperately wanted her uncle near. It was more than safety. He was a part of their family that had been missing all these years. Maybe not a father, but his presence gave her family strength. "Please Mama. The sheriff might change his mind and come after us, and the way that deputy treated you. I'd feel safer...with Uncle Cole here."

Her daughter's boldness caught Molly off guard. She stared down the road wishing that their home was closer. Clenching her teeth, she acquiesced. "Very well, if it will make you feel safe, but don't expect to invite him in like you did Jimmy. My kindness is not extended to killers."

Cole hung his head visible upset. "Murderer and killer. Is that what you think of me Molly?"

She could tell she hurt him and it gave her a guilty satisfaction. What happened at Crow Crossing fanned an anger that had been smoldering for years. She wanted him to feel her pain.

Molly sat stiffly. "It's how I'd feel about any man who takes a life."

She let her verdict hang in the air expecting a fight that didn't come. Cole knew it was useless to argue. For him, his brother's death was in the past, but women have a harder time letting go. She would not forgive or forget; that was Molly.

His silence angered her so she cut deeper. "We've done alright without you Cole. Ride with us until we reach home then be gone. You can only bring more harm to our family."

"Molly I'm not here to ruin your life, just trying to keep a promise. Claw at me if it makes you feel better."

Indignant, Molly tried to hurry the old mare with little success. It added to her frustration. "You can't live your life outside the law. Sheriff Brady had every right to arrest you."

Cole shrugged. "Badge don't make a man right."

She hated his logic. Having worked herself to the point of screeching in shear madness, Molly held her tongue and rode on. Other than the rhythmic clop of the horse's hooves not a sound was to be heard. It seemed like even the birds were honoring their truce. The silent tension weighted as heavy as their bitter words making it feel so awkward.

When it became apparent that talking was done, Jean consoled herself with the fact that at least they weren't fighting. The tenuous peace allowed her to breathe. With all that had transpired she found herself bursting with excitement.

Jean looked behind them. Jimmy was lagging way back. She wanted him closer...and to have her mysterious uncle only feet away, it was too much. Jean couldn't keep quiet any longer. Summoning her courage, she squeaked loud enough for her uncle to hear. "Do you know Jimmy?"

She could feel her mother tense and knew she was risking punishment when they got home, but she had to know. "You sent him out to help us."

Cole looked back at the boy before answering. "Jimmy! That's his name. No, I don't know him. He was peeking out the window like a fella' who cared more about you than being caught between me and the law. The boy showed grit."

The young girl turned her eyes back down the trail a warm glow coloring her cheeks. She smiled and stared whimsically off into the distance. What a morning! A handsome boy had gallantly risked danger for her and a notorious gunfighter was riding by her side; her uncle no less. An unfamiliar feeling of pride, and a budding romance, made her all giddy inside.

    Jean wiggled with excitement. She had actually spoken to her uncle for the very first time and he didn't seem so frightening. Even in Crow Crossing when facing down the rude deputy, he'd kept an even temperament, not like the wild killer she'd imagined. "Where you scared back there?"

Her question caught Cole off guard. He glanced at her then looked down the trail. "Ain't afraid of dying. It's livin' that's scary."

    Plagued with a young girl's curiosity, Jean persisted. "What are you afraid of?"

Surprised by her precociousness Cole shrugged. "Things."

"What things?"

He chuckled. "Just things?"

"What kind of things?"

    She wasn't going to let him off the hook. Cole looked at Molly before surrendering an answer. "Harm coming to your family. I made a promise to your daddy that I'd look after you."

Molly's eyes flashed. "If John was here you wouldn't have to look after us."

Her anger rattled like the lid on a teapot. "...and if that promise meant so much to you, where have you been all these years when a few extra dollars or a mended roof might have made a difference?"

    Cole defended. "I was doing what you said Molly...and I was figuring it out. We were just kids. But I've kept tabs on you. I've always kept tabs on you. That's why I've come back."

Molly fumed. "It's a bit too late don't you think?"

    Lowering his head, Cole softened his voice. "You've already decided it's too late, but I'll keep my promise just the same."

    He glanced to Jean. "Sorry little one, we shouldn't be fighting. It's a poor homecoming."

    Jean tried to be sympathetic. "It's okay. Grown-ups get angry a lot, but I know Mama don't mean nothing because she taught me that we should treat everyone we meet with respect. She says we don't know what road they've been down, and until we go down that same road, we don't have a right to judge. Isn't that right Mama?"

Molly cast a sideways glance at Cole then cast her eyes downward.

    Jean bubbled with the innocence of youth. "I also agree with Mama that you are real handsome."

Her face turning bright red, Molly hissed under her breath. "Jean Marie so help me if you don't be quiet..."

"Sorry Mama."

Molly glanced sideways long enough to see a grin spread across Cole's face. She blushed deeper, but Cole was smart enough not to embarrass her further, and they continued on without further bantering.

The Siringo's who had held back to defend the rear, galloped past heading home. It was near midday and chores were waiting. With a tip of their sombreros to the ladies, they smiled politely and rode on their way.

Jimmy and Will still kept their distance leaving the three of them along. Two women on a dappled plow horse riding next to a lean cowboy on a tall roan might have looked odd, but to Jean in all that was wrong something finally felt right. She couldn't put her finger on it. It was as though in some way her uncle had always been there like a picture turned against the wall. He was family held by a bond no anger couldn't break.

Leaning to the opposite side from her uncle, Jean hugged her mother and whispered. "Sorry Mama, but he is real handsome."

Upon reaching the broken gate of the Creed farm, Cole tugged Brazo's reins bringing the roan to a stop. Still embarrassed Molly kept her head down not sure what to do. Was she to say, 'Good day', or simply ride past him with her nose in the air and be done. Somehow she couldn't bring herself to do it. There was truth in what Jean had said about respect.

Seeing Molly hesitate, Cole offered a little respect of his own. "Your plow horse is pretty tall, would it be too much to ask if I could escort you as far as the porch and help you down?...show the kids that the grown-ups in our family can be civil."

Not wanting to appear the villain in front of her daughter, Molly sighed. Relenting, she politely nodded and reluctantly handed her reins to Cole allowing him to lead the mare down the lane. She had made the noble gesture, but inside she wanted to scream at Cole telling him it was no use, and she thought she might when two slender arms wrapped around her waist in a grateful embrace. "Thank you Mama."

Pulling back from the edge, Molly took a needed breath, finding forgiveness in a child's hug. She would not fight with Cole in front of the children again.

Except by night from the hilltops, Cole had not seen the farm in eight years. As they neared the home he was shocked at how much had changed.

The brightly painted house he dreamed of on lonely nights in faraway lands, was cracked and dulled to a dingy gray. The roof weathered by years of neglect had shingles missing and askew. A rag was stuffed in a broken window pane to keep out the elements, and the porch railing shy of spindles leaned precariously.

Across the yard the barn door hung on rusted hinges and threatened to fall. Cole winced. Apparently he'd not kept as good a tab as he'd thought.

Staring at the dismal scene he began to realize how hard it had been for Molly. Her anger seemed a little less unjust. Riding up to the rickety porch he climbed off Brazo and took one last look around before stepping to Molly's side. She saw the expression on his face and hid her eyes embarrassed by her own poverty, yet a part of her needed him to understand it had not been easy.

There were other emotions welling inside her. For Molly, Cole standing there brought back memories of better times when he used to drop by unannounced, usually with a gift of some sort; a cradle for the baby, a side of venison, or simple store bought scarf just for her. She remembered his strong laugh, and how he made her smile. Molly turned away trying to forget.

Knowing what must be going through her mind, Cole reached up and spoke in a soft voice. "You are home Molly. You've kept a roof over your head. Johnny would be proud."

Taking her by the waist he gently set Molly on her feet. His hand lingered for a moment, but he could see the fire smoldering in her eyes, and let go.

There was nothing more he could say. He dared not tell her he was sorry. She would take it as pity, so he stepped to the side and reached for Jean, but the young girl pulled back beaming. "No thank you Uncle Cole." She scrunched her shoulders. "I'll wait for Jimmy."

Cole grinned as the boys moseyed to the hitching rail. A twinkle danced in Jean's eyes. "Jimmy quit being so stand- offish, and help me down. If you got that black eye for talking to me, then that kind of makes you my hero doesn't it?"

Surprised by her boldness, Jimmy hid a boyish grin and dropped to the ground happy to be near her.

"You kids go in the house." Molly folded her arms and stood stiffly beside Cole waiting while Jimmy helped Jean down.

Once on the ground, Jean knew there were going to be words. She took Jimmy's hand. "Come on. You too Will."

Passing her uncle with an obvious glow on her young face, she almost gushed. "Thank you for seeing us home Uncle Cole. It was sure nice to meet you. I hope..."

A raised eyebrow from her mother told her the conversation was over. Retreating to the porch she pulled Jimmy inside.

Will slowly walked passed with wonder telling in his eyes. He was young and no words came to him, but a single finger reached out and brushed his uncle's hand as he hurried on to join his sister. He simply needed to know the tall man was real.

When the door closed behind them, Molly turned to Cole. "I'm sure this was very touching for Jean, but I have no doubt that you murdered the two men Sheriff Brady spoke of, and I don't want you around my children. Do you understand Cole? I want you to go and never come back."

Cole had expected no better. "I understand Molly. Now you understand this. I loved Johnny as much as you. He's my blood." Cole jabbed a stiff finger at the door. "As are those children. We are kin Molly. Hate me if you like but we're family. Do you understand?"

Lowering her head Molly whispered. "I understand." Then she looked up. "...but it doesn't change how I feel."

Cole grabbed Molly's hand, then reaching into his pocket he pressed a twenty-dollar gold piece into her palm. Molly pulled back. "Cole I can't..."

"Not a word out of you Molly Ann Creed. You buy Jean a pretty dress and Will a new pair of boots, something for yourself if you like."

Molly opened her mouth and closed it. She could tell by the determination in Cole's eyes there was no use arguing with him, and the truth was she desperately needed the money. It would take her the better part of the year to save that much.

Lowering her head, she turned to go, but Cole took her by the arm. "Molly, as long as I breathe, you needn't worry for money. I know you are too proud and too stubborn to ask, but maybe just knowing will give you comfort."

She clenched her fist. "Don't expect me to thank you Cole."

Molly tried to pull away, but he held her fast. "I'll stay away, but tomorrow Carlos and Miguel are coming over to make repairs. You can scream and be nasty if you like, but they are going to fix this place up just the same, so get used to it."

"Damn you Cole. You have no right."

Releasing her, Cole rebuked. "If I were hurting, you'd do the same for me."

Dumbfounded, Molly shook her head in disbelief. "I most certainly wouldn't."

Cole remained adamant. "Tell me Molly. When you risked your life jumping between me and Bob Olinger's gun back there, who were you protecting? Me or Bob?"

Stunned, Molly stood speechless. Cole mounted his horse and looked down. "Like I said, we are family."

Slamming the door, Molly pressed her back against it. "Damn him."

She opened her hand and stared at the shiny gold piece making sure it was real. "Damn his arrogant hide."

Overcome with emotion Molly's shoulders started shaking. She couldn't help herself, the tears came. It wasn't the money or the confrontation at Crow Crossing. Cole looked so much like his brother, it all came rushing back. How she missed John. The truth was she missed them both. "Damn him."

The door to the children's room opened and closed. Jean timidly crossed the room. Slipping her arms around her mother's waist she laid her head on her breast. Mother and daughter held each other in a quiet embrace tears rolling down their cheeks. Molly sniffed. "Why are you crying sweetheart?"

Jean looked up. "Because you are crying."

Cupping her daughter's cheek, Molly wiped away her tears with a thumb and a kiss. "Everything is okay."

The young girl returned her head to her mother's breast and stared at the door. "Don't be mad at me Mama, but I'm kinda' glad Uncle Cole lives down the road. It makes me feel like we can't be brushed away. Like you said, if somebody wants us gone, they are going to want it real bad now."

Molly needed to change the subject if she ever hoped to stop crying. "What about Jimmy. Is he staying for supper?"

Jean buried her head deeper. "Pete beat him up for being friendly to us; said the judge didn't like it, so Jimmy run off.

Lifting her face, Jean pleaded. "Can he stay in the barn tonight or a few days until he can figure something out. Mama, he's got no place to go."

Molly sighed and petted Jean's hair. "Poor Jimmy. Set another plate. Like it or not, looks like our little family is growing."

Bad Water
Chapter 7
Changes

Cold frosty light from a full moon filtered into the darkened hayloft painting three young faces with a pale silver glow. The hour was late and the only sound was the distant howl of a coyotes protesting the chill.

Jean had made no clandestine plan to sneak out and meet Jimmy in the barn after her mother had gone to sleep, but somehow it happened just the same. It had to be. In the spur of the moment she rousted Will from his slumber and ushered him through their bedroom window making him a co-conspirator.

In the uneasy silence of the loft large eyes evidenced young minds trying to come to grips with the incredible events of the day. They had witnessed the showdown at Crow Crossing. It was the closest the children had been to a real gunfight.

Their own father's death was a shadow that hung over them unjust and unspoken. Now to see his only brother, a notorious gunfighter, challenge the powerful faction which they had always felt helpless against offered some healing though they didn't quite understand.

Jean broke the silence. "I was so scared; him standing there cold as spring water facing down the sheriff and all his deputies. Never thought anyone could be so brave."

Without realizing it, Jean held tightly to Jimmy's hand as they huddled beneath the dark rafters. "...and that Bob Olinger was so mean to Mama, grabbing her, talking like no man should talk to a woman. I didn't care if Uncle Cole was as bad as they say, my heart was cheering for him."

Edging closer, Jimmy nodded. "I ain't heard nothin' but bad about Cole Creed from Pete n' the judge, but after seeing them badge toters rough up those farmers n' not carin' about their pride, I was pulling for him too."

The boy sickened. "I was there. The sheriff called everyone into Rubens to question us. Women too. Can you imagine...making women go into a saloon. Never heard of such a thing. Then Bob Olinger kicked ol' man Brody's chair right out from under him sending him sprawlin'. When Tom O'Donald protested, Bob slapped him across the mouth in front of Annie. Didn't even have the decency to double up his fist n' hit him like a man. He just slapped him like he was nothin'. Had Tom fought back, Annie would be a widow for sure."

Jean shook from a cold that wasn't there. "Poor Tom. Terrible for Annie too."

Her face brightening, she broke into an excited whisper. "I talked to him, Uncle Cole. I talked to him. It wasn't what I expected, but in a way it was. He was strong as tempered steel. When he spoke there was danger behind his words so you listened closely, but he let Mama claw at him like a she-cat when I knew he could of stop her. She calls him bad water but I'm glad he's here..."

Jean's eyes sparkling, "...glad you are here too Jimmy. Uncle Cole said how you worried about me."

A sheepish smile lit the boy's face then faded. "Don't know Jean. Me n' your uncle might both be bad water for you. Pete is bound to come looking for me. Not that he cares; just crazy like that. Wants it his way, mean as a wild boar. When he was 'wompin' on me, he cussed, n' said I best learn to stay away from them damn Creeds 'cuz the judge has plans for ya', especially Cole."

Jimmy turned and stared into the moonlight, a struggle waging inside him. For a moment Jean feared he might cry, but he swallowed a lump and squeezed her hand. "Jean I overheard something, heard it before I came to your house for dinner last week, but I kept my mouth shut ...'cuz I was on the Judges side and 'cuz...I was scared."

Overcome by emotions the distance between the young couple innocently closed. Jimmy leaned his forehead against Jeans. "Now I'm on your side...if you let me."

"Mush." Will rolled over and buried his head in the straw.

Jean snapped. "You shush Will...", then just as quickly softened. "Go on Jimmy. I want you on my side. Will does too. What did you hear?"

The boy took a breath. "Well the judge was talking with Pete and a few of the men; said he was bringing in a fast gun to deal with the great Cole Creed. Wade Bannock is his name. I've heard tell of him by the ranch hands. Bannock is greased lighten', real fast. Some say he's crazy, likes killin', part of the Seven Rivers Warriors gang. So they're gunning for your uncle. It don't seem right him being a judge to be doing that behind the law. Sending the sheriff is one thing but Wade Bannock is...well it changes my thinkin'."

His skin prickling Jimmy looked at the ladder trailing down into the dark reaches below. "If they knew I told they would kill me for sure, but Jean if I didn't something terrible might happen to you. It's just plum bad all the way around."

"Oh Jimmy." She took both his hands and sobbed. "What are we going to do? I can't tell Mama. She's already sick with worry though she tries to hide it from us."

The boy huddled closer. "I don't know Jean. I wish I was older so I could protect you, but I'm just a kid."

Jimmy blushed at his own honesty. He'd never held a girl's hand before and his heart was pounding in his chest. "Jean...you gettin' your Ma to let me stay here, well I owe you a lot...n' you bein' so pretty...maybe that beatin' was worth it. Least ways I'd take one again before I'd give up seein' you."

Her eyes shining, Jean melted. "That's sweet of you Jimmy. Divulging the judge's secrets, and what you did at Crow Crossing, why you've been protecting me all along."

Lifting her head, she boldly held the young boy's uncertain gaze. A feeling new and strange stirred inside her. Jean turned to her brother. "Will, you go back to the house and keep an eye on Mama...I'm going to stay a little while with Jimmy."

Sneaking into the front room young Will leaned his gun against the wall outside his mother's door. He turned the knob ever so quietly and pushed it open so as not to disturb her slumber. He just needed to assure himself she was okay. The moonlight shining through the small window outlined her delicate face in an angelic glow as she lay sleeping on her pillow.

She was his mother, strong and proud, he depended on her, yet laying there with her hands tucked sweetly beneath her chin she looked so fragile. It saddened him.

In the darkened room his blue eyes glistened with determination. There were bad men the grown-ups kept whispering about, and somehow he had to protect her; protect his family. Without a father, he was the man of the house, or so he'd been told for as long as he could remember.

Today, seeing his uncle stand tall, well it showed him there was a way. The young boy clenched his gun in silent promise, and another step was taken down the road to manhood.

Closing the door, Will slumped to the floor and leaned against it. He laid his rifle across his lap and let his sleepy eyes search the veiled corners of the room. The doors were latched and all seemed safe for now. He'd stay awake as long as he could. Yawning, Will whispered to himself. "Wish ol' Drifter was here. We'd show 'em."

The family clock on the mantle ticked away the minutes. He found it comforting. How loud the old time piece seemed echoing across the silent room as if it were talking to him, assuring him he was not alone. Will whispered back. "Hi Clock."
In response he heard the large kerthunk' it made at midnight. The chimes no longer worked, but the clock went on doing its job the best it could.

Will's weary eyes were drawn to it. It was not nearly so big as the church clock that stood in the parson's parlor, or even the one that hung on the store wall at Crow Crossing, but size didn't matter, it did what it had to do. The clocked clunked again at one o'clock, then two, but the boy didn't hear it. Somewhere in between he had fallen sound asleep.

"Will! Will, wake up." Brushing back his hair, Jean whispered in his ear. "Come on Will. It's almost dawn."
Blinking his eyes, Will struggled to his feet and looked to the window. The moon had set long ago leaving them in starlight. "You been in the barn all night?"
Lowering her head, Jean reached for his hand. "Come on let's get to bed before Mama catches us."

The two children stumbled through the dark to their door. Once inside Jean breathed easier. Her heart was beating wildly, she feared

Will could hear it pounding in her breast and would know what it meant. That was nonsense of course but she couldn't push the doubt from her mind.

Half asleep, Will climbed up into his bed without another word. Jean waited for him to face the wall, then taking off her dress she set it aside and slipped off her petticoat. Her eyes drifted toward the small window drawing her to it. A tender smile joined a million stars in lighting her angelic face as she rested her arms upon the sill. This was a day she'd remember.

Jean turned and looked at the door thinking of her mother and how young she was when she got married. With a long romantic sigh, the starry-eyed girl moved away from the window and danced to the center of the room where she spun full around. Yes, it was a day and a night she'd remember.

Climbing onto her bed, she lifted on her toes and placed a kiss on Will's cheek. He mumbled, but did not stir.

Returning to her feet, Jean picked up her nightgown, hugged it to her, then pulled it over her head and plopped down on her bed. She snuggled beneath the thick warm covers and tucked her doll under her chin.

Sleep would not come easy. Laying there with her eyes wide open she stared up at her brother's bunk. "Will...Will, I'm almost fourteen...and that's nearly fifteen."

Jean listened for a reply. All she could hear was her brother's soft breathing. He was lost in dreams.

"Come on children. Wake up." Molly stuck her head into the brightly lit room. The sun had been up over an hour but it was Sunday and she had kindly let them sleep in. "Come on get up. We've got a busy day. Like it or not, we are going to have company, and I want you kids on your best behavior."

Jean sat up in bed. "Who's coming?"

Molly picked up Jean's dress from the back of the chair, and plucked straw from the lace. "Your uncle is sending over Carlos and Miguel to do some repairs."

The words rolling so easily off Molly's lips caused her to pause. After all the years, it seemed strange to say 'your uncle' as if she was saying the O'Donalds, or Pastor Watkins, yet she had done it just the same.

Jean swung out of bed placing her bare feet on the floor. "Is Uncle Cole coming too?"

Molly's voice rose shrill. "No! He will not be coming here, not now, not ever. And those Mexican ruffians wouldn't be coming either if I had a say."

Jean giggled. "Uncle Cole told you who wears the pants! I'm glad." Setting the dress down, Molly's brow furrowed. "That's enough out of you young lady. There's oatmeal to cook. I've already started the fire in the stove."

Reaching up Molly shook her son. "Wake up Will. What are you doing sleeping in your clothes?"

The boy rubbed a fist to his eyes. "Don't know."

Molly brushed back his hair. "Probably don't know why your gun is outside my door either."

Will glanced at the empty peg on the wall. "I best let the chickens out."

"You best. Throw some hay to Queenie too, and get Bossy milked if you plan on breakfast. She's bellowing up a storm. You'd think somebody kept her up all night." Molly hurried to the door, but abruptly stopped and turned around. "I'm trusting you kids to be good." She looked straight at Jean. "Don't let me down."

"Mama they're here, Mama they're here." Jean burst through the front door breathlessly. "They're here."

The jingling of the tack told Molly that the Siringo brothers had come by wagon. "You kids stay inside."

"But Mama..."

"No buts."

Molly stepped onto the porch and pulled the door closed behind her as young eager eyes tried to peek through the narrowing crack.

Going to the top of the stairs, she stood stoically with her hands folded. Molly's long blue dress hung from her trim waist in perfect folds right down to heels of her shoes making her look taller than her five feet three inches. With her neatly combed auburn hair falling to the middle of her back and painted lips, she looked quite formidable. It was her intention.

Molly didn't know the Siringos', and while she was sure Cole would have told them to treat her with respect, she'd rather earn it.

The two brothers sat together on a sturdy buckboard piled with lumber and tools. Behind them trailed their horses. Each of the men wore traditional broad brimmed sombreros and sported shirts with large collars and loose sleeves that spoke of a Mexican flair. Their pants were tight with high black boots. Though they had come to work, to Molly they still looked very much like dangerous pistoleros.

"Ola pretty Senora." Carlos pulled the wagon to a stop at the foot of the stairs and locked the brake with his shiny boot. He smiled warmly. "Senor Cole said you would greet us with cold silence or hot lead."

His warm smile broadened into a hopeful grin as did his brother's. "...but I would rather we be friends Senora. It would make this beautiful day more pleasant, and it would be such a shame to ruin it with holes in my shirt."

Molly let her hands fall by her side. "I will not be friends with trespassers."

Miguel leaned in his seat looking past his brother. Younger of age, his voice was softer and very kind. "I understand Senora, but we have no more say about being here than you do. Senior Cole says go to the pretty Senoras, we go."

Carlos nodded. "Si Senora. Could you not take pity upon our poor souls and invite us to stay? A happy man works much quicker and is gone sooner."

Despite her anger, what the brothers said made sense. If they were going to be there she might as well make the best of it. Molly eased her stance. "Very well. What did Senor Cole...I mean what did Uncle..." Molly groaned, took a breath and tried again. "What did Cole say you were to do while you are here?"

The men smiled eagerly. "Everything Senora. Mend your fences, patch your roof, hang the barn door, repair your broken window, paint your house. Anything else you can find."

Molly looked astonished. Paint my house! Your list will take weeks."

"Si Senora. We come here every day until our work is done."
"What about Cole's ranch?"

Unconcerned, Carlos shrugged. "The cows eat grass. They go nowhere I think."

All of a sudden Molly's eyes narrowed. "Is part of your orders to protect me?"

The men looked sheepish. Carlos took off his sombrero and held it to his heart. "I will not lie to one so lovely. Senor Cole wants your home put right, but I think maybe your safety means more to him, no?"

Molly came to attention and barked gruffly. "I do not want any gunplay on my property. Is that clear?"

The men did not answer. She raised her voice and stamped. "I said is that clear?"

Awkwardly, Miguel joined his brother in removing his hat. "Senor Cole said that to keep you calm we should obey you in most things, but if trouble comes, shoot first, then when the bad hombres are dispatched, run from your temper. He said it is more deadly than lead."

Screeching, Molly turned around and stormed back into the house slamming the door behind her.

Carlos stared at the empty porch. "Little brother. I think you could have chosen your words more carefully."

Miguel hung his head. "Si."

A moment later the door opened again and Jean timidly stepped out. "Mama says she'd appreciate it if you would start by digging a new hole for the privy behind the house. That way you'd be out of sight, and if the sheriff comes, she'll have a place to bury you."

Bad Water
Chapter 8
Carlos & Miguel

By the fifth day of the Siringo brother's visits, the Creed family had pretty well adjusted to the cheery Mexicans of dubious origin. Jimmy, eager to earn his keep pitched in wherever he could. Even Will was staying nearby eager to learn the use of the many tools in the wooden carpentry box that Carlos unloaded first thing each morning. Men had been few in Will's life, just an occasional neighbor stopping by to lend a hand. Having Carlos and Miguel present everyday eased a longing in the boy.

Jean, not to be left out, routinely brought refreshments to the men served with a pretty smile. When pouring coffee into Jimmy's cup, her eyes would flash letting him know that with sweat on his brow and calloused hands, she viewed him as one of the men.

It was surprising how many repairs had been made already. Miguel being lighter than his brother repaired the roof with the help of Jimmy who delighted in dropping broken shingles off the edge to scare Jean if she unsuspectingly stepped off the porch. He'd yell 'Look out!' then watch her jump. He'd laugh and she'd scold.

Miguel and Jimmy also took on the huge task of re-hanging the barn doors and fashioning a new latch. When they were done, the old door was better than new.

Meanwhile Carlos and Will carved a wooden seat for the outhouse. To the young boy's delight, the older Mexican taught him how to use a planer and the drawing knife. These were tools of men that Will held with reverence.

Over exuberant in his new found skills, Will had to be cautioned by Carlos. "The hole in the seat is big enough my son. Any larger and your poor sister might be staring up through it screeching your name."

The boy laughed, then reached for the brace and bit. "Can we cut a moon in the door?"

An hour later with the crescent shape proudly ventilating the privy door, they moved on to other tasks, replacing the missing spindles in the porch railing, and completely rebuilding the stairs. This time flat stones were buried in the ground so the wood stringers supporting the steps wouldn't be resting in the mud.

Carlos also set Jean to work re-glazing the window panes. She enjoyed the challenge and was proud to learn skills of her own.

Through it all Molly had remained out of sight, staying indoors or going for solitary walks in the back pasture where she kept a quiet vigil from afar.

Though mid-February, it was an uncommonly mild winter and by late morning with a break in the weather the sun had warmed the house enough that the men and boys started painting. As brushes were dipped into the buckets, Jean skipped out onto the porch ready to work stuffed snugly into a pair of Will's old torn trousers.

Miguel handed a brush to the shapely young girl, and cast a knowing glance at Jimmy who was grinning ear to ear. "Be careful Jimmy. With a smile so big, you might get paint on your teeth."

Though Jimmy tried hiding his delight at having so pretty a working companion by his side, it was beyond him to do so. The two young kids worked together all day painting from the same bucket, and usually on the opposite side of the house from everyone else.

Will watched his old jeans sashay by for the third time and scratched his head. Carlos looked down. "What is the matter William?"

The boy shrugged and went back to painting. "Hope they didn't look that funny on me."

Carlos laughed out loud. "It is not the cut of the cloth my son. A kitten and a badger are both covered in fur, but no one would mistake the two."

By late afternoon as the tired workers were wearing down, the front door now freshly painted, opened and to everyone's surprise, Molly timidly stepped out carry a tray of thin sliced bread and cured ham.

While there was no smile on her face, a sparkle in her eyes showed a willingness to make peace. Carlos and Miguel glanced at each other happy they had finally earned their way into Molly's good graces.

"Eat up everyone, Can't work on an empty stomach." Molly set the tray down on a small table by the newly hung porch swing and stepped back as the hungry crew wiped their hands and accepted her peace offering with eager grins.

The men's gratitude eased the butterflies in Molly's stomach. It had been no small act on her part. A battle raging inside her, she had paced the floor all morning, hungering to be a part of the cheerful camaraderie outside. Peering through her window at the many changes she'd dreamed of for so many years was more than she could bear.

With a final growl Molly surrendered her defiant stance, rationalizing that the Carlos and Miguel should not be punished for Cole's sins. She did feel safer with them around and happier too. There was simply no sense denying it.

Molly turned and looked out over her farm. For the first time in years the old barn door could be closed to the winter winds. The privy was in its new location minus the flies, and the house with new shingles, a fresh coat of paint, and a railing that no longer leaned, looked almost brand new.

Carlos came to her munching happily on Molly's midday creation. "These are delicious Senora. What are they?"

Hiding her nervousness, Molly tried hard to be pleasant. "They are called sandwiches. Read about them in a cookbook by an Englishwoman."

The Mexican took a large bite and talked with his mouth full. "I think we will ask Senor Cole for enough paint to do the barn. Sandwiches, hmm. The mustard is very tasty."

Leaving the porch, Molly walked out into the yard and turned around. Everyone was in good humor and enjoying the meal. It had been a long time since the hearty laughter of men had brightened their home. She realized how much she missed it. Her thoughts were drawn back to a Fourth of July day when Johnny and Cole threw firecrackers at each other while laughing like little boys. The grandparents were still among the living back then, and with a baby in her arms, their small farm full of hope and promise had been the gathering place for family young and old; how she longed for it again.

Out of the corner of her eye, Molly noticed Jimmy and Jean taking their sandwiches to the barn. She would have to watch those two. A mother's intuition told her Jean had had her first kiss.

On the porch, Will sat close to Carlos. Often when Molly had peeked out the window, Will was by the older Mexican's side. She'd have to watch them as well. A boy needs a man in his life to teach him things a boy should know, and Carlos seemed a kindly fellow, but like Cole, he lived by the gun. She recalled that morning in Crow Crossing when Carlos plucked the badge off the deputy's shirt as if life and death were only a game.

Miguel seemed less a gunman than his older brother, more quiet too. While working, he'd spent time being a big brother to Jimmy. They joked and played, at least until Jean came out to help, then it was a whole new game, but always with a smile, Miguel understood.

Jean had been right; the men did make her feel safer. Still guns were like Giant Powder with a lit fuse. Eventually it would go off. Molly tried to put it out of her mind. The last four days had been good.

Returning to the porch, she called to Will. "Son, put the bridal on Queenie, I'm going to ride down to the O'Donalds."

Molly caught the concerned look on the brother's faces. "Don't worry. They live just down the road. And I seriously doubt Cole ever meant for you to hold me captive."

The deepening frown showed the men still had some misgivings. "Oh good grief. I'll only be gone an hour. I can't believe I'm even telling you this."

Carlos stood and came near her. "It is not Senor Cole. It's just that Miguel and me have grown fond of your family, of you."

Molly flushed. She had never considered this. Miguel saw her surprise and rose from the swing. "Si Senora. Maybe we are only two uncivilized Mexicans to you, but it has been long since we have been near a decent woman, or a proper home with children. You have something of great value. Senor Cole sent us here to work, but each night we stay longer because of the kindness your family has shown."

Searching for words, Molly stammered. "N..No, I don't think of you as...as…that way...uncivilized." She was left speechless, and bowed her head.

Carlos took Will's hand. "Come little caballero. I will help you harness the mare. Your mother, she will be okay I think."
When they were gone Molly turned to the younger brother. "I don't think of you that way Miguel. It is just the guns."
"I understand Senora."

Weary, Molly turned and leaned on the railing. "They have cost me and my children so dearly, I don't know how much you are like Cole, but killing outside the law is murder. I can't raise my children that way."

Coming to her side, Miguel's voice rose in a solemn tone. "If we are not like Senor Cole, it is only because of a lack of courage."

The Mexican went silent collecting his thoughts. "Si, Carlos and me, we kill much, but as soldiers in the revolution. Still, maybe too much. It is why we have come over the border. Pretty Senora I think that you do not know Senor Cole fought in our revolution too."

Molly raised her head in surprise. "No...I didn't. I mean we hear of the killings he's done, but not of war."
"Senora, he fought not for gold or glory, or to murder as you may think. He fought for the poor. Si, Senor Cole killed many, but as a soldier. I think those who write the legend of Cole Creed have forgotten this."

Miguel seemed to grow in stature, his words heavy with patriotism. "Senora, there were many families where the husbands and fathers were taken from them, butchered by greedy men. Senor Cole fought for these families, now Senora, being here, I think maybe I see with different eyes. Maybe I think he was fighting for you."

Surprised by what Miguel had to say, Molly left the porch and walked out into the yard. Without realizing it, her steps slowed until she was no longer moving. She stared down the road towards the old Jarmello place. The years had been difficult and they filled her heart with bitterness, but time and again, the man she hated most surprised her. Hard lines of black and white which she held so dearly all these years were fading to shades of gray. It confused her.

Coming to Molly's side Miguel touched her hand with an outstretched finger. "You will not understand him. I should tell you that when the fighting was over, and the canons were silent. Senior Cole tracked down and killed...or as you say murdered a wealthy generalissimo who left many widows in his wake. Illegal yes. It is why we fled, but what he did, gave some justice to those who will get nothing else."

Molly scowled. "No Miguel. No man has that right. You can't put yourself above the law then claim to be better than others who do the same."

Miguel nodded. "I understand Senora. I think that to Senor Cole, justice is more than mere words on paper or a tin star. Justice is greater than law."

Lifting her eyes, Molly searched the Mexican's face. She had not expected such conviction from a man who treated death so cavalier. Still he had not swayed her. Molly folded her arms and stood resolutely. "Tell me Miguel how does slitting a man's throat in the dark of night serve justice?"

Just then Carlos and Will came leading Queenie out of the barn. She was hitched to the buckboard. Will with an excited skip hurried to Molly's side. "Guess what Mama. The wagon is ours."

Molly looked to Carlos. He nodded. "Si Senora. Ol' Paz left us several wagons that are going to waste. Senor Cole felt...well riding a plow horse is no good."

Doubt telling on her face, Molly took a step back. Carlos could see her dander rising at the mention of Cole. "Please Senora. It is a small gift that cost him nothing. Think of your daughter."

The gift was too much. Cole would not try to buy her forgiveness, but he was arrogant, and cared nothing of her pride. It cut her deep.

Will tugged at her hand. "Please Mama please. I'm tired of walking everywhere. It will save on boots."

Looking down at her son's pleading face, Molly slowly relented. "Alright. I'm too tired to argue." She turned to Carlos. "It's just that we need one so badly."

Resigning herself to the gift Molly trailed a finger across the buckboard assuring herself it was real, then turned back to the Mexican. "Carlos, I refuse to be beholding to Cole. You let him know that."

"Si Senora."

Before she could change her mind, Carlos took her hand and helped her into the buckboard. Hearing the creak of the floorboard beneath her foot, Molly's mood swiftly changed. She wiggled getting comfortable on the seat. It was padded leather with a backrest.

Hiding her delight, she turned to the men. "I'll be back in two hours. You should have the painting done by then."

Carlos protested. "But Senora, you said..."

"Two hours Carlos. I'm still the boss around here."

Asserting herself, Molly looked down at her son. "Tell your sister to get her fanny out of that hayloft and back to work or she will find those tight britches will dance nicely to a willow switch."

Flipping the reins, Molly headed down the road. Queenie was a plow horse and took easily to the wagon.

Bad Water
Chapter 9
Tom & Annie

Her own buckboard! She couldn't help but smile. In a few short days, years of poverty had been wiped away. Cole had spent very little, but he had given so much. There would be time to deal with him later, but for now she'd enjoy her new found riches.

"Whoa Queenie." Feeling every bit the queen herself, Molly leaned back in the seat and relaxed. There was no hurry and she was so tired. Since Cole's return sleepless nights had been taking a heavy toll. The O'Donalds' farm was half way between her farm and Cole's. She'd get there soon enough.

As the wheels rolled beneath her, Molly shook off her fatigue and tried to remember why she was on the road. "She hadn't seen the O'Donalds since the incident at Crow Crossing and she needed to know Tom and Annie were okay.

Annie was her very best friend. There was a genuine love between the two ladies, and they were often inseparable. The frontier life was hard, and men didn't seem to understand how difficult it was for women. Often outnumbered twenty to one and isolated on farms, a woman might go months without seeing her own kind. Molly doubted she could have gotten through it all without Annie's shoulder. Now she wanted to be there for Annie.

The number of families living near Crow Crossing changed daily. So many left in the dark of night or simply disappeared. Like Grampa Charlie had said; the farmers were being swindled or bullied. She didn't want the O'Donalds to be run off.

Something had to be done about the problem. An answer had to be found. In the back of her mind she thought of Cole though she tried hard not to, refusing to believe he might be the only answer. There had to be another way.

When she turned into the O'Donalds yard, she spied Annie sitting alone on the porch wrapped in a blanket her hands folded in her lap. As Molly pulled to a halt, Annie stood and came down the steps. Her petite frame appeared fragile, aged beyond her twenty-four years. Reaching up, Annie touched a hand to the leather seat. "Hello Molly. You have a buckboard."

Molly rested her hand over Annie's offering a tender smile. "It's a long story. How are you?"

Annie looked back towards her house. All pretense of happiness drained from her face. "Oh Molly. I don't know."

Setting the brake, Molly climbed down and put her arm around Annie. "I heard what happened at Rubens."

A whimper escaped Annie's throat as she struggled for control. Fighting tears, Annie laid her head on Molly's shoulder. "Well at least I don't have to try and hide it from you. Guess everyone knows."

Molly brushed the tangled strands of strawberry blond hair from her friend's injured face. "How's Tom?"

Annie trembled. "He's hurting. Shamed in front of his wife. Won't talk much. I can't bare the pain in his eyes. Tom's a proud man."

The tears finally came. Molly hugged her. "Come on. Let's go inside."

Allowing Molly to lead her, Annie cautioned. "Tom will be distant, but I know he will want to see you. He's got to start seeing somebody. Ain't seen no one since that morning."

Molly stopped in her tracks. "You haven't seen anyone?"

Annie shook her head. "Just been down the road to leave Chad with Grandpa Charlie for a few days. We haven't told him."

"Then you don't know?"

"Know what?" Annie looked confused.

"Let's go inside."

Opening the door cast a bright light into the darkened room. The curtains were drawn. Tom sat in his leather chair gripping the arms tightly with his fingers. Beside him on the end table was a half empty glass of whiskey. He was not drunk, nor was Tom a drinker. The fact that the glass was there at all, spoke of the pain he was carrying.

Molly stepped close. "Hello Tom."

Tom didn't answer and hardly nodded. Annie closed the door behind them, then opened the curtains wide. She tried to sound cheery. "Molly's come to visit Tom."

The younger woman spoke to her husband as if he didn't have the facilities to comprehend.

Moving to the divan, Molly took a seat across from Tom. As she did she extended a hand beckoning Annie to her side. Annie sat down close and held Molly's hand in her lap squeezing it tightly.

If Annie looked tired, Tom appeared exhausted to the point of near collapse. His face was strained and gaunt. He probably hadn't slept in days. "Tom."

Molly waited. "Tom."

Stiffly, Tom turned his head towards her. "Tom, I heard what happened at Rubens."

The muscle in Tom's jaw twitched. His eyes reddened. "Then you know."

Molly could hear Annie weep. "Yes. I heard that you spoke up for ol' Mr. Brody when no one else would. Not only that, you tried to protect him."

Tom gave a start. He took a deep breath rattling with emotion. "That's what they are saying?"

"Yes Tom, that was brave of you."

Tom's mouth opened in a hollow draw of air that shook deep down in his chest. "Fat lot of good it did...cept' shame me in front of Annie."

Molly smiled softly. "Annie knows the kind of man you are. One who would help a friend no matter the cost."

Staring forward, Tom once more gripped the arms of his chair, the anguish inside him welling to the surface. "I wanted to fight back, but it wasn't in me. A man should fight, and I couldn't..."

Sliding from her seat, Molly knelt by Tom and touched his arm. "You're not a killer Tom. Bob Olinger is. You would have played right into his hands."

Tom shook his head. "Still I should have fought, not just stood there like a whipped schoolboy." He clenched his teeth. "I should of..."

Molly slipped her fingertips into his large hand, prying it from the chair. "Would you have fought if he'd hit Annie?"

Tom's eyes lit with fire. "Damn right I would have. Would have killed that son-of-a-bitch."

Reaching up, Molly turned his face toward her. "That's the difference Tom. Having a reason to fight. You're no coward. Annie knows that. She knows you would protect her with your life."

Tears streaming down Annie's cheeks, she rushed to Tom and hugged him. He pulled her into his lap. "Oh Annie."
Tom held her tightly rocking slowly, her face buried into his neck.

The sunlight shining in the window, lit Tom's eyes as he awoke from the darkness that had consumed him. Clearing his head, he took Annie's face in his hand. "I would kill for you Annie, or die for you."

He looked up to Molly who was now standing. "Thanks Molly. Thanks for being a friend n' helping me see it in a different light. Maybe I can sleep tonight."

Lifting her head from her husband's cheek, Annie's moist eyes sparkled. She didn't need any words to express her gratitude. Her misty blue eyes said it all.

Turning back, she kissed her husband and giggled. "See silly, it's alright. You're my man and not a killer. Bob Olinger can't hold a candle to you."
His voice husky with emotion, Tom laughed needing the release. "That sorry son-of-a-bitch."

Having her man back Annie started crying all over again. "Don't worry darling he will get what's coming to him. You wait and see."
This time it was Molly's turn to laugh. "He already did."
Her friends looked up with surprise. "What?" They both spoke at the same time.

Molly waited a second adding to their suspense. "Right after you left, Bob accosted me, bragging they were going to hang Cole."
She rubbed her arm remembering. "No sooner than the boast was out of his cowardly mouth than Cole himself came riding in from the south trail. He called Bob's hand."
Molly laughed again. "You should have seen Bob shaking like a whipped dog looking for a porch to hide under. It will be sometime before he shows his face around here again."

Tom came to his feet clapping his hands. "Good ol' Cole."
The three of them laughed and hugged. Suddenly Annie pulled away clouding with concern. "What did Sheriff Brady do?"

Beaming, Molly threw her arms wide and let them fall by her side. "Why he bawled like a cow past milkin' time; threatened he'd be back when he had more evidence, then slunk away with his tail between his legs. Couldn't leave fast enough. Everyone was laughing. Your friends saw it all Tom. They know. Think you should visit ol' Mr. Brody. Bet he'd like to thank you."

Molly wiped her eyes, realizing how tired she was. It had been a long time since she'd slept too. "I'll tell you the whole story when you come to visit, but I must be on my way before I drop."

Reaching out, Tom hugged both ladies to his chest. "Thanks Molly." He kissed her forehead. "I know it's not likely but if you see Cole thank him for me too."

A smile frozen on her face, Molly went silent. Cole; she realized she'd been singing his praise. "...not likely Tom, but if I see him..."

Turning out on to the road, Mollie headed towards home, then all of a sudden she whipped Queenie in a full circle, and went the other direction.

She didn't know why she had turned the wagon around, but there were things that needed to be said. It was her life, only Cole was pulling all the strings while she danced like a puppet. It wasn't right, and she'd make him listen as she had her say.

Her heart was pounding and her head was numb with fatigue. Like Tom she had slept very little in the past week making it difficult to sort things out. Sleepless nights had been spent in worry and doubt. Lost in a gray twilight of confusion, she was no longer sure who or what Cole Creed really was. He'd become a legend steeped in myth.

The story Miguel had told of Mexico left her dazed. Cole had stayed away, but he cast a long shadow she could not escape. He was there at every turn, in every thought. Had his reputation as a killer come from defending the poor in a foreign war? Had Cole been defending her all these years when she thought he didn't care? Was that what was bothering her? Molly didn't know and she had to find out.

Queenie was trotting; something the old mare seldom did. Maybe she sensed the urgency in her mistress's hand. Down the road, Molly could see the weathered sign above the gate that Paz Jarmello hung long ago. It read, Tierra Amarillo, Yellow Land. Others might have chosen a name more lofty, but old Paz was honest.

Straining her blurry eyes down the road, Molly could see the top of the trees protruding over a small rise. Memories of the large adobe house and out buildings sheltered by tall Cottonwoods rekindled in her mind. Years had passed since the last time she had ridden through the gate. In her youth she remembered it as a beautiful place with a courtyard and a stone fountain. There were many people living at Tierra Amaillo back then, but as the doom of the Mexicans was sealed by the encroaching gringos, neighbors hid their eyes pretending that no harm was being done.

Molly gave the reins an extra flick and Queenie responded. Dust rose from the wheels boiling in the late afternoon air. If Cole couldn't hear them coming, he was either drunk or dead.

Molly's breath caught in her throat. Cole was a marked man, and yet he sent the Siringo brothers to protect her when he needed their guns. It was part of the problem. He could anger her or make her feel guilty at the same time.

What if he was dead? It was a foolish thought bursting into her bewildered brain, but right now Molly was so tired she was having difficulty separating reality from a run-away imagination.

"Whoa!" Hauling on the reins she yelled at the mare coming to an abrupt stop amid clatter and a cloud of dust. The courtyard was barren and for a moment her fear that harm had befallen him loomed quickening her pulse. Just as she started to think the worst the door of the house flew open. Cole came out strapping on his gun. She had barely set the brake before he was by her side clutching her arm. "Are the children okay? What happened?"

Molly threw her hands to her face. She didn't know whether to laugh or cry. "The children are fine."
Forcing her eyes open against the fatigue, she stared forward. "Everything is fine...and nothing is fine."
Molly reached for Cole's hand. "Help me down."

Sure that only great danger would have brought Molly to his gate, Cole set her swiftly on the ground. "What's going on Molly?"

Shaking her head, Molly tried to summon her thoughts. She opened her mouth to speak then suddenly kicked him hard in the shin.

"Ouch!" Cole backed away dancing on one leg. "What was that for?"

Molly clawed at her hair and wailed. "I don't know!"

Turning her back on him, she bent her head to the sky. "Why did you come back?"

Cole stepped up behind her. "You know why I came back, to protect you."

"Well you sure have a funny way of doing it."

Molly took a stumbling step across the hard ground and stopped. "Death rides with you Cole Creed."

Whirling around, her arms fell weakly by her side; her shoulders slumped in total exhaustion. "You painted my house."

Molly stared blankly at him trying to make sense of it. Her voice rose with irony. "My children adore you and they don't even know you."

Throwing her arm wide, Molly wailed. "You gave me a wagon Cole. Do you know how badly I wanted a wagon?"

Once more Molly whirled around and faced away. "I'm not going to thank you Cole. I can't forgive what you've cost me...I can't forget what you are."

"Why are you here Molly?"

Turning quickly, Molly came back and stood toe to toe as if she were ready to fight. "I wanted you to know what you've done has made a difference. You deserve that."

Cole looked confused. "Isn't that like saying thanks?"

She shook her head violently. "No Cole. No, because I resent you so much. I hate everything you stand for...and I don't even know what you stand for...did you really go to Mexico?"

Molly edged closer. "You kill people Cole."

Suddenly tears came to her eyes. "Maybe you didn't pull every trigger, but people die around you...Johnny died following you. Can't you see it? I'm alone because of you. The children don't have a father because of you."

Wiping her cheek, she stood glaring up at him. "You need to go."

Cole hung his head. "Molly, if I stay or go makes no difference; this valley is going to be wiped out. I'm just trying to make sure you aren't wiped out with it."

"I refuse to believe that Cole. There's always hope. There has to be. My children...I can't..."

His frustration growing, Cole angered. "When are you going to wake up?"

Molly laughed though weary beyond belief. "Wake up to what Cole...that we are one big happy family? Should I just let you waltz into my life and climb in my bed like we are kissin' kin?"

"Molly!" Cole scolded, but she brushed him off. "I haven't had a good night's sleep since you came back. Do you know what it's like to never sleep? If you crawled into my bed, I don't think I'd even know."

Lost in torment, Molly's legs barely held her. "Don't tell me you don't have feeling for me. No man could so totally screw up a woman's life and not have feeling for her."

Cole took her by the waist sensing she was near collapse. He pulled her into his arms supporting her. "I have feeling of a kind for you Molly, but you can't hold a boiling kettle and not get burned."

"Oh that's hilarious."

Molly leaned her head against his chest and beat him weakly with her fist. "You play with fire Cole. You do what you want. You send men to my home. You don't care how I feel..."

"I care Molly. I care more about you than you will ever know."

Molly closed her eyes and stopped struggling. "Somehow I don't feel lucky."

Bad Water
Chapter 10
A Time for Truth

Coaxed from her slumber by the warm sunlight on her face, Molly moaned and forced open her eyes. She was in her own bed. Groggy with a dull ache in her head, snippets of her confrontation with Cole were fuzzy at best. For a brief moment she thought to dismiss them as a bad dream, but there was no escaping the truth, she'd actually gone to see him.

"Aaag!" Molly pulled the blanket over her head. What had she accomplished other than making a fool of herself? She moaned into her pillow. "What was I thinking?"

Curling into a ball, she hugged herself then suddenly tensed. Her arms were bare. Sitting bolt upright in bed Molly threw the cover back. She was in her Petticoat. "Jean Marie!"
Molly shouted for her daughter. "Jean Marie Creed."

With a flurry of light footsteps, the door flew open. Jean scurried in still in her nightgown. She closed the door behind her and came to her mother's side. "Morning Mama."
In no mood for polite sentiments, Molly growled. "How did I get in my bed?"

Searching for an acceptable answer, Jean tried on several faces but none of them seemed to fit. She looked down. "Uncle Cole brought you home; said you were suffering from exhaustion."
The young girl smiled hopefully. "You slept twelve hours. Uncle Cole said not to wake you."
"He did, did he?" Molly felt her blood begin to boil then remembered Cole comparing her to a tea kettle. She took a breath...and then another, refusing to let him get to her.

Searching about she spied her skirt and blouse hanging over the chair. Molly clenched her teeth. "How did my clothes get over there?"

Jean stared at them for a long time. "They're nicely folded."
"Jean Marie!"

The young girl jolted at her mother's terse rebuke then shrugged her shoulders. "Well...Uncle Cole carried you in. Your clothes kinda' got over there and you sorta' got over here."

Molly pounded her fist against the sheets. "Damn him."

Fidgeting nervously, Jean tried to be positive. "I'm sure he only wanted you to be comfortable. You are still fully covered, and it was dark...except for I held a candle."

Raging, Molly threw her pillow at the door. "He did it just to spite me!"

Jean looked confused. "Did you want to sleep in your clothes?"

Molly rolled her eyes. "No! I didn't want to sleep in my clothes...Oh, honey never mind. You run along. I got to get dressed."

Frowning, Jean cocked her head. "Couldn't you go back to sleep for a while. Uncle Cole said I should make you breakfast in bed."

Molly swallowed a curse. "Uncle Cole....I mean your Uncle Cole isn't in charge here, I am."

"But Uncle Cole left orders that you were stay in bed."

Molly's screamed. "Isn't anybody listening to me?

Tossing back the sheets, she rose to her feet. "How long did he stay?"

"Not long." Jean rose with her mother. "Just gave me some instructions, put some money on the dresser, told Will to keep his eyes peeled and left."

Molly lifted her foot and slid on her dress. "You didn't invite him to stay for dinner or spend the night?"

"Oh Mama...he said he already ate."

"Jean Marie..."

Storming out the front door, Molly spied Miguel nailing down a loose board on the porch. "Miguel I need you to drive me to Lincoln, I've got business to attend too."

Startled, Miguel missed the nail and hit his thumb. "Ouch!" Popping his bruised appendage into his mouth, he jumped to his feet. "Lincoln? Senora it is a long ride and a very bad place. Senor Cole would not..."

"Hitch the wagon. I'll get my hat."

She wasn't going to take no for an answer. Leaving Miguel speechless she disappeared only to return a minute later positioning her hat on her head. "Miguel are you ready?"

She pulled up short. Carlos was standing by Miguel, a look of stern disapproval darkening his face in a manner she had not seen on the cheery Mexican before though she always felt he was capable of it. His fearsome face trumped hers as did his size.

Fearing he wouldn't let her go, Molly defiantly stuck out her chin. "Is my wagon ready?"

Her voice was shriller than she intended. It embarrassed her. "Is it?"

Carlos stepped forward blocking her way. "Senora, please. Lincoln is no place for you."

He towered over her making her feel like a little girl. Taking a step back, Molly came to her full height, but it didn't seem tall enough. "I want to go."

The Mexican folded his arms across his thick chest and scowled. "We cannot protect you there Senora. Sorry. You must not go."

Her eyes suddenly burning, Molly began to shake. "Are you forbidding me to go?"

Carlos weighed the question then at length sighed. "No pretty Senora, but Senor Cole..."

Molly stomped her foot. "Then I don't care what Cole says, I'm going. Is Miguel going to take me or do I have to walk?"

Carlos looked at his brother, then back to Molly. "I will take you."

Startled, Miguel protested. "No brother. She asked me."

Lifting his hand, Carlos stood firm. "It is too dangerous. There may be violence, and there are not so many notches on your gun as mine."

Molly interrupted. "Miguel is taking me for that reason. I don't want gunplay. Carlos you stay with my children. They'll be safer with you."

Turning to his brother, Miguel assured him. "It will be okay. Maybe the Senora is right. You are ugly and you scare people." He grinned. "I'll be fine big brother."

The long road to Lincoln crossed a barren stretch of land making the distance seem greater than it really was. Molly was still angry at Cole for putting her to bed then leaving, though she didn't really know why. Unable to calm herself, she fumed at Carlos for nearly forbidding her from going to town, but in the end he let her have her way so she couldn't find a reason to stay angry with him either. Once again she'd worked herself into a terrible state. Embarrassed she hid

behind a snooty pout and peeked up at her companion through the corner of her eye. So far Miguel had remained silent. Sighing, Molly brushed the yellow dust from her sleeve. "Are you mad at me?"
The Mexican shifted nervously. "No Senora. Only worried for you."
"You think me foolish don't you?"
"No Senora." Miguel grinned sheepishly. "Si...little maybe." He grinned wide. "Much foolish."
Molly blushed then broke into an understanding smile. "Maybe I am. Cole has got me so confused. But I have to believe that there is an answer other than starting a range war. Men are the fools. When they lack the wit to work things out, they start shooting as if that's going to fix everything. Fools!"

Looking down the road, Molly threw back her shoulders. "That is why I'm going to Lincoln. I must do something before there is another killing. I fear that next time it will be someone close to me."
Miguel frowned. "So that is why we go."
"You don't approve?"

Pointing to a thin scar on his brown cheek, Miguel spoke softly. "When I was very young Senora, I chased a badger into his hole thinking maybe we could be friends. Before Carlos pulled me out by my heels the badger he clawed me pretty good. The badger did not think we could be friends. To him I was a boy and he was a badger. That was enough reason to want me out of his hole."

Miguel turned capturing Molly's eyes. "Senora, this is a big land, but it is a hole just the same filled with greed. There are badgers who do not care that you are a good woman. They want you gone."

The Mexican had politely made his point. Molly pondered his words as the wagon rattled down the road. With shy curious glances, she studied her strange companion. Miguel was a little older than her, yet his humble nature made him seem younger, and here he was showing wisdom Molly feared she lacked.

Gently, she touched a finger to his cheek tracing the thin line as if she were reading a poignant passage from a book. "Miguel there are many kinds of scars. Maybe I am sticking my head in a badger hole, but I must try. I'll risk a scar if it saves even a single life. My children deserve a chance."

Knowing he could not dissuade her, Miguel relented with his usual cheery grin. "Si, but if you find your badger disagreeable, let's pray I can drag you out by your heels before he scratches your pretty face Senora."

A giggle broke from Molly's throat and turned into a full laugh. They both laughed and the wagon rolled on. There would be no changing her mind, and the soft-spoken Mexican would not try. It gave her comfort that someone was finally listening to her.

When the laughter died away, Molly impulsively hugged Miguel's arm. "I thank you for your kindness...and for all you've done for me and my children even if Cole made you do it."

The wagon lifted over a rock bumping them together. Miguel smiled. "I think that if it were my choice Senora I would come to your farm anyway."

He grinned sheepishly. "When this is all over maybe you will need a ranch hand."

Molly held his arm more tenderly. "You would stay...look after me and my children? Do the things a man is suppose too?"

"Si Senora."

Moved by his noble gesture, she unconsciously leaned her head on his shoulder and tried to sort out her emotions.

At length Molly lifted her eyes to his questioningly. "If Cole and your brother rode away, you'd stay?"

"Si Senora...if you asked me too."

Molly stared off into the distance. Dark clouds hung over the white capped mountains. Winter was not done; heavy snows were sure to come to the valley walling them away. It was a lonely existence for a woman fraught with dangers. Miguel's offer to stay and protect her lifted a weight from her shoulders. "I could not pay you."

Miguel grinned at her then looked away. Molly pushed him. "What?"

"Nothing Senora."

She turned sideways and tugged at his arm. "What? I really want to know."

Turning briefly towards her, Miguel shrugged then looked back down the road. "I think you already know Senora. To a poor Mexican like me wealth and position are foolish dreams for which I care little, but the sparkling eyes of a very pretty Senorita, her warm touch upon my arm, that is worth more than gold. Seeing your beauty each day is payment enough."

Molly lowered her head truly moved. He left her speechless. Sensing her awkwardness, Miguel joked. "...but if you were ugly as a mule, I might reconsider the gold."
She smiled. "If I were ugly as a mule, you'd still be just as sweet, and say pretty words to make me feel beautiful."

As the trail rolled on, Molly's mood lightened. Laughing and teasing, she prodded Miguel about his childhood. She was genuinely interested. "How old were you when you went to war for your people?"
Miguel shrugged. "It is hard to say. There was always killing as long as I can remember, but we were poor and had no guns. One day two soldiers came. They saw our sister Maria in the fields. She was pretty, but just a peon to them. One of the soldiers lifted her into his saddle laughing vulgarly at what they planned to do with her. I ran to them pleading, but they knocked me down. Carlos was barely seventeen yet he came running like a man full grown. He pulled the soldier from the horse and shot him with his own pistol before he hit the ground. To see Carlos do this brave thing fired my soul. The other soldier was trying to raise his rifle. I stabbed him with a wooden pitchfork piercing his heart. It was over that fast. My brother and I said nothing. We just stared at each other. We were frightened, but for the first time we felt like more than poor farmers. We knew then in that moment we could make a difference for our people. They did not have to suffer under the tyranny of evil men."
Molly was stunned. "It sounds so terrifying."
Again Miguel shrugged. "Si, I guess, but now we had the soldier's weapons and horses. These riches changed our lives, and si, it was exciting too."
"...so you went on killing? Soldiers I mean." There was disapproval in Molly's voice that she did not hide.
Miguel nodded. "Si. We joined a small band and we killed as you say, but only to protect our village. We learned to ride and shoot. We learned war."
"You became outlaws?"
"Si. If that is the word you choose to use."
Molly's voice lowered as she tried to hide her thoughts. "...and you were joined by other outlaws...?"

Sensing the questions burning inside her, Miguel nodded. "Si Senora. If you are asking about Senor Cole, then si."
Molly flushed at being so obvious, but she wanted desperately to know so she did not turn away.

Miguel looked off in the distance as his thoughts turned inwards. "It was a border town, a small cantina. We were careless and the soldiers caught us by surprise. They rushed in cutting us to pieces. Much shooting, much confusion. We were in trouble plenty when a tall gringo rose from his table angry his drink had been spilled. I remember the blur of his hand reaching for that black pistol. A bottle was knocked over. Before it smashed on the floor, he emptied his gun."

Miguel shook his head still amazed. "When the smoke cleared our fortune had changed. Senora, we thought we were fast pistoleros. We did much shooting, some wounding, a little killing. But Senor Cole, he opened our eyes. The soldiers were not invincible. With this truth we became a real fighting force. Those were the days. We made a difference. Our numbers swelled. A retired general of some note was called up by the people. He asked us to join him. We were now an army of the people. From village to village they cheered us. The general he made Cole a captain. Many battles. No gringo or Mexican ever fought so hard for our cause. Villagers sang songs about him; pretty senoritas followed him through the streets hoping to win his heart. Carlos and me we followed him too. We follow him now."

His story over Miguel looked up. "Senora, do not think him evil. He gave us hope. We earned the respect of our enemies, and more important the love of our people."

Molly reached out and touched Miguel's hand. "I see your pride, yet so much killing."
"Si. But is it not better to die with hope than to live without it?"
"Yes Miguel. But isn't it better to live with love and not die at all? There is a better way."

The Mexican chuckled and nodded. "Si. That is what I tried to tell the badger."
They both laughed and Miguel squeezed her hand.

Forgetting about what lay ahead, the unlikely pair continued down the road enjoying a new found friendship. For now, talk was easy.

The road curved through low hills of dry grass and scattered scrub oak trees that limited their vision to the next bend. They passed an abandoned house by the side of the road. The door was burnt away and the charred roof had collapsed inwards. It was adobe clearly of Mexican design. Bullet holes riddled the mud brick. Once beautiful pottery now lay broken where it had been smashed against the walls no longer of use to the family who once lived there. Molly lowered her head. "I am sorry Miguel, but I don't want my people to wind up as yours did."
Seeing her genuine sorrow for his people, Miguel was moved and slipped his arm around her offering comfort. "Si Senora. We tried peace. It didn't work."
Molly leaned her head against him, a little less sure of herself.

Beneath the shade of the trees lining the road the buckboard rolled on. Molly held close to Miguel seeking his warmth and perhaps something deeper that she dared not put words too. Eight years had passed since John's death, eight lonely years. Trying not to think about it, Molly turned her gaze ahead.

Houses became more numerous, and as they passed a weathered barn the long Main Street of Lincoln loomed before them. Tall trees planted in rows and tidy homes both framed and adobe belied the more sinister nature of the picturesque community.

Except for the round stone walled Torreon, a tower built for defense, Lincoln looked little different than other small towns dotting the west.

Abandoning her thoughts, Molly senses heightened. There were people on foot and horseback, mostly men. Two women on the boardwalk stopped and stared at them, then leaned together whispering obviously upset.

Her skin prickling, Molly shrunk closer to Miguel. Something wasn't right. No one was engaged in social chatter, nor did they politely nod as she and Miguel rode by. Some of the courser men on the street were even scowling openly at them.

Suddenly it came to her; a Mexican with a white girl. Mixed relations where not uncommon in this small town, but with factions tearing Lincoln apart, little provocation was needed to set neighbor against neighbor.

Perhaps some knew who she was and might have guessed that the Mexican by her side was one of Cole Creeds pistoleros.

Miguel looked grim. "Never have I seen so many badgers. It may be you who drags me out by my heels."

He brushed Molly's hand from his arm. "I think you should not sit so close. My blood will ruin your pretty dress."

"Miguel!" Molly shuddered knowing full well what Miguel was saying. He was not an old Mexican uncle. Young and virile, their closeness only added more fuel to a volatile situation. She'd been leaning against him with the sentiment of their journey telling in her eyes. Molly scooted to the edge of the seat. "Let's hurry Miguel. Take me to Judge Brewster's office. It is near the big store at the opposite end of town."

Miguel snapped the reins as several burly cowboys stepped into the street as if contemplating stopping them. He nodded to the men with a comical smile and quickly headed on. "Si the Big Store Senora. I hear of it. The Murphy Dolan gang's hideout."

"Oh Miguel they are not a gang...not really."

Queenie broke into trot and they sped away. Molly struggled to breathe. Something was definitely wrong. It had to be more than her hanging on Miguel's arm. These men smelled blood, but why?

As they made their way up the street, a large two story house sitting back off the road on the right side came into view. Molly gripped Miguel's arm. "Hold on. That's Susan McSween."

A woman standing alone on the porch looked up in recognition. "Molly!"

Molly placed a hand on Miguel's shoulder. "Miguel stop, I need to talk with her."

Pulling the buckboard to a halt, Miguel jumped down and hurriedly helped Molly to her feet. With his hand close his gun and the other on the small of her back he ushered Molly quickly away from the road.

The blond haired woman met them half way across the long yard. Her hair was in disarray and the tired lines on her face told of someone who had not slept.

Without so much as a hello, she took Molly's hand. "Quick! Come inside."

Sensing the woman's urgency, Molly followed her to the house.

The door closed and bolted, Mrs. McSween nervously peeked through the curtains assuring herself that no one was following. At length she turned and embraced Molly then anxiously stepped back clutching her hands. "Whatever on earth brought you to town? Haven't you heard?"

Unsure what Susan was talking about; Molly shook her head. "Heard what?"

The woman's eyes teared. "It's terrible."

She paced the floor then returned. "Last night they murdered John Tunstall."

Molly jolted. "Oh my God Susan."

John Tunstall was no ordinary man. Killing down-on-their-luck farmers was one thing, but Tunstall was a prominent citizen born of British aristocracy. He along with Alex McSween and Old John Chisum openly opposed the Murphy and Dolan stranglehold on Lincoln. To murder a man of his stature was all out war.

Susan paced the floor again. "They just gunned him down. Dick Brewer and Billy Bonney saw them do it."

Molly nearly wept. "Oh Susan." She embraced her. "It's worse than I thought. Who did it?"

Distraught, Susan struggled for control, but her trembling hands betrayed her. "Them, all of them. Tom Hill, Billy Morton, Jessie Evans, others, but Jimmy Dolan put them up to it. It's his doing." She threw her hands to her face and sobbed. "If they'd kill Mr. Tunstall, then Alex is next. I'm so frightened."

Comforting her friend, Molly held her tightly. "Where is your husband?"

Susan tensed. "He's meeting with the Justice of the Peace to swear out warrants for the killers. Fat lot of good it will do."

Pulling away, she looked at Molly with concern. "Why are you here?"

Molly suddenly felt foolish. She glanced at Miguel then to her friend. "I've come to talk with Judge Brewster. Somebody has got to start talking."

Shocked, Susan shook her head. "The time for talking is long past. You should leave town immediately. You should take your family far away from this valley while you can."

Standing her ground, Molly remained adamant. "I have to give it one last try for my children. Once the shooting starts Cole won't be able to defend us against so many."

For a moment Susan eyes glimmered with a feeble hope. "Perhaps there is still a chance, Dick Brewer, Billy and others came by. They have formed a group called the Regulators. They are with Alex now and they will give Jimmy Dolan a fight. Yes, leave it to them. They can fight for Lincoln and Cole for the Alamo Valley. Please Molly for your own safety, flee while you can."

Hugging Susan, Molly hurried to the door. "It is all the more reason I must try."

With the door closed behind her Molly headed towards the buckboard knowing her mission was that much more desperate.

Bad Water
Chapter 11
The Big House

Wanting to be gone from Lincoln as soon as he could, Miguel helped Molly into the buckboard and hurriedly joined her. A sharp snap of the whip and the mare headed down the main road to a massive two-story building. A sign read, L. G. Murphy & Co. It was an impressive sight.

Wagons and horses tied out front evidenced the lucrative transactions both legal and illegal of the Murphy Dolan Empire. Beady eyed men, their guns hanging prominently, milled out front. With neither the cut of farmers or cowboys, a stench of evil stole Molly's breath. It wasn't hard for her to guess that this unsavory lot were members of one of the many outlaw gangs known to be on Murphy's payroll.

Directly across the street was a long framed building that housed Judge Brewster's law office and other business concerns. In many ways the two men were cut from the same cloth. Like Murphy, Judge Brewster was enterprising to use the word politely. It was whispered that the judge got a generous portion of his wealth from Murphy. And it was common knowledge that Brewster's court always decided in favor of the L.J. Murphy and Company frustrating good citizens to the point that they saw the law as a waste of time.

Miguel pulled the wagon to a halt by a hitching post. Across the street the men stopped and stared unashamedly at his shapely companion.

Sitting stiffly, Molly did her best not to make eye contact feeling more foolish every minute for having come to Lincoln.

Miguel hopped from the buckboard, sized up a man outside Judge Brewster's door, then taking Molly's hand helped her down. "No good Senora."

Molly was having doubts herself.

Once on her feet, she quickly pulled her hand from Miguel's and stepped away. "Thank you boy. Give the mare some oats and wait here. I shan't be long."

Molly spoke loudly in a most condescending manner. Miguel held her eyes briefly a bit amused then obediently nodded knowing her superior act was for his safety. "Si Senora. I take good care of your horse. We will need her plenty soon I think."

His humor did nothing to calm her nerves. Molly looked to the stocky man blocking the door. He was wearing a rusty badge hastily pinned to a filthy half tucked in shirt, casting doubt as to his being a real deputy. Molly came to her full height. "Is Judge Brewster in? I have business with him."

Taking his time, the man rolled his whiskered jaw in a manner reminiscent of a cow chewing a cud then puckered his stained lips and spit a chew of tobacco clear into the street. He wiped the brown drool from his chin and answered in a gravelly voice that rumbled deep in his throat. "Waaa' kinda business?"

Molly glared indignantly. "That is none of your concern." With that she quickly pushed pass him hoping he was too dull witted to accost her before she got inside.

Fortunately, she was right. Closing the door behind her, Molly found herself in a narrow hallway. To her left was another door with an overly large gold-leaf placard that read; 'The honorable Judge Warren H. Brewster.'

She knocked on the door, then opened it without waiting for an answer. Pushing the brass handle wide, Molly could see a large rounded man solidly built in a tight black suit that strained at the stitches. He was sitting behind a hand carved mahogany desk. With a gilded pen set, ivory handled letter opener and a hand painted humidor, each precisely placed, it all spoke of power and wealth.

Clean shaven with thinning peppered hair pasted to his prominent head as if it were painted on and clear piercing eyes too small for his face, he looked every bit an imposing magistrate. Another plaque set squarely on the edge of his desk left no doubt who he was; the Honorable Judge Warren H. Brewster.

As the infamous jurist rose to his feet, Molly noticed another man leaning against the wall opposite the windows in the shadows. He was young, lean, dressed in blue trousers and a loose red cotton shirt. An engraved pistol low on his hip seemed to be as much a part of him as his nervous fingers tapping on the pearl handle.

By the way the man's eyes narrowed questioning her presence as if he had every right to, Molly knew he took affront at her barging in.

"Do you have an appointment with the judge?"

His voice was as icy as his stare. Molly couldn't help but shrink before him. Unable to find her tongue, she nodded awkwardly.

He took a step towards her. "The judge doesn't see just anybody." Fearing he might throw her out, she stumbled over her words. "I...my, my name...I'm Ma, Molly Creed."

The two men stiffened. After a tense pause, the judge smiled, if that's what the expression on his plump face could be called. Certainly there was no cheer in it and his mouth never quite closed leaving you to assume he was about to speak even when he wasn't.

There was something unsettling about him. It was subtle. Beneath a paper thin facade of congeniality, a perceptible disdain made Molly feel most unwelcome. He cast a quick glance to the young man. "My, my, my. The Widow Creed."

He stood behind the desk. "In deed a surprise. My, my, my."

The judge spoke with a soft practiced southern draw though it was said he'd come from New York City. Fastidious, he was himself as carefully tailored as his suit, and like his suit, something didn't quite fit.

The trappings of his office, right down to his overly large diamond tufted chair held him high above the humble position of trust he held in rural Lincoln County.

Without taking his eyes off of her, he spoke as though passing judgment. "Wade. Look who just waltzed in to my office, Cole Creed's next of kin, pretty and fair."

Avoiding the tall man's stare, Molly quickly slipped into a chair in front of the judge's desk planting herself firmly. Her reply was quick and indignant. "Cole Creed is kin by blood only. I would not allow such a villain near my family."

The judge nodded pensively as if weighing the truthfulness of her statement. He settled back in his leather chair. "Very well, since you have so boldly come without an appointment, what can I do for you Mrs. Creed?"

Shifting uncomfortably Molly waited to answer until the judge's eyes traveled from her trim waist back again to her face. He did not seem the least bit contrite over his obvious assessment of her.

Taking one last breath to calm herself, she tried to organize her thoughts. "Judge Brewster with your permission I will not mince words. I'm sure you are well aware of the untenable position of the small farmers. With the high cost of supplies at the Big Store, there is no way they can make enough to meet the mortgages which are also held by L.G. Murphy, in short they are being starved and bullied out. You are an elected official and this should matter to you."

Despite her nervousness she had delivered her first sentence without tripping over her words. It bolstered her confidence. "I will not argue the injustice of this. I..."

The judge interrupted. "Actually my dear, I was appointed. I answer to the governor and not the farmers. It changes things. Don't you think?"

Molly wet her lips and tried to keep her train of thought. "Perhaps, but I am not here to argue. In a letter you wrote me last fall, you offered a paltry five-hundred dollars for my farm. Surely you must know it is worth five times that. If I were to accept your offer there would not be enough for me and my children to start over."

Leaning forward Molly nervously gripped the edge of the desk. "Judge Brewster, if you will only double your offer, I can give you something worth far more than my farm."

Molly paused to compose herself. She had one chip to play and she needed to choose her words carefully.

The judge folded his hands on the desk. "And what would that be Mrs. Creed?"

Instead of piquing his interest as Molly had hoped, his voice hissed with a growing impatience. "What is it you have that I could possible want?"

Used to politer treatment from men, the judge's terse cynicism left Molly unsettled. Her hands retreated into her lap as she struggled to raise her voice. "What I have is Cole Creed."

She searched the judge's face intently hoping to finally see some excitement upon hearing the offer she had ridden so far to make. Molly entreated. "Jimmy Dolan and his toughs can chase the farmers away, but no one can chase Cole Creed. He may be a despicable cold-blooded killer, but the farmers will rally around him, indeed they already have, good men like Tom O'Donald and others are talking. Dolan will have a fight on his hands that will only end with more killing."

Again Molly paused to let Brewster show some surprise but instead his face hung like a clay mask giving up nothing so she awkwardly continued. "Judge if you pay me the pittance I ask, I will leave this valley...and Cole Creed will follow me. I detest him as much as you, but I'll make sure he is gone for good from Lincoln County. No one has to die."

Without changing his expression, the judge cast a glance to the other man. "You hear that Wade; no one has to die."
He repeated himself. "No one has to die.".

Slowly rising from his chair, Brewster released a hollow laugh. "You misjudge me Molly. May I call you Molly? Indeed, Missus doesn't seem to fit one so childlike."

Folding his hands behind him he stared out the window. "I don't hate Cole Creed. Quite the contrary, I admire him. Yes, I do truly admire him."

He turned and faced her. "Oh he is a tenacious killer as you say, deadly as they come, but he's a man of honor. That's his only flaw. He can't be bought."

Molly's jaw dropped. "Honor! But you are a judge. Honor is what you've sworn to uphold..."
Brewster raised his hand dismissing her protest. "Oh you are precious aren't you? As precious as a new born babe suckling at your mama's breast. You still believe in right and wrong."
Amused he turned to the other man. "Wade she believes in right and wrong. How adorable. My, my, my."

From behind Molly, the man called Wade joined the judge in laughter. Molly pursed her lips. "I did not come here to be insulted."

Brewster, amused by the injured pout of his uninvited guest, calmly returned to his seat. "In my kindness, I offered you money long ago when you would have been wise to accept it, but you didn't even have the courtesy to reply, well things have changed. My how they have changed. Have you heard that John Tunstall is dead?" The judge sounded almost delighted. "So why dear child should I pay you when now I can just take your land for free?"

Molly was stricken. "Take my land? But, but Cole…he, he won't let you."

"Won't let me?" The judge leaned back in his chair and chuckled in a most sinister tone. "He won't let me?"

Brewster shook his head. "Granted, Cole is fast enough to scare away the sheriff and a few deputies, but there are men faster. Men like Jess Evans, and young Wade Bannock here. Indeed, Wade could empty his gun while Cole's stood in leather."

The judge paused, assessing the woman before him. "You see my starry-eyed dove; Cole is not as invincible as you think. That, and he's always on the losing side. You farmers are the losing side. Cole knows that, but like I said, he's got that ugly streak of honor."

Molly was speechless. She'd come expecting to reason with a man of the law bound by honor, and sworn to uphold it. "But…"

Reaching the end of his patience the judge's voice rose in anger. "Frankly I am tired of you dirt farmers and of the great Cole Creed. He has killed too many men to just let him ride away hiding under a woman's skirt."

Molly's eyes flashed. "You sent those two men after Cole? The ones found in the river."

The judge sneered. "If they were the only men he killed, I could forgive him, but this has been going on for some time between him and me. Yes sir, he has cost me dearly in both money and pride. Do you hear me? Cole has hurt my pride!"

Brewster pounded his fist on the desk. "So justice be damned. I will see Cole Creed tried, convicted and hung by the law that you hold so dearly."

The gunman behind her coldly added. "Or shot through the head for resisting arrest."

Molly's face reddened. She'd been such a fool. The last hope she held was utterly dashed. "What about the law…what about us farmers, my children?"

Reaching across the table, Brewster took Molly's small hand in his. "Why if you were smart, you'd run. Run girl. Just run!"

Incredulous Molly eyes grew wide with disbelief. "Run? But I have no money. My children would starve."

"Oh come now, don't be so melodramatic. Pick wild berries like you primitive folk do; suckle your babies at your breast if food is scarce, but run."

Mortified, Molly tried to pull her hand back but he wouldn't let her. She stammered. "I, I have a daughter nearly fourteen, a boy eleven, I do not suckle them as you so crudely put it...let go you are hurting me."

The judge released Molly and leaned back in his chair, his devilish eyes once more drinking her in. "A fourteen-year-old girl? In full bloom! Bet she's as pretty as you. Is she?"

He did not wait for an answer. Shifting from one thought to another, Brewster continued. "First I offered you money and you refused it. Then I advised you to run, and here you sit. Out of the kindness of my heart I'll make one last offer."

No longer hiding his vulgarity, Brewster's spurious smile hung on his jowls like a hungry wolf. "Stand up child and turn around...slowly. I want to look at you."

"What?" Molly couldn't believe her ears. "I most certainly will not!"

The judge leaned closer. "Shall I have Wade stand you up?"

Molly froze.

"Wade stand the pretty lady up and turn her around slowly for me."

Cringing, Molly gripped the arms of the chair. "No! You will not touch me." Her voice cracked. "...I'll do it."

Furious, Molly rose to her feet glaring daggers at the men. It was useless. Their evil was beyond her comprehension. Showing her contempt, she whirled quickly around. "There!"

The judge sneered. "Now do it again child...slowly, like I told you." Brewster would not be denied.

Her face coloring with humiliation, Molly resigned herself to her fate and moved slowly under the men's scrutiny. Turning full circle, she stopped and sneered at the judge. "Are you satisfied? Do you find some worth in a dirt farmer now?"

"Indeed I do." Brewster nodded his head in approval. "Nicely put together. Very nicely. Many a lonely cowhand would happily surrender his hard-earned pay for what you've so richly been endowed with."

Molly wanted it over. "I've done as you've asked and endured your insults. I'll find no justice in your court. Good day Mr. Brewster."

She turned to go, but the judge boomed. "Stop!"

His voice grated in his throat almost a growl. Molly froze in mid stride knowing it was not a request. In Lincoln County Judge Warren Brewster was the law and there was no appeal.

Her hand on the doorknob she resisted as long as she dared then obeying the judge's command, Molly turned to face him hating it all the more because the judge knew she had no choice.

For a moment she tried to remain brave, but unable to hold his intimidating glare, Molly faltered and cast her eyes down.

Brewster stood silently letting a minute pass until she was thoroughly cowered. "There my child. That's better."
He played his words out slowly. "Don't you want to hear my third offer?"
Molly was sullen. "Go ahead have your fun at helpless woman's expense if it makes you feel powerful. Tell me your third offer so I can be gone from your sight."

The judge bristled. "I find your snotty attitude most disrespectful." His fingers strummed on the desk like an angry parent, then clenched into a fist. "...and I am powerful. That you will learn my pretty."

An undercurrent of rage shook his massive frame as it boiled near the surface. "You think the Creed name makes you special, you think you can waltz in here and demand justice from me."

Rising, Brewster leaned across the desk and shoved his nose at Molly. "Lincoln County is a gold mine for men of vision and power to reach out and take as they see fit."
Throwing his arms wide he looked upwards as if towards heaven, his voice ringing like a traveling preacher. "Men like Mr. Murphy, Jimmy Dolan...and myself, Judge H. Warren Brewster. Yes! All we have to do is brush away the Creeds of the world."
The judge shoved his nose closer to Molly causing her to retreat. His voice dropped to a whisper. "You are dust."

His mood ever changing, Brewster could hardly contain himself "How dare you stroll into my office proud and arrogant offering me a deal and then have the temerity to presume to tell me my duty? You are dust."

The judge pounded his desk. "Now turn around again, only this time surrender your pride and submit yourself to my inspection."

Numbly, Molly obeyed feeling naked beneath his stare. Consoled, Brewster looked at Molly approvingly. "You are a lovely speck of dust, and dust that sparkles could be gold dust in the right hands...
He looked down at his hands slowly cupping them together. "My hands."

It was as if he could see the tiny flakes sparkling on his fingers. He raised his head. "Oh there would be riches for you. You and your daughter would be bathed in scented water, dressed like dolls in satin and silk. You'd have beautiful rooms, wallpapered with mirrors, and high feather beds. All your needs taken care of."

Brewster cocked his head. "Does it not sound like heaven Molly?"

Molly stood dumbfounded, not understanding what he was talking about. The judge smiled condescendingly. "I'll explain my dear child. You see I have financial interest in a charming brothel in Leasburg, but women are so scarce. It causes me difficulty as you can well appreciate. It was what Wade and I were discussing when you barged in, an answer to my prayers. God truly loves me."

He saw the disbelief register on her face and pressed harder. "Why with all the lovelorn cowboys and homesick soldiers you would do your country a great service as well as turn me a tidy profit. You see Molly, unskilled as you are, easing the suffering of these wretched souls; an angel of mercy is truly all you are suited for so don't discount my generous offer. Your worries will be over dear child. No more killing...No one has to die." The judge lifted an eyebrow. "Save for Cole Creed that is, but after all you hate him. Consider his death a down payment."

Molly shook visibly, her legs barely able to hold her. She struggled to breathe. "A whore? That's your offer? A whore? And what of my son?" The judge merely shrugged. "He's dust."

Livid, Molly wanted to strike him. "You are a horrible man. I thought Cole was bad, but now I understand."

Molly backed to the door, her voice raw and thin. "Thank you for opening my eyes. I hope you rot in hell."

Brewster showed no emotion. "Does this mean you refuse my final offer? Pity. We could have done it the easy way. Pity, pity."

Unable to contain her anger, Molly screeched. "Have you truly no human decency? Your offer is absurd; absurd as you standing there with your pot belly in an ill fitted suit. Whore! The farmers will fight. You don't know who you are dealing with."

Brewster exploded. "Absurd. You call me absurd!" The judge shrieked. He was not a man to scoff at. "No my little harlot, you are a paper thin girl in a fat man's world, a pretty veneer with no substance, a paper doll to be undressed as it pleases others, that is your only value. It is you who have no idea who you are dealing with...but very soon."

Reaching behind her Molly fumbled for the door handle in disbelief. "I am not a whore, and neither is my daughter."

The judge smirked. "You are if I say you are."

Bannock stepped over and caught Molly's arm, his face wicked with amusement. "I could take her there now. Ride out, fetch her daughter, kill Cole and be done with it."

The judge shook his head. "Too messy Wade. Got to handle it by the law. Cole will take some thinking. For now, just sweep this pretty little dust out of my office. She won't go far, too stupid to run."

Finished, the judge returned to his chair, and started shuffling papers with not so much as another look at her. His mind was on to other matters.

Bannock grinned. Gripping her tightly, he lifted Molly onto her toes and danced her into the hallway slamming the door behind them.

Having never been manhandled, it left Molly speechless. Her eyes wide, she tried to pull away, but Wade reached out digging his claw-like fingers into her cheeks. "Not through with you yet." Chuckling hideously, the gunman pulled her close, his acrid breath burning her nostrils. "This is for Cole. Tell him I'm coming. Tell him what I did."

Bannock ground his whiskered mouth into Molly's soft lips causing her to whimper. Panic nailed her to the wall. Sliding his hand inside her coat he grabbed her breast and shoved her roughly against the wall pressing his kiss further.

Imprisoned by his weight, she trembled against him betraying her terror. Bannock sneered into her shattered face then ran his tongue across her lips. "Tell him. Tell the great Cole Creed that Wade Bannock violated his womenfolk."

Molly tried to scream, but he pressed his thumb deep into her throat until she gasped. Enjoying his cruelty, he squeezed tighter until her eyes bulged. "Now maybe you understand."

Jerking her from the wall, he brutally threw her to the floor. Molly landed with a heavy thud and turned her eyes upwards fearing he was not done with her. Bannock dropped his hands to his hips letting his evil laughter ring from the walls.

There was a heavy thump outside the door. The narrow hallway suddenly burst with light. Twisting her head Molly saw Miguel, the unconscious deputy laying prostrate at his feet. Her brave protector pushed inside, his hand opening by his gun. "No!" Molly grabbed his wrist and pulled herself up. "No Miguel!"
Pushing him backwards with all her might, Molly kept her body between him and the gunman. "No. Take me home...now!"

Her frantic expression pleading more than her words, Molly backed Miguel out the door and shut it quickly. She knew this brave Mexican would defend her with his life, but he was no match for a man like Bannock. "Help me into the wagon. Please."
Sick with fear she scrambled for the seat. "Please Miguel. Hurry!"

Trying to sooth her, Miguel lifted Molly up, and grudgingly climbed beside her. "Senora did he hurt..."
"Just go." Molly sobbed. "Go!"

The door flew open. Bannock stepped onto the boardwalk. He was still laughing. "Greaser, you bring her back anytime she wants a little loving."

Miguel's fists tightened on the reins knowing the gringo needed a bullet in a bad way. Molly clutched tightly to his arm. "No Miguel." The brave Mexican looked down into her pleading eyes. She beseeched. "If he kills you, I'll be at his mercy."

The gunman's laughter taunted, but Miguel hauled on the reins, spinning the wagon around. His love for the girl was greater than his lust for vengeance. He eyed the arrogant man. "Gringo, it is not your day to die, but soon."

In a heartbeat Bannock's laughter turned to insanity, his face contorting with rage. Molly yelled at the mare. "Go Queenie, Go." In response to the familiar voice the horse bolted into a run.

Speeding away Molly looked behind her. The insult from the Mexican had incensed the vile gunman. Even at a distance Molly could see murder in his eyes. "Faster Miguel."

Bannock stepped into the street his hand reaching for his gun, but luck was with them as another wagon crossed between. A dozen yards more and trees lining the street blocked the evil man from their view. For Molly it wasn't enough. She wanted to be done with Lincoln, have it far behind. Her heart cried for home where she'd be safe, nearer to Cole. The truth hurt, but she didn't care. What a fool she had been.

Bad Water
Chapter 12
Starlight and daylight

An hour passed yet Molly's stomach churned with a sickness she doubted would ever go away. How could anyone be so cruel?

She hated the gunman for what he'd done to her, but she found the judge even more despicable. The law which she held so dear; that gave her fragile world security, was merely an end to a means for him. Worse than Wade Bannock's violation, Brewster had stolen her peace of mind. How could she ever feel safe again?

Molly shuddered at how calmly he offered to make her a whore as if he was doing her a favor. Dust! Her children were not dust and Jean would never be used for the pleasure of men.

A cold breeze stung Molly cheeks reminding her that winter was still upon them. She stared off into the distance trying to forget the terrible ordeal.

The evening sun laid low on the horizon, its fading orange light surrendering to the gray shadows spreading balefully across the land. A whore! How dare he. Molly retched, nearly vomiting. What a fool she had been.

Miguel placed a hand on her back rubbing gently. Fuming himself, he had not said a word since Lincoln. He had wanted to kill the gunfighter, instead he rode away. His first responsibility was to protect Molly, still it left a bitter taste. He looked down. Seeing her pain, Miguel set his anger aside. She was all that mattered. "Are you okay Senora?"

Molly lifted her head. Humiliation telling in her eyes, she nodded hesitantly. "Thank you Miguel. I'll be...okay."
She covered her face and burst into tears. "I've made a horrible mess of things."

Reaching out Miguel pulled her to him. "Cry on my shoulder if it will help. No children here to see."

Molly fell against him releasing her tears. He hugged her tenderly. "You will be okay Senora. I have no tools to fix such things, but when I get you home, maybe a soft blanket by a warm fire will soothe the hurt."

Crying openly, Molly struggled to breathe. "Oh, Miguel I feel like a fool. Those men. How could anybody be so evil?"

Miguel shook his head. "In Mexico while fighting unspeakable cruelty, I asked the same question."

Wiping her eyes, Molly sniffed and looked up. "And?"

Miguel stared at the disappearing sun. "There is no limit to the evil in men's hearts. Yet neither is there a limit to love."

His face shining with the last golden rays, he turned to her and softly smiled. It was the most honest smile Molly had ever seen. It warmed her very soul and pulled her closer to him.

Miguel tenderly raised her chin on his finger. "Love is greater than evil. It has substance. This gunman back there may have thrown you to the floor, but you are stronger than him, for you are love."

Molly's eyes glistened. Reaching up she wrapped her arms around Miguel's neck and kissed him softly on the cheek. "Thank you. I needed to be reminded of that."

The young man blushed. "I think pretty Senora, you have made me a very rich fellow, or at least one greatly overpaid for a few honest words."

Molly smiled and placed a second kiss a little closer to his lips, then released him. "No really Miguel. I thank you for your kindness. I don't know what I would have done back there without you. Or even now." She playfully shoved him. "...and your soggy shoulder. You've been so..."

Miguel jolted as if a man stricken. Molly stared not understanding, then the distant crack of a rifle echoed across the barren land.

Screaming, Molly threw her arms around Miguel pulling herself to him. "No!"

Her hand came away covered in warm blood. "Miguel!"

The brave Mexican snapped the reins sending the mare into a run. "Take them little one. Kill the horse if you must. Senora, I lov..."

Miguel slumped in the seat.

With no time to think, Molly grabbed the reins and whipped the horse faster. She looked to her side. "Miguel, Miguel!"
He did not answer. Molly shouted the mare onwards. "Yah!"
She looked behind her expecting to see riders, but in the brief seconds since the rifle cracked the sun surrendered its last light shrouding them in blackness.

The shot had been at a distance, like the one that killed her husband. She couldn't let it happen again, not to Miguel. "Yah..yah....yah!"

The old mare did her best to obey, but it was a long way home and she was already covered in lather. "Yah, go Queenie." Molly cried. "Go...please."
Tears rolled down her cheek drenching her blouse.

Swallowed by the dark, no speed was fast enough. She placed her hand on Miguel. He was warm and his muscles yielded to her touch so she told herself he was not dead, not yet.

Molly slapped the reins and prayed out loud. Queenie was taking air in great gasps, age was against her. The wagon bounced recklessly down the road. "Hurry Queenie."
How far the old mare had run Molly could not tell. The horse was weaving from side to side her tongue hanging out.

Spent herself, Molly slowed. "Sorry Queenie, she cried. "You've done your best." Running her fingers lovingly through Miguel's hair Molly sobbed. "...but maybe a little more...just a little more Queenie."

Carlos walked to the gate as he had done many times for the last hour. He paused and stared down the road. They should have returned a long time ago. His horse was saddled, but he delayed, hoping that all was well and that he was just being an over protective big brother. Miguel was family, and the beautiful senora was a rare flower whom he could not imagine anyone wanting to any harm, so he waited.

Drawn by an unseen hand, Carlos stepped anxiously into the lane one more time. Had there been something? A sound? His eyes strained against the night. For a brief second a star near the road blinked out, then another. He heard a fragile squeak from a woman's throat. A dark shape stumbled and fell only to get up again and struggled towards him.

Carlos broke into a run. "Senora...Molly."
Upon hearing the Mexican's voice, the woman collapsed. In an instant Carlos was by her side. He scooped her up from the dirt. "Oh Senora."

Her slips were gone and her dress was shredded from her terrible ordeal. How long had she run?

Cradling her to his chest, Carlos headed through the gate. "Hold on a little longer my child."
Her throat raw from gasping for air, Molly croaked. "Miguel." She tried to lift her arm to point behind her, but she hadn't the strength.

Hurrying as fast as he could, Carlos made his way to the house. A light was on. He hollered. "Senorita Jean, Senorita..."

The door flew open as Carlos reached the steps. "Mama!"

A warm damp cloth dabbing gently at her face roused Molly from her slumber. Without opening her eyes, she moaned weakly. Speech was beyond her. Reaching up she touched a soft hand. It was Jean. "Mama."
The young girl shook as her eyes filled with tears. "Oh Mama."

Slowly Molly rolled her head towards the voice. She parted her lips but could not find words for her torment. Weak beyond all measure, Molly lay in her daughter's arms. She dared not remember...Miguel.

Broken in body and soul, Molly drifted off hiding in the dark reaches of her mind where pain was dulled and thoughts forbidden. Lost in a perpetual night, fear like a distant wind moaned evil across the hilltops never reaching the valley below, here huddled in the space between dreams she was safe for a while.

From time to time she'd stir but never truly wake. In her delirium she was aware of Jean's constant presence and Annie's too. It calmed her. When the winds came too close and she tossed fitfully, gentle hands on her shoulder would press her into the pillow. 'Sleep...sleep', and so she did.

Hours passed or was it days. Familiar voices came and went, at first like whispers from afar, then slowly, ever slowly they spoke to her clearly calling her from the dark. At last it was time. Molly heard the door creak. Reaching deep inside, she found the strength to force open her eyes. As her vision cleared, Carlos stood before her bathed in evening light. She could see the pain etched in his face and she knew. Rolling her head into her pillow Molly wailed.

The older brother sat on the bed beside her. Reaching down he gathered her in his arms. She cried like a fragile child. Ever so tenderly he placed a kiss on her forehead. "Rest Senora. They can hurt him no more."

When Molly woke again she could smell vegetable soup wafting from the kitchen. Rising slowly from her pillow she sat up in bed. Her hands were bandaged. A sharp pain reminded her she had fallen down many times during the long nightmare that brought her home. Her bare knees were skinned and raw, as were her feet.

Clutching the sheet to her, Molly tried her voice. "Jean." It was a little more than a scratchy whisper, but her attentive daughter was vigilant. The door opened and Jean stepped through carrying a bowl of soup. "Mama get back in bed."
Molly shook her head. "Please dear, get me something to put on."

The young girl stood her ground. "No Mama. You eat some soup first then we will argue."

Relenting, Molly crawled back under the covers. She reached out for the bowl then remembered her hands. "Guess you will have to feed me."

Jean took a place by her patient's side. With a heart full of questions she dared not ask, she put a spoon to her mother's lips. "Sip slowly Mama."
The tears on their cheeks spoke of shared grief. It was a hard thing. Miguel was gone, but for now they would not put words to it.

Molly waited patiently as Jean wiped her chin with the edge of the spoon, then accepted another bite. "Has Annie gone?"
Jean nodded. "She had to get home to nurse Polly, but she'll return."
"Is Carlos here?"

Jean shook her head. "No...no Mama, he went to pull Queenie from the road."
"Oh Jean!"

Taking a napkin, Jean blotted a tear from her mother's cheek and tried to change the mood. "If you keep crying you will get your soup wet."

Molly lowered her eyes. "Did...has...never mind."
The young girl understood. "Just for a bit Mama. He helped Annie with your bandages then he tore out of here like..."
Jean wiped her own cheek on her shoulder. "Here. Take another bite."

Raising her bandaged hand, Molly pushed the spoon away and looked intently at her daughter. "Like what?"

Slowly resting the spoon in the bowel, Jean's voice lowered to a frightened whisper. "Think somebody is going to pay before the day is done."
"Was he angry?"
Jean set the bowel down. "That was it Mama. Not so much as a hell or a damn when he saw your torn body. Uncle Cole's mind was already set. I fear something real bad is going to happen."
Molly sobbed. "What have I done?"

Bad Water
Chapter 13
A Dark Horse

Heavy dark clouds hung oppressively over the mountains blotting out the sun. As if the morning was not dismal enough, a cold fog drifted hauntingly above the damp earth as if the spirits of dead had come to pay their last respects.

A small funeral service was held in the yard beneath a lone pine standing near the road. It was just a tree, but today it was given the solemn honor of marking the final resting place of Miguel Julio Albano Siringo.

Tom O'Donald with the help of the boys, dug the grave in the early hours before dawn. Their black silhouettes worked silently in the thin gray light. The somber ringing of the pick and shovels echoing off the walls of Molly's room told her the hour was near.

When they were done, Tom was kind enough to carry Molly out and set her in a chair on the porch. Annie tucked a warm quilt around her and squeezed her hand before joining the others by the grave.

After the men and boys lowered Miguel's pine coffin to his grave, Annie sang an old church hymn soft and sweet. When she finished Jean stepped beside her and began 'Amazing Grace'. She was growing up so fast. It brought more tears to Molly's swollen eyes.

As her daughter's melodic voice rose on the frigid air her sad refrain was joined by a low cadence of hoof beats. Appearing out of the fog, Cole rode into the yard and quietly dismounted.

He removed his hat and bowed his head, but stayed apart from the others. Molly lifted in her chair. He looked both handsome and deadly dressed in black. How tall he seemed.

While the women wept Cole stood cold as iron though Molly knew he hurt no less. Poor Miguel had followed him out of Mexico. It had to play on Cole's mind.

The hymn sung, Tom bowed his head and lead them in a prayer; ashes to ashes dust to dust. With the Amen solemnly given, Cole climbed on his tall roan without a word. Molly held her breath wondering if he'd ride to the porch or at least tip his hat to her, but he did neither.

When it was all over they slowly drifted from the grave, Tom comforting Annie, and Jimmy wiping Jean's tears. Will stood stoically awhile longer then followed the rest leaving only poor Carlos kneeling by his brother's marker.

Returning to the porch, Tom gathered Molly in his arms and carried her back to bed. Annie waited for him to leave then sat beside Molly holding her hand, letting her cry her last tear. "You best get some rest."

She kissed her softly and started to leave the room.

"Annie wait..." Molly went silent and turned her head towards the wall.

Returning to Molly's side, Annie petted her hair. "What is it darling?"

Molly's lips twitched as she struggled to speak. "...no one mentions Miguel in my presence...do they blame me for his death?"

She sobbed and burst into tears.

Annie's heart ached for her friend. She pulled Molly into her arms and held her head to her breast. "No sweetheart...no. We are trying not to cause you anymore pain."

"Oh Annie..."

Molly laid quietly in Annie's embrace, her eyes staring across the room. At length she found the courage to speak what was burning in her heart. "Cole...he didn't stay very long."

Squeezing Molly tightly, Annie rocked. "No...no he didn't darling, but he carries a heavier burden than the rest of us...thankful he came at all."

Molly lifted her head. "What Annie? What's happened?"

Annie pulled Molly back to her breast. "Best you rest."

Sniffing back her tears, Molly pleaded. "I have to know. He just rode away without a glance in my direction. He blames me?"

"No baby. Not Cole." Annie kissed her forehead. "He protects you."

"Then what Annie?"

Her brow furrowing, Annie leaned her head against Molly's. "Oh darling, Cole's gun had already spoken. Guess you don't know it, but he warned them long ago; you don't mess with Molly Creed he said, or you buy a one-way ticket on a train to hell. Said it before he went to Mexico."

Annie took a breath. "The night after Carlos found you, the judge's barn burnt to the ground. They say a dark rider on a tall horse back-lit by the flames watched it burn. Three men pursued him into the hills. They never returned. Tom says it's rugged country covered in snow, and if their bodies are up there, it will be spring before they are found if the wolves don't get them first."

Annie held her close and rocked her. "It's started Molly. They say no one had ever seen the judge so crazy."

Holding Molly as tight she could Annie shook her head in anguish. "There's more Molly. Story goes that before dawn a herd of Murphy-Dolan cattle, over six hundred head, stampeded turning over wagons, trampling out buildings and fences. Something had spooked them bad. Some said Indians, but in the morning when the drovers returned from rounding up the cattle, they found a sombrero hanging on the judge's gate. It was whispered to be a warning from Cole. Eyes for an eye Molly. Eyes for an eye. Yes, it's started."

Lifting Molly's tear stained face, Annie looked into her eyes. "That's why Cole didn't come near you. He knows how you feel and he carries the stench of death."

A week had passed since Carlos had found Molly in the road. She was young and her physical wounds healed quickly. Most had already faded or disappeared completely, all but one thin gash on her knee. It would leave a scar. Tracing it Molly thought of Miguel. He was right about him having to pull her out of a badger hole, only he never told her it would cost him his life. She had not considered that. Thinking back, they'd tried to tell her but she refused to listen. Bowing her head, she allowed a few last tears knowing guilt would be her constant companion for a very long time.

Stepping timidly onto the porch, Molly shaded her eyes against the sun not quite sure she was ready. Geronimo, their old red rooster was crowing off in the distance hearkening the new day. A few crows flittering along the fence post added their cries. Life went on.

At the top of the steps, Molly hugged herself against the chilled air. She was wearing a white laced dress. It was a special dress that fit her fragile mood.

The sound of a hammer ringing solemnly in the barn drew Molly across the yard. She lifted her skirt and hurried with quick light steps. Days had passed in long silence. Having hardly spoken a word since the dreadful night, her heart beat faster knowing she must make peace with Carlos, but not knowing what to say.

Molly paused at the door resting her finger tips gently on the freshly painted wood. Against the deep red stain her white dress burst with the brilliance of the morning light.

The ringing of the hammer stopped. As her eyes adjusted she saw Carlos and Jimmy looking up from their work. Taken by her angelic appearance, Jimmy was the first to speak. "You look beautiful." He blushed, realizing he spoke his thoughts out loud.
"Thank you Jimmy." Molly blushed too.

The boy looked to Carlos, then brushing the sawdust from his trousers, he stood and edged toward the door knowing the conversation that needed to happen didn't involve him. "Guess I better roust Will and get the chickens fed."
Scooting past Molly, he couldn't help staring; her eyes sparkling and the soft winter sun playing in her hair. "Sure's a pretty dress Mrs. Creed."
A quick smile was given and Jimmy was gone.

Molly stepped into a patch of light in the middle of the straw covered floor and folded her hands before her. Carlos watched her without speaking. His eyes held kindness yet Molly's fingers still fidgeted nervously. "What are you building?"

Carlos gestured to a corner of the barn with a small window. "We are turning the back stall into a bunkhouse for Jimmy and me."

Tossing a handful of nails into a bucket he stood. "The boy needs a bed."
Carlos set the hammer aside and stepped close, almost touching her. "Cole and I decided I should stay here until the bitter..."
He paused and forced a smile. "...well, that I should stay here."
"So it's come to that?"

Molly turned so he couldn't see her eyes. "You are going to stay to protect me after the suffering I have caused you?"

Throwing her hands up, she covered her face. Her heart was full of apologies and gratitude and so much more she wanted to say but it hurt too much. Carlos took her by the shoulders and turned her around. "There now, pretty Senora. We buried our sorrows. Today is for the living."

Molly hung her head letting her long soft hair cover her face. "You were right Carlos; I shouldn't have gone to town."

Pulling her towards him, he let Molly rest her head on his shoulder. "Who's to say what is right? Maybe you shouldn't have gone. Maybe I should have stopped you. Maybe...It does no good little Senora. We do the best we can. Is that not what you tried to do?"

Wrapping his arms around his fragile charge, he held her gently. "I've seen a lot of killing. What I learned is that good men die. I have to be okay with that. It is something I cannot change, even if it is my only brother."

Molly sniffed and found a smile. "How did you and Miguel get so wise?"

Carlos stroked her hair. "The hard way...the hard way."

Bad Water
Chapter 14
Growing Up

The old brass kerosene lamp flickered with a dim yellow glow on two empty bunks in the children's room. Will had taken his bedding and moved in with Carlos and Jimmy. In his quiet manner he said not a word to his sister, but as she watched him go, Jean knew her brother would not return to their small room again. Since the day he was born this room had been a safe harbor, but that is not what boys are meant for. Jean dreamed of one day becoming a mother, but for Will it was different. With danger baying at their walls, it was time for boys to become men.

Jean stared out the window saddened by her loss. Like most boys Will buried his fears deep inside. With Miguel's death he spoke even less. The night Carlos brought their mother home, Will stood quietly in the shadows watching as she and Annie bandaged her wounds. Jean saw him there out of the corner of her eye, rigid, his fist clenched by his side, the pain of their mother etched on his young face. He only ventured near when his uncle came. Before Cole left he knelt by Will and told him to be strong, that he was the man of the house and his mother needed him. That was all.

Though Jean would not have guessed it possible, she already missed her brother's teasing and lack of patience for her feminine ways.

The last several hours she had tossed and turned, but found no solace in dreams so she paced the floor. Their valley was dying and so much was left unsaid. Feeling smaller every passing minute, Jean yearned for someone to tell her everything would be okay, but her mother was locked away in her own pain, and mostly slept needing to heal in body and soul.

Unable to take the silence any longer Jean crept into the big room and quietly open the back door. A cold blast of air caused her to shiver. She braced herself. At last she could breathe. It felt good. With bare toes poking beneath her thin cotton nightgown, she crept out onto the porch and hugged her cheek to the tall post. Closing her eyes, she took a frigid breath and slowly released it.

Feeling better Jean cast a glance behind her. This night their small home felt like a prison. She couldn't go back inside.

Assailed by her fears, Jean suddenly leaped from the porch and raced across the yard to the barn. It was a wild impetuous dash. Once inside, she pulled to a halt knowing she shouldn't be here, but the desperation in her heart pushed her forward. On tip-toes she made her way through the dark to the bunkhouse door; the straw muffling her tiny steps.

Pressing her ear close to the wall, she could hear the Mexican snoring in his bunk. She was comforted by his presence, but he still scared her. If he caught her he would surly say; 'Little senorita, you get back to bed where you will be safe.', but he couldn't understand the fear in her heart; from that, her little room couldn't protect her.

Jean glanced over her shoulder making sure no one was watching then she stooped and peered through a crack in the boards. A small pot belly stove with its door open glowed red in the corner, warming the room. In its wavering light, she could see Jimmy lying uncovered on the lower bunk against the opposite wall from Carlos. The flames danced on his bare skin painting his firm young muscles in light and shadow. Her heart quickened. How she wanted to be with him right now.

For a moment she thought of sneaking in quietly, taking his hand and together stealing off to the loft where they could be alone.

No. She knew Carlos would wake. It was hopeless. Frowning, Jean turned and looked at an empty stall behind her. Old Queenie was gone, ridden into the ground by her mother in a desperate attempt to save Miguel. And poor Miguel, a quiet hero she had thought invincible now lay buried not far away. His death unearthed old memories. She recalled the terrible night they brought her father home, and now Miguel dying the same way. It left her searching for answers. Would it happen again? Was this how they would all meet their end? One by one?

Moving away from the door, Jean ducked under a railing and leaned her head on Brownie. If she couldn't be near Jimmy, she'd be close to his horse. Adopting a pout, she wrapped her slender arms around the pony's neck seeking comfort.

She thought of her mother. Whatever happened on the trail that night had injured her the most, once so strong, now all she did was cry. She could hear her through the walls.

Their family was caught up in a storm that threatened to sweep them all away. No...not everyone, not her uncle. He alone stood unwavering holding the evil at bay.

Jean had seen him just three times, and only briefly, never to really talk. If there was any strength that could keep them safe it was in him, yet with all that was left unspoken her uncle was more a legend than reality. She had to know.

Alone in the dark, Jean suddenly had an overpowering need to be near him. Her urgency grew to a panic. Taking the bridal from a nail on the wall, Jean slipped it over Brownie's head and with trembling fingers fastened the square brass buckle against the horse's cheek.

The young girl hadn't told herself she was actually going. Seeing her uncle was strictly forbidden, but each step while innocent in itself, took her closer to him.

Jean gently slipped the wooden rail from its cradle, then climbing onto the side railings, shifted her weight onto Brownie's back. She took a breath then leaned against his neck. "Come on boy, we are just going for a little moonlight ride."

Jean prodded him with her bare heels and whispered. "No one needs to know."

The horse's hooves fell silently on the hay covered floor. For the first time she was glad they had no barking dog to tattle on her midnight misadventure.

Once outside the barn the cold autumn night turned her breath to steam. Her nightgown while warm enough for a cozy bed seemed wispy thin and she shivered, yet the cold inside her was far worse.

Putting the chill out of her mind, Jean coaxed Brownie forward. To the left Miguel's cross caught the starlight. Jean looked back at her mother's window. "I am almost fourteen."

Her mind made up, she turned and urged the pony through the gate. "Go boy."

Tierra Amarillo was only a mile over the next rise, not too far. She could be there and back before anyone would know.

It all seemed a jumble. She had so many questions swirling inside her that could only be answered by one man. Was wanting the truth so bad?

Her own farm at last out of sight Jean gave the gelding his head. "Go!"

Brownie was eager to run. With the crisp air stinging her cheeks, the young girl's heart beat in unison with the falling hooves. She was on the road alone in the dark of night beneath the stars, the wind tugging at her flowing gown. What she was doing was forbidden. Jean smiled feeling strangely akin to the uncle she never knew. This night she rode free following her heart.

All that was dark and evil seemed far behind her. Shivering she laid her slender body close to the pony seeking his warmth. "Just you and me Brownie. We can hide amongst the stars."

Jean let out a yell for joy. It was an act of defiance. She had always obeyed, trusting in the strength of others. An inner voice told her it was time to find strength in herself. The past was fading and the future unsure. If she were to ever be more than a little girl, she had to choose her on destiny.

Yet as she got closer to the gate, the stories of her uncle being a murderer played in her mind. What if he really was a bad man, one who would kill little girls all alone? No, that was silly. Her mother said he wouldn't hurt them, but what if..? She didn't have a real question, only youthful fears looming like demons in the night.

The road seemed longer than she'd remembered. Maybe it was the lay of the land playing tricks with moon shadows. Yes, that was it. Moon shadows. Jean rode on.

To the north of the road a stand of dark pines came into view. She would have ignored then but Brownie paused in his gate and turned his head. Pulling the reins Jean came to a stop. Her heart was pounding knowing deep down what she was doing was wrong. Were eyes watching; disapproving eyes that would find her out?

Breathing heavy, puffs of steam curling about her, she looked behind, then back to the foreboding woods. She gasped! Had something moved? Fear prickling her skin she searched deeper beneath the ghostly branches. Suddenly a rider dressed in black on a dark horse pushed out of the trees.

A scream caught in Jean's throat. She kicked frantically with her heels. "Go Brownie! Go!"
Obeying her command, the pony bolted to a dead run. Without a saddle the young girl held tight. Fighting terror, she summoned all her courage and peered over her shoulder. The rider was whipping his horse, pushing him faster. "Go Brownie!"

She was light and riding bareback. Brownie was young. There was a chance. Again she glanced behind her. The rider was gaining. He rode a powerful stallion. Jean prayed that Brownie could hold his lead.

Between gasps of air, old fears set her heart pounding. Her father, Miguel and ol' Paz. were all killed on the road at night. Was she doomed to be next? Why hadn't she obeyed her mother? Tears flowed backwards across her cheeks. "Go Brownie!"

Up ahead the gate to Cole's ranch appeared out of the dark. Jean pressed her head tightly to the horse's neck and closed her eyes. "Please..."
The pony responded with greater speed. Jean could feel his hooves digging against the road. "Please, please..."

When she opened her eyes again, they were almost there. Behind her she could hear the big horse gaining. She dared not look back.

Jerking hard on the reins, Jean headed Brownie into the gate, but her turn was too sudden and the pony's speed too great. He reared sending Jean flying backwards through the air into a large juniper beside the road. The stiff branches covered in thick green needles broke her fall. She slid to the ground with a hard thump, landing in a sitting position. The shadowed rider was off his horse and next to her before she could escape.

Scooting backwards, Jean screamed. "Don't you hurt me. My Uncle is Cole Creed, meanest man who ever lived and he will kill anyone who touches me."

The stranger stepped back. He stared a moment then broke into a big grin. "Shucks ma'am, I wasn't going to hurt you. Jes' seein' if you are alright."

Stunned, Jean wiped her eyes. She could see the man's face now. He was really more of a boy, maybe eighteen or nineteen and rather handsome, not a villain at all. His big cheery grin instantly calmed her fears, but left her embarrassed. Her nightgown had caught on the tree and slid up leaving her legs completely bare. She quickly pulled it down over her knees. "Then why were you chasing me?"

The boy reached out a hand and helped her to her feet. "Why were you running?"

Jean stomped. "It doesn't matter why I was running. You had no business chasing me."

Taking the liberty to dust the twigs from her back, the boy did his best to appease her. "Sorry, but not every day a fella' gets ta' see a pretty little girl riding half naked beneath the stars. Kinda' romantic."

Jean nearly screeched. "I ain't pretty, or little, or a girl...I'm fo...sixteen. And I sure ain't naked so take your sinful eyes off of me."

She pulled away. "And stop brushing me. If Uncle Cole saw you touching me that-a-way he'd kill you for sure."

The kid dropped his hands to his side. "Well I will disagree with you about not being pretty. Think you are about as pretty a night flower as I've seen, but if your uncle is as bad you say, I best give up right now and ride along with you so he can kill me proper."

Jean was completely flustered not knowing if he was teasing or crazy. He smiled again and reaching up, wiped a tear from her cheek. She slapped his hand. "Stop touching me."

"You are crying."

"I'm not crying. It's the wind." Jean hurriedly sleeved the evidence from her face. She stared defiantly. "I'm not crying."

Regaining her composure, she brushed past the strange boy and stood next to Brownie. Jean started to lift her foot then realized that in a nightgown it wouldn't be lady-like. She frowned at the boy. "Well don't just stand there. Help me onto the horse's back."

Taking her by the waist, the young man lifted her onto the pony, then turned and mounted up himself. "The next time you steal a horse, steal a saddle too."

Jean hissed and headed Brownie down the road. "What makes you think I stole the horse?"

The boy prodded his mount alongside her then eased into a steady gate. "Guess I know a thing or two about horse stealing."

He flashed his big grin. "When you stepped up to the pony it was like you knew him, but weren't best friends. Girls are always best friends with their ponies; hug 'em and such. You know. You also said, help me onto the horse, not my horse. I'd say ya' stole, or borrowed if you prefer from a friend. A young feller maybe?"

Looking forward, Jean brushed the tangled hair from her face. "You think you are so smart!"

"No ma'am. Jes' know horses...and pretty girls."

Jean started to stick out her tongue, but decided it wasn't something a sixteen-year-old would do. "I told you I'm not pretty. I've got a long nose."

The boy did know a few things about girls and figured his pretty companion was fishing for compliments, and he was happy to oblige. "I think you are right pretty. Heck, them ancient Greeks had long noses and they made statues of them cuz' they was so pretty."

A pearly smile betrayed Jean for a brief moment, but she quickly hid it beneath a scowl. "Bet you never even seen a Greek stature."

The boy looked down right hurt. "Did too, in Santa Fe once...well a picture of one; read about them though. The book said they were beautiful and had long noses. They ran around in their nightgowns too. Maybe that's it, you are a Greek goddess riding around in your nightgown. Why you're so pretty you could be Apple-dite"

Jean nearly screamed. "Stop talking about my nightgown, and it's Aphrodite."

Her companion grinned. "See, and smart too. Long noses are a sign of intelligence."

"No, they are not. You never read that. They are just long."

Patting his horse, the boy defended. "Poncho here is intelligent and he's got a long nose."

"You are impossible."

Jean tried to stare forward, but was drawn back to her companion's clear blues eyes sparkling beneath the newly risen moon. He was staring back, and she was old enough to know he was admiring her too. Jean tugged at her nightgown which had ridden up as she straddled the pony. "Well you best stop looking at my leg or..."

The boy laughed. "I know your uncle Cole will have my hide."

"Well he will."

She knew the boy was mocking her so she defended. "He's a bad one. Fast as Jess Evans or Billy the Kid."

The boy gave her a minute to calm herself. "Why are you out riding in your nightgown? Don't you have no clothes?"

Jean's eyes flashed. "Of course I have clothes. Don't be stupid."

Offended, she rode on with her nose turned up. The boy waited a moment. "Well?"

Turning on him, Jean snapped. "Well it's none of your business. I can go riding in my nightgown if I want. A girl shouldn't have to worry about men...Boys! Skulking around in the dark spying on her from behind every bush."

Continuing in his usual manner the boy let another moment pass while he pondered her answer. He finally shrugged. "I heard of sleepwalking, ain't never heard of sleep-riding...maybe that's what you were doing; explains why you fell off your pony back there. Maybe high-strung Greek girls with pretty noses sleep-ride..."

Jean's voice rose shrill. "I am not high-strung, and you made me fall off my..." She suddenly stopped. "I know what you are doing. You are like all boys; you like to tease. We will talk no further about my nightgown or why I'm out riding after dark."

The boy nodded accepting her wish. "Yes ma'am, high-strung and pretty as a pixie flittering beneath the stars. Right romantic, a just end for a man...excuse me, a boy about to meet his end at the hands of your most dangerous uncle."

Jean smiled once more only this time she couldn't hide it. She liked being compared to a pixie flittering beneath the stars. It did seem romantic. "If you silence that silly tongue, maybe I'll just ask him to give you a good thrashing before he sends you packing."

Just then the adobe hacienda came into view. It was larger than she's imagined with many windows and doors set back under a roof supported with stone columns. There were numerous buildings and corrals. A thought came to her that Uncle Cole had enough room for her whole family.

Jean had not planned things this far, and didn't know what to say to her uncle about why she was here so late at night. He'd be angry with her. The boy's presence was no longer a bad thing. She could put the blame on him. He was a ruffian who chased her through his gate. It was partly true.

Jean turned to the boy. He was charming but he liked playing games. A gleam came to her eye. "My uncle is going to be angry when he hears you've been fresh with me."

Guiding his horse nearer to Jean until their legs brushed, the boy grinned. "I know what's going on in that pretty little head. Been reading your face and you are in more trouble than me. You can shift the blame, but I don't think your Uncle Cole will believe I dressed you in your nightgown."

Blushing, Jean snickered. "Well maybe you stole me from my bed."

Turning serious, she faced her companion. "You know my uncle, don't you?"

For the first time, the smile faded from the boy. His eyes looked past her to the adobe house where a lamp burned yellow in the window. "Not sure anybody knows your uncle. Some men are like a river running deep. Try hard as you can, you will never understand them Miss Jean."

The young girl's mouth dropped open. "How do you know my name?"

He teased her with a wink. "Might be that I keep track of all the pretty girls in Lincoln County...dress and undressed." He pulled the reins letting her catch up. "Or maybe your uncle has been bragging about his only niece; saying she's as pretty as she is smart, that her eyes, always full of questions, light up like dewdrops on a morning glory catchin' the mornin' sun. Guessin' I'd be agreeing with him. You are pretty...nosy."

Reaching the porch, the young man suddenly hollered in a comical shrill voice. "Uncle Cole, oh Uncle Coooole, best come on out. A pert little lady here says you n' I need to commence ta' shooting at each other."

A brief moment later, the door opened framing Jean's uncle in the lamplight from a table near the door. He wasn't wearing his gun nor did he look too concerned. Taking in the scene he ducked his head and stepped onto the porch. "I ain't your uncle, and if I was, I'd shoot myself."

Cole turned to his niece. "Jean what are you doing out here half naked?"

The boy nearly burst. "See! See what I told you, see! Pretty n' half naked."

Jean scrunched her nose. "Oh shut-up. I don't even know who you are."

The boy took off his hat and started to introduce himself, but Cole interrupted. "Kid what the hell is going on?"

Offering an overly innocent smile, the boy shook his head. "Don't know myself. I guessed she fell from heaven. Found her in a bush hanging like a Christmas angel only she was shooting off your name like a double barrel scattergun."

Jean bristled. "I wouldn't have been in the bush if you hadn't chased me."

The boy's grin broadened. "Go ahead and tell him the part where I scooped you up n' stole you from your bed..."

Screeching, Jean defended. "I never said I was going to tell him that..."

"Enough!" Cole reached up. Taking hold of Jean, he set her firmly on the porch, then turned to the boy who pushed his pony close to the girl. "Billy you coming in?"

Jean knees nearly buckled. "Billy!" She looked at her uncle then back to the boy. "You are Billy the Kid?"

Bowing low in the saddle the boy reached out and gallantly raised her hand to his lips. "Shhhh, mustn't let the saintly know you've been cavorting with ne'er-do-wells. They might take away your wings."

He grinned at her starry eyes then turned to Cole. "No sir, looks like you got some family business to attend too. I'd recommend a good hard spankin' over your knee to curb that fiery temper."

As the kid backed his pony away he smiled adoringly at the girl. "With your niece being sixteen and in the flower of life, I might pay her a call if you don't mind me courtin' your kin."

Raising a brow Cole stared down at his niece. Jean look up, her large brown eyes pleading with him not to embarrass her by revealing her age. Cole held her under his scrutiny a moment longer then turned back to the boy. "No, I don't mind, but her mother breathes fire when it comes to gunfighters so beware."

Accepting the warning, Billy tipped his hat, "See you Miss Jean. Next time you go sleep riding maybe I'll wake you with a kiss."

With that he headed out at a merry gallop. A hundred yards down the road he broke into a silly made-up song about a midnight angel with a chili pepper for a tongue.

Awestruck, Jean watched the wild youth until he disappeared. "What was he doing here Uncle Cole?"

Stepping to her side, Cole rested a hand on Jean's shoulder. "Being a friend I think."

He then turned the girl to face him. "The question is; what are you doing here young lady?"
Tilting her head, Jean tucked both hands beneath her chin and shrunk back. "Don't be angry. Please don't be angry. He chased...well no...I, I just..."
Jean stopped and lowered her eyes. "I just had too."

Cole shook his head and ushered her inside. "Come little princess."
Stopping in mid stride, Jean mouthed the word, 'Princess', and looked up. "My daddy used to call me that, didn't he?"
Closing the door, Cole offered a knowing smile. Jean's voice softened. "I had forgotten."

She edged closer and took his hand. "That night they brought him home...I remember now, it was you, wasn't it? I thought my daddy was asleep. Mama was crying. You were tall and scary."

She stared in wonder at her uncle. His strong face and deep voice were like an old book thrown open. Snippets of memories awoke in the forgotten recesses of her mind. "Mama said my daddy was a lot like you. Strange! I can remember him now. I can see his face again clearly; like you, but younger...and not so sad."
A light danced in her eyes then faded as she tucked the memory away for another day.

Turning, Jean walked to the center of the room and spun full around. "It's bigger than I expected. How many rooms?"
She looked up to see her uncle towering over her, his arms folded. Jean ducked her head. "I know, what am I doing here?"

Her mind had been tormented with questions when she sneaked away in the dead of night, now it was totally blank. Try as she might, all she could think of was how cold the tile floor was beneath her bare feet. Lifting on her toes, she took several timid steps forward then stopped short. Her soft brown eyes moistened. "I...I'm..." She started trembling. Something about her uncle demanded the truth. She took a breath. "I'm scared Uncle Cole."

Suddenly Jean rushed forward and threw her arms around him. "I'm scared."
She buried her face against him hiding her tears. "I'm scared. Don't be angry."

Cole tensed. Little Jean had no idea the door she had pried opened with her simple hug. He had fought wars, charged canons without wavering, and now a mere child shook him to his core.

The famed gunfighter slowly reached down and wrapped his big arms around her. A promise to his brother had brought him home, but this young girl holding so tight had finally given him back the family he'd lost.

Lifting his head to the rafters, Cole closed his eyes, memories of Molly burst vividly before him as if it were yesterday. She was not much older than Jean, young and pretty, sitting on the fence railing laughing hysterically as he lay in the dirt after being bucked off a wild bronc' he had ridden just to impress her. He remembered them racing their horses along the river banks, picnics beneath the trees, a stolen kiss.

There was sadness too. Like when Tucker her old lop-eared hound died. Barely thirteen she stood there weeping as he poured the last shovel of dirt onto the grave. So many memories; he'd buried them all until now.

Filling his lungs with a ragged breath, Cole looked down and smoothed Jean's hair. "It's okay Princess. I'm not mad at you."
She stepped away and wiped her tears with a tiny fist. "You won't let anything bad happen to us, will you?"

Taking Jean by the shoulders he knelt before her and lifted her chin so they were eye to eye. "Jean you are no longer a baby. There are hard times coming. You need to know this."

"But..." Jean protested. "...you are a famous..."
Cole poked a finger to the side of her mouth making her smile. "You want to know you are going to be okay. That isn't a promise anyone can make."
His blue eyes glinted. "But you have something much better than a promise. Princess, there are a lot of good people looking out for you. Me, Carlos, that young boy of yours, Will..."
Cole thumbed over his shoulder at the door. "...even Billy, and don't forget your Mother. She's looking out for you most of all."

Pulling his niece closer, he grew serious. "Jean, there are bad people out there who would hurt you. What I need is a promise from you."

He cupped her face and held her tenderly. "If ever you are in danger, you will fight with all you might. No matter how hard, or terrible, or scary it is, you will survive until I come for you."

He brushed the hair from her eyes. "Will you make me that promise? You will never give up?"

Jean nodded. "I promise."

She threw her arms around his neck. You promise me you will come?"

Holding her close, Cole whispered into her hair. "I promise sweetheart. As long as I draw a breath. I will come."

Sniffing away the last of her tears, Jean touched her hand to her uncle's face tracing the age lines with her finger. "Tell me about my father."

Cole smiled as Jean pleaded so earnestly. "Mama just says he was brave and handsome. Guess that's what all mothers say."

Folding Jean's small hand in his he gave it a kiss. "Guess she's right, though most men don't care about being handsome; too prissy. A good man should be doin' what's right, not parting his hair in front of a mirror. Your father was strong and brave, but he liked to laugh. Boy, he liked to laugh. I remember one morning when we were kids right here in this valley, and a black bear come sniffing around the door huntin' for food. Instead of your daddy slamming that door shut, he opened it wide and invited that ol' bear right in just so he could play a joke on gramps who was sound asleep well past milkin' time. It was quite a joke. Well your daddy got a woopin' and granny a new bearskin rug. You used to play on that rug when you were little."

Jean clapped her hands. "I remember. Tell me more..."

Bad Water
Chapter 15
Bad Company

Sitting on the porch swing, Jean pulled her blanket around her and stared down the road. It was early morning and her pretty head was swirling with a million thoughts. Off in the distance a single shot carried over the grassy hills. Jean recognized the sharp crack of her brother's small-bore rifle. He often hunted early before the wild creatures went into hiding.

The hollow sound of boots on the porch stirred Jean from her thoughts but she didn't need to look up to know it was Jimmy.

He stood quietly beside her until it made her uncomfortable. She snapped. "What?"

Mocking her with a comical snarl, Jimmy slumped beside her and rubbed his hands on his knees. "Strangest thing. I brushed Brownie down real good last night, and this morning he's covered in dried lather."

Digging her toe into the porch, Jean shrugged her shoulders. The boy waited a minute then took her hand, his clear gray eyes following hers off into the distance. "Why I bet Brownie must have run a full mile down the road to lather like that."

Jean remained tight lipped for a moment then leaned her head on his shoulder. "I came looking for you last night, but you were asleep."

The boy was glib. "Usually am at night."

Jean elbowed him. "Saw you through the cracks."

A shy grin parted her lips. "You always sleep in the raw?"

Jimmy grew a bit red. "Carlos put too much wood in the stove so I kicked the blanket back. What do you do on hot nights?"

Leaning closer, Jean snuggled against him. "Jimmy, if Mama didn't have me n' Will to look after do you think she'd go away?"

Turning with a sudden flush of emotions, she took both his hands. "I mean there wouldn't be no reason for her to stay...always taking care of us, this farm. She's doing it for us."

"Guess that's true Jean, but where would you go?"

Jerking free, Jean jumped to her feet livid at the boy. "I meant you and me ya' dumb cowboy!"

She stomped to the railing. "Boys! You said if you could, you'd protect me. That's almost like a proposal."

Jimmy came to his feet sputtering. "Gosh Jean, I meant where would we go. Of course it would be us...if we had a place to go."

Jean softened just enough to hint she might forgive him if he didn't make any more stupid mistakes. "...and we'd take Will with us. Right?"

"Of course Jean, but where?"

With a head full of fanciful ideas the young girl once more turned and stared down the road, determination narrowing her brow. "You leave that to me." Her mind racing, she took Jimmy's hands again. "I want you to find two more horses...with saddles, and a place to hide them until we can get away."

The boy was stunned. "You want me to steal horses?"

"It ain't stealing. You said ol' Pete owed you back wages, just takin' what's yours. An' after that beating he gave you. I think he owes you a little extra."

Jean dared not let Jimmy squirm out of her plan. She threw her arms around his neck and pressed an affectionate kiss to his lips. "Thank you Jimmy I knew you would be my hero."

As the bewildered boy struggled to figure out how he'd gotten himself into this mess, Jean pulled away. "Now you be off and do what you promised. I've got thinking to do."

It was midday when Will came back struggling under the load of a small deer he had gutted and clean. Jean met him by the back fence and held the gate open for him. "Kinda' puny."

Will frowned. "Eat hay."

Jean folded her hands meekly. "Didn't mean anything by it. You done good."

Rubbing his shoulder, Will limbered his arm. "Could use some help carrying it."

Jean shrugged. "Sorry, Carlos has gone off to talk with Uncle Cole."

Will pulled a face and Jean's eyes grew wide. "Surly you didn't mean for me to touch that poor dead thing?"

Knowing it was useless, Will shook his head. "Did Jimmy go to Uncle Cole's too?"

He stared accusingly. "Appears everybody is going to Uncle Cole's lately."

Jean's heart fluttered wondering if her brother knew. She put it out of her mind. "No. Jimmy went...elsewhere. Besides you know what Mama said about Uncle Cole...bad water n' all."

Eager for peace, Jean held out her hand. "I'll carry your gun for you...if it ain't bloody."

The boy remained deadpan as he handed her the rifle. "Don't strain yourself."

Wanting to change the subject, Jean waited until he hoisted the deer onto his shoulders. "Do you think we could make some of it into jerky? ...be good for traveling."

Will eyed his sister suspiciously. She was being nice. That usually meant trouble. "You sick?"

"Will Creed I'm just saying we ought to be prepared. Like if we had to leave suddenly...you know, if we just had too..."

She turned and hurried towards the house, her voice rising in frustration. "I don't know why I always got to do the thinking. It's bad enough that I've tried to be nice when you are just plain mean."

When she got to the porch Jean turned around and hollered. "Cut the deer up in the barn. Mama's heating up some water for my bath so don't you come in without knocking...and make some jerky...lots of it."

Slamming the back door behind her, Jean spied her mother pouring the last bucket of hot water into the washtub.

Molly straightened and frowned. "You are getting too old to be yelling at your brother. Could hear you all the way in here."

Jean stepped close to her mother then faced the other direction. Molly instinctively started undoing the tiny button on the back of her dress. "You are fourteen next week, it's about time you start acting like a lady."

"Mama, have you ever been to Colorado?"

Molly slipped the dress off her daughter's shoulders. "Colorado! What's going on in that pretty little head?"

Jean wiggled her hips letting the dress slide to the floor then stepped out of it "Just wondering, never been anywhere."

"Well do your wondering in the tub. Carlos might be back anytime, don't know where Jimmy's off too."

Molly stuck her hand into the water testing it. "Perfect. I'll be out back planting some tulip bulbs Annie gave me. Holler if you want me to wash your hair."

"Thought you said I shouldn't holler."

Molly tweaked Jean's nose. "Don't be impertinent or I'll make you holler long and loud. She scooted her daughter towards the tub with a swat to her backside. "Now take your bath."

Jean waited for the door to close, then finished undressing. She paused for a moment in front of the oval floor length mirror hanging on the wall. Her mother was right. She was a young lady. It was no longer proper to wrestle with her brother; maybe yelling at him wasn't lady- like either.

She smiled thinking of how Jimmy treated her special when she dressed frilly with ribbons in her hair. Yes, hollering would have to go.

Breaking into a saucy grin, Jean wiggled her hips. There were other ways of getting what she wanted.

Testing the water with her toe, she eased herself into the tub and leaned back thinking about her secret plan. She felt guilty for even considering running away, but she was trying to save her family. Her mother would be so hurt...and angry, boy would she be angry. Still, if she and Will ran off to Colorado her mother and Uncle Cole were sure to follow. It was the only way Jean could see after what Uncle Cole had told her.

Lost in thought, Jean rubbed the bar of lye soap in her hands until it lathered then she soaped her arms. 'Colorado.' She'd heard stories about Colorado and she knew if they followed the morning sun it would lead her there. She'd make extra biscuits in the days to come. With the jerky, and maybe some cheese it should get them through. Perhaps some hard-boiled eggs cradled in straw would extend their food for a few days on the trail.

Her mother often wrote to an Aunt Myra who lived in Telluride which was due north of them. It seemed as good a place as any, and there were stories of gold nuggets as big as a man's fist. There was no gold in Lincoln County, only poverty. Jean muttered out loud. "If poorness was a stone, we'd be buried under them."

The morning was gone and the sun was half-way across the sky. Jean had sent Jimmy away almost five hours ago. And while she tried not to worry about him, an uneasy feeling tightened her stomach. She tried to put it out of her mind. It was just two horses, the judge had plenty.

Jean went back to playing with the soap and dabbed the bubbles on her chin making a beard like she used to do when she was young.

The tub was small and Jean could no longer slid down and put her head beneath the water. When she was little their mother bathed her and Will together in it, now her legs hung over the edge, her toes touching the floor.

She once saw a picture of a real bathtub in a Montgomery Ward's catalog that Mrs. Hayes kept at the store in Crow Crossing. Jean frowned doubting that there was a real bathtub in all of Lincoln County. Maybe they had them in Colorado.

Bending her knee to her chin, Jean started soaping her leg. She pointed her toe admiring her own form. Her leg was no longer the fat and pudgy limb of a child, but that of a young woman, delicately tapered. She thought of Jimmy and smiled, happy for the gifts nature had given her. How easily the boy submitted to her wishes all for a simple kiss. She giggled, but her brow quickly furrowed. He should have returned by now.

Just then Jean heard a horse galloping into the yard. It had come fast and stopped abruptly just outside the door. This alarmed her. Carlos and Jimmy always took their horses to the barn. Placing her hands on the edge of the tub she straightened her arms and craned her neck trying to peer out the window.

All of a sudden there was the stomping of heavy boots on the porch then violent pounding on the flimsy door. "Open up inside Widder' Creed. I wanna' talk ta' that daughter of yern'."

Dropping back into the tub, Jean screeched and instinctively folded her arms across her chest. It was ol' Pete and he sounded drunk as hell. "Open up, ya' hear."

He pounded again only harder shaking the door in its frame. It suddenly burst open with a terrible bang. Jean screamed. "Mama!"

"I'm here baby." Molly hurried through the back door as Pete swaggered into the room carrying an uncorked bottle in his hand. His eyes were bloodshot and his hair stuck out like a wild man.

Shaking his head to fight off the effects of the alcohol, he took a few more steps then blinked in astonishment at Jean huddled in the tub.

Drunk as he was it took a moment for him to comprehend the situation. Slowly a huge grin spread across his face exposing a mouth full of long uneven teeth. "Well lookie' here." His words were slurred. "No wonder Jimmy done run off. Found himself a piece of sugar candy."

Molly rushed between her daughter and Pete. "You are drunk. I will thank you sir to leave my home this instant."
She pointed a stiff finger at the door.

Taking a swig from his bottle, Pete stuck out his arm and swept Molly aside. "Nothing doin'. I may be drunk, but I sure as hell ain't blind drunk."
He stumbled closer to the tub leering unashamedly. "I hear tell this youngin' knows Jimmy's whereabouts. Stupid sweet on her he is. Can see why."

In the foreman's stupor he figured he had every right to be in the Creed home, though the sight of Jean curled in a tub full of suds was sufficient pay for any guilt such a man might have.

Molly reached for his arm but he shook her off and swayed over the tub. "Bet he'd do anything you'd ask? Wouldn't he?"
The foreman Shouted. "Wouldn't he?"

Throwing his head back, Pete raised the bottle to his mouth. Liquor spilled down his neck drenching his sweat stained coat. "I'm gunna' skin the boy good this time n' maybe stretch his neck, fool boy hangin' with Creeds. Ha ha, hanging with Creeds, do ya' get it?" His jest reminded him of why he'd come to the Creed home. The foreman's eyes narrowed accusingly. "Someone stole two of the judge's horses. Ranch hand saw Jimmy skulkin' around earlier." Pete waved his bottle at Jean. "Bet this lil' vixen knows what he's up too, or even put 'em too it. Jimmy ain't got the gumption on his own."

Molly eyes darted to Jean. The young girl ducked her head the truth plain on her face. Pete saw it too and grabbed at her leg. He missed as Jean pulled her knees tighter against her chest. Stumbling backwards to keep his balance Pete's arms flayed. "Get out of the damn tub little Missy. You tell me where Jimmy is or I'm gunna' whip your ass 'til ya sing like a canary. N' if ya' put that boy up to it God help ya'." Once more he flung his arms wide. "Nobody steals the Judges horses especially no damn Creed. Now get up fer' I drag ya' up n' beat the truth out of ya'."

"No you won't!" Molly threw her small frame against the inebriated man trying to push him out the door. "Leave my house you drunkard."

She struck at him with her side of her fist, but Pete was crazy drunk and felt nothing. Intent on the girl, he shoved Molly hard knocking her into a chair and onto the floor. She laid where she fell, stunned.

In the old man's diminished capacity holding to one thought was a struggle. The theft of the judge's horses was pushed from his mind by the sight of the naked girl cowering before him. His voice rolled with perversity. "Stand up like I told ya'."

Justice no longer mattered.

Eyes wide, Jean whimpered shaking her head in a feeble protest.

Enjoying his power, Pete lifted his bottle and poured the brown liquor over Jean washing the soap suds from her skin. "Let's see what ya' hidin' 'neath them bubbles that done turned Jimmy's head.

There was no stopping him now. He licked his lips. "Pretty as a Louisiana whore."

Regaining her senses, Molly crawled to the tub and threw herself over her daughter. Outraged, she turned her face upwards. "Leave her alone you drunken fool. Cole will kill you for sure."

Pete kicked the tub and laughed. "Cole Creed, he's livin' on borrowed time."

Insane with lust he emptied his bottle over the both of them, then took a final swig and threw it aside. "Gunna' give ya' a taste of what the Judge has in store for you Creed women." Bending, he grabbed Jean by the ankle, delighting in her screams as he dragged her from the tub.

Pulling backwards, Pete lifted his head and froze, looking like a disheveled scarecrow with bulging eyes. Inches away from his face was the long barrel of a small-bore rifle.

At the other end of the gun, young Will stood resolutely eyeing Pete down the sights. The boy uttered not a word, but there was no mistaking his intent.

Letting go of Jean's leg, Pete spread his hands wide and slowly stood up. "Easy boy. That thing might go off."
Will nodded. "Might."
Less arrogant and more sober, Pete took a step back. "I din't mean your sister no harm. Jes' come fer' answers."

Unmoved, Will tipped his barrel upwards repositioning his bead on the man's brain. Pete wiped his mouth nervously. His eyes darted to the naked girl. For an old man past his prime she was a prize too tempting to lose. He would never get this chance again.

Something snapped inside of him. Turning back to the boy, an ugly grin spread across his whiskered face. "Can't blame ol' Pete. The man's eyes pulled back to Jean, his word coming long and slow. "...she sure is invitin' laying there all vulnerable n' pretty like...so tasty...all soaked in whiskey."

An evil chuckle gurgled in his throat. He had to have her. Drawing courage from the bottle, Pete's smile twisted in an evil sneer as he faced the young boy standing in his way. He took a menacing step forward. "You wouldn't shoot me, not ol' Pete. Why you is just a mama's boy. Ain't got no papa. Bet your mama tucks you in at night."

Will remained motionless. The old man edged half a step closer. Lowering his hands, he looked ready to pounce. "Give me the gun child. Soft as yo' sister I bet. It ain't in ya' ta' kill so you hand that cannon over, an' ya' run-a-long n' play."

A deathly silence followed where Pete fully expected the ill-bred child of a dirt farmer to obey his command. The clock on the mantle clicked three seconds more. His cheek pressed to the gunstock Will didn't budge. The foreman's eyes turned crazy shaking in their sockets. It was too much. Exploding with rage, his voice reverberated from the rafters. "I'll stomp your ass into the floor. Who the hell you think you are defyin' me?"

With slow deliberation, Will laid his thumb over the hammer and cocked it back. "Bad water."
The drunken man shook with incomprehension. "What the hell does that mean? Give me the God-damn gun."
Will's blue eyes glinted. "Take it."
"Why you little..." Without warning Pete grabbed for the barrel. In the same instance the gun thundered in Will's hand, its deafening

roar shaking the room to its timbers. Smoke filled the air and curled beneath the ceiling.

Pete staggered back clutching the side of his neck, blood oozing through his fingers. "He shot me! The little bastard shot me." Will calmly chambered another round as the bewildered man retreated to the door. "He shot me...I'll get you for this you damn filthy Creed."

Pete jabbed a threatening finger at Molly. "The judge has got plans for you n' your girl, but I get the boy."

Seeing the blood on hand, Pete screeched and slapped it back to his neck. "Damn you kid."

Bewildered, the old man stared longingly at the girl he'd never have then staggered stiff legged onto the porch. His bold threats crumbling to a whimper. "Only wanted to touch her...had every right. Horse stealin's a hangin' offense. Jus' you wait."

Molly ran to the door as Pete awkwardly climbed onto his horse. He looked in no condition to use the Winchester tucked in the scabbard beneath his leg but Molly shouted her outrage intent on putting the fear of God in him. "My son can shoot the head off a turkey at a hundred yards so you ride hard and don't look back." She followed him into the yard "...and if his uncle heard that shot you better ride while you can breathe."

Pete stared past her to the doorway. The rifle was still aimed at his head. With one hand clutching his neck, he spurred his pony. "Whore! You'll be sorry."

Running back up the stairs, Molly slammed the door and bolted it. She dropped to her knees and embraced her son. "You go around to the side of the house and keep watch. We will talk later." Pushing him toward the back door, Molly scooped her trembling daughter out of the tub and into her arms. "It's alright baby. He's gone."

"Mama I'm sorry." Jean burst into tears. "I'm sorry. I sent Jimmy to steal those horses."

"Why Baby?"

Jean wrapped her arms around her mother's neck. "So we could run away and you wouldn't have to protect of us."

Bad Water
Chapter 16
Butterflies

𝕵ean sat on the sofa in her nightgown with her feet tucked beneath her watching Molly pace the floor. The grief on her mother's anguished face brought tears to the young girl's eyes.

Molly stopped in front of her. "Didn't you learn anything from my mistake? Miguel is dead, and now Jimmy's wanted for horse stealing. Are you proud of yourself?"

Molly shook her head. "Guess it's something in us Creed women. We condemn the men for fighting then we jump right in behind them pushing them into the storm."

Jean ducked her eyes and sniffed. "I'm sorry Mama."

"Sorry won't save that boy from hanging." Molly resumed pacing. "I'd whip you good if ol' Pete hadn't already put the fear into you. Maybe I should have let him..."

"Mama!"

Molly stopped in front of her again. "Do you know what that drunk would have done if your brother hadn't..." Once more the pounding of hooves could be heard in the yard. Molly rushed to the window. "Thank God."

Hurrying to the door she unbolted it and threw it open. Carlos had Jimmy by the arm dragging him up the stairs. "I found him down in the river bottoms. Sent the horses' home."

He shoved Jimmy through the door. "Fool kid."

Jimmy rubbed his arm when Carlos let go, and cast an injured look at Mrs. Creed. He saw the disapproval on her face. Hiding his eyes, he hurried to Jean's side and sat quietly fearing the wrath that was to come.

For Molly the worry and frustration were too much. It had to stop. She couldn't stand anymore. "Jimmy, come morning you find someplace else to live. I won't have a horse thief bringing trouble down on my family."

Jean jumped to her feet wailing. "Mama it wasn't his fault. Please Mama. I made him do it."

Molly placed her hands on her hips. "You tell me how a girl your age got a sixteen-year-old boy to steal horses. Tell me! Is Pete right? Have you been shaming us in that hayloft?"

"Mama."

Lowering her head, Jean wept.

Near tears herself Molly snapped. "You are right Jean, it is your fault, but no good comes from the judge's ranch. They are just a gang of thieves and his boy is one of them. He proved it. Instead of protecting you, he let you seduce him."

"Mama that's not fair."

"Neither is you bringing the judge's wrath down on our family."

Jean clenched her fists. "Then I should go...and...and you too Mama. Nothing good comes from our farm either."

Bursting into tears, Jean ran out the door. "I'm going with Jimmy."

Molly started to follow then stopped. Carlos reached out a hand and squeezed her shoulder. "Maybe we should all leave this farm."

For a long moment Molly stared silently after her daughter, then slowly turned and backed away. "No! I'm going to hold this family together."

Her anger unabated, she looked at the boy sitting lost and alone. "Jimmy do you care for Jean?"

Jimmy came to his feet. "Yes ma'am. More than my own life."

Molly held his eyes. "Then you won't take her with you, will you?"

Dropping his head, Jimmy's voice broke. "No ma'am."

His voice broke. "I'll go alone."

The worried lines in her face easing, Molly turned away. "That's what I needed to hear. Go tell Jean you can stay until they come for you. Don't think I'm doing you a favor. It may not change anything."

Jimmy's heart leaped. "Yes ma'am."

He scooted towards the door. "Thank you."

Gripping the knob Jimmy paused. "Mrs. Creed, Jean didn't...I mean...she's a good girl. I was just stupid."

Molly remained firm. "I know how she can be when she wants her way. You just remember. When you leave, you leave alone.

With the kids gone the room grew painfully silent. Carlos turned towards the door ready to leave, but Molly caught his hand. "You're not going to tell Cole are you? If he heard what happened to Jean, he'd start a war for sure. The valley would be in flames."

Carlos rested his hands on his hips and shook his head. "Not sure what to do Senora. What you say is true, but if they are coming, they are smart enough to go after Cole first. He should be warned."

Molly clutched her throat. "Do you think they are coming tonight?"

"Don't know Senora. This Pete hombre shot, horses stolen. If they want an excuse they got it."

Looking out the open door, Carlos stared off into the graying expanse. "Not that they need any excuse. They are murderers. Last night they burned out the Ramirez. Poor Antonio barely had time to escape with his family into the hills."

He turned back and faced Molly. "...but the Ramirez are Mexicans so nobody is going to make much fuss I think."

Molly wrapped her arms around herself and seemed to shrink. "They come in the dark then vanish. How do you fight what you can't see? It's like nailing a shadow to a wall. Nothing sticks and with all the outlaw gangs, there are too many of them to even accuse."

Her shoulders drooped. "And who would convict them if they were caught? Certainly not Judge Warren H. Brewster."

Carlos slowly walked out onto the porch and leaned against the railing. "Si Senora. You may not like it, but if you are looking for justice, you will only find it in Senor Cole's gun."

Molly shook her head. "Then I'll not find it."

Moving past him, she searched her small farm with the cold realization of how quickly it could all be taken away. Her eyes came to rest on her son sitting in the dry grass beneath the empty buckboard that Queenie used to pull. How lost he looked in the purple hue of the dying sun. Stepping off the porch she put the violence out of her mind. "Do what you think is best. I need to tend to my children."

"Hey Will."

Molly got down on her knees and joined her son under the wagon. Her voice was soft. "Guess you got a powerful lot on your mind right now."

She leaned over and placed a tender kiss on his cheek. "I want you to know what you did was a terrible thing...but it was the right thing."

The boy did not move. His blank stare seemed turned inwards. Molly smoothed his hair. "You saved your sister. That's what matters."

Will's mouth twitched as he tried to put his thoughts into words. His voice showed little emotion. "Like killin' a deer. That's all."

Slowly turning his head, he lifted his eyes to meet hers. "Only the deer didn't deserve to die."

Appalled, Molly pulled back. "No Will. You don't have the right to judge Pete or to want him dead."

"But I do Mama. He's pure mean. I only turned my shot because I knew you'd be upset if I killed him."

"Oh son...do you want to grow up like your uncle...having people fear you?"

Will shrugged and looked far away. "Better than fearing them."

Dropping her arms to her side, Molly tugged at the dry yellow grass. "Will, you might not understand this, but being afraid of others is not as terrible as being afraid of yourself. It's the kind of fear that kills your heart."

She reached for her son. "You die a little with each life you take. Remember that."

Scooting away from her, Will took his rifle and crawled out from under the wagon. "Better than dying all at once."

The boy stood and walked into the night.

Her face heavy with sadness, Molly slowly got to her feet and watched him go. From the long shadows behind her Carlo's voice turned her around. "Senora, the boy, he kills something every day. You do not think about it for you are a woman, but he thinks about it. I know because I was once a boy. Do not judge him too harshly. Killing is part of life, at least a boy's life. With each kill he makes, he is preparing for that day when he will have to protect those he loves. For Will it was this day."

Carlos stepped beside her. "He is only eleven and you will always see him as your little boy, but this day he became a man."

The early morning light, not so bright as it had been even a few short days ago, did little to warm the small bedroom. A haze settled over the valley.

Haunted by dreams of Pete Briscom dragging her naked from the tub again and again, Jean had thrashed about all night. Anxious for some peace of mind, she had refused to wake, but now with the pale sun shining in her eyes she groaned a last protest and struggled to her feet taking her blanket with her.

Weary, Jean looked forlornly at her bed knowing it was no use. With her blanket tucked beneath her chin, she stumbled into the big room. It would be another hour before her mother woke. For now, she'd have to endure the uneasy silence alone.

Lifting the lid of the breadbox, Jean found a single flour biscuit left over from the night before. It would do. Nibbling the crumbling bread, she paced the floor still protesting the morning. It was cold and gloomy. She frowned and taking up the poker, she stoked the smoldering fire, then watched it as it burst into flames.

Dropping the poker on the hearth, Jean's reluctant steps carried her to the side door where she stared blankly through the small panes. To her surprise Jimmy was up. He was leading Brownie out of the barn saddled and ready to ride.

Her heart suddenly beat with a young girl's fear. Hurrying on to the porch, she closed the door behind her. "Where you going? Not leaving are you?"

With her mother's threat echoing in her mind she had to ask. Jean moved to the edge of the steps. "You wouldn't leave without telling me goodbye would you?"

Jimmy looked up and grinned, surprised by her concern. "Thought we talked about that last night. Just taking Brownie for a little ride. Do it most mornins' but you are usually still in bed getting your beauty sleep so you wouldn't know."

Jean scrunched her nose knowing he was teasing her as much as scolding her for sleeping too much. "Well I'm up now. Where you heading?"

Jimmy cast a glance over his shoulder. "Just up on the hill. Won't be gone long. Need a little time to think."

Stepping off the porch, Jean raised on her toes and gingerly crossed the frosty ground. "Take me with you."

The boy looked surprised. "You are in your nightgown."
Jean shrugged. "Got my blanket. Pretend I'm an Indian. Besides you said we wouldn't be gone long."
A grin spreading across his face, Jimmy pulled the brightly colored blanket close to her cheeks. "I never said 'We'."
Leaning into him, Jean smiled coyly. "Bet you meant to."
Jimmy knew it was no use bantering with her. "Guess I did."

In one quick move he picked Jean up and swung her high onto the horse's back, blanket and all. "Whoa!" She landed with a jar, surprised by his strength. He was growing up which to Jean kind of meant they were both growing up. As Jimmy swung into the saddle before her, she wrapped the blanket around him, then buried her head against his back and closed her eyes.

Their trail led through the back pasture and across a small stream that was little more than a trickle a few feet wide. Paper thin sheets of silvery ice hung delicately just above the water as if floating in the air. Brownie's hooves splashed a narrow path shattering the fragile decoration. A few weeks ago the ice had been strong enough to support the horse's weight. Spring was coming on.

Making their way higher up the winding trail, Jean ducked her head dodging branches of wavy leaf oak. The once green foliage had turned from the bright yellows and reds of last autumn to dull rusty browns by winters end. With branches mostly bare, a thick mat of damp leaves softened the fall of Brownie's hooves.

High above the valley their trial meandered into the loftier hills bordered by stunted pines forever green. The changing seasons matter not to the old trees.

Wrapped in her Hudson Bay blanket woven with warm fall hues she felt more akin to the aspens, their slender branches now bare. She would need the warmth of spring to feel alive again.

Jimmy was a growing boy caught somewhere in between. Jean tried to decide if he was a limber pine or a sturdy oak. She ran her hands down his strong arms, and decided he was more like the oak.

His strength made her feel safe. A soft smile lit her face knowing Jimmy needed her too.

Climbing up on the ridge, her quiet young man weaved his horse through the trees and came out in a clearing that opened to the east where there was a little more sun. He reined Brownie to a stop.

Jean hugged tighter and peered over his shoulder sensing that they'd reached their destination.

From here she could see the entire valley. Far below two rivers joined, the Ruidoso winding down from the steep mountain divide, and the Hondo flowing south into the desert. These rivers brought life to the valley. Dotted alone their banks were the small farms where families had staked their claims hoping for a better life that sadly had never came. Still it was beautiful and the evil lurking beyond their humble home seemed far away.

Jimmy stared reverently for a long time then swung from the saddle and helped Jean to her feet. She looked up into his eyes but the boy's gaze was already elsewhere. Releasing her, he turned and walked silently to the overlook. There was a chilly breeze. Stuffing his hands into his coat pockets, he stared uneasily, his breathing quickened leaving puffs of steam swirling in the air.

Jean came to his side and snuggled under his arm. She hesitated a moment respecting his privacy then folding in front of him she laid her chin upon his chest. "Guess this is your hayloft."

Acknowledging his companion with a quick glance, he faced forward. "It's so big Jean, and I don't know if there is a place in it for me."
He shrugged. "Maybe it's being an orphan, but I just don't seem to fit."

His lips quivering, Jimmy filled his lungs with a deep breath of the crisp mountain air. "After ma died, no kin ever wanted me...Pete took me in more to help him, and he made it clear I was livin' off the scraps of others. Even your ma ain't happy about having a...a horse thief in her home."

Filling with emotion, Jimmy glanced down. "You letting me stay in your barn was about the best thing that ever happened to me...your ma telling me to leave was the worst." The boy clenched his jaw. "If I live or die, nobody cares. It hurts."
Jean wrapped her arms around his waist and held tightly. "I care."

Returning her hug, Jimmy scoffed. "You're a kid."

"I am not. I'm a woman...well a young woman." Jean climbed onto his boots and lifted on her toes. "Almost as tall as you."

He kissed her forehead. "Ain't discountin' you Jean. Heck, you are the only one who does care. Without you..."

A lump tightened his throat silencing him; he stared back into the distance struggling against the tears threatening to come. Jean turned her head aside not wanting to embarrass him. "Brownie cares."

She looked up and smiled. "You got a horse, a saddle, and a pretty girl if you hadn't noticed. That's more than most men around here."

Turning his eyes downward, a doubtful grin lit Jimmy's face. "You saying you are my girl?"

Wrapped in his arms, Jean playfully pinched his side then shook her head. "No...I'm your woman."

The young couple burst into laughter and hugged tighter. Bending, Jimmy scooped Jean up. "Come on. We best get back before your ma wakes, then I really won't have any place to call home."

Following a deer trail beneath the gnarled trees growing from the bank, Will looked over his small shoulder. In the distance he could see the thin wisps of smoke rising from the chimney of their home.

Before him the slow-moving Hondo seemed to wander on forever. Alone with his thoughts he struggled to come to grips with what had happened the day before. Will understood his sister's desire to leave the valley even if she did go the wrong way about. That was Jean.

Seldom did he venture this far from home in search of game. If he shot a deer there was no one to help him haul it back, but today his doubt carried him onward as much as the hunt.

Though only eleven, there was a toughness in the boy far beyond his years. Since the day he took his first step there had always been chores and responsibilities. A family alone had to eat to survive. Each member pulled their own weight. Even at an early age he understood the different roles of men and women.

Will's hand slid down the worn stock of his faithful rifle. It was the only connection he had with his father. To him it was more than a gun. It was an obligation handed down from father to son; a bequeath of strength and obligation. He was to stand in his father's stead, to feed and protect his family. It was a bond with a man he never knew.

His mother and sister did their best yet it was beyond them to understand what was missing for him. Nor did they realize how much the hand of his uncle mussing his hair on that fateful morn in Crow Crossing meant to him. A man like his own father had come into his life; a fearless hero feared by many, but for Will this tall stranger eased the emptiness that gnawed at him.

Though he'd never dare say it to anyone, in the boy's heart his father had returned from beyond the grave. It was seeing Cole stand against the sheriff that gave Will the strength to protect his sister.

The boy looked down the Hondo one last time, then turned. From now on he'd hunt closer to home.

It was late when Molly woke. The night had come and gone without incident, she hoped the day would do the same. Not feeling much in a mood to do anything, she took her time getting dress before going about her chores.

There was plenty to do, but nothing urgent, mostly busy work to keep her from going crazy. She heated water and washed some laundry in the same tub Jean had bathed in the day before. It was just a tub, but it was full of memories. She'd bathed her children in it since they were babies, heck; she'd bathed in it herself. It seemed funny how the most simple things become precious when they were about to be taken away.

Somewhere beyond the meadows, a distant rifle shot cracked and trailed away. Molly stopped. The distant rumble of Will's gun was something she heard most mornings, but over time she had come to put it out of her mind. After yesterday she would never hear it quite the same. She saddened. Would even this simple yet cherished sound of her life vanish like her neighbors; grow silent as her son?

Angered by the thought she threw the dirty laundry into the tub. One by one Molly scrubbed each article of clothing harder than necessary fuming at the injustice. With each rag brutally washed she'd wring them by hand as if it were someone's neck.

When her basket was full she stomped to her feet then paused.

It would do no good to get all worked up. Taking a breath, she quietly carried the laundry out the front door and down the steps to the line where she started hanging up the sheets. The frost had melted from the ground and a gentle breeze of thin desert air quickly stole the moisture from the fabric. With a little luck the clothes would dry on the line.

"Thank you Mama."

Jean's soft voice came with a welcomed hug from behind. "Thanks for letting Jimmy stay."

Molly cast a reproachful eye over her shoulder. "You didn't return to your room until very late last night."

"We just talked Mama. Honest...had to forgive each other for what we'd done."

"Help me hang these clothes sweetheart, then let's take the buckboard to Crow Crossing. It's Saturday if you hadn't noticed, and...well, we've missed a few weeks. When we are done with the laundry, Will can hitch up Carlos's mare."

"Are you sure you are ready Mama?"

Molly nodded her head. "Life goes on. It may be scary as hell, but it goes on."

Holding a clothespin between her teeth, she pinned a sheet to the line with another, then popped the one from her mouth. "...I think only you and I'll go alone this time. We don't always need to be relying on your brother. We're Creed women. It takes more than an insult or a dirty old man to send us into hiding."

"Yes Mama."

Jean took her petticoat out of the basket and draped it next to the sheets. "Mama, everything has changed."

She paused and lowered her voice. "...the way ol' Pete looked at me..."

A tiny smile tugged at the corners of her mouth. "...and the way Jimmy looks at me. I've changed."

Molly stopped hanging the laundry. Reaching out a hand she combed her fingers through her daughter's hair. "Boys grow quietly into men, but with girls...well it's like butterflies suddenly spreading their bright colorful wings on a glorious morning breeze for all the world to behold. You are forever changed."

Releasing Jean, Molly dug back into the basket. "If your father were here, you'd always be his little princess, but other men will look at you differently. They will admire your curves wanting to see more than is proper. Some will want you, but one will love you. The hard thing is telling them apart."

Jean hugged her mother's arm. "Mama....some good came out of what Pete did."

Molly rolled her eyes. "I suspect so, but only a Creed woman could see it that way. Most women would be hiding under their beds crying buckets of tears. You are a strong girl Jean, but it's also what gets us Creeds into trouble; we don't have the sense to come in out of a storm."

Hanging the last pair of trousers, Molly looked up. Outside the gate, Cole Creed sat his tall blue roan silently watching them. He had promised he'd leave her alone. Good to his word, he stayed on the road. Molly knew it took some doing, she also knew he'd come to make sure they were okay.

Without turning her eyes away, she handed the basket to Jean. "Take this to the house darling. Walk proudly, not like you've been beat."

Casting a smile to her uncle, Jean hurried across the yard heeding her mother's wisdom. She knew she was the reason he had come.

Untying her apron, Molly cautiously made her way to the gate. She held his cold stare trying to read his face. It was like clawing at stone. More than anything she feared his hair-trigger temper would explode and he'd ride off to Lincoln with guns blazing. If there was any hope of avoiding more killings she'd have to choose her words carefully.

Molly's heart quickened as the distance between them closed. His smile could warm a girl's heart, and just as easily his piercing eyes could wilt her like a flower under a hot desert sun.

A few more steps brought her closer. He wasn't giving up anything. This time words alone would not be enough. She'd have to sweeten them with honey. "Hi Cole. Guess I know why you came. Carlos told you?"

As he often did, Cole remained silent a long moment before speaking. "No, Tom O'Donald. I was the last to hear."

There was bitterness in his words, but at length he softened. "Guess I know why."

Edging closer, Molly gently rested a hand on the roan and looked up, her anxious eyes pleading. "Cole, Jean's okay. Will took care of it. You'd been proud of him."

Cole shook his head. "I know what those pretty brown eyes are asking Molly. I'm not the killer you make me out to be, but sometimes..."

He looked away. "I hear more than you might expect."

His tone was accusing. "Hate me if you like and talk about me behind my back, but don't hide things from me. It will come to no good."

Lowering her eyes, Molly nodded. "Deal."

She looked back up. "Does that mean you won't kill ol' Pete?"

Cole stared down the road taking his time. "Mean's I won't kill him today, but if this Pete feller happens to cross my path somebody will be hanging his soiled trousers on the line."

A smile of relief lit Molly's face. "Thank you Cole."

Molly leaned in closer. "Cole, I've asked you to keep your distance. You know why. No point in going there...and maybe I've spoken unkindly at times..." Her voice began to break. "...but there is hurt...and I'm afraid of you Cole, afraid of what you might do. Don't judge me too harshly. It's hard to be beholding to you, needing you, and wanting you gone."

Her hand inched across the stallion toward his leg then stopped. "Cole, about not hiding things; do you know a man named Wade Bannock?"

The roan came to attention as his master tightened the reins. "I do."

Molly looked up wanting him to read what was in her heart while at the same time fearing he would. "He treated me unkindly Cole. Said to tell you about it. He's got an evil laugh I don't think I'll ever forget."

Unconsciously she brushed a finger to her lips remembering the man's cruelty. "From now on I'll tell you what I know, but it's to keep the peace, not destroy it. You stay away from him Cole."

Cole let his hand fall by his side. Reaching out a finger, he gently touched her hair. "I appreciate your concern Molly. Now I'll be honest with you. If they brought Bannock in, time is short."

Molly gave a start and looked up not wanting to believe, but Cole's steel blue eyes affirmed his declaration. He turned his horse around. "Something is pushing them, something bigger than me. I think they got careless and want to hide their mess. You stay close to home."

Molly trembled. "Surely Cole somebody will stop them..."

"They're the law Molly. When they come, it won't be to protect you."

Cole whipped the reins and headed off at a gallop leaving Molly standing in the road.

Slowly walking backwards, she watched him ride away. She should have felt a sense of victory, another killing had been averted, but inside her there was a longing she hated to acknowledge. "Damn you Cole."

Molly turned and headed towards the porch. Cole had told her to stay home. He had said time was short but he didn't say how short. Was it days or months? She had no idea, and probably neither did he. "Come on Jean let's load up the wagon and get to Crow Crossing."

Jean could see the troubled look on her mother's face. "What's wrong Mama. Is Uncle Cole going to kill ol' Pete?"

Molly hurried into the kitchen with Jean at her heels. She grabbed a basket of fresh eggs and bread. "No, he won't kill Pete. I sweet talked him, like you did Jimmy, guess I'm a fine one to lecture you. Let's go."

Bad Water
Chapter 17
The Storm

Cole pushed the blue roan through the stunted pines and up the ridge. The stallion's hooves found purchase in the crumbling earth. Patches of hard frozen snow slowed their progress on a trail. Time was growing short. Cole wanted to be done with it.

His brow was furrowed with concern. He had tried not to unduly worry Molly about Wade Bannock, but the young gunfighter's presence signaled the beginning of the end. Cole's old threat would no longer keep her safe.

Not only did the Murphy Dolan faction have the law on their side, they had every outlaw band, and the military so it seemed. Cole had spotted a company of Buffalo Soldiers out of Fort Stanton Heading towards Lincoln. It was well known that Murphy, Dolan, and Sheriff Brady had all mustered out of the army. None of this bode well for the Regulators. The numbers were stacking against them. And now Wade Bannock, a fast-hired gun. They were going to end it and end it quick.

It was April Fool's Day, and Cole found irony in it. He laughed under his breath in spite of their impending doom.

Crossing a low ridge, he pulled to a halt in a shadowed crevasse beneath an overhanging rock. The trail looped back in a narrow gully of fractured rock hidden in the pines. He would wait here as he had many times before. Molly had no idea how much time he spent in the saddle keeping her and the children safe.

His time fighting in Mexico had taught him many things. While Carlos stayed close he patrolled the hills in military fashion. It was his presence that kept Murphy and Dolan's forces at bay. They knew if he caught them in small numbers they would quietly disappear, and so now Wade Bannock was brought in to challenge his control over the valley.

The next move was Murphy and Dolans. All he could do was wait like he was doing now. There isn't a lot of choices when you are out of options.

Cole did not have to wait long. Down the stony trail weaving through the Ponderosa pines, the cadence of hooves making slow progress rose and fell. It was two horses by the sound of it. Cole had only expected one. Out of habit, he loosened his pistol in its holster.

The plodding hooves grew louder. Making their way over rock and root, two riders came into view. Both men were leaning heavy in their saddles appearing worse for the wear.

The young man out front raised his head and forced a smile. "Ola old man."

Edging the roan forward, Cole nodded grimly. "Billy."

Billy tried to sit tall, but flinched and went back to leaning against his pony's neck. Beneath the gathering clouds, Cole squinted taking in the scene. "Kid, looks like you got shot in the ass again." Ever cheerful, Billy offered a painful chuckle then glanced to the man behind him. "Frenchie here took one too. We are a matching pair."

The boy nudged his horse alongside Cole. "...Believe it or not, we won."

Billy looked back at big French clinging to his saddle horn. "...least ways today. Tomorrow who knows."

Gritting his teeth, Billy tried once more to smile. "Town is in need of a new badge toter if you want the job, though I figure your first duty would be huntin' me. Put nine rounds into Sheriff Brady this mornin'."

Billy closed his eyes against the pain then continued. "Sorry for beatin' ya to it. Know how much you had your heart set on killing the bastard. We done in Deputy Hindmann too. Quite a shootout. Some folks a mite upset."

Billy cautiously looked around. "Surprise they aren't on our trail."

He turned back to Cole. "...yours too amigo. Have you heard about Bannock?"

Cole nodded "Heard."

He stared down the trail contemplating the situation. "Damn."

Turning back to Billy Cole sighed. "There's no way out of it for you now kid unless you hightail it back to Texas."

Billy put his hand on his leg and it came away wet. "Gunna' hold up at San Patricio for a spell, but as long as Mr. McSween is still in the fight, I reckon as I'll stay."

Cole accepted Billy's answer knowing he'd do the same.

The boy saw the resignation on his friend's face. "Don't worry. Me n' the Regulators will watch over Lincoln. You watch over Alamo Valley, and we'll go on looking out for each other like always. We ain't dead yet."

Billy tensed against the pain. "We best be goin'. You too Mr. Creed. I wouldn't leave that pretty little niece of yours unprotected too long. Ya never know when I might show up."

Taking up his reins, Billy shook his head. "Yes sir, a sorry affair." Without another word, the wounded men pushed their ponies down the left trail looking more dead than alive.

Watching them go Cole patted his horse. "Yes sir Brazo, hard days are coming fast.

With Miguel's death and Molly's injuries, weeks had passed without money or provisions making a visit to Crow Crossing all the more urgent. The mortgage had to be paid. Letting the farm slip away after all they'd been through would be tragic.

Molly could have asked Cole for the needed funds, but she had her pride. More importantly she wanted to believe she and the children could make it on their own.

Loading her basket into the wagon, Molly turned to the three males standing silently watching her with concern. "Will, you can stay home this time. Plenty of chores to do. Carlos you work Jimmy until he's too tired to even think about doing a young girl's bidding."

She scowled at the boy. "Don't just stand there, help Jean into the wagon, she's a lady if you hadn't noticed, and you've got some growing to do if you want to catch her."

Carlos understood Molly's blustering. Going to Crow Crossing would take courage after what she'd been through. She had to do this on her own if she were to ever feel safe again. It was why Will wasn't going. The boy had proven himself, and now Molly needed to know if the same strength was in her. Jean did too. This was one trip the women would make alone.

Helping Molly onto the seat of the buckboard, Carlos tempered his words. "Do what you need to Senora, but there is a reason why I'm here. If you are not back in three hours, I will come looking for you."

Molly nodded, feeling a bit like a child being scolded. Still his concern was warranted, and his promise of protection secretly welcomed. "It's only Crow Crossing. I'll be back soon."
Carlos patted her hand reassuringly then stepped away. Molly snapped the reins. "Getty-up."

Wrapped in a blanket Jean leaned on her mother needing to be close. It was one of those moments where she wanted to be a little girl again. Someday she'd spread her butterfly wings, but growing up takes time, so for now the safety of her mother's shoulder would keep her home.

Molly slipped her arm around Jean in a forgiving hug then toyed with her frayed collar. "I think it's about time we get you a new dress."
Jean filled with excitement, her eyes beaming. "Really Mama?"
Molly nodded. "It's your birthday present...from your Uncle Cole."
Jean wiggled closer. "That makes it even better. I wouldn't want to take money we need for the farm."
She giggled. "I think I'd like a yellow dress."
Surprised, Molly almost laughed. "A yellow dress?"
Turning, Jean clutched her mother's arm. Yes, something bright and pretty. I'm tired of blue and gray."
Molly expression showed little hope. "I doubt Mrs. Hayes has a yellow dress. Maybe we can buy a nice blue print, and order in a yellow one. Let your uncle buy you two dresses."
"Oh Mama do you think he would?"
"Baby I'm sure he would." There was satisfaction in Molly's voice. "For all the frustration he's causing me, maybe we should buy us both a dozen dresses and put them on his tab."
The girls both laughed. Jean hugged her mother. "A dozen dresses, that's silly but it would be a sight to see...a dozen dresses."

They rode on enjoying the quiet time together. Jean lifted her face to her mother knowing a kiss was waiting for her forehead. She smiled gratefully then closed her eyes as if she were going to sleep. "I think he's lonely."

Molly looked down in surprise. "What makes you say that? You've hardly know him."
Jean's heart skipped a beat realizing she almost revealed her midnight ride. "Oh...just because. Havin' everybody afraid of him. It must be lonely."

She snuggled closer. "Did Uncle Cole ever have a girl?"
This time it was Molly's heart that fluttered. "...Once."
A smile lit the young girl's face. "Did she love him?"
When her mother didn't answer, Jean opened her eyes and looked up. "Did she?"
Molly's voice trailed to a whisper. "Yes...but that was a long time ago."

Jean thrust her arm from under her blanket. "Look Mama."
Not far ahead the O'Donalds were coming down the road. Easing the mare to the side, Molly made room for their buggy to pass. Tom pulled to a halt. "Mornin' Molly."
His voice was heavy causing her concern. "Morning Tom."

Molly smiled at Annie who was nursing Polly. The child was getting big, but food was where you found it and right now it was scarce for everyone. "Morning Annie. My she's growing up."

Annie returned a polite smile but nervously looked to her husband. Molly could feel a tension. "Is something the matter Tom?"
The O'Donalds looked at each other then back to Molly. After an awkward pause, Annie spoke. "It's Grampa Charlie. With all you had to deal with we didn't want to..."

Molly suddenly grew alarmed. "Is he okay? Is something wrong?"
Tom tried to remain calm. "He's gone Molly. We found him dead, the day of Miguel's funeral, and you being...well you know."

Tears came to Molly's eyes. "I thank you for protecting me. Seems like everyone is. What happen? He appeared in good health."
Tom's jaw tightened. "Don't know. Just found him dead in his yard. Maybe a heart attack."

Molly searched their faces. "There is something else isn't there?"

Annie leaned on Tom's shoulder and sobbed.

Taking time to comfort her, Tom wrapped his arm around Annie before answering. "There were a lot of horse tracks in the yard. Might have been a reason for his heart giving out."

Tom lowered his head. "Like a lot of folks around here, guess we will never know."

"Oh Tom, Annie, I'm sorry."

"Does Cole know?"

Annie sniffed and wiped a tear. "Yes. He dug the grave, very kind of him. Two funerals in one day. We buried Grampa not far from Johnny. Just came from placing flowers by the headstone. Laid one on Johnny's too."

"Thank you."

Molly prodded the mare forward until she was adjacent to Annie. "Jean and I will drop by tomorrow, bring a venison roast with fixins'."

Annie smiled. "I'd like that. The boys could use a good meal and I could use some company...you be safe."

Fighting back tears Molly snapped the reins sending the horse on down the road. Would it ever end? She tried to count those who were gone. Giving up she grew angry. Cole should have told her about Grampa Charlie while they were being honest. "Damn him."

"What Mama?" Jean wiped her cheek and sat up.

"Oh nothing baby."

Studying her mother's face Jean frowned. "You are mad at Uncle Cole again. Why?"

Molly whipped the reins wanting to be gone. "There's a lot happening in the valley that he's not telling me."

"Mama you told him to stay away."

"Well he's not, is he?" Molly caught Jean rolling her eyes and quickly added. "Maybe it's our own fault." She put the emphasis on maybe and shoved her nose at her daughter. "Both our fault, yours and mine, but *maybe* if he'd quit treating us like children, leaving us in the dark, then *maybe* we wouldn't be running off doing foolish things."

Jean let a moment pass then politely scolded. "Like you hiding Uncle Cole from me. I'm not a child anymore either Mama."

Stung by her daughter's honesty, Molly slipped an arm around her and spoke softly. "I love you baby, and I'm just trying to protect you."

Snuggling back into her mother's arms, Jean closed her eyes one final time. "Guess that's what Uncle Cole is doing; protecting us, and loving us Mama." The young girl's voice trailed off into a whisper. "...he loves us."

Molly looked down at her sleeping daughter's head bouncing on her shoulder. It came to her that Jean was almost as tall as her. Her baby had grown up and somehow she had missed it. Jean was right, there were too many secrets. Molly remembered a saying her own mother used to quote, 'Secrets are an invisible flame that burn.' No good ever comes from secrets. Molly stirred uncomfortably; she had hidden the children's only uncle from them all these years justifying it by telling herself everybody had secrets. Cole certainly had his. Her face clouded. Murphy and Dolan had their secrets too. Only theirs might be the death of them. She wondered if they were behind Grampa Charlie's death.

With the Indians on reservations, Murphy and Dolan had managed to secure the army beef contracts to keep them fed. The Alamo valley was broad and opened with the Ruidoso running through it, a perfect place to graze a large herd of cattle if the small farms were gone. Thing was, Murphy-Dolan held the mortgages on most of the farms including Molly's. It was rumored that building the big store had put the two men heavily in debt so they'd sold deeds to raise cash to pay off the bank. Now all they could do was squeeze the farmers again and get the land back without buying it so they could sell it again or run beef; rumors and secrets.

As for the families who had vanished. The law said it was the rustler, and not Murphy Dolan. Maybe it was rustlers, heaven knows there were plenty of them, but rustlers would have no reason to drive the farmers out. Molly sighed and spoke her thoughts out loud. "It's what you know and what you can prove."
Jean stirred, but kept her eyes closed. "What Mama?"
"Nothing sweetheart...just nothing."
"Mama, it's not the same here anymore."
"I know baby but it's all we got."

Bad Water
Chapter 18
Clouds

Coming over the final ridge, Molly pulled the buckboard to a rolling stop. A lot had happened since the last time she came to Crow Crossing, none of it good. An uneasiness fluttered in her stomach making her feel a bit silly. It was only Crow Crossing.

The familiar row of dark buildings rose from the boardwalk. Molly had been coming here since early childhood holding onto her mother's hand. The low roofs and inviting doors had always been a place to meet neighbors, but this morning something was different. There were horses and wagons as usual; men milling about, then it dawned on her. She didn't know any of them. Her eyes scanned the length of the boardwalk. Not one horse was familiar.

Snapping the reins, she cautiously coaxed the mare forward.

"Clouds."

Molly was distracted. "What dear?"

Jean points to the sky. "Clouds. A storm is coming Mama. Can't you feel it in the air?"

Her brow furrowed, she gave a quick reply "Yes dear, I feel it. We will do our business and get home."

Molly pulled up in front of the store and stopped. She paused and nervously looked down the boardwalk. There was no ringing of blacksmith's hammer, nor smoke in the chimney of the eating house. The only sound was course laughter coming from Rubens. Molly tied off the reins. "Jean, stay with the wagon baby. I'll be back shortly."

"But Mama. My birthday dress."

Molly squeezed her daughter's hand. "Just wait."

Climbing down, Molly took her basket and quickly made her way up the steps. The men milling out front, stopped to stare at her. They were hard-bitten men. Some scowled, others leered. None tipped their hats. She hid her eyes and made her way through them.

Just as she started to lift the latch, a voice called to her. "Hello Mrs. Creed."

It was young Bobbie Maxwell. He was Jimmy's age only taller and more muscular. His voice was cold lacking the cordiality accorded women by boys his age. Still, his was the only face she knew, so she welcomed his presence. "Morning Bobby."

Instead of replying the boy stared with the same disconcerting grin as the men. It unnerved her. She nodded once more and hurried inside.

Closing the door, she looked up. Three tall cowboys talking to a fourth man turned and faced her. As they parted Molly nearly screamed. Behind them stood the ignoble Judge Warren Brewster.

Seeing the look on her face, Brewster's eyes sparkled with a sinister pleasure. "Well, well, if it isn't Molly Creed, the angel of justice and decency."

Molly instinctively shrunk back, frantically looking left and right trying to figure out what was happening. She suddenly realized all the shelves were empty. Everything was gone. "W-where is Mrs. Hayes? What have you done?" Molly's voice betrayed her fright.

Clearly amused by Molly's rattled demeanor, the judge did not bother to answer. Instead he spoke dispassionately to the men. "Boys you will have to excuse us. You got your orders now get this job done and we will be gone from this depressing place."

Brewster followed them to the door. He started to close it behind them when he suddenly stopped. His face glowed with devilish delight. "My, my, my."

Something set the gears spinning in his morbid brain. "So that's you lovely daughter? Even prettier than I imagined, all filled out."

The color drained from Molly's face. "I've come to do business with the Hayes, not discuss my family with the likes of you."

"One moment." The judge stepped out onto the boardwalk and pulled the door behind him. "Bobby..."

The boy's name was the last word Molly heard before the door shut. She looked around the room. Not so much as a candle or a jar of preserves remained. The store had been completely emptied.

A shudder went through her. Right now Jean was out there with that horrible man. Molly rushed to the door when suddenly, it opened again. The judge stepped back in and closed, it locking them inside. Molly retreated to a corner.

"Come here Molly."

Backing against the wall, she shook her head. "Where is Emma? I want to see Emma."

The judge folded his hands. "The Hayes are gone. Seems like they were a mite careless with who they extended credit too. I convinced them California would be a healthier climate."

Brewster waved his hand gesturing to the store. "I'm the new proprietor...for the time being. Actually if you must know my dear, it's because of you that I had to take action against the Hayes, and all of Crow Crossing for that matter. Pity."

Utter confusion colored Molly's face. The judge gloated. "When you came to my office and threatened that the farmers would rally around the renowned Cole Creed, well I couldn't take that chance my dear. I've seen it happen before. Mr. Murphy and Mr. Dolan are counting on me, and even in my esteemed position it is not wise to displease them. Yes, this empty store is completely your fault. Poor, poor Emma. How she cried."

The judge took a moment to look at the barren walls pleased with himself. He turned to Molly with one thought replacing another. "...and that ruthless kin of yours, he insults me. My new barn went up in flames. It was the largest barn in all of Lincoln County. You can understand my dismay...and three more of my men have gone missing, but no matter, the men I can replace. Indeed, I already have. Still I must teach Cole Creed a lesson he will remember. The problem is he is a hard man to hurt, and that is where you come in my dear child."

He pointed. "I see you brought a basket of eggs. How adorable." He cupped his hands beneath his chin mocking her. "...what would Emma have given you? A dollar? A whole dollar! Pity, pity."

Brewster knew exactly what the money meant for her. He taunted. "How will you ever pay your mortgage? Tisk, tisk."

Walking back to the window, the judge appeared in no hurry. "You see, I told you I'd get your farm without paying for it. You truly should have taken me up on my very kind offer to relocate you and your most fetching daughter to Leasburg." He shrugged. "No matter. As I said, you are what I say you are."

Turning back to the window, the judge smiled. "Yes, she will make a pretty little whore."

Her face turning crimson, Molly cursed. "You dirty old man, you will get your damn money."

Reaching into her bag, she threw a fist full of coins on the floor. "There!"

The judge glared at Molly's affront as she bolted towards the door threatening as she went. "Keep your filthy hands off my daughter you vile..."

"Stop right there!"

The judge boomed with the self-assured authority that he honed in his courtroom, halting Molly in her tracks. Her face turned crimson knowing she dare not oppose Warren Brewster. He carried no gun, but the judge was a man whose depravity had no bounds and he had the law to back him up, making him as deadly as any killer.

His voice once more honey sweet, Brewster curled a finger. "Come here Molly. There is something I want you to see."

Hesitantly, Molly went to his side fearing the worst. He placed a finger under her chin. "Look my pretty."

Slowly Molly lifted her eyes and stared out the window as ordered. Jean was being helped down from the wagon. Her daughter smiled innocently as Bobby Maxwell set her on the ground. Jean started to step away but the boy held her firmly by the waist asserting control over her. Relenting she chatted cheerfully, oblivious that anything was wrong.

In the midst of the young people's captivating conversation, Bobby suddenly turned his head towards the window. His cold dark eyes stared right at them, a sinister grin upon his face. The judge nodded to him. Bobby did the same, then turning back he pulled Jean closer in a too familiar way. She resisted for an instant, but the boy was charming and forceful. His hands slid higher up her body until his out stretched thumbs were dangerously close to her breasts; his fists clutching the fabric of her dress. As Jean's lips moved in unheard pleasantries, the boy looked back at the judge as if waiting a signal.

"My, my, my. How that boy wants to please me. It looks as though your daughter might have her first client, and she doesn't suspect a thing. Poor stupid child."

Horrified, Molly tried to push through the door, but the judge grabbed her wrist and jerked her back hard. He twisted her arm upwards buckling her knees in pain. "Just stay where you are. All it will take from me is a wave of the hand and your little girl will find her handsome Bobby Maxwell...shall we say, not so handsome."

The judge leaned his head to the side as if imagining what could happen. "Indeed, her cheap dress is so flimsy I suspect it will fall right off leaving her completely bare in front of all those lonely desperate men, like Burk there. He was in prison until a few short months ago. No telling how long it's been since he's had a woman. And Toby Rollins, he's wanted in Texas for raping a Mexican girl, but Texans will hang you for any little thing. Now the tall man with the scar across his eye, that's Bud Spence, he strangled his wife and child; no reason, just felt like it. Yes Molly, they are all deputies sworn to uphold the law, my law. No telling what they might do upon seeing such a tender flower in all her glory. Give you goose bumps."

Molly's skin beaded in cold sweat as a sickness washed over. "How can you be so evil?"

The judge shook his head. "Evil? Why it's kindness my dear. You see, in a war..." He paused and held her eyes. "Make no mistake it is a war, and in war men die, but you can't kill women. People get upset. Makes bad press. They send in U.S. Marshals, it gets messy. So you have to do something else with the fairer sex, don't you? It's kindness Molly. Men die, but no matter how disrespectful you are to me, you get to go on living, though I do believe we will have to relocate you after I've taken your farm. Can't leave two helpless women uncared for."

Brewster folded his hands in mock thought. "Yes, out of mercy I will have to declare you wards of Lincoln County and find you suitable housing...perhaps in Leasburg, even change your names, legally of course. No one will ever find you."

He let his threat sink in, then bobbed his head. "Yes, kindness! Why I'm a bona fide humanitarian."

Molly tried to pull free. "I'm a grown woman. You can't do this..."

The Judge pulled her back to him. "If I produce a document saying your name is Jezebel and you are seventeen...well what do they know in Leasburg; just lonely men with silver eager to partake of your delicacies...and your daughter's."

"Please no. Don't hurt her. Please." Molly tugged at his sleeve. "What do you want from me?"

Putting his arm high around Molly's waist, Brewster pulled her to him. "Ask again dear, only sweeter, and put a 'sir' on the end."

Her eyes turning fearfully to her daughter, Molly dared not resist. She swallowed the bitter taste in her mouth willing to do whatever it took to save her child. "What do you want from me? ...Sir."

"There. That's better. Servitude becomes you." He touched a fat finger to her cheek and let it slowly trail down her soft neck to her blouse. "Not so high and mighty, are we now?"

He pulled her closer. "Are we?"

Molly closed her eyes tightly. "No sir."

"That's right. Not so high and mighty at all. You see Molly you have no idea how offensive it was having you stroll into my office. Me the high and honorable Judge Warren H. Brewster, having to bargain with a dirt farmer, and a woman at that. Why you might have just as well thrown a bucket of shit on me."

Incensed, he shoved her backwards. "Now get down on the floor and pick up that money you threw in my face."

Brewster jabbed a finger at his feet.

Molly made no attempt to defy him. Dropping to her knees, she obediently began picking up the scattered coins as she wept.

The judge gloated. "There is something exhilarating about seeing another human being on their knees. And so much better when it is you Molly."

When she had gathered all the coins, she held her hands up hoping to appease him. Brewster stepped backward. "Crawl to me Molly."

Lowering her head, Molly did as she was bidden. The judge chuckled. "Look at you now, like dust upon the floor."

Taking her chin Brewster hissed with a voice both cold and threatening. "Don't you ever throw anything in my face again. Is that understood?"

Tears flowing, Molly meekly nodded.

The judge swung his arm wide batting the coins from her hand scattering them across the room. Molly cowered, but he grabbed her and jerked her to her feet. "You think your little pittance matters to me? It's you I want Molly, your pride...your vain pride."

Holding her tightly, he toyed with her lace bodice pressing it aside. "You do have some bodily worth; a warning for the contemptuous Cole Creed, and a small financial remittance for my suffering...why you are trembling. Do I make you tremble child?" Struggling to breathe, Molly whispered yes. The judge pushed her hair back. "What's that? I can't hear you."

It was all Molly could do to keep her feet beneath her. "Yes sir...you make me tremble...please don't hurt her."

She sobbed. "Do what you want with me, just don't hurt my daughter. She's been through enough."

Releasing his grip around Molly's waist, the judge took her by the shoulders and held her at arm's length. "That's a girl. Stand there, feet together and behave yourself. Now that we have an understanding. We do have an understanding, don't we?"

Molly nodded.

No longer caring if she answered, the judge played with her top button, rolling it in his fingers before pushing it through the fabric. Molly closed her eyes.

"Such a pretty harlot. Don't close your lovely eyes darlin'. They are your most precious asset revealing so much, as if you were completely naked."

His hand lowered to the next button. "I merely wish a glimpse of what I am buying. Then you can be on your way."

At last Molly understood. Pulling free, she stepped back her lovely eyes hiding nothing. With a hand that no longer shook, she reached up and unfastened a clasp on her skirt letting it slide to the floor. "You bastard."

The judge stared approvingly. "Yes my little trinket. I most assuredly am."

He rubbed his hands, "…but a rich bastard. Now reveal all your assets, it looks to be a most profitable day."

Jean turned at the sound of the metal latch. The door to the store slowly opened. Molly came out head down, her face hidden beneath her hair.

Pulling away from the boy, Jean called to her mother. "Where's your basket, my new dress?"
As if coming out of a trance, Molly suddenly rushed to the wagon. "Get in Jean, we're going."

Offering her hand, Jean waited for Bobby Maxwell to help her up, but her mother screamed. "NO! Don't you touch her. I'll kill you if you do you son-of-a-bitch."

Jean was stunned. "Mama!"

"Get in the wagon Jean. Now!"

With a confused backwards glance to the boy, Jean hurried and climbed up. Her mother snapped the reins causing the bewildered girl to fall back against the seat.

As the buckboard spun around Jean heard Bobby laugh. It was cruel. She didn't understand. Behind him a large stocky man in a black suit came out of the store. He appeared to have no interest in them at all. Instead, he waved his arms to the motley cowboys summoning them to him. Lightening cracked and the rain started to pour.

Jean clutched her mother's arm. "Mama what happened."
The wagon bumped and Jean held tighter. The sound of glass breaking turned her head. Beneath the black rolling clouds, the men were throwing torches in the windows. "Mama, they are burning Crow Crossing! They are burning it down!"
Molly whipped the horse. "Let it burn."

Bad Water
Chapter 19
Into the Darkness

Thunder cracked and rolled down the long valley as a bolt of lightning tore a jagged path across the dismal sky. Molly welcomed the rain drenching them in the open buckboard. She doubted she'd ever feel clean again. *'There is no limit to the evil in men's hearts.'* Miguel's word echoed in her mind. Judge Brewster said it was a war, and you can't kill women so you humiliate them, killing them within.

Yes, she understood now, though she felt a bullet would have been much kinder.

The wagon slowly rolled to a stop as the horse waited for a command to continue. Jean looked down at the reins hanging limp in her mother's hands. "Oh Mama."

Taking up the straps, Jean urged the horse onward.

Behind them the unearthly red glow of Crow Crossing lit the black smoke swirling upward to the clouds. Jean ached inside. The row of humble dwellings had been an endearing part of her childhood, and Emma's store was their sole source of income. What would happen to them now?

Furious, she snapped the reins. "They wouldn't have burnt Crow Crossing if Uncle Cole had been here, no sir. They'd a been backin' their horses and blubberin' goodbyes."

Staring off into the distance she wondered where he was now. She looked up with the desire of a young girl's heart. Down the road she spied a man on a horse riding out of the fog. For a moment her heart leaped, but no, the rider wasn't tall enough to be her uncle. A few yards closer and she could see it was Carlos. He had come looking for them as he'd promised.

Drawing up alongside, the faithful Mexican read their faces; Molly staring blankly, her once beautiful hair matted to her face, and Jean bravely wiping the rain from her face. His eyes saddened. "Poor little angels."

Jean lowered her head, knowing they'd never be allowed to leave the farm alone again.

Taking off his coat, Carlos draped it over Molly's shoulders then spoke to Jean. "Senorita let's go plenty fast."

Reaching out he slapped the horse's rump sending it on its way. As the buckboard moved past him, he looked back at the foreboding glow and muttered beneath his breath. "Not good."

The door to Molly's bedroom creaked opened. With her head down, she slipped silently into the great room wearing her white laced dress. It was the second time in two weeks she wore it. Her hair was neatly pulled back in blue satin ribbons making her look both beautiful and fragile.

She gave a quick sideways glance, but avoided eye contact and went straight to the stove where she poured herself a warm cup of coffee.

Carlos waited, giving her a moment to get comfortable with everyone watching her. Stepping close he put a gentle hand on her shoulder. "The storm has passed Senora."

Molly lifted her eyes and stared out the window. "I don't think so."

Holding the cup in both hands she took a long sip. for a while she stared quietly in deep thought then raised her voice. "Will, Jimmy, you boys got chores to do. Best get to it...Jean you help. There's more to you than being pretty. Now outside with all of you."

She waited until she heard the door shut behind them, then setting the cup down she turned in Carlos's arms and leaned against his chest. The Mexican smoothed her hair. "What happened to you Senora?"

Molly shook her head. "No! Don't ask."

Wrapping her in a big hug, Carlos granted her wish. "Cry if you need to little one."

She sobbed softly accepting his comfort.

At length Molly took a breath and looked up. "Why are you here? You know what's coming."

A familiar smile broke across his broad face. "I have a job to do." Molly shook her head. "You'd die for me and my children?"
"Senora. I would die for what is right. Does it matter if it's here or a distant battlefield?"
Her eyes moistening Molly lifted on her toes and placed a kiss on Carlos's cheek and spoke softly. "Moments before Miguel was shot, I placed a kiss on his cheek. I can do no less for you. It is all I have to give."

Carlos touched his face. "You kissed my brother. To know this gladdens my heart. He did not die in vain. Neither will I."

Gathering her in his arms Carlos hugged her, laughing. He lifted Molly off her feet and spun her full around then set her back down. "If you choose to not speak of this evil deed, then enough of this sadness. You are strong Senora. You leave here and face bad hombres but always you return. Men will die, but I think Molly Creed will live a very long time."

Molly conjured a faint smile. The brave Mexican was right. Brewster could not kill her. He said so himself. And she'd never submit. "Carlos, it is time I swallow my pride for my children. Tonight will you go to Cole and tell him I need enough money to pay off the mortgage, all of it. Tom can take it into Lincoln so I don't have to ever see that bast..."
Molly bit her lip. "...it's over three hundred dollars. Tell him I am asking him for it."

"Si Senora I'll do this for you. Only in swallowing your pride, I think you maybe have found it."

His face grew somber. "Though I would rather you leave this rancho while I am alive to see it."

The storm returned to Molly's eyes. She pulled away. "Maybe there will be a time, but this farm is all I have Carlos. You must understand. If I left, how would I feed my children? For you it is easy. All a man needs, is a horse and gun. Children need a bed at night and walls to keep them safe. Your jeans are suited for the trail, not so a dress. Sagebrush would tear it to shreds and I'd be stripped naked aga..."

Molly stopped in mid-word throwing her hand to her mouth. The pain on her face told Carlos the rest of the story. He reached for her. "Poor Senora. I should not have let you go. I am sorry."

Pushing away, Molly shook her head. No! You cannot protect me from all things, and I won't be a prisoner to my own home."

"But Senora, tell me who did this..."

She shook her head. "No Carlos. There will be no more bloodshed, not on my account. They cannot kill me so they try to break me, but I won't be broken."

Picking up her coffee, Molly walked out onto the porch. The rain had subsided, but dark clouds remained. Carlos came and stood beside her. She searched around for the children then cocked her head in thought. "We are strange family, us Creeds. Cole is as dark and as dangerous as they come, evil by my judgment, but I know he loves us. And here I am a stubborn woman with two children and a horse- stealing orphan, fighting a battle I can't win."

Molly drained her cup and set it on the railing. "...and you, a scoundrel and a pistolero. You are part of our family as well...and I know you love us too."

Hugging herself, she breathed in the cool moist air. "Love is all we have."

Her large brown eyes filled with emotion. "Miguel said, 'Love is greater than evil.' I have to believe that. Without it there is no hope. You say you fight for what's right. We will fight for love, and we will do it here."

Several hours had come and gone and with them Carlos. He built a roaring fire before he left. The house was warm. Molly carefully folded her white dress and placed it in the bottom drawer of the hand carved oak dresser her mother left her. It was one of her many treasured possessions that made their humble house a home. The men could never understand how difficult it was to walk away from so many memories. To them the farm was just wood and paint.

Reaching out a loving hand, Molly touched the picture of John. The farm was their dream. Leaving it would be abandoning him. She couldn't do it. Who would tend his grave?

Drifting across the room, her fingertips trailed over the embroidered table cloth toying briefly with the folded bills Cole had sent back with Carlos. The farm would finally be hers. 'Bless him'.

The thought gave her a twinge of discomfort for thinking it, but, 'bless him anyway'.

Molly turned and stared into the mirror at her own image, her pout reflecting back to her. "...and damn the judge."
She swore out loud. "Damn him to hell."

Slipping the straps of the lace petticoat off her shoulders she let it fall to the floor, then placing her hands on her hips she turned left and right. After two children, her stomach was still flat and smooth. She looked admiringly, assuring herself that after thirty hard years she was still beautiful. The thought came to her that with ribbons in her hair, she maybe could pass for seventeen. It gave her both comfort and grief. "Damn you Brewster to the darkest reaches of hell. I am beautiful and you cannot soil it. The ugliness you wrought is your own."

Facing the mirror, she threw her shoulders back and stuck out her tongue dismissing Warren H. Brewster as pathetic fool whose violation had done her no harm.

Freed from the guilt, Molly bounced onto the bed like an innocent child and crawled beneath the covers. They felt cool against her bare skin. Tonight she'd sleep naked. It was her act of defiance.

The long troubling day had left her drained to say the least. Snuggling deeper into the sheets, her eyes closed surrendering to fatigue as a stout breeze rattling the window carried the harsh world outside into her dreams. Molly saw herself running in a field of tall dry grass, only now the sheet was her white dress, then a sheet again, or something somewhere in between barely clinging to her. Her slender back was exposed, and behind her the field was aflame. She could feel the heat upon her flesh.

Curling above the stocks of grain, thick black plumes belched to life. An ominous cloud of smoke overtook her. Growing in size, it transformed into a sinister face with deep eye sockets. She could hear its cruel laughter. "My, my, my." it said.

Her heart pounding, Molly ran faster, but it was hopeless. Caught by the flames, her sheets vanished in a shower of sparks that glowed red against her skin, then vanished. The laughter grew louder. "You are flawless and will fetch a pretty penny."
Roaring at its own humor the evil cloud drew nearer. "Run my sensuous beauty, but you cannot escape..."

Near panic, she tore through the tall yellow field in long strides with the taunting voice thundering above her. An evil tongue of smoke and flame licked at her flesh, then abruptly the laughter stopped.

Through the wavering fumes Molly's tear-filled eyes spied Cole, dark and brooding upon his tall horse. If only she could reach him.

Angered by the intrusion, the smoke growled, "No!" Stretching out a thick tendril it curled around her smooth white skin snatching her feet from the ground. Cole's gun was suddenly in his hand, the hammer cocked back, but he dared not pull the trigger for she had forbidden it. He sat helplessly waiting. Was killing justified now?

Coiling about her, the smoke lifted Molly higher. Soon it would be too late. Struggling against everything she believed, every oath she'd made, Molly screamed "Shoot! Cole shoot!" Cole's gun boomed. In slow motion the accusing bullet tore a deadly path, its deep luster reflecting the all-consuming fire. Molly watched mesmerized as the heavy slug plowed through the evil cloud. Blood red flames spurted forth searing her skin, but the tendril loosened its grip letting her body slide free. Limbs outstretched, she was falling, falling, falling.

Molly bounced on the bed coming to an upright position. She was awake and gasping for air.

Kicking her feet from the covers, she ran to the door and threw it open. Before she realized it she was standing on the porch clutching the post trembling as she struggled to breathe.

Fearing her dream was true she frantically searched the fields. No. There was no wall of flames. It was only the acrid smoke of Crow Crossing stinging her nostrils, that, and nothing more; a childish nightmare.

Rubbing her nose in protest, she longingly stared westward wanting Cole to hold her, to touch her, to assure her she was beautiful. Her cheeks flush. "Damn you Cole." She whispered lovingly. "I hate you so."

Pressing her hands to her face, Molly stumbled into her room and crawled back beneath the covers. She knew she'd dream again. She'd run the final distance to the tall horse fearing what she would do.

Pulling her knees to her breasts Molly hugged them tightly. She felt small and alone. "Damn you Cole. Why won't you force me to leave this accursed valley so I can hate you forever?"

Black coals lay strewn across the midnight landscape. Dying embers pulsed a faint red glow. The rains came, but not soon enough to save Crow Crossing. Dreams to ashes and dust to dust.

Yet from death comes life, and winter's bitter winds would soon spread the charred ruins far and wide offering a rich soil where tender blades of grass would in time erase all traces of the people who dwelt here; their stories lost to the ages.

Through the damp smoldering cinders, a tall man walked silently leading his horse. He had seen such ruins before, war was not a stranger. Kneeling he picked up a blackened hinge protruding from the rubble. It was all that remained.

His face sullen, he knew it was not fire that burnt Crow Crossing to the ground, it was petty hatred. From the gold fields of Colorado, to the land of the Apache, and the far off battlefields of Mexico, he'd seen the ravages of fools. Men who warranted no mercy.

He'd watched good men die and suffered the grief on the faces of widows left behind. "Not here." Cole swore beneath his breath. "Not my family."

Clenching his jaw Cole rose to his feet and blew the stench from his nostrils. His fast gun had spoken many times in defense of the innocent and all it had gained him was the revulsion of his fellow man...and his own kin. Still, he would honor his oath to his dying brother. Somehow he'd keep Molly safe so she could go on hating. The irony was not lost on him, but if being reviled by an angel was the price he had to pay, then so be.

A high pitched whimper turned Cole's head. From the shelter of the brush lining the edge of the ravine, two shiny eyes at ground level hopefully edged towards him. Cole smiled. "Hello Drifter. Looks like you need a new home."

Bad Water
Chapter 20
Six Feet of Ground

"**M**ama come quick!"

Molly lifted her head from the pillow, her senses dulled. "What...what?"

She rubbed her eyes. Jean tugged on her arm. "Hurry."

Sliding from the covers she protested. "I have to put on some clothes."

"Hurry Mama."

Jean tore out of her room and through the front door, leaving it wide open. Stepping into her dress, Molly could see Carlos and Jimmy hurriedly mounting their horses. She grabbed her shoes and ran barefoot into the yard with the buttons up her back still undone. "What's happening?"

Jean had already climbed behind Jimmy. Carlos reached down extending a hand. "They're running cattle in the cemetery."

"No!" Molly climbed up behind him and looked down at her son. "Will, don't you follow. Stay here."

Kicking their horses, Carlos and Jimmy bolted from the yard. Molly tried to slip on a shoe, but it tumbled from her hand. Frustrated, she threw the other one aside and held on.

At full gallop, the cemetery was only minutes away. Molly looked over Carlos's shoulder. In the distance cowboys with lariats were driving the cattle across the graves. She cried, "The headstones!"

As the dense herd pushed forward under the drovers prodding, the white picket fence and graceful trellis gate tipped over disappearing beneath the grinding hooves. Molly cried out. "No!"

They were not the first to arrive. Off to the side, Annie stood in her buggy her hands to her face. Tom was at the edge of the herd waving his arms trying to turn them.

The dirt farmer's shouts of outrage mattered little to the hardened cowboys. Their whistles and whips raised above the bellowing herd forcing them onward.

Carlos slapped the reins. "He's going to be trampled." Driving his horse between Tom and the cattle, he drew his pistol from the holster with a quickness that surprised Molly. It thundered in his hand, dropping the lead steer.

Suddenly all was quiet. The report of his .44 brought man and beast to an abrupt halt. With men in front and in back of them, the cattle stomped nervously not sure where to run.

Not missing a beat, Carlos slipped his Winchester from its scabbard and tossed it to Tom. Jimmy had lowered Jean beside Annie who was running to join her husband.

Sliding off the rear of the horse, Molly jumped down. "Shoo cows!" She waved her arms chasing the frightened animals away from the closest graves. Distraught, she punched the flank of a massive steer with her fist. "Get!"

Annie ran to her desperate to help, but there was little they could do. In anguish they searched the ground. The wooden markers were gone. Molly ran several steps forward looking left and right. Nothing! Throwing her hands to her head, she spun full around. The simple graves were trampled beyond recognition.

Out of the dust behind the herd, the drovers cautiously made their way through the cattle. There were eight cowboys all told, lean rugged sunburned men used to taking on trouble if there was a day's wage to be had. As the distance closed, a scratchy voice snapped. "Ya' gunna' have ta' pay for that steer." It was Pete Briscolm's. Like a bad penny he kept turning up.

Her heart aching, Molly faced the line of cowboys. She wailed. "Why? In God's name why?"

"Judge bought the land." Pete spit his chew at Molly's bare feet. "You're trespassing."

Molly jumped back avoiding the spittle. In doing so the loose sleeve of her unbuttoned dress slipped, baring her shoulder. She quickly pushed it back in place, but not before Pete laughed vulgarly. "Looks like your dress is falling off...again."

Molly fumed at him, not for embarrassing her, but for discounting the lost graves. Jean rushing to her side. "Leave my Mama alone, you...you...dirty old man."

Seeing the young girl, Pete showed his yellow teeth and turned to his drovers. "This little one too, sight I won't forget. Something about the Creed women, can't keep their clothes on."

The men roared with laughter as their foreman expected them to.

Carlos edged his horse closer. "Senor, it looks like you can't keep your tongue in your mouth. Be careful. You might lose it."

The laughter died down. Pete's eyes narrowed. "What'd you say greaser?"

He spat again, motioning at the imposing line of wranglers. "Maybe you ain't too good at math...being a Mex."

Using the barrel of his gun, Carlos pushed his Sombrero back and offered a congenial smile. "Senor, it's not how many you shoot, it's who you shoot first."

Pete fidgeted in his saddle and cast a wary glance at his men. He doubted any of them could match the Mexican, still he had his orders.

The metallic sound of a rifle turned his head. Tom levered a round into the Winchester. "We just buried my Pa. Ya' got no right." Indignation strained the voice of the grieving farmer. Though a peaceful man, he was ready to fight. "This cemetery is God's land, ain't something the judge can buy."

It was three guns against eight, but Pete wasn't sure it was enough. Something told him the Mexican wouldn't back down, and his pistol was already drawn.

The surly foreman was the sort who would gladly take his boss's money, and willingly dispense his cruelty, but he would not die for him. That was what separated him from the Mexican; honor.

Biding his time, Pete carefully chose his words. "The judge ain't without heart. We will give you a few minutes to collect what you want before we run you out of here, but there's one more thing..." His face souring, he jabbed his finger at Jimmy. "We are taking the boy for horse stealing."

All eyes turned to Jimmy. Stunned, he swallowed hard. Jimmy knew the judge's men had every right to take him, but at the moment he was more frightened of falling back into Pete's hands. He'd be beaten for sure.

Carlos looked at the boy then turned with an icy stare. "You have no proof."

It galled Pete having to banter words with a Mexican. He snarled angrily. "We got proof enough to haul him into court...the judge's court."

Pete laughed and the drovers joined him.

Carlos remained unswayed. "I think Senor two graves lost are worth more than two ponies found. No?"

He cocked his gun. "If you all empty your pockets; we can come up with the difference."

"What!" Outraged by the Mexican's audacity, the foreman bellowed in disbelief. "What?"

"Si, just six feet of dirt, and a few wooden boards, but to these families they are beyond value. My offer is a generous one, no? Empty your pockets."

Pete cursed and threw his hat to the ground. "I ain't going to pay you a god damn penny you thievin' greaser."

Molly caught the glint in Carlos's eyes. He was done talking. "No!" She screamed at the top of her lungs, stopping the confrontation cold. Killing was senseless. Her voice trailed away burdened by the futility. "No...the graves are gone. All the money in the world won't bring them back."

She looked at the broken ground searching in desperation, a cry escaped her throat. "Senseless."

The men scowled uneasily at the barefoot woman standing bravely before then. There was something about her that demanded respect. She boldly stepped towards them. "Is it not enough that good men have died?"

Some of the wranglers fidgeted in their saddles. Molly tugged at her dress barely hanging on. "Are you proud of yourselves for shaming women?"

A few of the men lowered their gaze. Pointing at Jimmy, Molly scolded. "Must you now prove your strength by bullying a child?" Her eyes burning in the dust-filled air, she searched their faces. "I know some of you. We went to school together. Look at yourselves. Hank Thompson, you use to pull my pigtails, and sit beside me in church, and now you would trample me and my children into the ground."

The cowboy's eyes darted between childhood friend and his foreman, then closed under the weight of his guilt.

All the wranglers sat their horses a little less tall, all save the unrepentant foreman. His heart was a cold as a gravestone.

Fighting back tears, Molly spread her arms wide no longer caring about her dress. "Look at me for God sake! Have you lost all decency? This is hallowed ground. We don't want your money. Just leave us alone. Go."

A long silence followed where the dishonored men would have willingly turned their horse away if only someone would lead them, but none had the courage to be the first.

Pete scowled at the drovers fearing one might. He alone had no such conscience and cruelly barked. "You heard her Mexican. Ya' ain't gettin' a copper penny, and I ain't moved by her tears, n' I still want that boy. Turn 'em over and we'll leave you to your graves. That's our only concession."

The foreman's eyes narrowed, he meant to hold his ground.

Unimpressed, Carlos's voice rolled in husky proclaim. "Then you have chosen a good place to die. The boy, he stays."

Stunned by what was happening, Jean ran to Jimmy's pony clutching his leg. "Come on Jimmy, take me home. Take me home now. They got no right."

From behind her rose a familiar laughter. "That's right Jimmy, take her home like a good little boy. We know the women wear the pants in the Creed family."

It was Bobby Maxwell. Jean whirled around. "You shut your face Bobby."

Sneering, he looked down at the feisty girl. "What's a matter? Wasn't my kiss yesterday sweet enough for you?"

Balling her fist, Jean stomped. "You never kissed me!"

She looked back to Jimmy. "That's a lie."

Eager to prove his manhood to the wranglers, Bobby boasted. "Sure I did. Don't you remember? When I lifted you from the wagon."

He defended his accusation. "She smells like flowers. Doesn't she Jimmy? Bathes in sweet lilac water. Ask Pete. You can smell it in her hair and on her lily white neck."

Jean's face reddened at being talked about so brazenly in front of the men.

Not without a measure of guilt, she wavered. Even though Bobby hadn't kissed her, she had flirted, enjoying his attention and yielded to his touch.

Cringing beneath the judgmental stares of the drovers, she looked up fearfully to Jimmy, pleading with her eyes.

For what seemed an eternity, the boy held her gaze asking for the truth. Jean's heart beat unsure of what the truth was. For the first time words failed her, but her injured look was enough; Jimmy came to his decision. Lifting his head, he faced the larger boy. "You're a damn liar Bobby. Jean would never kiss a coward, least ways one as ugly as you."

The face of the youthful braggart filled with rage. Turning bright red, he jumped to the ground and charged forward. "Get down off that horse. No one calls me a liar or a coward."

Showing his mettle, Jimmy grinned. "I also said you was ugly."

With that Jimmy dove off his horse, tackling his old friend in midair. The boys rolled in the dirt to the cheers and hoots of the cowboys. "Go Bobby. Knock 'em down."

Choking on dust, Bobby came up first and caught Jimmy on the jaw with a hard right hook that spun him full around. He loaded his fist ready with his next punch, but Jimmy found his feet and ducked, delivering a blow to Bobby's stomach as the larger boy's fist caught air.

Jimmy followed up with another to Bobby's nose sending him stumbling backwards. Bobby swung wildly three times stirring the dust.

Someone shouted. "Get 'em Bobby." Another yelled. "Kick his ass." The boy did his best and swung a glancing blow at the top of Jimmy's head.

Coming under Bobby's punches, Jimmy delivered a jarring uppercut to his ribs. Dazed and bewildered by the smaller boy's onslaught, Bobby fell against a steer, then finding his balance swung out catching Jimmy above the eye, but too late to stop another hard right to his nose which made a loud crack!

Blood gushing down his face, Bobby staggered more from shock than the punch looking as if he was going to cry. "You son-of-abitc..." Jimmy caught him again, a painful blow just below the sternum emptying the larger boy's lungs.

His heart no longer in it, Bobby threw several short jabs to keep his assailant away but he left himself wide open.

"Here's your kiss." Jimmy fist shot straight out landing square on Bobby's mouth. The taller boy went down. It was over as quickly as it started. Size and strength was no match against a boy fighting for love. The goading of the men died away. No one wanted to cheer for a loser.

Knowing his ex-friends temper, Jimmy reached down and pulled the pistol from his holster then threw it away. "Did you kiss her Bobby? Tell the truth or I'll stomp my boot through your face."

Bobby covered his nose. "I didn't kiss her."
Jimmy raised his fist menacingly. "Say it louder so everyone can hear."
Air rattling in his chest, Bobby obeyed. "I didn't kiss her."
"You lied?"
Shamed, the boy struggled to his feet mumbling. "So I lied."

A long silence followed as the truth was acknowledged. Bobby glanced nervously at the men, then stared at his feet. Pete cursed. "It don't matter if he kissed the damn Creed brat or not. She's nothin' n' you're still a horse thief. We are taking you to the judge."

Suddenly, one of the drovers pointed down the road. "Look! Somebody's comin'. Ridin' hard."
Annie shaded her eyes and gasped. "It's Cole."

A murmur rose from the men. "Cole Creed." The name played down the line.
Carlos grinned. "He heard my shot. I think maybe he is hungry, but not for cows."

That was enough for a wrangler named Mort Darby. He backed his horse out of line. Pete growled where are you going Darby?"
Turning his mount, the cowboy retorted. "Din't hire on to fight Cole Creed...come on Hank, let's go."
His sidekick was only too eager to join him. As the two men broke rank, a third spoke up. "I'm comin' too."
Pete cursed "Ya' damn Cowards. Pick up you pay."

Their advantage dwindling. The foreman nervously searched the line of men fearing the others might bolt while at the same time wishing he could follow the fleeing cowboys.

Molly's abhorrence of death set her heart pounding. Cole had not witnessed her abuse before, but this time, standing before these men, tear stained, barefoot, her clothes in disarray, she knew he'd slaughter them all.

Acting quickly, she grabbed Pete's reins. "It's bad enough you trampled his brother's grave. Listen to me. If he finds out your name, he'll kill you for what you did to Jean."

Turning Molly pleaded with Carlos. "Please. No more killing." Whirling around, she begged the men. "Please let it end."

Every eye was now upon the rider fearing what was going to happen next. Straining against the collective tension, a cowboy broke the silence. "He's sure comin' fast."

Stepping out in front of the drovers, Molly wrenched her hands. She had to stop him.

Twenty yards away Cole pulled to a halt next to Annie's buggy. It was then Molly noticed a long gun barrel sticking out behind him. "Will!"

Cole lowered Will into the buggy and waited while the boy hunkered down taking aim. Then, cold as ice, Cole looked up in a way that set her heart trembling. He urged the tall roan forward at a slow steady gate, his right hand hanging by his deadly gun.

He was an imposing figure; a man to be reckoned with. It was what Molly had always felt. In his presence hung a shadow of death.

She hurried forward grabbing the bridle of the roan. Cole..."
He kept moving forcing her to dance alongside. "Cole, it's okay." Ignoring her, he took in the wreckage. "It don't look okay."
"Please Cole, no killing. Not in front of Jean."
Cole spoke up, not caring who heard. "Better to kill 'em all now than have them kill us later."
The Cowboys shifted uneasily in their saddles, knowing the gunman before them didn't make idle threats.

Coming to a stop, Cole's icy stare searched the faces of the nervous men. Some cowered. "Whose cattle are these?"
Molly answered for them. "They were taking them to the river when they spooked. Wasn't nobody's fault."
The strain in her voice made him doubtful. "What about that boy holding his nose? Nobody's fault?...and that dead steer?"

Carlos grinned proudly. "I shot him."

The Mexican could see his answer did not satisfy his boss. "Si, for looking cross-eyed at me."

He pointed his pistol. "Like that one."

Without warning Carlos fired again dropping another steer. The roar of the gun nearly panicked the herd. They bellowed and stomped nervously in the confined space. Others bolted kicking up their heels throwing dust into the air. For a brief moment, it was pandemonium before the shouts of frantic drovers could steady the herd.

While seemingly an insane act, Carlos played his part shrewdly. His actions served a twofold purpose, the latter being merely to unnerve the men.

Jumping out of the way Molly screamed. "What the hell are you doing?"

Cole cut her off. "Molly don't you cuss."

Incredulous, she swung her fist in the air. "Cuss? He nearly starts a stampede and you tell me not to cuss. I'll cuss if I want too." She turned back to Carlos. "Are you crazy? You could get us all trampled."

She whirled around venting her frustration. "Men!"

Cole eyed the Mexican hiding his amusement, then turned and faced the drovers. "Who's in charge here?"

Everyone instinctively looked to the very queasy foreman crouching in his saddle. Cole stared long and hard making the old man's skin crawl. "What's your name?"

Pete swallowed and stammered. "It..it's...it's Bob, Bob Wilson."

Cole noticed the bandage on his neck. "Sure it ain't Pete?"

Turning peaked, the foreman shifted his eyes uneasily to the boy in the buggy who had his sights on him, then back to Cole. "Na...no sir. Bob Wilson."

Scowling, Cole nodded to the dead steer. "That's the judge's Brand."

He looked down at Jimmy standing by his horse. "Jimmy, you worked for the judge. Do you know this man?"

The boy hid a grin, and took his time answering, letting his tormentor chew bitterly on every second. Pete stared at the boy he had beaten many times, only now it was he who was pleading for mercy.

After a long wait, Jimmy answered. "Yes sir, I know him, know him well. He's...Bob alright. Pete is a worthless drunkard. Most likely back at the ranch sloshed like a fat pig in fermented slop." He turned to Pete. "Ain't that right Mr. Wilson?"

Pete glared daggers at the boy. Jimmy smiled and asked again. "I said, ain't that right Mr. Wilson?"

Seething in silent rage, Pete muttered. "Yea boy...that's right."

The old man hoped his humiliation was over, but Jimmy wouldn't let it go. "Tell me Mr. Wilson, do you know of any reason why I should return with you?"

Pete gritted his teeth. "No."

Picking up Pete's hat from where he'd thrown it, Jimmy offered it to him. "When you see Pete you tell him for me that he better stay away from Miss Jean. Will you do that Mr. Wilson? Cuz' I'll kill 'em if he ever touches her again. Do you understand Mr. Wilson?"

His face bitter with contempt, Pete growled. "Sure kid."

Cole had heard enough. "Well what you want to do Mr. Wilson? You want to fight it out, die here in a cemetery, fitting as it may be, or do you want to take your cattle and go?"

Pete dug at his collar. "Don't want to fight you Mr. Creed. Just as soon go if you got no objections."

"I have plenty, but the lady thinks you are worth saving, so you owe your lives to her."

Molly took a deep breath, then to her dismay, Carlos pushed his pony forward. "Senor Bob generously offered to pay for the damages."

Taking off his sombrero, he held it out to the foreman. The older man's face twisted with hate. Reaching into his pocket he took out a wad of bills and threw them into the hat cursing. "Take the money. Nearly a month's pay."

"Gracious amigo." Carlos nodded and proceeded down the line of men. "It is a big sombrero. let's fill it for the pretty lady. She will say a prayer for your souls."

Cole turned back to the foreman. "Mr. Wilson. There's six feet of ground here that is Creed land. You tell the judge anytime he wants, he can have six feet of his own. Happy to oblige."

The gunman's eyes narrowed. "...and if I ever see you or the Judge's cattle up here again, he'll be missing a herd and puttin' out a help wanted sign. Is that clear? Mr. Wilson."

Eager to be gone, Pete nodded. "Yes sir. I'll tell him."

Backing his horse away, Pete snapped at Bobby Maxwell. "Whatcha' standin' there bleedin' on hallowed ground for? Get ta' your saddle. Let's move this herd."

Pete looked down at Molly. He'd come to drive her out, instead she saved his life. It was a bitter pill to swallow.

As the penniless drovers pushed the herd from the cemetery, Jean looked at Jimmy. He was leaning against his horse regaining his strength. Stooping she picked up his hat and dusted it off, then timidly came up behind him. "Here."
Her voice was meek and trembling with doubt.

Turning, Jimmy took the hat from her hand then climbed into the saddle without a word. Jean's eyes darted nervously fearing he might leave without her. His silence made it seem as if he might.

Jimmy took a deep breath to clear his head then pulled his hat down over his eyes ready to ride. When Jean thought she couldn't stand it any longer, he smiled and reached down a hand. "You coming?"

Molly stood barefoot in the dirt watching Carlos examine the steers he shot. She walked over to him and slapped his arm hard. "What were you thinking? You are supposed to protect us not start a range war."
Cole interrupted. "You and the O'Donalds each get a steer and some cash. It's the only justice you're going to get."

Molly opened her mouth, but Cole cut her off. "Before you start whining; it's not about feeding you, it about making them pay. Every inch they take has gotta' cost 'em a yard."
Putting her hands on her hips, Molly fumed. "Look at me Cole. Do you think a kind word right now would kill you?"

Cole smiled obligingly. "You sure are pretty Molly...with your dress falling off. You want to explain that?"
Molly opened her mouth and closed it. It was no use. She scowled at both men, then went back to searching the ground. Neither of them understood how much making the other side pay had already cost her.

Bad Water
Chapter 21
The Ride Home

Searching the trampled earth, Molly found a third piece of Johnny's marker. With trembling hands, she fitted the broken shards together and reverently brushed the dust away.

Carlos came to her side and rubbed her shoulder. "Do not fret Senora. I can put it back together."

Lifting her face, Molly nodded gratefully then looked around at the ruined ground her heart breaking. The cemetery had been a sanctuary for her. She had come here when she needed to talk with Johnny, to tell him about their children and face her fears. It was all gone. She sobbed.

Carlos understood her grief. "We will put his marker next to Miguel's under the tree in your yard so you can see it from your window. It is his spirit that matters, and it has always been with you. I think maybe he would prefer the farm where he can watch over you."

Molly's eyes thanked him for his kind words. They helped.

Gently taking the pieces of wood from her, he put them in his saddle bag. "Senora, there is only sadness here. You should ride home with Senor Cole. Tom and Will can help me cut up the beef. We will load it into the buggy and be along later."

Casting a scornful glance at Cole, Molly retreated shaking her head. "No thank you, I'll walk."

Cole led his horse over. "Not barefooted you won't."

When he reached out for her, Molly pulled away. "Don't...I can climb up on my own."

Grudgingly she put her foot in the stirrup and swung into saddle making no attempt to hide an indignant pout. It was never easy with Cole. He was always too close or too far with tension grating in between. Now when she needed tenderness he was hard as iron.

She scowled down at him then started to slide back to make room in the saddle when he swung up behind her.

Reaching his arms around Molly's waist he took hold of the reins. Molly went rigid resenting being locked in his embrace. "I want you to know I'm doing this under protest."

Cole leaned in pressing his lips close to her ear. "You usually are." His warm breath stirred Molly's hair, robbing her mind of any clever retort. "Don't make fun of me."

He flipped the reins then rested his hand close to her stomach. "I'm not Molly. I take you very seriously."

His words were kind enough and offered some consolation. As her temper started to cool, Cole's arms squeezed her in a definite hug. She tensed and scolded. "Why did you do that?"

"Sorry. I got to thinking about Johnny's grave, you facing those men, and nearly being in a gunfight. You've been through a lot this morning, and...maybe I could have been a little kinder. Sorry."

A perceptible smile tugged at the corner of her mouth before she could stop it. He cared, and as much as Molly hated to admit, it mattered. She felt bad for snapping. "It's okay. Maybe I needed a hug."

Molly allowed his affection and rode quietly remembering old times. He often hugged her back then. How she loved it when he'd greet her at the door. Laughing, he would pick her up and twirl her around. "How's my little Molly," he would say.

There were happy times when she welcomed his strength. Other men had hugged her, but not like Cole. In his arms a girl felt both safe and frightened.

Lost in pleasant thoughts Molly suddenly realized she had been leaning against him and quickly sat up. He chuckled softly. She felt his breath on her bare back and blushed. "Don't you be staring at me."

"Hard not to Molly. Sunlight coloring your ivory skin, why you are the prettiest thing in this whole dang county."

"Your flattery has no effect on me so save your words." She knew it was a lie the moment it left her mouth.

Molly could feel his eyes upon her. It sent a shiver down her spine. Cole had always made her feel beautiful. She let him stare a moment longer. "That's enough."
She leaned back against him. "Don't try your sweet talk on me." Cole joked. "We said we would be honest with each other. Just letting you know you are pretty."

Getting comfortable, he placed his hand flat upon her stomach. After a moment she casually placed her hand over his seeming not to mind.

He was right, she needed comforting. "Cole, what happened back there...like you said, it's a lot for me..."
Her voice trailed away to a soft whisper. "...Thank you."

Molly leaned sideways in his arms and looked up at him. "...and thank you for not killing those men."

Her lips where close to his face and she resisted a sudden impulse to reward him with a kiss. Embarrassed by her own thoughts, she quickly turned her head, but not before Cole laid a kiss of his own alongside her cheek. It stunned her. "Cole Creed, don't you be kissing on me."
He laughed. "You almost kissed me."
"Why I did no such thing!"
Cole shrugged. Your lips puckered...all sweet and cherry."

He was teasing. Molly tried to pull away and only wound up snuggling deeper into his arms. "That doesn't mean I was going to kiss you."

Knowing he didn't believe her, she protested. "You know I hate you."
Cole smiled. "I know."
"Well I do."
He gave a chuckle that trailed away into regret. "Then I apologize for kissing you."

Even more flustered Molly settled back against him. "Well you should be sorry."
Shaking his head, he corrected her. "I didn't say I was sorry, I just apologized for doing it."
"You are hopeless." She giggled despite herself. "...and you got no business kissing me."

Cole let a moment pass as he pondered her rebuke. "There are a lot of reasons for kissing a girl."

Molly waited for him to explain then grew impatient. "Such as?"

Giving it deeper thought, he rested his chin close to her head. "Because he's a guy and she's a girl. That's reason enough. Then again, he might be compelled to kiss her because she's as pretty as a field of wild flowers on a spring morn."

Teasing, he tapped a finger to her nose and lowered his voice. "...or she may have an unsightly wart, but the poor fellow loves her in spite of it."

Molly elbowed him, knowing he meant her temper.

Growing philosophical Cole changed his tone. "Could be that he admires her pluck even though she's a mite confused...or maybe Molly, he's always been crazy in love with her because he's a damn fool."

Cole pulled away, his voice growing bitter. "Pick any reason, they all might be true."

Molly took a deep breath and stared forward not knowing what to say. Love and hate where dangerous companions.

Though she resisted, she found herself falling back into his arms. His hand still rested on her stomach. Entwining her fingers with his she silently pulled his grasp tighter around her and closed her eyes needing desperately to be held.

"Shoe."

Molly opened her eyes. "What?"

"Shoes in the road." He lifted her bare foot with the toe of his boot. "I'm guessing they're yours."

Sliding off the back of the horse, Cole stooped and picked up the closest shoe. For Molly, seeing him hold it so carefully seemed sweet in an odd sort of way. How small it looked in a hand more suited to a heavy gun.

She had seen him as a killer and nothing more. Watching him now Molly remembered there was another side to him that she had forgotten. The memories came with a twinge of guilt.

Returning, Cole tucked her shoe under his arm and capturing her dainty foot in his hand, he carefully brushed away the dirt.

Moved by his gentleness, Molly sat quietly as he slipped the shoe onto her foot and laced it up. Finished, he walked a short distance and picked up the other shoe.

Examining it, Cole raised it to his mouth and blew the dust off the shiny patent leather. He rubbed a spot with his thumb and blew again. Satisfied he turned around only to find Molly was standing by the horse on one foot, hanging onto the saddle for balance. The hardness had left her face. She was staring silently waiting for him to return, her dark eyes awash in emotions he could not fathom.

Going to her, Cole knelt and slipped her foot into the shoe. After he laced it, he held it tenderly struggling with feelings of his own.

He took a breath and slowly stood. The low morning sunlight shining beneath the brim of his hat lit his steel blue eyes as they searched her face trying to understand. For a brief moment she met his gaze then turned her back to him. "Could you fasten my dress?"

With a sigh, he took the two halves of the feminine garment in his hands and lifting them from her shoulders he stared longingly at her delicate back. She was the serene beauty missing from his violent life, but to her he'd always be a killer.

Burying his heart, he pulled her dress together and carefully fastened each button one at a time. "There. All put back together."

Molly turned in the space of his arms, her head down. She paused waiting for something though not sure what. His hands were upon her waist. She felt herself leaning into him and pulled away. "Can we walk for a while?"

Cole summoned a smile and released her. "I guess so."

As they turned and faced down the road, Molly quietly slipped her hand into his. Neither of them in any hurry, they walked without speaking.

In the safety of their silence feelings too long buried stirred inside them. He squeezed her hand. She leaned against him.

Beside the road a field lay barren. With the coming spring it would burst forth in wildflowers, their soft pastel petals a new beginning. Molly thought of Cole's bold words. Did he really love her? Not as kin, but as a man loves a woman. The answer either way could only lead to more hurt. Still...

"You're home."

Molly stirred from her thoughts. Cole repeated himself. "You're home...I'd walk you to the porch, but the woman who lives here hates me."

Molly started to protest, but how could she take back her words after all that she had said? Contrite, she bowed her head.

Accepting her silence as affirming the painful truth, Cole let her warm hand slip through his fingers. Before she could sort out her emotions, he climbed into the saddle and sadly looked down. "I know it doesn't mean much coming from me, but eight years alone is too long for a woman to go without being told how pretty she is. So for what it's worth, you are more beautiful than the first time I held you. There is something about you Molly. Maybe it's because you have the courage to be beautiful in a world where it's dangerous to be so. Anyway, it doesn't matter, but I thought you should know. Goodbye Molly."

Putting his heals to the horse, he was gone.

Molly stepped into the middle of the road her voice trembling. "It matters."

Bad Water
Chapter 22
Darkness & Flames

About midday the menfolk came riding in, the butchering done. Bringing the buggy to the porch, they made several trips through the front door piling the kitchen table high with the different cuts of beef, and then they headed off to the Ruidoso to wash up.

Evening was coming on and the women had worked throughout most of the afternoon salting the meat and packing it in barrels. Helping her mother with the pickle was one of Jean's responsibilities and she dutifully rubbed the bay salt into each cut of meat even though her thoughts were elsewhere.

With a knowing smile, Molly nudged her teasingly. Jean blushed. "Well Mama I think that was the most romantic thing. Jimmy fighting for my honor."

Reaching into a small crock, the young girl added a dash of saltpeter. "He sure whipped that no-account Bobby Maxwell, whipped him good."

Molly chided. "Don't you be thinking two boys rolling in the dirt, pounding each other senseless is romantic. It's shameful."

Turning the meat over, Jean filled her hand with more salt. "But Mama, don't you think Uncle Cole riding in like that at the last moment, making Pete eat crow after him insulting you was kind of romantic?"

Indignant, Molly defended. "Cole is a ruffian who cares nothing about my honor."

Jean peeked out of the corner of her eye giggling. "I saw you walking back holding hands. He cares about something."

"Jean Marie!" Molly snapped. Backing away from the table she angrily wiped her hands on her apron. "Don't be cheeky. I was...he was...well..." She stamped her foot. "He was merely escorting me like a gentleman should."

Risking her mother's ire, Jean quipped. "Some ruffian."

The sun was settling behind the hills as Jean made her way across the yard to the barn. Looking up at the hayloft she spied Will dangling his feet out the high door, his rifle lying in his lap. She felt sadness for her brother. Only eleven and he'd already used his gun to protect their family. His childhood was lost. "Hey Will."

Taking his self-appointed position seriously, he scanned the road before answering. "Hey."

Jean leaned against a cedar post and tucked her head sideways. "See anything?"

"Nope."

For Jean her brother was like most boys, few of words, but looking up at him she remembered what he'd said before he shot Pete as she lay curled in the tub. 'Bad water.' She couldn't blame him for trying to be like his uncle, nor would she tease him about it. With Lincoln County aflame, Will hadn't had much of a childhood, still if it had not been for his courage, things would have turned out a lot worse for her.

"Will, you should come on down and stretch your legs."

The boy made a face. "You want to get Jimmy up here so you can be alone?"

Sticking out her tongue, Jean sneered wishing some boys had even fewer words, at least brothers. She had tried to be nice. "Will! You get down here or I'll tip the ladder and you can stay up there all night."

Marching into the barn she went straight to the bunkhouse as the guys now called it. Before knocking she stopped, adjusted her dress with a necessary wiggle and fluffed her hair. "Jimmy?"

"I'm here." The voice came from behind startling her.

She whirled around. Jimmy was brushing his horse and grinning. She clutched a hand to her throat. "You scared me."

Dropping the brush, Jimmy waited for her to come to him. "I thought you were helping your ma pickle the beef?"
Jean shrugged not so innocently. "Guess she didn't want me underfoot."

The boy's hand was resting on a wooden rail. Jean looked around to make sure they were alone, then slid her fingertips up the post until they touched. "I didn't kiss him."
Jimmy shrugged. "I know. Bobby said so."

Stepping closer, Jean held his eyes. "I want you to hear it from me, and not someone who was under threat of being stomped." She grinned shyly. "...by my man."
A bit embarrassed by her boldness she scolded. "Though two boys rolling in the dirt, pounding each other senseless isn't romantic. I think you are ruffians."

Glancing over his shoulder, Jimmy spied Will leaving the barn shaking his head. Jimmy turned back to Jean. "Ruffian? Maybe you shouldn't be hanging out with the likes of me; orphan and ruffian, you being so much better..."

Jean's haughty expression crumbled in distress. "No Jimmy, I didn't...I mean..." She reached for his hand. "Well maybe I like ruffians."
She softened. "...a lot."

Grinning, Jimmy pulled her toward the loft. "Then maybe we got something to talk about. Must be some reason why you came in here."

A blush telling on her cheeks, Jean gathered her skirt and hurried up the ladder. When Jimmy poked his head through the hole, she was already kneeling in the straw, her eyes large with anticipation. The boy teased. "You ain't going to get all mushy on me 'cus I slugged Bobby are you?"
Jean pulled a face. "No!"
Folding her hands in her lap she toyed with her fingers. "...I'd already forgotten about that...*Jimmy!*"
Realizing she blurted out his name a bit too excited, she calmed herself and started again. "Jimmy...ah..."

The words wouldn't come. Jean lowered her head and went silent, but Jimmy lifted her chin. "What is it Jean? Creed women ain't never had trouble sayin' their thoughts."

They both snickered. Taking a straw in her hand she held it to her lips. "Tomorrow's my birthday."

Jimmy groaned. "Don't give a feller much warning."

Jean slumped into a pout. "With all that's going on, not sure it matters. Least ways I don't expect no one to make much of a fuss over it. Guess I'd feel guilty if they did."

Reaching for Jimmy's hand she held it close to her breast. "So...well...I..."

Frustrated with herself Jean blurted. "So that's why I want to spend tonight with you." She started talking fast. "Kind of a birthday party...nothing else. We don't need no presents or cake. I just...well I'm fourteen and in most places that's marryin' age."

She blushed. "Not that I want to get married, but if I can't have a real birthday, then I should at least be able to...to...well be with the boy I..."

Suddenly she felt miserable, she had revealed too much. Tears came to her eyes, and she felt foolish. "Guess I should get back."

"Jean!"

She looked up to see Jimmy grinning. Folding her hand in his, he pressed her fingertips to his face. "See this cut I got protecting your honor...don't you think it deserves a kiss?"

Jean burst into a huge smile. Throwing herself into his arms, she planted a kiss, full on his lips, knocking him over backwards into the hay.

Jimmy caught his breath. "That ain't where I was punched."

Pulling her hair out of his face, Jean gave him a quick peck. "My aim was off. If you want accuracy, kiss my brother."

Done talking she landed another kiss, long and hard, pushing his head into the straw. With their lips crushed together, Jimmy mumbled, "Happy Birthday."

Tossing in her sleep haunted by the dream from the night before, Molly thrashed beneath the sheets, kicking the blankets to the floor. Chased by smoke and flame she rolled from side to side seeing Cole's gun flash again and again. "No." She murmured, but the deadly proclaim of his gun would not be silenced. It rolled like thunder.

With a sudden jolt Molly sat bolt upright and froze. Something woke her.

Every sense keenly alert, she listened intently It came again; the distant pop of gunfire. "No!"
Molly threw back the sheet and jumped from her bed. "Jean!"

Running to the door in her nightgown, Molly called to her daughter's room. "Jean get up."

Out in the yard, Carlos was saddling his horse. Barefoot she ran to him. "Carlos, what is it?"

The Mexican shoved his Winchester into its scabbard. "Plenty shots coming from Tierra Amarillo."
Molly threw her hand to her mouth and backed away. The unrelenting barrage echoed as if from a distant battlefield. "Oh Cole."

Instinctively, Molly searched for her children. Will was standing silently in the shadows on the porch holding his rifle at ready. Jean came running out of the barn carrying her shoes, with Jimmy close behind, pulling on his shirt.

"Look!" Carlos pointed. A red glow lit the frosty haze that lay across the top of the low hill. He cursed. "They are burning him out."

Rushing to Carlo's side, Molly clutched his arm. "Go to him. Go!"
Carlos shook his head. "I can't Senora. I must stay and protect you."

Five shots rang in rapid succession sounding as one. Carlos turned his eyes back to the terrifying glow. "It is Cole. I've heard that before. He is still alive."

Molly pleaded. "Please Carlos. They will not come here until they kill Cole."
Unsure, Carlos hesitated. "I don't know Senora."
"Please Carlos. I'll take the children into the hills. The boys are armed. Please go."

"Si." The Mexican nodded and climbed into his saddle. "Get dressed plenty quick Senora. Pack food and water. Take Jimmy's horse and the mare. Wait by the spring until I come for you. Hurry!"

Whipping his horse, Carlos tore out of the yard and was soon swallowed by the night.

Molly turned to the children. "Jean, get your shoes on. Will, Jimmy, saddle the horses and grab extra ammunition, all you've got. Be ready to ride."

Rushing back into the house, Molly slipped off her nightgown and struggled into a dress. Her finger fumbled frantically trying to reach the buttons behind her.

"Here Mama."

Shaking visibly, Molly stopped and allowed Jean to fasten her dress.

The muted gunfire continued. Molly threw her hands to her ears. "Will it ever cease?"

"Done." Jean hurriedly stepped back. "Maybe it shouldn't...means Uncle Cole is still alive."

Molly grabbed two shawls and put one over Jean's shoulders. Fill the canteen from the horse trough, it will be faster. I'll get a sack of food."

By the time the women had finished, the boys were already waiting in the yard. They had the good sense to fold some blankets behind the saddles.

Jimmy lifted Jean onto the blanket then putting his boot in the stirrup swung up before her. Molly climbed from the porch onto the mare with Will behind.

It was time to go, every second was precious yet for several minutes they lingered in the dark listening intently to the distant battle in disbelief. Jimmy spoke out loud. "Must be some fight. Sounds like thirty guns or more."

A rifle cracked three times further north. Jimmy stood in his stirrups. "That's Carlos. I know the way he levers his rifle."

Unable to bare it any longer, Molly turned the mare and headed for the back pasture. "let's go."

Twenty minutes had passsed, and no one had spoken. The night they feared for so long had finally come.

Molly and Jimmy pushed the horses up the last rise. They were now in a high fork between two steep hills overlooking the valley. Their tracks would be lost in the cow pasture far below where Molly had the presence of mind to follow the creek for some distance before striking out for the spring. They were safe for now. Dismounting, they silently walked one by one to the edge.

From their height they could see that Tierra Amarillo, Cole's beautiful ranch, was burning. As they watched in disbelief, a huge plume of flames leaped into the black sky as the roof of his house caved in.

The gunfire stopped. Molly held her breath fearing the worst, then the shooting erupted again. They hadn't got him yet. Whoever they were, they had not caught Cole off guard, and he was proving tough to kill.

Mesmerized by the terrible glow it was impossible for Molly and the children to pull their eyes away. They were standing outside the gates of hell looking in knowing one man alone held back the flames that sought to engulf them all.

With every hated rifle crack they feared it would be the last, signaling the battle was over, their hero fallen. It was too much. Jean leaned her head on Jimmy's chest and cried. Molly rested her hand on Will's shoulder. "Come on children, let's roll out the blankets."

Pulling the bedrolls from the horses they went about their tasks without speaking. Jimmy helped Jean down onto a blanket and dropped beside her. Molly did the same for Will. Their hearts heavy, they tried to comprehend the battle far below, but it was futile. Unbearable minutes passed as the shots cracked and rumbled. Molly whispered her thoughts. "Some kind of man...you give it to them Col..."

Realizing she'd spoken out-loud, Molly eyes flashed at the children. "Well he is. Now best get some sleep..."
Just then the shots stopped abruptly. Everyone held their breath waiting while the deadly silence ticked away.

Without a word everyone got to their feet and walked once more to the edge. The battle of Tierra Amarillo was over. Thick angry smoke tinted red curled and belched skyward.

No one dared say the words that stabbed deep at their hearts; somewhere in the ruins below Cole Creed lay dead buried beneath the burning timbers. Jimmy pulled Jean to him comforting her sobs.

"Let's get some sleep children." Molly ushered them back to the trees. They looked so tired and numb, not knowing what to think. Through it all Will had remained silent uttering not a sound. Molly ached for him. It was too much for a young boy.

She brushed his hair, then looked to Jean. "We got to finish salting the beef in the morning. Plenty to do. Jimmy and Will, you remember to milk the cow and let the chickens out. With all the meat, don't think you will need to go hunting. Save your ammunition..."

A tear rolled down Molly's cheek. She wiped it away unashamed. "Good or evil, he came back for us, deserves a few tears."

Turning away from the children she looked towards the valley wondering what was to become of them. She told herself now was not the time for crying.

Molly guessed it was already several hours passed midnight and she had no idea when or if Carlos would return. She didn't see how.

As the children lay curled in their bedrolls, she quietly rose to her feet and stood watch. Sleep was not for her. Alone she sobbed and walked further into the dark. "...oh Cole."

He had told her she was beautiful. She had told him she hated him. For the first time she truly regretted her cruelty, but it was too late. Growing angry at herself, Molly shook it off. Feeling sorry would do the children no good. Still, she couldn't erase his caring face from her mind.

Shivering from the cold she was about to return to her blanket when her eye caught an uneven row of faint torches coming down the road from Tierra Amarillo. Her throat tightened. She knew now beyond any doubt that Cole had lost.

Molly glanced over her shoulder at the children but did not wake them. The enemy was burning them out. Their farm was next and it would be a sight too horrible for them to see.

When the riders reached her gate they turned in as she knew they would. Their home and all that she owned, would be reduced to ashes. Her heart aching, Molly held her hand to her mouth watching the riders pull to a halt.

Agonizing over what was sure to come she waited for the vultures to throw their torches through her windows. The tiny dots of lights circled her house then some broke off and entered barn. They would burn it too..., but to Molly's surprise, the row of torches turned around and left, heading back the way they came. For whatever reason, her home had been spared.

The marauders had not found her nor did they pursue them into the hills. She exhaled. For this night it was over, but no matter what she could not stay. They would surely come again.

Turning, Molly walked back into the trees and silently wept. It would be a long night and she would stand her guard though the lonely hours.

Molly leaned her head against the tree weary beyond all measure. All the years wasted, her hatred burning inside her like poison. How many times had she wished him dead? The irony was she could not justify it with how much she missed him.

"Mama, look!" Jean jumped to her feet pointing. "It's the O'Donalds. They're burning."

Everyone hurried from their blankets as shots erupted and quickly died away. Jean burst into tears. "Annie and the children."

Dashing into the trees, Molly returned with Brownie. "Jimmy, I'm taking your horse."

Jean ran to her mother pleading. "Mama you can't go!"

Suddenly calm, Molly placed a kiss on her daughter's cheek. "Annie needs me."

"But Mama."

Molly shushed her. "Don't worry baby. They won't hurt me."

She hugged her daughter. "There is a reason why they skipped our farm. "They have different plans for me...and for you."

Jean looked confused. "For me?"

As soon as the words left her mouth, she understood. "Oh Mama."

Molly quickly climbed into the saddle and looked down at her children. "If I don't return by morning, the three of you take the mare and ride out of here. Stay to the back roads. Go to Colorado like you planned."

She smiled softly. "It was a good plan Jean; sorry I couldn't see."

Molly looked to the taller boy. "Jimmy when you leave you take my baby with you. Build a life for yourselves and forget this place."

Lastly Molly turned to her own son. She had no words that would help him. Blowing him a kiss, she whipped the reins and rode away.

Leaning against the horse's neck, Molly raced at a dangerous speed across the hilltop and down into the icy meadows. Hell had opened up around her. From the ashes of Crow Crossing, to the flames of Tierra Amarillo, and now poor Annie's door, fire sought to consume them.

In anger and fear the word had been given; burn them out, and so this night had come. Their once pristine valley lay covered in a thick choking haze.

Molly had held to the last when everyone had told her to run, and now she was running, but into the flames.

There was less than half a mile to go. If the raiders were still at the O'Donald farm, her arrival would certainly draw their attention. Molly knew she was the greater prize. She would let them see her then try to outrun them. If captured she would barter her own life for that of her friend. This ride was for Annie.

Molly's head was clear. The flames of Tierra Amarillo had burned away her hate. Here at the end she'd fight for her family and friends. For some her change of heart had come too late. Now she would try to make amends.

As Molly pushed her pony across open meadow, there was no doubt in her mind that Tom was dead. He was a good man, but not a killer. He would have perished in the first volley. Her only hope was that the riders whoever they were, be they the John Kinney Gang, Jess Evans, the Seven River's Warriors, or worse the Selman's Scouts, would have some decency and not harm women and children.

Married young, Annie was little more than a child herself. Petite of frame with large innocent eyes she looked far younger than her years and was often mistaken as Jean's friend, and not Molly's. Maybe the men would see her that way and take pity.

Having lost her own husband to violence Molly knew well how distraught Annie would be. It grieved her. She whipped the pony faster, driving it down into the last ravine. Coming up out of the draw, she pulled to a sudden halt. Just ahead was the main road which she had to cross. The flames from the O'Donald home spread an orange light across the field to where she now stood. She gave a start. A score of riders back lit against the nightmarish scene were coming fast straight at her.

Praying she hadn't been seen, Molly acted quickly and pulled the horse back down the slope dropping below the ridge. Concealed by night and shadows, she laid on Brownie's back keeping her head low. All she could do was wait.

The pounding hooves growing louder and louder. It sounded like they were coming right over the top of her. As they reach the road, the very ground shook until she thought it would burst asunder.

Molly felt a terrifying urge to bolt, but just when she started to tug on the reins the ground stopped shaking. The horsemen were riding away from the evil deed they'd done. With each passing moment the hoof beats faded. Luck was with her. She blew the air from her lungs calming herself.

For several minutes Molly waited making sure all was clear. Then cautiously she pushed Brownie out of the gully. Moving to the edge of the road, she searched both ways. To the east she could see the last of the riders disappearing down the banks of the river. Looking to the west there was nothing.

It was now or never. Molly whipped the reins. "Go Brownie!" The young horse shot across the road, its legs stretching in great strides.

Staying to a line of trees Molly made for the dying flames. Tom and Annie's home was not far from the main road. At a dead run a swift horse could cover the distance in a minute.

Drawing closer, Molly gazed in horror at the smoldering shell of the home she'd been to so many times. Flames leaped out of the empty sockets where two windows and an inviting door use to stand. The charred porch swing hung awkwardly by one slender rope burning like a candle's wick.

Molly pulled to a stop. She was still a long way off, but in the middle of the yard laid Tom's body lit by the flames. He was a big man. Molly had expected it, but seeing him there was unbearable. "Oh Tom."
Her words broke into sobs. "Poor Annie."

Slowly Molly pushed the pony forward knowing she had to help Annie yet desperately wishing it were all a terrible dream.

She had only gone a few paces, when the horse shied. Molly looked down beside the road. "Dear God no!"
There in the dry grass lying face down was little Chad, a bullet hole between his shoulder blades. They had shot the boy as he ran.

Molly leaped from the saddle and knelt beside him. Her hands trembling, she touched his small arm. He was dead. "Oh, Dear God."

Near Panic, Molly looked around listening for Annie's cries for her family?" Had the murderers taken her?

Lifting from the grass, Molly hurried forward on foot, her eyes searching every shadow. Seeing nothing she moved faster, and faster, she was running now into the yard her mouth agape. At the far edge of the porch, Molly stopped abruptly as if struck by a bullet herself. "No...No!" Dropping to her knees, she cried out loud. "No!" There, lying at her feet was the nearly naked body of little Annie. Her beautiful eyes opened as if staring to heaven. "No Annie. Not you!"

Molly beat the earth. "No! No! Dear God no! Monsters!"

Annie's twisted body lay like a shattered doll where she'd been thrown to the ground, the flickering light aglow on her porcelain skin.

Wounded beyond all measure, Molly reached for Annie's hand, wishing, hoping in vain, but no, her dearest friend in all the world was dead. "Oh Annie."

Ever so carefully, Molly brushed the dust from Annie's cheek, and tenderly wiped blood from a serpentine cut on her lip. Who could be so cruel?

With trembling fingers Molly closed Annie's eyes then lifted her long strawberry hair from the dirt, and spread it across her breasts covering her the best she could. Tom loved her hair.

Leaning forward, Molly placed a gentle kiss on Annie's forehead and another to the jagged cut on her lip wanting to kiss it away. Maybe then she could pretend her friend was only sleeping, but no the serpentine scar remained, Annie was dead. "Oh, dear Annie. I'm so sorry."

Bowing her head, she wept over her friend. "My dear precious heart."

Drenched by her own tears, she wailed. "Annie, Annie...Annie." Molly looked to the sky. "It's not fair God. A soul so lovely should not have been taken before her time, not this way. Oh Annie."

Molly collapsed sobbing, sobbing... She suddenly froze. A faint sound pulled her from her torment.

Turning her head, she listened intently, her eyes searching the night. A short distance away beneath the barren willow trees hanging over the pond Molly could barely make out the fringed roof of

Annie's buggy. The sound came again...the shaking of a rattle. "Polly!"

Jumping to her feet, Molly tore across the yard and through the reeds, then down a shallow slope, her heart pounding until she feared it would burst.

As she got closer, she spied blankets and clothing piled on the ground. Tom and Annie were planning to escape. They had heard the gunshots at Tierra Amarillo, only they had waited too long.

Molly edged closer, fearing to hope. She rested her hand on the buggy and peered inside. Tucked beneath the seat was the wicker basket that Annie used to carry food for those in need. Coming from it was the cooing of a child.

Ever so carefully Molly slid the basket from beneath the seat. Snuggled in a blanket was little Polly smiling and shaking a toy doll that rattled.

With quivering hands, Molly lifted the child to her breast. "There, there sweetheart."

The child was not crying. She did not know the meaning of death. There was no way she could understand her family was gone.

Bad Water
Chapter 23
The Taking

The valley was at peace now. Silent stars paid homage in the inky black sky. Holding the sleeping baby to her Molly pushed the pony onward. Much of the night was spent burying her friends. She dug a shallow grave in Annie's garden where the ground was tilled. Molly laid Annie and Chad in the grave herself, then used Brownie to drag Tom. It was a grizzly task.

She had cried all her tears, and now what time was left was for the living.

Coming out of the valley she urged her tired mount up the last ridge. They would wait for Carlos until dawn. If he didn't come, she'd load their belongings into the wagon and head for Colorado.

At length, woman and horse, both weary came to a stop beneath the oak trees. They had reached the spring. Dropping from the saddle, Molly looked for her children. Will was watching from the beneath the shaggy branches of a distant tree. There was enough light to see his eyes turn to the baby. He understood.

Molly waited for him to rush to her like a little boy would; instead he slowly walked to the edge of the knoll staring vigilantly into the distance.

She grieved. How long had it been since she heard him speak? When was the last time he slept? Caught up in a nightmare, he was drifting away and she didn't know how to reach him. If she tried to talk it only drove him further away. Her heart ached.

Slumping to her bedroll, she looked to her daughter. Jean lay fast asleep beneath a blanket curled on Jimmy's shoulder. How she envied her. Worn to the bone, Molly laid down beside them with the baby asleep in her arms and closed her eyes.

When Molly awoke, the pale morning light was playing out across the frosty hilltops. A light snow had fallen. She frowned. Carlos had not returned though she had not really expected him to. No one could survive the horror of the night.

Not eager to face the truth head on, Molly decided they would wait awhile longer. She pulled her blanket close and looked out across the empty valley. There was no one left but her. In a little while she'd be gone too. She thought of all the people now departed who told her to leave. It broke her heart. How could she have been so blind and so stubborn?

Rolling his head, Jimmy yawned and blinked open his eyes greeting the morning with the reluctance of youth. He took in his surroundings and combed his fingers through his thick black hair. Molly stretched out a loving hand to him and patted down a tuft that was sticking up. Even he had not escaped her anger. Appreciative, the boy looked up and noticed the baby in Molly's arms. The sadness on her face told the rest.

Jean stirred, but did not open her eyes. Hidden in the safety of sleep, she snuggled deeper against Jimmy and kissed his neck muttering. "Love you."

The boy glanced nervously at Molly knowing she must wonder how intimate they'd become. Molly returned his fearful gaze with a tender smile wanting him to know the only thing that mattered now was that they were alive. She gently handed him Polly. It was her way of saying, I trust you.

Jimmy carefully laid the baby between him and Jean then rubbed his finger across her tiny cheek. Molly knew someday he would make a good father.

Getting to her feet, she took her blanket and walked over to son. He had stayed steadfastly in his appointed spot.

Not wanting to intrude, Molly silently stared off into the distance by his side bravely facing the new day. For now, they would not talk about what had happened. She knew it was not his way, but youth could no longer hide him.

Kneeling, Molly shared her blanket and kissed his cheek. She softly whispered. "This will all pass, and a day will come when you can be boy again."

The boy slowly turned his head and searched her eyes doubting her promise. His face hardened, and he looked back out over the valley resuming his quiet vigil, his rifle clenched tightly in his young hands.

Molly kissed him again then stood for a moment beside him before walking back to the trees. Jean was awake and cuddling the baby to her, tears streaming down her cheeks. She looked up as her mother approached, needing to see the truth in her eyes.

Bending, Molly smoothed the baby hair. "She's got a new family now."

Jean sniffed and tried to speak softly to the orphaned child, but her voice broke with pain. "It will be okay. You are mine forever and always."

Holding the baby in her arms Jean looked more like a young mother than a big sister. It would take time to sort things out.

A breakfast of biscuits and cheese washed down with cool spring water seemed to lift their spirits as much as could be expected. The sun cresting over the eastern hills lit the golden patches of dry grass nestled between the dark pines. Winter was on the high mountain and the day was coming fast.

Molly knew they could wait no longer. The men were gone; Miguel, Tom, Carlos, her Johnny, and Cole, all gone. On this cold day she stood alone for the very first time. The survival of her children depended on her.

Summoning an inner strength, Molly got to her feet and squared her shoulders. "Listen to me."

She waited as one by one as they shook off their shrouds of gloom and turned their heads. "We have to leave the valley. It is not safe anymore."

Molly folded her arms trying to hide the shaking in her hands. "I need you to be brave, braver than you have ever been."

Standing before them, Molly reached out a finger and tenderly brushed a lock of hair from Jean's forehead. "There will be a time for grieving, but to survive we must fight with all our strength. That must be our only thought. We are going to Colorado."

The children's eyes darted to each other. Molly's words gave them hope. Jean reached for her mother's hand and kissed it, then held on.

Molly looked at Jimmy. The boy nodded. "Ain't nothin' here. Family is with you and Jean, Mrs. Creed."

Stepping to the center of the circle, Molly continued. "It will take provisions to get to Colorado, so we have no other choice, but to ride down and pack the wagon with food and what belonging we can take. There is great danger, but we have to take the risk. No doubt they are hunting for us now, and if we remain here they will find us."

She could read the question in the children's eyes so she tried to assure them. "I don't know when they are coming back. Still it's early, and hopefully we have time, but no time to waste. Let's go."

Keeping to the shadows of the trees and narrow ravines where they could, the ragtag family pushed their two horses down the mountain. No one spoke. For the first time they were truly alone; no heroes were left to fight the battles. What strength there was, they'd have to find in themselves.

Looking behind her, Molly watched the sunlight dance on Jimmy's pistol hanging prominently on his hip. In spite of his age, it gave her comfort. It was a symbol of strength that was theirs.

Behind him Jean held the baby in one arm while clinging tightly to Jimmy with the other. From the beginning the two of them had sought comfort in a fledgling romance against her will, and now she realized how fortunate Jean was to have Jimmy. The boy had courage.

Coming out of the pines the trail leveled and for a time they were visible. Molly searched the distant road for riders. The land appeared abandoned, not a breath of wind to bend the dry grass, or a single bird to take wing. It gave her little comfort.

The two horses dropped down into the last draw then climbed the bank and made their way into the lower pasture where they slowed to a walk. Skirting around the barn they approached the house from the back. Jean cried. "Look Mama, the door has been kicked in." The splintered boards laid broken on the floor. Had the marauders tried the latch, they would have found it open. The Creeds like most families in the valley did not hide behind locked doors.

With no other choices, Molly cautiously urged the mare forward. Halting by the porch they could see through the open doorway. The late night's visitors were long gone. Molly breathed a sigh of relief.

"Come on children let's hurry. Jimmy and Will, you hitch the mare to the wagon then pull it up here. Jean, come with me. We will pack some food and gather what belongings we can."

The two women carefully entered the house. With the door gone and no fire in the hearth, it was cold and strange leaving them feeling like intruders in their own home. They didn't belong there anymore. It was just as well, they needed haste. Molly wanted to be far away by nightfall.

She glanced to her daughter who was holding her arm. "Hurry Jean. Grab as much salted beef as you can carry, and the sack of beans. Pile everything on the back porch for the boys."

Molly hurried to her dresser and started gathering warm clothes suited for the trail, and her white dress; she'd take that too. Her arms full she paused; it would be the last time she'd see her dear bedroom. It was where her children were conceived and born. In this tiny room she and John had spent their first and their last night together. He told her to sleep and kissed her goodbye, never to return.

Setting her bundle on the bed, Molly picked up their wedding picture and held it lovingly to her breast. No one would ever know how painful this was for her, or understand why she had stayed when every fiber of her body screamed go. A tear rolled down Molly's cheek. Wiping it she hastily gathered up her belongings and hurried out the door.

The boys had the wagon by the porch and half loaded when she came out carrying her precious bundle with the picture on top.

Along with the food, Jean had packed her grandmother's china and tea set. It was to be hers someday. She blushed feeling foolish about packing something so silly, and glanced at her brother fearing he'd disapprove.

Without uttering a word, Will carefully took the tea set from Jean's hands. Setting the box in the wagon, he placed a board across the gate to keep it safe, then stepping back he found a smile for his sister letting her know he understood. Picking up his rifle, he hurried away.

As an afterthought, Jimmy ran back into the house and returned with all the bedding he could carry. Throwing it into the wagon he took a moment to spread it out. "It will make the ride more comfortable, and there's enough room to lie down if anyone gets tired."

He looked at Jean holding the baby, his thoughts were of them. Setting a pillow in place, the young man scrambled out and mounted Brownie ready to ride.

Molly held little Polly up to Jean then climbed up beside her and took the reins. It was time to go. She looked around. "Will?" Suddenly they were aware the boy was gone. "Will! We have to go." When he did not answer a cold sinking feeling tightened her chest. "Will!"

Frantic, Molly jumped down. Jean, holding the baby quickly followed, both their hearts suddenly racing. Molly's voice cracked in a strained whisper. "Will! You answer me."

Cautiously she edged around the side of the house with Jean pressed to her side.

Peering past the corner, Molly screamed. "Will!"

In front of the house were five horsemen. Three she knew. One was Pete, one was Bobby Maxwell, and the last, the despicable gunman Wade Bannock. Her heart sank. Will stood bravely on the porch his rifle trained on the gunslinger.

Bannock droned with indifference. "Tell the boy to put the gun down or I'll kill him."

"Will!" Struggling to breathe, Molly edged closer to her son. "Will put it down."

With his clear blue eyes holding a steady bead on Bannock's head, the boy didn't budge.

Pete, having already earned respect for the unflinching youth, nervously rubbed his bandaged neck and shook his head. "Don't know Mr. Bannock. That Brat's got the drop on ya' n' his uncle's nerve. I wouldn't twitch if I was you. Keep him calm, I say. We can catch 'em later on the trail."

The gunman looked incredulous. "You seriously mean to say he could shoot before I could drop him?"

Pete continued scratching his bandage. "He kin shoot all right, fast on the trigger he is n' he can take the head off a turkey at a hundred yards. You ain't but five. Don't spook 'em I tell ya'. He's loco."

Less sure, Bannock stared hard at the boy, then his face turned ugly. "Don't matter. He can't get all of us with a single shot rifle. Either way he's dead, an I'll be damned if I will let a snot-nosed kid tree me."

The gunfighter turned back to Molly. "You want your boy riddled with bullets, it's your choice. We're runnin' out of time."

Molly knew men like Bannock didn't back down. Near panic she turned back to her son. "Please Will, it's no use." She took another step. "Listen to me. Put the gun down."
Unflinching Will stood ready to fight. His duty was clear; protect his family.

Impatient, Bannock yelled. "Tell him to toss it, now!"
Molly glanced at the gunfighter her eyes begging for understanding, then back to the boy, her voice shaking. "Will please put it down." She was next to him, kneeling, her hands outstretched. "Give me the gun Will."
Unwilling, the boy held his ground as if made of stone.

Tears rolling down her cheeks, Molly gently touched her fingers to the barrel. "Sweetheart, they will kill you. I lost your father. I couldn't go on living without you...please son, give me the gun or I'll die too."

Will held a moment longer wanting so desperately to protect his mother, but knowing he couldn't. He was just a boy.

His young heart breaking, Will slowly released the trigger, and bowed his head.

Molly slipped the rifle from Will's hand and tossed it to the ground, then took a hollow breath. It was over.

She buried her head on her son's shoulder. "Oh Will."
All was lost, but she'd saved her son. In utter despair she'd found victory.

With the danger past and eager for vengeance, Pete spit. "Shoot the little Creed bastard or let me. He's got one comin'."
Molly jumped to her feet, a mother's rage burning in her eyes. "You harm my child and so help me I'll see you hang, you sorry son-of-a-bitch."

Bannock smirked. "I just come for you and your daughter. The boy ain't none of my concern."

Clutching the baby, Jean hurried to her mother's side. "Mama."
Pete pointed at the girl and cackled. "That's the little dainty I was tellin' you boys about, jus' skin n' whiskey. Saw her I did, every inch of her. I weren't lyin', see, n' I'd a had her if it weren't for her crazy brother."

Molly pushed her daughter behind her and glared at the foreman. "I wish Will had killed you when he had you in his sights. I wish he would have blown your head clean off."

Bannock raised in the saddle chuckling. "Dangerous boy you got there, n' a right pretty daughter, but the trouble she's in ain't Pete's fault. You brought it on her by acting high n' mighty n' pissing off the judge. He's not the forgiving sort, n' a bit twisted too if you hadn't noticed."

The gunfighter reached in his shirt pocket. "Speaking of which..." He unfolded a piece of paper. "Judge has something he wanted read to you."

Holding the paper high, Bannock took an official air:

"Whereas Molly Creed being a homeless female without means of support, it is decreed that she and one Jean Creed being of like disposition shall be lawfully assigned wards of Lincoln County. And whereas she has shown poor judgment and restraint by trespassing in the Judge's office, shouting profanity and showing total disrespect for the law, and whereas she shamelessly disrobed in a front of said judge in a place of business; flaunting herself in order to garner favors from a public official, and whereas she has consorted with notorious criminals, and harbored a horse thief, and whereas she has taken possession of stolen cattle and currency, it is deemed necessary and good by this court, that Molly Creed be institutionalized in Leasburg for not less than three years where her talents can be retrained to better serve the citizens of the county. The same verdict shall be rendered upon Jean Creed for the crime of horse stealing, so ordered on this day April 2, 1878 by the honorable Judge Warren H. Brewster presiding."

Molly stared incredulous. The judge's decree left her sick and speechless.

Bannock folded the paper and stuffed it back into his pocket. "You got to admire his humor."

Looking down at Molly, the gunfighter soured. "The incident yesterday in the cemetery set him off, but mostly he ranted about your disrespectful mouth. So now I got to ride ta' hell and back because of your waggin' female tongue. Not too happy about it."

He nodded behind him. "Brought two extra horses for you, now get on 'em. You can cry all the way to Leasburg if you like, but you are going just the same."

Shaking with anger, Molly took the baby from Jean and handed her to Will. She brushed his hair. "You take care of her son. Know I love you."

The boy quietly took Polly from his mother, but his eyes never left the gunman.

Stepping back to her daughter Molly wrapped her arms around her. "Kill us if you must, but we are not going with you."

Annoyed, Bannock shook his head. "You know I ain't gunna' kill you. Judge intends ta' make a little money off ya' while indulging his sick humor, so you can ride sitting up or tied over the saddle. Makes no difference to me."

Not waiting for her to answer, he nodded to the two men. "Buck, Toby, tie 'em to the horse with their asses in the air."

Turning to face the grinning hooligans, Molly clutched her daughter tightly. "You keep your filthy hands off my baby or I'll kill you so help me."

Her empty threats only made them laugh, but as the toughs stepped onto the porch young Jimmy from the edge of the house summoned his courage and kicked his pony forward. "Don't you touch them."

"Shut-up boy." Bannock snarled. "...n' while you're at it, unbuckle that gun n' throw it on the ground. I'm losing patience mighty fast."

Jimmy held firm. "You ain't taking Jean."

A cry escaped the girl's throat. She threw her hands to her face knowing full well what was about to happen. "Nooo' Jimmy please...I'll go..."

Jimmy glanced nervously from the gunman to her then back again, his face growing hard. "He ain't taking you."

Jean saw the love in Jimmy's eyes and knew there was no stopping him. He would do what a man had too no matter how hopeless.

Jean leaned her head against her mother. "Mama."

Molly knew it too. He'd become a man and die in the same moment. Holding her daughter closer, Molly covered her ears. "Be brave baby."

Bannock knew the look as well. "Don't be a fool kid. I don't like killin' children. Ain't good for my reputation."

His mind and his heart set, the courageous boy let the reins slide from his fingers. "I love you Jean." His words hung in the air like a dying man's confession, then for the love of a girl he went for his gun.

The boy was fast, his hand a blur, but Jimmy barely cleared leather before Bannock answered his challenge sending lead and flame tearing through the air.

Jimmy flew backwards off his horse as if struck by a sledge hammer. Arms flung wide, he hit the ground hard landing face down. Everyone stared in stunned silence. A wisp of dust settled over the boy as the terrible deed registered in their minds.

Slowly Jimmy lifted his mouth from the dirt, but his strength was gone. Stretching out his hand to Jean he collapsed and laid still.

"Jimmy!" Jean screamed and tried to run to him, but Molly held her tight. "No baby. It's no use."

Her heart holding a pain no child should bear, Jean crumbled against her mother's breast, stretching her own hand to the fallen hero.

Molly held her daughter tightly, and stared grief stricken at the courageous boy, wondering if it would it ever end.

Pain turning to anger she lifted her head to the gunfighter, the smoking gun still in his hand. "Women and children! That's what you will be known for; a killer of women and children. You coward..."

Her screams of rage, broke the spell that held them frozen. Buck and Toby rushed forward pulling the distraught girl from her mother's arms.

"No!" Molly kicked and clawed at the man named Buck. His burly arms were around her waist from behind groping her as much as restraining her. Twisting frantically, Molly elbowed him sharply in the eye. Buck yelled. "You bitch."

He slapped her hard across the face then grabbed, ready to throw her over his shoulder. Bannock fired a shot into the air and aimed his pistol at Will. "Touching. Now you two whores get on the ponies or I'll kill the boy."

Molly looked helplessly at her son. It was no use, she slumped in defeat. Her worse fears had come true. She had failed to save her family.

"Get her in the saddle Buck n' keep your damn hands off her. She ain't for you." Bannock waved his gun emphasizing his order.

The fight gone out of her, Molly allowed the man to lead her stumbling to the horses. Buck roughly lifted her up and set her down hard. Toby tossed Jean face down over the saddle, but Molly protested. "Let her ride. She'll give you no further trouble." Bannock shrugged. "Set her upright Toby. We will see if she behaves."

Will stood stoically on the porch holding little Polly in his arms. If looks could kill, every man would have been swallowed by hell's flames.

Unnerved by the boy, Pete turned to the gunfighter. "Well ain'tcha' gunna' kill 'em. Leave no witness."

A screech caught in Molly's throat, but Bannock pointed his gun at Pete. "Ain't nobody going to harm the kid, you old drunk. That boy is insurance that these whores will behave themselves."

He turned to Molly. "Ain't that right. If I let the boy live, you will do as you are told won't you?"

Staring heartsick at her son, Molly nodded her head. "Yes. I'll do as I'm told. Just don't hurt him."

The gunfighter pushed his horse to the porch and glared down. "My name is Wade Bannock. You remember it. Remember it good. Someday they'll write songs about me."

Unimpressed, the boy stared like a wolf cub ready for his first kill. Bannock frowned uneasily. He was used to men cowering in his presence, and here a mere boy faced him with cold disdain. "What's a matter with you kid? You ain't right in the head."

Bannock waited, but Will held his eyes unwavering. Bannock whirled his horse around. "Kid ain't right."

With a final disquieting glance over his shoulder he tore out the gate. The other men kicked their ponies following their young leader.

Standing steadfast with the baby in his arms, Will never took his eyes off of them as they rode away. He whispered cold. "I'll remember."

Bad Water
Chapter 24
Heartbreak

Grief. There was little else. It robbed her of thought and so injured her heart she felt it would surely stop. Molly struggled to stay in the saddle, and at times even that seemed too much.

Her family was torn asunder. Will was all alone with a suckling baby to care for. And Jean, poor Jean crushed beneath unfathomable grief was being carted off to a brothel where she'd spend her life as a whore paying for her mother's sin.

Molly wept for them all. Poor Jimmy, a boy who only wanted a family, senselessly gunned down before her daughter's adoring eyes. He proved his love only now there was no family to love. It was more than Molly could bear.

How many had died since last night, she dared not count. Everyone who loved her had come to a terrible end.

Had she left when she had the chance they would have followed her, but in her self-righteousness she had angered a very powerful and petty man. The judge proclaimed her a whore and thus it was so. She had no more say than a cow at milking time. Her life was over.

Molly closed her eyes. Her mind and body began shutting down. The world around her grew dim, sounds faded with the coming of eternal night. Every fiber of her existence willingly surrendered to a painless black abyss. She wanted to die, let her life end now, escape from the judge's purgatory, and find some small victory in death.

Wavering in the saddle threatening to fall, she stopped breathing, how wonderful it felt. All she had to do was let go.

It was possible to die of a broken heart. She knew that now. When suffering is more than the mind can bare, the body will surrender to end the pain.

The others died fighting for love, she was no different, other than her heart still loved. A tiny flame yet flickered inside her. What was it Miguel had said? 'Love is stronger than evil.' That was the unconquerable truth. Her heart still loved, and love does not die. Love was the essence of who she was. Miguel said that too.

Molly for good or ill was a Creed, and inside her burned a flame that the mightiest storm could not subdue. As long as she drew a breath there would be no surrender. Somehow she'd save her children. As much as she abhorred violence, if her last and only choice was to kill, she would shed her saintly garb, and take up the serpent's skin of her husband's brother. Using feminine guile, she would succeed where he had failed.

Her children needed her now more than ever. Molly's defiant heart pounded sending blood coursing anew through her veins; she opened her eyes and rose in the saddle. The judge was gravely mistaken if it thought it was over. Today Molly Creed would fight, and those who underestimated her because she was a woman would pay the price.

Burning with resolve Molly turned and looked at Jean, her young and tender face now gaunt lost in a hell of her own, but she was alive. Molly vowed then and there that her daughter would be no man's whore.

Their simple life had been stolen from them, but they still had fight in them. Her brave son was free. Will knows how to hunt. He had kept them feed through summer and winter, and he would do the same for Polly. They would not starve. The farm was still there. He had shelter and a milk cow for the baby. Will would figure it out. It was not in him to fail. He too was a Creed.

Somehow she'd find a way to rescue her daughter and escape. Molly needed a plan, and just as quickly it came to her. She was not as strong as the men. Women never were, but still they survived and at times triumphed. Her greatest strength was that she was a woman. Today that sensual virtue would be a cloaked dagger she'd drive deep into the minds of the unsuspecting men. She'd play the coquette, the vixen, whatever it took to drive a wedge between the men. Divide and conquer, she would find their weaknesses and use these against them.

With a light kindling in her eyes, Molly assessed their situation. Her wits grew keen like a cat on the prowl. If an opportunity availed itself, she'd be ready. If none came, she'd make her own.

Molly lifted from crushing despair to a deadly huntress. That was the Creed spirit. There would be hell to pay for any man who got in its way. Just like Cole, she would take them down one by one.

It was going to be a long ride to Leasburg and with winter's gloom, a slow pace fit the mood. The main road west spread out as it slowly wound through the valley. Later on it would grow steep and narrow following the Ruidoso deep into the mountain, but here there was enough space for wagons to pass each other. The party of five men and two females bunched together with Molly and Jean surrounded by their surly captors. It seemed unnecessary since Buck and Bobby held their reins.

Bannock dropped back until he was riding just a little in front of Molly. He'd been brooding since they left the farm. In his mid-twenties, his hand had the speed of youth, yet enough years were behind him to hone his skill to a deadly proficiency few could match. Though younger than the other men in the party, his reputation with a fast gun made him the undisputed leader.

To Molly he was the bull to be nutted. His volatile temper kept the other men in sway, but being young, his confidence was on the surface so to speak. Bannock was a man in stature only. Inside he was still a boy trying to prove himself. If she could bring him down the band of misfits would fall apart.

Bannock glanced back at her. "That son of yours ain't right in the head, too stupid to know when to back down."

Molly almost smiled. The gunfighter's encounter with an eleven-year-old child was still bothering him. It was exactly what Molly was looking for, a chance to sharpen her claws.

Mustering her confidence, Molly tailored her reply with an inflection of indifference. "It's his Creed blood. Like his uncle, he will fight to the bitter end."
She gave a wry smile. "You are lucky I stopped him. Pete was right; he would have killed you like one of them mindless turkeys. Guess you owe me your life."

Bannock shifted uneasy in his saddle. "You are crazy as he is."

Kicking her horse Molly settled by Wade's side and sat erect. "Maybe so, we are both Creeds."

The gunfighter shot back. "You married in. You ain't no Creed."

Cocking an eye Molly shot her advisory a smug grin. "You are wrong...again. The Creeds are a close family. Cole and I are distant cousins. Way it's done out here, few women folk. Me and Cole got the same great granddaddy so maybe you better be watching me too."

Bannock eyed her uneasily. "Like I said, you are all crazy." Molly took it as a compliment, then changed the subject. "So why now?"

"What?" The gunfighter looked surprised.

Needing to understand what was happening, Molly pressed for answers. "Last night's raid. Taking us captive. Why now? Why not a month ago, or a month from now? Something must have scared Murphy and Dolan pretty bad."

Interrupting, Pete cackled from behind. "Sure did. Lincoln is in flames. Sheriff Brady is dead along with his deputy. Billy the Kid got 'em.

Pete, wanting to be more important than he was couldn't contain himself. "...n' the army is involved. Washington's takin' note so we got ta' move fast, leave no witnesses."

Wade growled. "She don't need to know."

Beginning to understand, Molly scoffed. "So that's it. Just wipe everybody out and it will be over."

Pete pushed his horse in closer. "Na' it ain't over. Murphy is dying of cancer n' that crazy Billy the Kid escaped. Says he is gunna' get 'em all, n' he's fast as Wade here..."

Bannock nearly burst. "I said she don't need to know...n' the Kid couldn't lick my boots. Now shut-up!"

Wade kicked his horse forward fuming. "I could take the kid and Cole Creed at the same time."

Deflating Wade's boast, Molly chided. "Like Billy taking Brady and his deputy...only he's done it."

Ignoring her, Bannock rode on in silence for a moment longer then turned again. "That day at the Judge's office...you didn't tell Cole about me abusing you. How come? You ruined my plans."

Molly sneered. "To ruin your plans."

Wade chuckled. "You sure got a mouth, don't you?"

Thinking to himself, he laughed. "Lips so soft n' sweet, n' noisy as a bayin' hound. Some mouth."

She flushed with anger remembering his cruel kiss, she sneered. "A mouth with teeth, best you not forget."

Molly let the bantering end. However, some good had come of it. The gunfighter learned she could hold her own. Bannock wasn't the kind of man who could handle being bested by a woman in a battle of wits. From now on he'd treat her with more respect.

The party slowed as they reached the broken gate of Tierra Amarillo. Bullet holes riddled the wooden arch above the entrance. Apparently the late night raid had ended with the attackers still full of unrequited rage so they took it out on the gate.

Wade Bannock, his face growing sour, slowed to a halt without even realizing it. The cruel humor that was his usual demeanor shifted to one of uneasiness. His eyes darted nervously scanning the hills.

The gunman's behavior puzzled Molly as she watched his every move, then with a sudden realization her heart leaped. Unable to contain herself Molly rose in her stirrups. "You couldn't kill him could you? You couldn't! Cole is still alive."

She shouted with joy. "Cole is still alive. That insufferable son-of-Creed is still alive!"

Bannock flared. "Shut-up!"

His eyes wild, he turned on Molly, but quickly swallowed the bile rising from his gut. An outburst would only prove her right. Countering, he tried to brush it off. "Dumb luck, but I got a dozen men on his trail. It's only a matter of time."

Bannock knew she was not dissuaded, and snarled defensively. "I'll bring ya' his ears when I bed you in Leasburg."

Ignoring his insult, Molly bounced in the saddle laughing for sheer joy. "Cole is alive. Bless his evil heart. Bet the Judge is mad as hell."

Bannock wasn't the kind of man to be laughed at, especially by a woman. He grunted a cursed. "Shut-up! I said I'll get 'em."

Pushing her irate advisory to the brink, Molly jeered. "You crawled in with an army in the dark of night, everything in your favor and you couldn't take down Cole Creed. Odds aren't going to get any better..."

"I said shut-up whore!" Bannock's face turned blood red. "I would have got 'em if it weren't for that back-shooting Mexican, cut down two of my men n' opened up a hole when we were closing in for the kill."

Jerking on his reins, his horse stomping, the gunfighter could hardly control his temper. What should have been an easy victory and his greatest triumph, had slipped through his fingers. He shook with rage. "Filthy greaser."

Molly's eyes flashed again. Bannock had too much contempt for a dead man, she couldn't hide her excitement. "Carlos got away too didn't he? He did, didn't he? You were just shooting holes in the night so they got bored and rode off. Bless them both."

"Not before I put a bullet in the Mexican, if he ain't dead, he's dyin'."

Molly couldn't hold her tongue she was so happy. "He'll die laughin' most likely."

Bannock lost it. Standing in his stirrups he screamed like a mad man. "Shut-up, you filthy damn whore. You filthy..."

Molly had pushed the young killer too far. Coming out of his saddle he raged. "Take off your shoes."

"What?" Molly was shocked.

Reaching her horse, He roughly grabbed Molly's ankle and pulled her shoe off her foot all the while shouting orders "Bobby, get the girl's shoes."

The boy looked confused, but did as he was told. "Ah…yes sir."

Erratic, Bannock shifted to the other side of the horse and snatched Molly's other shoe.

Pulling her foot away, she protested. "Stop it. Why do you want our shoes?"

Stomping like a wild boar, he yelled again at Bobby. "Bring 'em here boy, NOW!"

Bobby hurriedly jerked the last shoe off Jean's foot and running forward handed them over.

Cursing a storm, his fingers jerking erratic, Wade hurriedly tied the laces together then climbing back into his saddle he kicked his horse under the arch. "Damn whore."

The gunman flung the shoes up over a splintered board. They came to rest dangling in the air for everyone to see.

Bannock turned back to Molly. "That's my calling card, me, Wade Bannock calling Cole Creed out. When he sees them, he'll know who's got his women folk. If I can't find him, he will find me."

He shook a fist in her face. "You just don't know when to shut-up do you?"

Molly curled her bare toes against the cold stirrup. "Damn you, I want my shoes."

Bannock laughed demonically. "With your mouth a flappin' at me, you're lucky it ain't your dress up there, but don't you worry." He pointed to a sack hanging from the pack horse Toby was leading. "Judge has got you new shoes and two satin dance hall dresses. When we get to Leasburg he wants me to parade you through town adorned all la-te-da to drum up business. Wants your first day in town to be real profitable."

Tears stung Molly's eyes. "You are a bully and a coward. Give us back our shoes. We can't cross the desert barefoot."

His nerves raw, Bannock was young enough that it riled him being called a coward. "Shut-up damn-it! Or I'll strip ya naked so help me n' dress you n' your brat like the whores you are right here n' now. Men would like that, wouldn't they?"

Molly fell silent knowing Bannock was crazy enough to carry out his threat. She glanced fitfully at the slavering faces of her captors, it made her skin crawl. She bowed her head. Their shoes were lost.

Bannock laughed harder. "Not so funny now is it whore?" He waited a moment demanding an answer. "I asked you if it was funny now ya' stinkin' barefoot whore?"

Molly lowered her head and muttered. "No it isn't funny."

Her humiliation gave the young man satisfaction. It was enough for now. Wanting to be gone from his place of shame, Wade waved his arm for the party to follow, then headed out at a gallop. Pete held by Molly's side long enough to laugh in her face. "Whore," then he whipped his horse and hurried ahead to join the gunfighter.

Molly assessed what she'd done in risking Wade Bannock's fury. It cost her her shoes, but it left Bannock less sure of himself. He'd be chewing on her taunts dulling his edge. Maybe it was worth the price.

Volatile and erratic, Bannock had blundered. His failure to get Cole was a slap to his reputation, and reputation was everything to men like him.

Molly looked down the trail. It was five hard days to Leasburg. As bad as her plight was, she had reason for joy. Cole was alive, somewhere he was out there, and no matter how many men were tracking him, she knew he was coming for her. It gave her hope.

The egotistical gunfighter wasn't her only concern. Since their capture, the judge's lecherous foreman and young Bobby hadn't taken their eyes off Jean. Each had designs on her for different reasons, and now she was within their grasp.

Pete was old, aged by liquor. Time was running out for him. The day he burst in on Jean laying in the tub was likely the first time he'd seen a naked girl in years. She was a vision he'd obsess over until it drove him crazy with desire.

Bobby had the fire of youth and Jean was a beautiful girl, but of greater concern he had been humiliated by Jimmy. Taking Jean would be his only way to reclaim victory over the dead boy. Pete or Bobby, either way, Jean was in danger.

If either of the two miscreants found the courage to make a move, Molly guessed it would be after they made camp for the night. Bannock might stop them out of sheer meanness, but if he weren't so inclined, it could go very bad for Jean.

Molly looked up the trail. Somehow she would have to get back in Bannock's good graces. That meant no matter how distasteful, she had to be nice to him, and that carried a danger of its own.

Her predicament wasn't much different than Jean's. Being a woman held risk, and not unlike Jimmy thirsting for vengeance, Wade Bannock dreamed of adding Cole Creed to the notches on his gun. In his twisted mind, abusing her would be the same as striking out at Cole.

With Bannock hungering for fame and the judge wallowing in vengeance, humiliating her served both ends. Like Jean, she was caught between a rock and a hard place.

Pete and Bobby, or Bannock and Brewster, it didn't matter. They all had their plans, but Molly's mind was set. Her captors would never get them to Leasburg.

A pall of silence hung over the uneasy troupe. It was more than the evil deed that darkened their journey. Among such men there was little talk. They were loners who brooded inwards about the bitter injustices heaped upon them and how one day they'd have their revenge. A quarrelsome lot, their festering hatred would often erupt in angry insults at each other then go silent only to start again later. Angry scowls hung on their sunburned faces like a bad coat of paint. The only time they laughed was at someone's misery.

Molly measured each one of the men. While Bannock, Pete and even young Bobby had their calculated intent, the same couldn't be said of Buck or Toby. The two saddle tramps knew even the most destitute whores would look upon them with disdain. They would never know the love of a woman. Rape was the only answer to their torment. They were a low breed of men who reacted with animal instinct, striking out wherever they could. Their mindset was no better than a pack of dogs. If the lead male attacked, they'd attack, but on their own, were unlikely to do so. Jean was in little danger from them unless Bannock in one of his fits tossed her to them like table scraps.

The day was half gone. She'd have to do something soon. Bobby still led Jean's pony, but Molly had snatched her reins back from the witless Buck when they left Cole's gate. While she was not so foolish as to try and make a run for it, having the reins could work to her advantage.

Molly turned her attention to the old man. Being the judge's foreman, Pete pretended to be equal in stature to the gunfighter. Indeed, he had been riding next to Wade most of the morning. However, Pete was slowly slipping back, either to get away from Bannock's foul temper or to be closer to Jean. Molly kept a wary eye on him. It caused her blood to boil seeing him staring at Jean and licking his lips as if she were a piece of raw meat. It was time to end his fantasy.

Their party continued climbing higher up the mountain. The trail narrowed and rose a good four feet above a stony dry wash it followed. Strewn with rock the old water course divided the land east and west by the nature of its treacherousness. It simply wasn't worth the effort to cross it. This gave Molly an idea.

Pete kept slowly falling back, his obvious attention now completely on Jean. It was unlikely he'd try anything on the trail, but he clearly intended to stake his claim over the young boys, that, and his crude nature, would certainly add to Jean's torment.

Trying not to be noticed, Molly nudged her horse forward coming quietly alongside him. The horses kept their slow plodding pace up the mountain, and step by step Molly edged her pony closer bumping Pete's mount forcing it near the steep bank.

At some length the old man grew distracted from his perversity by Molly's proximity. She bumped him again, causing him to snarl at her, but as he did, Molly stared past him her eyes suddenly wide with disbelief. Pete whirled around fearing Cole Creed had come to the rescue.

With his back to her, Molly raised her bare foot and kicked the old man hard in the rump sending him flying out of the saddle.

Screaming in a high voice, Pete sailed through the air and over the bank. He hit the ground hard knocking the air from his lungs as he bounded to a painful stop amid a cloud of dust.

Startled by the commotion, Bannock whirled around his pistol drawn. Molly shrunk in her saddle appearing sweet and demure while Buck and Toby edged closer chuckling in amusement at their companion's misfortune.

Bannock looked down at Pete. "You been drinking ya' old fool?"

In agony Pete raised his head from the rocks groaning as if from a mortal wound. Air rasped in his throat as he struggled up from the dirt rubbing an injured shoulder.

Molly watched him assessing her handy work. The combined height of his horse and the stony ditch was not enough to kill him, still, at his age it would leaving him nursing nasty cuts and bruises all the way to Leasburg.

Spitting grit from his teeth, Pete cursed and tried to point an accusing finger, but his bloody limb would not bend. "That bitch, that filthy whoring bitch kicked me in the ass."

Wade turned to Molly who smiled back all too innocently. His brow furled. "You promised you'd behave. Batting her eyes, Molly shook her head. "Did no such thing! I promised to do as I was told."

Smiling coyly, she looked down at Pete who was stumbling out of the gulch. "You never told me I couldn't kill Pete."

For the first time Bannock broke into a genuine laugh. The other men joined in. Bleeding and covered in dirt, Pete scrambled up the bank swearing. "Ain't funny you two-bit harlot."

Ducking past his horse he went for Molly. "Wait 'til I get you..."
As he reached for her, Molly kicked hard catching him with the flat of her foot in his face knocking him back and blooding his nose, but he charged in again. "Bitch, God damn bitch..."

Bannock cocked his gun and aimed it at Pete's head. "Get back in your saddle ya' ol' drunk."

The injured man pulled up short. "What?"

"You heard me. Judge want's her pretty."

Outraged, his hands still outstretched, Pete sputtered. "You gunna' let her get away with what she done to me?"

Bannock holstered his gun. "Teach ya' to be more alert, unless you like having your ass kicked by a girl. Either way you keep your paws off her. Now climb on your horse or I'll leave you here."

Pete looked like he was going to burst, but there was nothing he could do. Shaking with hate he bared his yellow teeth at Molly. "It ain't over whore, ain't over by a long sight."

Turning his horse around, Wade reprimanded Molly. "You ride up front with me so I can keep an eye on you."

When Molly obediently came along side, he added. "Looks like there is more to you than I guessed."

He studied her face for a moment with new regard then spurred his horse.

As their party rode on Molly twisted in her saddle and stuck her tongue out at Pete just to piss him off. If the foreman ever had the men's respect, he'd lost it. Ill tempered, he would nurse his wounds both inside and out. One thing Molly knew for sure, Jean was no longer in his thoughts nor was he in any condition to take advantage of her, at least tonight.

Not only was he bruised and battered, true to character or lack of it, he had already guzzled half a bottle of booze then crawled inside to ease his pain and humiliation. He'd be lucky to stay in the saddle at the rate he was drinking.

Unfortunately, that left the field wide open for Bobby. He'd be harder to deal with. The boy was keeping a short leash on Jean's reins, drawing her more to his side than trailing behind him. It was only the young girl's wall of grief that kept him at bay.

"I'd sure like to see Cole's face when he finds your shoes hanging on his gate."

"What?" Molly was distracted from her thoughts. Bannock's comment surprised her. He was still chewing on her insults from the morning. Obsessing seemed to be a trait of his.

She refocused. "I mean...I'd like to see it too...right up to where he puts a bullet between your eyes."

Bannock tensed, but controlled his temper. "Tall boast, but Cole Creed is just a legend who's outlived his time; ain't no match for me."

Molly had heard as much from others. When it came to a fast draw, Bannock was a hair-trigger few could match. Worse, he was erratic and no telling what would set him off. Wade Bannock could be laughing one moment and a murderous rage the next. His volatility made him dangerous, his gun made him deadly. It was why the judge brought him in.

Wade waited for her to argue with his boast just so he could prove her wrong. When she didn't, it aggravated him. "Cole Creed is a farmer who got good with a gun, but I'm a professional. It's how I make my livin'."

Tilting her head Molly quipped. "Must not be too famous. I've never heard of you."

Bristling, Bannock shot back. "What would a whore know about gunfighters?"

He quickly calmed himself, then defended. "Besides, my employers been havin' me to do my work quietly. I don't get the credit I deserve...but after I kill the great Cole Creed, you will know of me, everyone will know of me. Men will be buyin' me drinks, and women will swoon, you'll see."

Molly feigned indifference. "It will take more than a fast gun to kill Cole Creed...guess you've learned that already."

A deep shade of scarlet rose from Wade's collar as his infamous temper boiled. Without warning his hand shot out so fast Molly had no time to react. Grabbing her by the neck, he jerked her to him. "You ain't learned when to shut up."

He shoved her back into her saddle, then stared forward chewing his anger.

Clutching her throat, Molly gasped for air. She'd pushed him too far. It was a foolish mistake. Staying in his good graces was the only way to keep Jean safe from the other men. Shaken, Molly tried to make amends. "Sorry." The single word rasped from her lips, it was all she could manage.

Molly held back until she regained her composure then cautiously nudged her pony to his side. Keeping her head down and her tongue silent she gave the gunfighter time to cool.

They rode another mile while Molly paid penance. At length Bannock got his anger under control. "A woman is like a gun with blanks. You are impressive to look at but when put to it, you ain't nothin' but noise n' smoke."

He jabbed a finger at her nose. "You'd do better to close that smart mouth of yours and try being meek. It will get you farther with me."

Molly nodded her head accepting his scolding. He was right. She was playing a dangerous game, and while she wanted him off balance, it was folly to openly oppose him. A direct attack would only get her hurt, she'd have to be more subtle.

Bantering with the killer was wearing on him, but from now on she'd have to play it cute. It was like feeding candy to a bear, and if that's what it took to keep him distracted while giving him a stomach ache, she'd do it.

Time was not on her side so Molly waited as long as she dared, then adopted a sugary sweet voice. "Mr. Bannock. I'm sorry for offending you. Still, you can't expect me to be happy about what you are doing to me."

The apology given, she let it lay for a moment knowing he couldn't fault her for resenting Leasburg.

Feigning sincerity Molly chose her words carefully. "I want you to know it is the judge I blame, not you. He is the one making you do this terrible thing...to me."
She added an injured pout.

Out of the corner of her eye, Molly studied her opponent trying to gauge if he believed her. Bannock was a killer without conscience, yet he was also egotistical and she guessed correctly that he saw himself as a hero in his own right. It would explain his anger when she scoffed at him.

The game continued. Molly pushed her horse closer until their legs touched. "The judge is a wicked man who treats people like pieces on a chessboard to be moved or discard at his whim. The only difference is you are a valued knight, and I a mere pawn. He knows you are the only man who can topple the opposing king, something he can't do without you."

Young and eager for praise, there was a perceptible change in Bannocks demeanor. Molly's flattery garnered her a sideways glance. "What you say is true about the judge...n' me. He needs me. Ain't nobody else got the guts ta' do what's got to be done. Jess Evans turned him down flat. So did the others, I'm the only one who can end this game in a checkmate as you say."

Bannock turned and looked her square in the eyes. "...but the judge gave you ta' me. You are my payment for this ride to hell n' back, and I'm going to collect. So you best get use to the idea." Molly lowered her head. "I know."

She waited letting her silence acknowledge his claim, then cautiously countered. "...but he also expects you to get me and my daughter to Leasburg unharmed."

Bannock sneered. "Don't think me a fool. I know what you want...keep your daughter safe, that's it ain't it? Your problem is the only thing you have to barter with is you. Keep that in mind when you dangle your feminine charms lookin' for favors. You are baitin' your own hook."

He watched Molly shift uncomfortably, and laughed. "Not so happy about paying the price when it's you that's legal tender. So tell me you ain't no whore."

Molly hung her head. Bannock's cruel jest had enough truth to cut deep. It was a long way to Leasburg, and at the same time dangerously near.

Bad Water
Chapter 25
A Flower Most Feminine

The five surly men worried little about their female captives escaping. The idea was absurd, but it was on Molly's mind, though at present she was inclined to agree with the men. Barefoot and defenseless, she couldn't conceive of it working, yet it seemed their only hope.

For some time, Wade Bannock had lapsed into deep though. Though stoic on the outside, always trying to be the tough gunfighter, his jaw would twitch in half frowns and shallow smiles, betraying a man living in his own mind.

The gunfighter's daydreaming went on for some time, then as if his companion had been part of the conversation he'd been having with himself, he just started talking out loud.

"Met him once you know."
He glanced at Molly. "Guess I wasn't much older than your boy. Never forget it. He rode into town one day when Digger was liquored up. Hell, Digger was always liquored up. Digger, he was the undertaker until they caught him stealing gold teeth from the dead, so he stuck ta' dealin' cards mostly; meanest son-of-a-bitch that ever lived. Never saw him smile.

"Didn't think nobody could take ol' Digger, but that mornin' Cole Creed not much more n' a kid himself climbed off his horse n' dressed Digger down for kickin' an old hound in the street. Can you believe it; for kickin' a dog. Digger was mean that way, use to bust up my ma some, me too when he'd come home drunk.

"Ya didn't push Digger so he pulled on Cole, got his pistol out and a bullet through the chest for his trouble. Digger's gun went off shooting himself in his own damn foot."

Wade laughed remembering. "Took him a bit to die. I laughed then too. Walked right up to him lying in the dirt and laughed in his face 'til his eyes rolled back in his head. Still he was the only Pa I ever knew.

"When Cole realized I was Digger's son, he took me home and apologized ta' ma. Told her he was right sorry; gave her some money, all he had. Ma invited him in n' fixed him some pepper pot soup. Told him not to fret, the farm was hers now and we'd be alright without Digger drinking all the money.

"Still it was a sight to see. Digger was fast as greased lightning, and Cole Creed beat 'em. It was like time stood still. His hand was hangin' at his side then holden' a smokin' gun n' Digger was dead. Knew right then n' there that someday I had to best Cole Creed; prove I was as good as the man who killed Digger.

Molly stared in stunned silence. There was nothing she could say.

By late afternoon they had left the Ruidoso. The pine covered hills with patches of snow buried in the shadows, slowly gave way to a arid climate of cactus and sage. They had crossed over the rim.

Beneath the falling hooves of the weary horses a parched soil crumbled to dust and caught the breeze. It added to Molly's distress. There was no cover here to hid them if they were to escape. Maybe after dark, she thought, but knew that would be too late.

Bannock was pushing hard giving her little time to think. He had declared the price she was to pay. He knew she'd do anything to save her daughter. Instead of taking her by force, he'd make her beg to be his whore. Molly sickened. If there was an answer she had to find it by nightfall.

Her mind was racing now. No stone could be left unturned. If only she had a weapon. Her captors had guns and knives, but these were the weapons of men, and took a strong hand. Even if she could get a hold of one, they would just take it from her. No, the blade and the bullet were not how women fight. She would have to find ways more subtle.

Then it came to her; a weapon most feminine. She almost smiled; poison. Yes, poison. History is replete with stories of women resolving unpleasant situations with this most genteel assassin.

Molly looked around. Lining the trail were the robust desert plants that had adapted to the harsh land, tall pungent sage dispersed with rabbitweed, chaparral and greasewood to name a few. A dandy like Wade would think nothing of such useless weeds, but not so Cole Creed. Cole had lived among the Apaches and learned their knowledge of herb-lore. The Indians used these resilient plants as medicine, but in higher quantities they could be deadly.

Molly had to think. Chaparral was used as a medicinal tea. It killed intestinal parasites and much more. In sufficient quantities it was lethal, but slow acting and had a bitter taste that would be easily detected. Chaparral would do her no good.

As they followed the trail, Molly's eyes searched each and every weed trying hard to recall what Cole had told her. There was something he had said that scratched at the back of her mind. They rode on, her eyes darting feverishly. Bannock took her silence to mean she was sulking over his besting her. He inwardly gloated. For now, it worked to her advantage. Molly kept searching and trying to remember. 'Think.' She whispered to herself.

Suddenly there it was! A plant they had passed many times which she'd discounted because she couldn't remember its name. This early in the season no blooms were to be seen only the unassuming plant dotting the small ravines. It was easily overlooked among the more sinewy species. Yet there beside the road as if heaven sent, a single lavender blue flower most feminine; the larkspur.

It was as though it was calling to her; 'Here I am, the answer you've been searching for.'

Cole's words came rushing back. She remembered him giving her a sweet bouquet of larkspur. Taking one in his hand, he had gently placed it in her hair and told her that the larkspur was like a woman; beautiful yet deadly. He laughed and said its spell worked quickly.

Molly was surprised she'd forgotten. He'd picked the flowers for her before his brother had made his intentions known. Cole had been charming that day, telling her she was like the larkspur, delicate and beautiful, yet with the strength to survive.

Had he only found the courage to tell her he loved her, how different life might have been? Had he not hesitated, but he did, and the next day Johnny came to her professing his heart. She accepted his affection as much out of frustration with Cole as for her love for Johnny.

The past was written and could not be undone, but she could take the wisdom Cole had given her and use it to save the daughter who might have been his.

Molly's heart raced. If somehow she could gather enough larkspur to spike the evening coffee, it could be the chance she was searching for. In her mind she doubted the dainty larkspur would kill the burly men, but hopefully if her plan worked they'd be in no condition to force themselves on her and Jean.

Just ahead a small ravine cut across the trail. It was deeper than most and meandered into the foothills offering some seclusion. In its sandy bottom a dry watercourse carved from rock by the infrequent rains held just enough moisture to tempt life in the harsh desert. Here among the purple sage larkspur grew more abundantly. "Stop!" Pulling the reins, Bannock came to a halt. "What?"
Molly fidgeted uncomfortably. "I...we..."
Not known for his patience, Bannock barked. "What the hell is it?"
Looking startled, Molly blurted out. "Maybe you men can go on forever, but we girls have to answer the call of nature."

Bannock rolled his eyes. "Now?"
Conjuring a demure voice Molly persisted. "If you'd just let Jean and me ride up this draw, I'm sure we can find some privacy."
"Nothing doing." Bannock shook his head. "You can walk, but you ain't taking the horses."

Her lower lip curling into a pout with as much distress as she could fain, Molly pointed her toe. "On those stones and thistles in our bare feet? Our tender flesh would be cut to shreds."

Groaning, Bannock leaned in his saddle and held out his hand. "Climb on" He pulled her into his lap. "I'll take you up the draw." Bannock turned to the boy. "Kid, grab the girl."

Without asking why, Bobby pulled Jean sidesaddle in front of him then rode up and fell in line behind the gunfighter.

Jean's eyes were wide, not sure what was going on. Molly spoke reassuringly letting her know everything was okay. "We are just having some privacy dear." Molly looked doubtfully up at Wade. "You are going to let us have privacy aren't you?"

Bannock shook his head in disgust. "There are things a feller don't want ta' see. Just do your business and be quick."

The dry ravine went straight for about sixty yards before turning up a bend that offered some concealment for the women. Young shoots of larkspur were growing in abundance. At last there was hope.

Bannock eyed Molly suspiciously. "You got a twinkle in your eye. What's going on in that pretty little head?"

Molly swallowed. She'd been too obvious. Needing a distraction, she quickly stared over his shoulder searching left and right.
Wade barked. "Now what?"
Molly shrugged. "Oh nothing."
His hand on her waist, Bannock pulled her tightly against him. "I said what!"

Risking his temper, she scanned the hills once more before pressing her face close to his and lowered her voice to add a hint of danger. "Nothing...it's just that this is Apache territory, and Cole being friendly with the Indians..."
Stretching out her leg, Molly daintily lifted her skirt exposing a bare foot. "...and no doubt wanting to return my shoes..."
She leaned in even closer her eyes scolding. "...that somebody stole, well this is a good place for an ambush."

As her captor tensed, Molly tucked her chin and smiled ever so sweetly. "If I was going to kill you, I'd do it here."

The gunfighter instinctively searched the hills. He hadn't considered this. The speed of his gun and their strength of numbers suddenly dwindled. Wade looked back at the boy and growled. "Come-on kid hurry up."

He tightened his grip on Molly. "You think you're cute don't you?"
Molly smiled demurely. "What do you expect from a girl whose legal tender?"
Bannock groaned. The little kitten curled against him had claws. She was toying with him, but what she said had merit. Cole Creed could be anywhere.

Putting his heals to the pony he droned sardonically. "Cute and legal tender, both fit you quite well, as does whore. It's what you are...or will be after tonight."

The gunfighter was callous. "You may protest, but women are like water, they take the form of the vessel that holds them, just like your body shaping to mine right now."

He pulled her closer to prove his point. "Once you settle into Leasburg, you will know what you are and you will accept it. A few good tumbles on them clean white sheets and you will finally learn to curb your tongue."

When they reached the bend, Bannock took another look around then returned his attentions to Molly. Holding her a little too familiar, he lowered her to the ground. Bobby did the same with Jean who hurried to her mother's side.

Before Wade let go of Molly's hand, he delivered a terse warning. "You women be quick, and no tricks or so help me I'll tan your hide, and you'll be riding back missin' more than your shoes." Looking most innocent, Molly stepped away accepting his scolding.

As the men rode out of sight, Molly heard Wade tell Bobby to keep his eyes peeled. She breathed a little easier. His attention was elsewhere.

Molly turned and hugged her bewildered daughter. "Oh, Jean. You have to be very brave if we are going to get out of this. Do you understand?"

Jean looked up into her mother's face. "I do Mama. It's just Jimmy..."

"I know sweetheart. It's hard, but we got to be harder. There will be time for crying, right now remember you are a Creed."

Molly kissed her cheek. "Help me gather flowers."

"Flowers? There are no flowers Mama."

"Well plants. As many as you can. I'll explain later. Now hurry."

Using her skirt for a basket, Molly started picking all the larkspur she could carry. Her hands worked quickly breaking stems as she sidestepped up the ravine gathering more plants. "Come here baby."

Undoing Jean's buttons, Molly stuffed the deadly leaves between her blouse and petticoat. The hand-me-down dress fit loose and Molly was able to stash a decent quantity without her looking lumpy. Still there was danger. Bobby would be close to Jean even touching her. He mustn't notice. Patting everything into place she buttoned Jean back up. "If that boy's hand gets too close, you...well you distract him. Do you understand?"

"I understand Mama."

Molly carefully arranged stems in her own clothing, added a few sprigs of grease wood and chaparral as well. She worried more about Wade Bannock than Bobby.

When she had stuffed as much of the plants as she dared, Molly adjusted her blouse and gave Jean the final once over. "I think that's all we can risk." Standing on her toes, she yelled. "We're ready."

As the sound of the horses grew near, Molly cautioned her daughter. "Act like nothing has changed. Cry if you can."

Tiptoeing from rock to rock, Molly made her way down. Her heart beat wildly. This was her only chance to save her daughter. Any slip up and all would be lost.

As the horses came into view, she was relieved to see the gunman still searching the hills.

Upon reaching the women, Bannock gave Molly a look that warned she better not be up to any mischief.

Staring him straight in the eyes, Molly joked. "You still have your scalp."

He sneered. "You've still got your mouth."

Playing the deadly game Molly innocently wiggled her hips and watched nervously as his expression change from scrutiny to animal lust. Both carried a danger, but this time the gleam in his eye made her breathe easier. He was no longer suspicious and Molly intended to keep it that way.

Coquettishly, she stepped on to a rock in front of him and lifted her arms waiting with a practiced smile. Men carry weapons of steel; all that a woman has she is born with. A youthful thirty, Molly was quickly learning she could be adorable if needed, a weapon of great value in a man's world.

As crude as Bannock was, her feminine charms were having their effect. Desire telling in his eyes, he reached out and drew her into the saddle before him.

Molly held her breath fearing he might hear the rustle of the leaves against the fabric. As soon as the horse took her weight, she leaned away from her captor.

Not liking the distance, Bannock kicked his horse causing it to lunge forward. Caught by surprise, Molly instinctively threw her arms tightly around his neck to keep from tumbling backwards. He laughed. "Falling for me are you? Can't wait for night?"

Angered, Molly pushed her hands against his chest. "No! I just don't want to be close when Cole puts a bullet through your brain."

Bannock countered. "The great Cole Creed wouldn't back-shoot. He's a living legend and too noble for that. No, he will ride in bold as day and when he does, I'll put him down like an ol' toothless lobo past his prime."

The horse picked its way over a large bolder jolting the two of them back together. "...and while you are being cute, remember it's that smart mouth of yours that's got him killed. If it weren't for you he'd a never come back."

Molly shifted uncomfortably. "He's not dead yet."

Bannock grinned. "n' you ain't bedded yet, but both are as sure as rain."

The gunfighter rode on amused by his own wit. He chuckled out loud. "It was your stayin' when you shoulda' run that's put Cole in harm's way. Why it was 'cuz of you that he turned to the gun in the first place. It's 'cuz of you that he locked horns with the judge, and it's you that is leading him to me right now. It was always you Molly. It's you who's gunna' kill him, kill the legend. My bullet will just put the poor ol' bastard out of his misery."

Molly swallowed back tears knowing everything he said was true. It hurt. The truth had been doing that a lot of late. She took a breath to calm herself. There was no time for crying, they were locked in a deadly game of distraction and misdirection. If she could keep Wade's mind going in a dozen different directions, if she could win their freedom, then Cole wouldn't have to face Bannock, she could make it up to him; this time she'd take Cole's hand and leave Lincoln County for good.

Steeling herself, Molly cooed sensually. "About killing and cuteness..."

She pressed her face close to his. "You thought what I did to ol' Pete was cute didn't you...when I nearly killed him..."

Letting the gate of the horse bring them closer, she brushed her nose softly against his cheek. "...you like your women feisty, so you wouldn't punish me if I really did kill that ol' lecher? Would you?"

She looked up at the gunfighter with large innocent eyes as if asking for a piece of candy. Bannock laughed in spite of himself. "You really are full of surprises." He laughed again. "If you can kill the ol' codger without me catching you, sure knock yourself out."

Molly smiled gratefully. "Good. It will give me pleasant thoughts to distract my mind while you are having your way with me. You wouldn't want me to get bored now would you?"

"There you go with that smart mouth again. It's going ta' cost ya'."

Yawning, Molly looked away disinterested while tactfully putting distance between them, but Wade, supporting her bottom with a roaming hand felt her weight shift and pulled her back to him. Molly had no choice but to accept his vulgar advances. She feigned indifference hiding the truth that inside her every nerve was on fire.

Enjoying the curves of his captive, Wade suddenly slid his hand up to the small of her waist. Molly's heart jolted, she could hear and feel the larkspur crush against her. Near panic, she grabbed Wade's hand and clapped it firmly to her breast, and scowled. "There! It's what you want, take it. I'm tired of playing your game."

Her quick action had kept the rustle of the larkspur from registering in his brain. "A dying man, ought to have his last wish."

A surprised grin telling on his face, Bannock squeezed her breast and rolled it in his fingers. "You ain't timid, I'll give you that."

He tightened his grip until she winced. "Tender, but ain't timid."

Molly closed her eyes and fought to calm herself. The larkspur, only a hairs breath from his filthy reach remained undetected for the moment.

By the time they returned to the others Bannock had had his fun. The alert gunfighter returned his attention to the road and what lay ahead. His obsession with killing Cole Creed consumed his thoughts. Without a further word, he lifted Molly into her saddle then slapped his reins eager to ride.

Molly glanced quickly at Jean to see how she fared. The boy had indeed followed the gunfighter's lead. As he put Jean on her pony, his hands were all over her in a clumsy manner that betrayed his poor character, but Jean was adeptly fending him off. To keep the larkspur undetected, she allowed his hands to slide across her chest. Bobby had proven himself a liar and now a thief.

Catching her mother's eye, Jean nodded letting Molly know she was more than okay, she had found the will to fight. She was a Creed.

Bad Water
Chapter 26
Nightfall

On this evil day Molly had worn many faces. Some of them honest, others tasked her very soul. Wade Bannock had torn her family asunder. Carrying out the Judges orders did not excuse his despicable deeds. He reveled in the misery he dealt and the pleasures he stole. Molly cursed him silently. "Drink from the tears of your victims. Tonight I'll serve you a brew more deadly."

If all Molly had to do was play him a fool by dangling herself in front of him, she would, yet something told her he was quite the opposite. A man doesn't live long in his profession by being stupid.

All be it twisted, Wade Bannock had a quick mind. Perhaps he warranted her harmless or found her cute antics entertaining, so be it; more subterfuge. This night she'd fight with all she had, he was going to take her anyway.

Yet, Molly cringed in her own skin feeling dirty for the kindness she bestowed him. For hours she had ridden beside this despicable brute as a willing companion playing her part in the masculine and feminine dance. She had thrown her tantrums, cajoled, and flirted; doing everything short of offering herself to the man who would deliver her into a life of prostitution.

Bannock had derided her as currency in which they'd trade. It was a battle of strength against beauty. For now, the trick was not paying too much too soon.

As they came over a low rise of yucca and sage, Wade veered from the main trail, leading them down into a shallow vale were an abundance of trees grew by a warm spring known to travelers. The water stayed lukewarm all year around never freezing over in the winter so it was a welcome haven for anyone following the dangerous trail.

Tall cottonwoods replaced the endless junipers stretching out behind them, the last vestige of the eastern mountains. Over the next rise the harsh desert began in earnest, spreading bleakly clear to Leasburg.

Here there was still beauty. With the heated breeze off the dry desert and the warm spring waters, the air was still pleasant enough that a fire and a blanket would make the night bearable.

The sun's last yellow rays reached up from beneath the horizon shooting shafts of amber light into the graying sky. Time was rapidly running out.

Pulling to a halt by the water's edge, the horses lined up and drank their well-earned fill. Wade barked. "We camp here."
His command was for everyone, but a raised brow turned to Molly let her know here in this spot their game would end. She felt her skin prickle.

Bannock threw his leg over the saddle and came towards her. Not waiting for him, Molly quickly dropped from the horse's back robbing him of the chance of touching her. "If you got a pot, I'll fix the coffee."

Without waiting for an answer, Molly looked up at her daughter. Bobby was already reaching for her. "Jean get down on your own. That boy's a mite fragile, you don't need his help."
Taking several fast steps, Molly was by Jean's side as her feet touched the ground. "Help me make the coffee."
Molly glared at the boy. "If you want to fill your hands, get some firewood and be quick."

Bobby frowned. "Don't tell me what to do."
Molly went nose to nose with him. "I'm telling you." She jabbed a finger at the trees. "Now either you gather the wood, or bring me a switch 'cuz you are a long way from being a man."

Her bold insult evoked laughter from Buck and Toby. Even Pete chuckled. Embarrassed, Bobby hurried off to do as he was told.

Wade watched the exchange with amusement. Not letting Molly have it all her own way, he strutted over and lifted her chin until she stood on her toes then thumbed her nose. "Scare away little boys if you like, but don't forget your place woman. While you are making the coffee, fix dinner too."

Spinning her around, he faced her towards the pack horse and gave her a firm swat on the bottom. "Now get to it before I take a switch to you."

Blushing, Molly scurried to the animal while hiding her embarrassment among the sacks. He enjoyed treating her like a child and giving her a taste of her own medicine.

Bannock had the bold confidence of a powerful man and though she hated him, it made her heart quicken. He was taking his time roping her in, knowing full well she'd eventually share his blanket.

"To hell with him." Fumbling with the cords Molly untied the first sack, but her fingers quickly retreated. Instead of the provisions she expected, there before her eyes were the satin dance hall dresses Wade had taunted her with. Touching the silky fabric made the reality of her impending life suddenly very real.

Slowly reaching up, she couldn't help stroking the alluring dress of vibrant color and ornate texture. Sinful and sensual, the form fitting gowns with intricate black lace bordering the low cut cups took her breath away. Life on the farm was one of simple cotton, drab and functional. Like most farm girls growing up Molly had secret fantasies of such scant attire, dreaming of how beautiful she would look dancing before a crowd of adoring men, her sunburned skin powdered lily white, kissed with rouge, and silk ribbons in her hair.

The beautiful dress called to her, 'Here I am, your childhood dream, your destiny'.

Molly gently lifted the delicate fabric with her fingertips. Her breath halted as new and frightening emotions warmed her blood. The dress had the power to transform her. By merely touching it she felt fragile like a music box figurine.

Her slender bare limbs bejeweled in sparkling trinkets and bobbles, she'd be an object of desire, her identity stripped away replaced by the single word; Whore. "No!"
Pushing the material back inside Molly swore a silent vow. "No. I'll never accept that name."

She quickly refastened the sack. They could decorate her in garish feathers and revealing lace; stand her on tables before pawing men, but no dress would change her. She was Molly Creed.

Turning to the other sack, she hurriedly fished through its contents retrieving a slab of salt pork, a smaller sack of pinto beans, another of flour biscuits, and a third of coffee. In the bottom she found a frying pan, and a large dented coffee pot.

With her arms loaded, she made her way to the clearing where Buck and Toby were building the campfire. The men were strangely silent, the air heavy with tension. Their cold stare told her they knew what the night held in store for her.

Her eyes darted nervously to their faces, but they held blank stares. She could try to speak to them; let them know she was a person, but it was no use, she no longer existed. Lowering her head, she let them feast on her as they went about their work.

When the men finished the fire, they dusted their hands and moved away content with watching her from a distance.

Bobby, not wanting to be seen doing a woman's bidding waited for the men to go. He nervously stepped beside her and dropped his load of wood then hurried off without a word. She could feel the strain in him too.

Having done as he was told, the boy hid in the shadows beneath a tree festering his humiliation, while staring across the clearing at Jean; his eyes never leaving her. Molly's will hardened. This night the boy would drink coffee with the men.

The fire crackling, Molly dropped to her knees and went right to work. Jean came to her side carrying forks and tin plates she'd retrieved from another sack. Molly smiled reassuringly. "Here Jean, fill the pot and pan with water from the spring."

Taking a forked stick, Molly positioned the hot rock so she could balance the coffee and beans over the flames. Working quickly, she took a knife and started slicing some salt pork to put in the beans.

Her head tilted so her long brown hair hid her eyes, she searched the clearing. When she felt no one was watching, Molly set the knife aside and quickly loosened her buttons.

Trying to act natural she slipped the larkspur from her blouse and hid the sprigs and leaves beneath the folds of her skirt.

Before Molly could button her dress back up she heard the scuffing of boots behind her. Out of the corner of her eye she caught the glint of firelight dancing on an amber whiskey bottle dangling from Pete's scabbed hand.

She clutched her blouse close just as the old man leaned down close. His hot breath stank as it blew her hair. "I'll get you for what you done to me..."

Pausing in mid-sentence, his eyes darted left and right fearfully searching the dark for Bannock. Molly belonged to the gunfighter. Even Pete knew that.

Assured that they were alone, he pushed his rough lips to her ear. "Wade will have you tonight. I ain't no fool, but my times comin'...or should I say your time is comin'."

Wanting him gone, Molly stared forward saying nothing, but the foreman's hand was on her shoulder, his thumb digging painfully into the hollow neck. "You busted me up pretty good, but whiskey heals all pain." He chuckled. "...septin' what I'm gunna' do ta' you n' your precious little girl. Extract my pound of flesh from her too, I will. In Leasburg I'll be her best customer. You will hear her cries through the walls. Chew on that."

Turning her head upwards, Molly pressed her warm lips to Pete's stubbled cheek in a kiss that froze the old man cold. He flinched and sucked in air sucked. The sharp blade of Molly's cooking knife was shoved deep against his groin. She whispered softly. "...and before we reach Leasburg you may wake up gagging in the night, your shriveled manhood shoved down your throat. Chew on that."

The stunned foreman stared down in disbelief. Molly's large brown eyes shined back deathly sweet. She pushed the sharp blade upwards breaking his skin.

Jumping away from the terrifying blade, Pete stumbled backwards before regaining his balance. Every injury she caused him this day suddenly ached. Rubbing his bruised shoulder, he grimaced and shuffled off visible shaken. "Bitch."

Molly sneered. "Jerk!"

She was now more than ever committed to her plan. Jean returned shortly with the water and knelt by her mother ready to help.

The men were off by the base of the large cottonwoods getting liquored up. Between sips they'd leer in sideways glances at her and Jean. Vulgarities were whispered, then followed by laughter. It had started; a slow descent into the debaucheries of the night. Molly glanced at Jean. "To hell with them."

She furiously chopped at the meat. "Let them get drunk. It makes it easier."

Huddled together, the women quickly transferred the larkspur from their clothing to the coffee pot then filled it with grounds and water. Jean popped on the lid. "Mama how do you know it will work?"

"I don't know baby. Maybe it won't, though from what your uncle told me it should at least make them sick as dogs. Then again, it may do nothing. I don't know."

Unsure, Molly added all that was left of the larkspur to the pot, then crushed the green tendrils of chaparral she'd hidden and added it to the pinto beans hoping the strong taste would not be noticed.

She cautioned Jean. "Don't eat or drink tonight except for biscuits and water. Only pretend."

Jean nodded.

There were some hot peppers in the food sack. Molly generously added these as well hoping it would mask the flavor of the chaparral, and with a little luck cause even greater distress for the men. With the peppers, chaparral, and larkspur, it was a triple punch. Molly glanced at Jean. "That ought to do something."

As a finishing touch, she spit into the pot. Watching her mother, Jean leaned close and did the same. It was done.

Bad Water
Chapter 27
Bitter Stew

"Come and get it." With a nervous glance to each other the girls stood holding a plate in each hand which they kindly offered to the approaching men. Bannock took a hearty bit and quickly sucked in air. "Damn woman. This is hot."
Molly pulled a face. "I used the ingredients you had. If you don't like the beans go hungry."

Wade took another mouthful braving the peppers. It didn't actually taste too bad, and a day on the trail left him famished. "Pour me more coffee whore; gotta' wash down these Mexican fire coals down."

Buck woofed down his fourth spoonful and smiled approvingly. "Pretty damn good. How'd ja' make the gravy?"
Molly looked pleased and handed him a steaming cup of hot coffee. "I crumbled some biscuits in the water and boiled some fat." She forgot to mention the seasoning was finely diced larkspur.

Just out of firelight, Molly caught young Bobby trying to force down the fiery meal just like the men. His mouth hung open in pure anguish. She bit her lip hiding a grin.

Holding back until the last, Pete stepped out of the shadows hungry as the rest. Molly handed him a plate with a wicked smile. "Save some room for your late night snack."
Taking his meal, he quickly hurried away.

Molly and Jean made sure that everyone of their captors was on their second plate before they pretended to eat. She filled her cup a quarter full then held the pot high. "More coffee?"

Wade held out his cup, his eyes glinting. "Damn good meal."

Handing Molly his plate, he traced a finger across her cheek and down her neck. "Right tasty, but I reckon there are delicacies even sweeter that shall be savored this night."

He toyed with her blouse pulling it off her shoulder. The red glow of the campfire danced on her skin quickening his pulse. He added. "...n' hot as these beans no doubt."

Abruptly turning around, he hollered at Pete. "Old man, break out your bottles. One for each of us, n' don't pretend you ain't got none. The saddle bags on your pack horse are full ya' ol' sot. Tonight is for drinking."

Grumbling, Pete went to the pack horse, then stumbled into the light and handed Bannock a bottle before stomping away clutching two more to his chest.

Molly started to shrink back, but Wade caught her by the wrist. Pulling her towards him, he downed his coffee, then twisted the cork from the bottle with his teeth. "Here."

Taking Molly roughly by the cheeks, he tipped her head back and poured the hot liquor into her mouth.

She jerked away spitting the vile brew while rubbing her bruised cheeks. Wade laughed. "Have some more."

"No!"

The gunfighter feigned disappointment. "What's a matter? You don't want to party?"

Molly spit again. "That whiskey has gone bad. Can't you tell?"

Wade took another swig and swished it in his mouth before swallowing. "Tastes okay to me."

Leaning forward, she pretended to sniff the bottle in Wade's hand then pulled a sour face. "My father was a brewer. I know bad whiskey. It's tainted. You will all get sick as snake-bit hounds."

Molly's father was a teetotaler, but Bannock had unwittingly offered her a cover when and if the men started feeling the effects of the larkspur.

She held the pot before her. "If you are going to drink that poison, you best counter it with more coffee."

Wade belched, then patting his stomach, yelled at Pete. "Ya' ol' drunk, ya' been buying cheap whiskey."

Buck, leaning up against a tree, took a swig from his own bottle. "He dint' buy em', stole a whole damn wagonload from the Apaches last fall. Been drinkin' ever since."

The drover looked around. "Reason enough for them to lift our scalps if they is out there."

Wade released a smelly burp and took another drink. "Hell I've drunk worse."

Molly tipped the coffeepot for all the men. "You boys better have some more Joe, before you get too drunk to know what you are doing."

The men laughed. An unholy glint in his eye, Toby answered for all of them. "Oh, we know what we is doin'."

With one drink after another, and coffee in between to cleans their palate, the men continued jugging the whiskey all the while laughing and making crude jokes.

Buck leered at Jean, with a sideways glance to Pete. "So ya' soaked her in whiskey did ya? Bet it's still on the little whore's skin iffin' we run dry."

He laughed vulgarly and the others joined in. Molly tipped the pot to his cup. "Here, have some more coffee."

Distracting him with an enticing smile, she overfilled the cup scalding his hand. He jumped back. "Damn it whore!"

Molly put her fingertips to her lips. "Oops."

Molly added more water and grounds to the pot then set it back on the fire. Wanting away from it all, she slipped into the shadows masked by the men's raucous humor which continued to grow louder.

Moving farther away, she found a log by the stream and dropped with fatigue. Reaching the stream, her fingers dipped into the dark water. Molly cupped her hand and lifted it to her lips rinsing the bitter taste of the liquor from her mouth. Like her father, she didn't care for strong drink, and tonight above all nights she must keep her head.

Calming herself, Molly watched the ugly scene unfold. The men were getting very drunk and laughing at their own belches. Not far from them Jean was pressed against a tree her eyes wide with fear. At her tender age she had never experienced crude men eyeing her and talking about her the way they were, still Jean was holding up.

Fourteen! It then struck Molly that today was Jean's birthday. A pain stabbed in her heart. "Poor child. What a terrible party."

She felt like crying. Fourteen...but watching her daughter face the men bravely like a woman and not a child, she realized there was strength in her. Jean was growing up.

Molly started to stand and go to her, when suddenly Bobby loomed from the bank of the spring blocking her path. He was crocked and scowling. "St..sta..stay woman."
He put a strong hand on her shoulder pushing her down onto the log. Towering over her, he tried to stand straddle- legged with arms folded in a manly pose of authority, but too drunk to manage, he dropped to his knees and rubbed his face struggling to collect his thoughts. "Jimmy was my friend, but he never shoulda' pulled on Wade Bannock. He had no chance." The boy whimpered. "No chance."

Looking like a parent, Molly shook her head. "Do you know why Jimmy had to try?"
Bobby wailed. "I ain't no coward if that's what you is sayin'. You...you Creeds have shamed me."
Molly held his eyes until he looked away. "You shamed yourself Bobby."

"Shut your mouth." He snapped angrily. "You are done tellin' me what ta' do."
He burped and stared across the clearing at Jean. "It's all her fault." Waving his hand, he pointed an accusing finger. "Pretty n'...she makes a fella want her so bad he will do stupid things to get her attention...just wanted to touch her."
Bobby gulped a breath of air. "...don't matter. Ta' make right what Jimmy done to me...n' so the men will stop makin' fun of me, I gotta' take Jean. You know that."

Shaking her head, Molly scolded. "No Bobby, you don't."
The boy gripped her tightly by the shoulder. "I said shut-up. Ya' don't talk 'less I tell you too."

Bobby swayed, but caught his balance. "...and after what you done, threatening to switch me, everybody laughing, I'll take you too."
"Bobby!"
Taking him by the wrist, Molly pried his fingers from her shoulder. "You used to be a good boy. I babysat you when your mama was dying. Do you remember? And now you behave like this. What happened to you?"

Bobby jerked his hand free, shame telling in his eyes. "This God damn county happened to me. Ain't no good in it."

He struggled up to his feet. "...n' ain't no good in you. Women are whores. All of you are damn whores jus' like Pete says... so I'm takin' Jean and I wanted you to know why. I have to... I... I just have to..."

Molly came to her feet. "Sounds like a scared little boy with a guilty conscience to me."

The truth stung. Shaking his head, Bobby hollered. "I said shut-up woman. Pete...yeah, Pete, he...he sent me over here, said I should take you right now, prove to Mr. Bannock that I'm a man. Said Mr. Bannock would like me then."

Bobby's breathing came heavier. "Pete says you are a whore hidin' under decent women's clothes...says every farmer in Lincoln County has had ya'."

In a sudden impulse he grabbed Molly's blouse in his fist and ripped it off her right shoulder.

Eyes bulging he stared dumbfounded at her exposed skin then he began to shake. Consumed by his crime, he grabbed the other half of her blouse. "Whore. Like Pete said..."

Frowning, Molly pushed both her hands against his chest driving him backward. "Bobby stop it."

Losing his balance, Bobby yelled in surprise and tumbled over backwards into the stream taking her blouse with him. He landed in a tremendous splash and came up flailing and gulping for air.

From the other side of the clearing the belching and laughing stopped. Turning toward them, the men stared in surprise. Pete alone had a sinister grin.

Gathering her skirt in one hand, Molly wrapped her other arm over her breast and hurried past the fire to Jean. The situation had just gone from bad to worse.

Bannock watched dumbfounded as Bobby struggled up from the spring soaking wet with Molly's blouse still clutched in his fist.

Blinking the stupor from his eyes the gunfighter turned and faced Molly. His brain in a fog, he struggled trying to pass judgment on what happened, but it was beyond what wit he had left.

Toby staggered forward swinging his bottle. "She looks right pretty in her lacy top. Think Bobby done made some improvements. Jes' needs ta' lose her skirt n' we 'kin get this shindig on."

He punctuated his assessment with a horrific belch that droned on for several seconds.

Pete and Buck laughed. Wade joined in the merriment then swaggered up to Molly. Seeing her petticoat and bare limbs set his heart pumping alcohol and larkspur through his veins.

Drunk as Wade was their cat and mouse game required too much thinking. His base animal instinct took over. Reaching out, he tucked his fingers into the waistband of Molly's skirt and ripped it clear away.

Aghast Molly backed away as the men hooted and cheered. Laughing, Pete clapped his hands and danced a jig. "Pluck her like a chicken."

Molly's torn skirt dangling on his fingers, Bannock grinning like a fool, held it high and turned full around to the roar of the men. Caught up in the cheer he played his part. Bowing low he tossed the shredded dress into the fire.

The white slips of Molly's laced petticoat hung nearly to the ground. She was still covered, but for the drunken cowboys used to cattle, a pretty woman in her undergarments was a rare sight to behold. Their blood boiled.

Wade burped. "That fool Bobby finally done somethun' right." The men laughed louder as Bobby stormed into the circle dripping wet. He lunged, full of anger, towards Molly for pushing him into the stream. Only now the men were cheering him.

Stunned, Bobby stopped in his tracks, reveling in the praise he had so long hungered for.

Pete slapped him on the back. "Atta-boy Bobby. Pluck her like a chicken."

Not wanting the approval to end Bobby pointed a finger at Jean. "Gunna' do the same to her, the teasin' little bitch. Pluck them both like chickens."

Pete hooted and pushed the boy towards her.

Jean backed away pleading. "Bobby we go to church together..." To Bobby, everything out of her mouth disgraced him. He raged, "Shut-up...we got church right here. Your mama done baptized me n' washed away my sins. Now Jimmy's precious little angel is gunna' sing for the congregation."

Wiping the water from his face, he lunged at Jean. "Let's see your pretty wings."

The roars of encouragement rose then faded to perverse silence as the men stood eagerly waiting. The boy was going to give them the flesh they wanted. Wade grinned wide, "Best get to it son. Tonight you become a man."

"No!" Molly screeched and rushed towards her daughter, but Buck and Toby caught her wrists and held her back. Struggling, Molly threatened. "Bobby, don't you touch her. Don't you dare..."

It was no use, her curse trailing off, she dropped her head weeping. "Leave her alone...please."

Jean shrunk against the broad trunk of a cottonwood, her eyes darting from man to man unable to comprehend how they could let this happen.

Swaying, Bobby grabbed the top of her dress with both hands and jerked downwards. Jean screamed as he ripped it completely off.

Dropping to the ground, she sobbed, her bare shoulders shaking. "Bobby!"
Nothing in all her life prepared her for this. Tears streaming down her cheeks she looked up at the boy, her beautiful eyes asking why?

Appalled by his own deed, Bobby backed away. They'd been childhood friends, now her torn dress hung in his hand. Overcome by his evil deed, the boy cried aloud, his face flushing red. Then catching himself, he looked up into the questioning stares of the grown men.

Embarrassed, he sought to cover his outburst. Following Bannock's lead, Bobby threw the tattered garment into the flames and unleashed his humiliation on Jean. "Get up bitch...get up! I gotta' do this..." He grabbed her by the wrist and dragged her to her feet. "You get up. Dance for us men."
Jean cried and tried to pull away, but Bobby staggered backwards, pulling her near the fire. "Dance you, d-damn-it."

Having her dance was all the young boy could think of. Then in the midst of all that was unholy something very small happened; a tiny thing. As Bobby pulled the shattered girl to him, he felt the warmth of her fragile hand in his. She was suddenly little Jean once more, his childhood friend, and not a whore like Pete said.

Bobby's eyes filled with horror. "Jean...I'm...I'm..."
Releasing her hand, he shook as a sickness washed over him. "I can't..."

Whirling towards the men, he balled his fist in protest. "I can't...I ain't like you...I, I..."

Bobby backed away crying like an injured child. Utterly ashamed he turned and ran into the night.

For a long moment the men stared in stunned disbelief watching him disappear. It was an awkward spectacle that put a damper on their fun. Angered, Pete hollered after him. "Damn little crybaby. Maybe you can't but we sure as hell can."

Licking his lips, he looked down at the young girl eager for his chance.

Jean's eyes wide with terror, wrapped her arms over her breasts as the old man dropped his bottle from his hand and staggered forward.

Buck pushed Molly towards her daughter. "You dance too whore. Gunna' have us our own burlesque show...always wanted ta' see one. You twirl pretty-like, n' let them slips stand out like petals on a flower."

He clapped a tune with his hands and turned to his friend. "Toby get out your harmonica let's have some dancin' music."

Free from the clutches of the men, Molly grabbed Jean's wrist and snatched her away. Glaring at Pete she slid closer to Bannock desperately hoping he would stop the vindictive lecher.

Wade, dealing with a growing queasiness in his stomach, had been content to simply watch the men humiliate their captives, but visions of Molly's swaying naked to music drew him into the fray.

As Molly drew close, he reached out and ripped a laced strap from her shoulder bearing more flesh. "You heard what Buck done told ya'. Dance!"

Wade staggered and steadied himself. "Let's see yo' pretty legs."

Wetting his lips, Toby spit a foul taste and put the harmonica to his mouth. He struck up a bad rendition of Turkey in the Straw that was not to Bannock's liking. The gunfighter waved his bottle silencing him. "No, no. I want somethun' soft n' sweet n' slow. Play Red River Valley."

Wade slid his hand down the length of Molly's arm. "I want you ta' move like that winding river. Twirl 'til them slips on your hips stand straight out. Now dance."

Molly and Jean huddled together knowing full well that to dance would drive the men into a frenzy. Their scant garments would be plucked and torn just like petals from a flower. Molly clutched at Bannock's arm. "Our bargain?"

Wade reached out and ripped the last strap from her shoulder. "Hell woman, you can't make deals with the devil. Dance."

The judgment given, Toby filled his lungs with the smoky air and blew the first note, then instantly followed up by hurling vomit all over the harmonica and his hands. He dropped to his knees and vomited again.

"Jesus Christ!" Wade jumped out of the way of the splatter, too late to save his boots. "What the hell Tob'..."

Suddenly without warning Wade retched too. Grabbing his stomach, he emptied its contents into the fire. It was a bazaar sight. There was enough whiskey in his belly that his vomit fueled the flames sending them curling into the night air as if Hell had opened its gates.

Molly wrapped Jean in her arms and yelled at Bannock. "See what I told you; tainted whiskey."
She still had the presence of mind to hide their deed.

Bannock blew the slime from his nose. "Pete, you lousy bastard, I'll..."
He dropped to his knees cursing the foreman, but Pete had already crumbled by the spring. On his hands and knees half in the water, he was bucking like a cat gagging on a hairball. The stench of vomit started a chain reaction among the already queasy men.

Buck ran from the circle but didn't make it far before he grabbed his stomach blowing beans several feet through the air. He stumbled and fell face-first into his own filth.

A loud death like moan turned the girls. Staggering from the light, Toby clung with both hands from a tree branch convulsing in dry heaves.

As Molly and Jean withdrew in disgust, his knees buckled but he kept his grip on the branch struggling to stand. The exertion was too much and his trousers darkened from the discharge of his bowels. Almost simultaneously his body convulsed exploding its contents from both ends coating him from chin to boots in the process. He convulsed again only now there was blood dripping down his face and neck.

Wade lay curled in the fetal position vomiting out the side of his mouth in a pool of smelly mud. "Damn you Pete..."

A full bottle was within his reach. In agony he hurled it into the campfire. The bottle exploded in brilliant flames that rose to the top of the trees setting the dry leaves ablaze. Smoke swirled and sparks showered about them as the tree burned.

Frightened, Jean pulled back against her mother whispering. "Mama we killed them."

Molly shook her head. "Not hardly, but let's go."

Taking Jean's hand, Molly cautiously led her around the edge of the camp. Barefoot and terrified, the girls hurried to the picket line where the horses were tied just beyond the firelight. Molly pressed close to her daughter. "We don't have time for saddles. Just get a bridle."

Their hearts pounding, they quickly slipped the bits into the horse's mouths, then led the animals farther into the dark. "It's now or never."

Her hands shaking so bad she could hardly control them, Molly boosted Jean onto the back of her pony. Freedom was seconds away. Suddenly out of the dark a fist caught Molly's hair jerking her backwards. She fell screaming. "Ride Jean...aaah!"

Howling like a crazed animal, Wade Bannock twisted his fist tighter into Molly's hair driving her into the ground. She fought back. "Run baby, go..."

Bannock shook her until she thought her neck would snap. She screamed in pain.

Horrified at seeing her mother thrown to the dirt, Jean cried. "Mama, nooo!"

Whipping her pony forward, she kicked at the gunfighter trying to break his hold, but Bannock caught Jean by the ankle dragging her viciously to the ground. "Where do you whores think you're going?"

Jerking Molly to her feet, he in turn grabbed Jean's hair and danced them before him. "Ya figured I'd just lay there n' let you pretties ride away?"

Wade Bannock was made of tougher stuff than Molly had guessed. He retched, but steadying himself, he dragged them forward and wretched again.

Angered by their attempted escape, Bannock jerked the girls apart then slammed them back together. "I said you could kill Pete.

If you are behind this, I'll hang you upside down by your ankles and whip your bare hide 'til you bleed."

Near panic, Molly cried. "No it was the whiskey, I told you."

As he dragged the girls back to the campfire, they passed Bobby sobbing at the trunk of a tree. Seeing them approach, he hurriedly wiped his eyes and struggled to his knees. Wade threw Jean down in front of him. "Here's the brat. Take her if you're man enough, but if you let her loose you'll be wearing her shiny dress and pleasuring the men come mornin'."

The boy took Jean's wrist then bent over and heaved so hard she feared he'd expel his entrails.

Bannock stormed past the firelight. Indifferent to the prostrate men strewn near the campfire, he marched at a furious pace towards the spring.

Dragging Molly with her head bent to his waist, he threw her face down into the water. As she tried to rise, he kicked her hard in the rump sending her flying. She came up soaking wet and screaming. "You bastard."

Trudging into the stream, Bannock shoved her face under the water. He let her fight for a moment then dropping to his knees beside her he stuck his own head under the surface. When he rose up, he brought Molly with him. She was gasping and crying. "I hate you. I hate y..."

Wade shoved her head back under water, then pulled her up again. "Never thought otherwise."

Sliding back to the bank, Wade released Molly, letting her fall by his side. He sucked in a deep breath of air trying to clear his mind. "The judge let it be personal; let you Creeds get to him. To me you are just a whore...let you play your games 'cuz it amused me."

Molly pulled back sobbing, but Wade pointed to the ground in front of him. "Come here."

A cry broke from her throat, refusal was futile, she crawled from the water's edge and went to him. "I truly hate you."

Soaked to the skin, Wade pulled Molly into his lap, and brushed the matted hair from her damp face. His hands slid down her slender neck and over her bare shoulders tracing her curves. "Soft n' pretty."

Pulling her over him, Wade leaned back against the sand and pressed his lips roughly to Molly's. "Remember our first kiss?"

Not expecting an answer, he tucked his thumbs into the top of her Petticoat and pealed it down to her hips intent on having her, when all of a sudden he threw Molly off of him and vomited again. "Damn that rot gut. I'll kill that ol' man myself."

Trembling violently Bannock wiped his mouth on his sleeve looking like he might draw his last breath. He gagged, but refused to give up. "Get over here."

Pulling her petticoat back up Molly did as she was told. Bannock folded her against him. His strength gone, he tumbled over sideways pulling her tightly to his chest. "Damn-it to hell."

Shaking with convulsions, he draped a muscular arm over Molly imprisoning her beneath him, his powerful fist clutching her throat. Bannock burped a foul smell and closed his eyes. "Damn-it to hell."

Overcome by the poison he sought refuge in sleep, yet enough meanness remained in him, he never drifted so deep as to forget the girl buried beneath him.

Molly struggled then relented. It was useless. When she tried to rise, his fingers would tighten about her neck.

Tears rolled down Molly's cheek. In the distance she could see Bobby on all fours heaving his guts. Jean was kneeling beside him rubbing his back caring for him. Fearing for her daughter she wanted to yell; tell her daughter to run, but Bannock would silence her before she got a word out.

As much as Molly abhorred death, tonight more than anything she wished Wade Bannock dead.

Bad Water
Chapter 28
Creed Justice

A cold sun bathed the early morning campsite in a hazy red glow that danced on the swirls of smoke and the steam curling off the water; a silent requiem for their night of hell.

The weary men laid strewn where they had fallen, chopped down like cords of wood in a rotting forest. Jean was fast asleep with Bobby's head cradled to her breast.

Since the first gray light Molly pondered the unholy scene still locked beneath Wade Bannock's arms. He stank. She closed her eyes not wanting to face the new day. It would only bring them closer to Leasburg. She had failed.

Behind her there rose a rattle of pans. "Bitches!" Ol' Pete cursed at the top of his lungs. "Damn them evil bitches."

Awoken by the foreman's unwelcome discord, the camp struggled to life. Wade released Molly and fought his way up to a sitting position. He rubbed his head. "What's the hollering? I got a buffalo stampede in my brain."

Pete stomped towards them his eyes spitting hate. The disheveled old man, his shirt unbuttoned and sparse gray hair sticking up like whiffs of smoke, thrust the coffee pot at arm's length. "Look at this!" "Bitches." Cursing at Molly as she raised on a stiff arm, he dumped the contents of the pot over her head. She screeched and tried to brush it off but not before Wade saw that there was something more than coffee grounds. He grabbed her arm and shook her. "What is this?"

Pete threw the pot at Molly, hitting her square in the back. "I'll tell ya' what it is. The bitch poisoned us with larkspur."

Struck by the sudden realization behind last night's decent, Bannock roared like a bull coming out of a shoot. Thundering to his full height, he threw Molly into the air. She landed hard on her feet, her knees buckling beneath her. Before she could fall, Bannock slapped her hard spinning her head sideways. "You scheming whore."

Recovering from the forceful blow, Molly pulled her hair from her face and stared defiantly at the two men. There was nothing she could do now to save her hide so she smiled bravely. "You told me I could kill Pete."

Glancing at Pete, Wade blustered. "Didn't say you could kill the rest of us damn you."

Molly lifted her chin. "Like you said, don't take it personal."

Wade raised his hand. "You little..." Molly closed her eye against the impending blow.

"He's dead."

Wade's hand froze in mid strike. The gunman turned towards Buck who calmly walked up staring blankly at them, his hands stuffed in his pockets. "Tob's dead."

Buck shrugged and halfheartedly nodded behind him. "Over there, lying in his own shit."

Shaking with fury, Bannock squeezed Molly's arm until she cried out. "You are hurting me."

Ready to kill, he hurled her to the ground so hard the impact knocked the air from her lungs. Gasping, Molly struggled up on her elbows, but a swift kick from Wade's boot sent her rolling to the water's edge. He stood over her intent on making her pay.

Her chin in the stream, Molly tried to crawl away but Bannock's heavy boot came down on her slips pinning her to the ground. She lifted her head and sputtered. "Go ahead. Kill me. Do it you bastard."

The gunfighter doubled his fist letting it waver in the air then stopped. "No I can't kill you. Besides, that would be too easy..." He leaned over her. "...but I can do worse."

Wade beat his fist into his hand. "I'm going to deliver you and your stinkin' daughter to Leasburg just like the judge said. You are gunna' have the biggest damn parade a whore ever had."

Molly raised to her knees. "I'll never wear that dress."

The gunfighter spit. "Then you'll ride through town bare ass naked like Lady Godiva. That aught ta' drum up business."

Bannock turned and yelled at the top of his lungs. "Bobby you get that little slut down here right now."
He glared at Molly. "When I see the judge, I'll hand him a thousand dollars you n' your brat make on the first day. You will be lucky to see the second."

Grinding his boot down firmly, Wade jerked Molly up by her throat tearing her slips away. He shoved his face into hers. "Poison me! You Creeds are too stupid to know when a little fear is good."

Bobby came timidly holding Jean's hand. She was still in her petticoat, untouched from the night before. Wade sneered at the boy in disgust. "That girl done stole your balls son, if you ever had any."
He glared at Jean. "Time to pay for your mama's sins."
The young girl shrunk against the boy. Bobby nervously glanced down at Jean then squeezing her hand he cleared his throat. "Please Mr. Bannock, she ain't never hurt nobody."
In no mood for heroics, the gunfighter snapped. "Shut up and hand her over."
Bobby bit at his lip. "She's better than us. You got no right..."
Scoffing at the youth, Bannock let his hand fall by his gun. "Whatcha' gunna do ya little crybaby; stand by her all noble like your dead friend did? Stupid kid."
Bobby stood rigid for a moment longer then his shoulder began shaking. Hiding his eyes in shame, he whimpered. "Please sir..."

Bannock waved his arms. "Get the hell out of my sight you damn coward. Go pick some flowers if they don't scare ya' too much."
Wade grabbed the boy by the arm and jerked him away from the girl. "I said get."
He kicked the boy with the side of his boot adding to his humiliation.

Bobby stumbled backwards a tortured protest on his face, but he ducked his head and shrunk away.

Disgusted Bannock scowled at Pete and Buck. "You too, go bury Tob' if you care, or throw him in a ditch."

Seething with anger as the men hurried to go, Wade turned and swore at the girls. "Damn the lot of ya."
His face snarling a threat, he jabbed a finger at the ground. "You whores stay put."

Stomping away in long strides he covered the distance to where the supply sacks were piled at the base of a large tree, then just as quickly returned carrying one of them. "Stupid Creed bitches."

Reaching into the sack, he shook it violently, and let it fall away as he raised his arms high. In his hands he held two very small satin dresses, one red, one blue, both trimmed in black lace with stiff black crinoline slips.

He grinned at Jean. "Take off your clothes. I'm going to be your first customer."

Panic-stricken the girl froze. Bannock clenched his teeth. "I said strip."

Not waiting he thrust out his huge hand ripping Jean's top down to her hips. So stunned by his violence, Jean stood wide-eyed, unable to scream or even cover herself. Molly gathered Jean in her arms and cradled the child to her breast. She was suddenly calm. "Don't fear him baby. He's nothin', just a bully."

Speaking softly, Molly smoothed Jean's hair. "It will be okay. He doesn't want you. It's his pathetic way of letting me know who's in charge."

Turning, she stared bravely at Bannock. "Let's stop the game."

Bannock laughed. "Maybe you ain't so dumb after all. Saves me some time n' your pretty little daughter a whole lot of pain."

His eyes narrowed. "Are you willing to pay her price?"

Molly pushed Jean behind her and squared with the imposing man. "You want to be the one who makes me a whore. Alright, let me dress my child then I'll settle my debt right here and now."

The gunman stood gloating. He let a finger trail down her cheek. It was indeed what he had intended. "Oh, you will pay...with your last shred of dignity. No doubt about that. It's a weakness in you Creed. You are good to your word."

Wade grabbed Molly forcefully by the shoulders and pressed his lips to her bending her over backward so brutally she whimpered in pain.

Releasing her, he shoved the scant red satin dress into her arms. "Dress your little girl and send her off to play with Bobby while I play with you."

The smug grin on his faced said he knew he had won. He took several steps back then folded his arms waiting.

Hiding Jean behind her the best she could, Molly wiped the tears from her daughter's cheeks. "Come on baby it will be all right."

Letting Jean's petticoat slide to the ground, she pulled the red satin dress down over her head and adjusted it into place. "Cry if you need to. No shame in that."

With the tender care of a loving mother, Molly meticulously laced up the ribbons as if it were a Sunday dress. "There."

Turning her around she placed a kiss on Jean's forehead. "You look real pretty."

Molly slid her hands down Jean's arms. "You will need something for your feet."

Reaching into the bag that lay on the ground, Molly fished out a pair of fancy black shoes and handed them to her daughter. "Here baby you take these into those trees yonder and have Bobby help you tie them up. He won't hurt you, not anymore."

With a glance behind her, Molly hugged Jean tightly and whispered in her ear. "Make him take you out of here...now! It's your last chance. You can do it. I'll buy you the time."

She lifted Jean's face, capturing her eyes. "I won't be going to Leasburg."

Jean fell on her mother's shoulder. "Mama..."

Molly held firm. "You are my victory. Do as I say and no matter what you hear, don't look back. You do this for your Mama."

Tears drenching her cheeks, Jean nodded silently. She would live for her mother.

Molly kissed her. "Run baby."

Her heart breaking, Jean turned and rushed from the circle of the trees.

When her daughter was out of hearing range, Molly turned to face her tormentor. She shot him a wicked smile. "You do what you wish Mr. Bannock. Take more than your just pay because I want you to know when you are done, you owe a debt to my daughter. Like Bobby said, she's done no one any harm."

Wade Bannock hung his hand from his gun belt delighted by the hell Molly was about to suffer. He looked down admiringly at her bare legs. "Before your poison took its toll last night, I do believe you owed us a dance. Dance for me Molly. I want to see sunlight and shadow paint your bare skin as I christen you a whore."

Reaching into his pocket, he threw a silver dollar on the ground. "Dance for your pay."

Smiling bravely, Molly knelt and picked up the coin, every second buying Jean time. "Thank you kind sir." Then slowly stepping back she lifted her chin high. What she was about to do would have been unthinkable a few short days ago, but for her daughter no price was too high. Molly's world had changed. Who she loved and hated had changed. In the end, she had changed. Standing here at the edge of ruination, Molly was the strongest she'd ever been. Brave men had died, yet she remained to the end.

Molly took one more step back. On this ground she'd fight her greatest battle, but never again would she be afraid. She nearly laughed at how comical it was. After all Bannock's effort, what will he have gained?

Knowing she could stall no longer, Molly lifted her slender arms letting her graceful movements flow sensually. She'd keep her promise.

Cupping her hands over her breasts she tucked her fingers in the top of her petticoat. "If you'd be so kind as to lay me down on this before you abuse me, I'd truly appreciate it."

Her eyes lowering in a false blush, she slowly pealed the feminine garment down her slender hips shifting them left and right. The last dance had begun.

Releasing the fabric from her finger tips, it slid down her legs to her feet. Molly casually stepped out of it hesitating for a brief second in all her glory, then kneeling, she quickly clutched the petticoat to her and slowly returned to her feet.

Holding Bannocks eyes, she wiggled again, teasing. Buying every second she could, Molly demurely let the petticoat float to the ground then pointed at it with her toe. "There's your evil bed, you pathetic bastard. Find what victory in it you can. I will surrender my body but not my soul."

Mocking the gunman's own stance, she placed her hands on her hips and stared brazenly at him letting him know he held no fear for her.

Molly was beautiful, but Bannock was not the kind of man who valued beauty. He cared more for winning. In his lust for fame, he had wanted to humiliate her, to cower her, but Molly's courage cheated him, so now he would simply take her to spite Cole. There was still that. Bannock let his eyes drink from the lovely vision a moment longer. "I said dance."

Stretching her arms above her head, Molly lifted on her toes and slowly turned full around and around, twirling faster and faster, then coming to a sudden stop she faced him and grinned. "Ain't no music. The harmonica player is dead."

Wade admired her pluck. Snatching her wrist, he pulled her to him. His hand slid unjustly over her naked body, cupping her breast. It was not merely the pleasure of touching her, but more to let her know he could. In this moment he proclaimed his first victory over a Creed. It was a name he both hated and revered.

Instead of crying out in rebuke of his touch, Molly taunted. "For your sake, I hope you are better with a gun than you are with women."

She laughed in his face. "So you got a breast in your hand, you are just a little boy playin' at being a man."

Angered, Bannock backhanded Molly hard, knocking her to the ground. She landed on her hands and knees. Regaining her senses, she brushed her hair from her face and wiped the blood from her mouth.

Raising up on her knees Molly touched a finger to her lip and slowly traced the serpentine cut made by his ring. Her beautiful eyes darkened like a storm. "You killed my friend?" Molly dabbed at her own blood. "Annie had the same cut on her lip."

Unashamed, Bannock grinned remembering. "Your friend was a mite fragile." Taking a menacing step, he closed the distance. "Told you I like it rough."

Molly threw back her shoulders and came to her feet. "Then you will love this."

Shoving her hands against his shoulders, she lunged, knocking him off balance, then quickly taking a step back she drove her knee hard into his groin.

Bannock's eyes rolled upwards in agony. He dropped to his knees, but as he fell, he backhanded Molly hard across her cheek, spinning her full around.

She landed cat-like, her fingers coming to rest on a thick branch lying in the dirt. Grasping it, she swung the branch at Wade's head with all her might.

At the last second, the gunman caught her wrist deflecting the blow. It scraped down his jaw leaving a trail of bloody scratches.

Bannock struggled up pulling her to him. "Damn you whore." He squeezed her wrist until she dropped the club. Capturing her slender waist in his hands, he lifted her easily off the ground. "Oh you are going to be such fun."

Wade bit at her breast, but Molly grabbed his hair in her fists and shoved his head back then threw herself forward sinking her teeth into his ear. Howling, Bannock raised her above his head trying to tear her off. As he did, she spit his bloody earlobe into his face and laughed at his rage. She had chosen death over being any man's whore. Molly would go down fighting.

Furious, Bannock twisted her in the air intent on dashing her to the ground. He'd rape her broken body, but he would have her.

"Boss."

The gunman froze with Molly clutched in his grip above him. He roared at Buck who had walked in on his play. "Get the hell out of here ya' piss ant."

Not sure what to do, Buck took a step back. "There's a rider comin'."

Growling, Wade let Molly slide to his hip and held her firmly with one hand as he angrily waved Buck off with the other. "Get rid of him damn it, and don't come back."

Buck took another step away. "He's riding a tall blue roan."

For an instant Wade froze. The beautiful girl dangling in his arms, no longer mattered. Releasing his grip, Molly slid to her knees.

Bannock stared down the road, but his view was blocked by the trees. He turned back to Buck. "Is it...?"

Buck couldn't pull his eyes away from the naked girl. "I think so. I think it's him."

In less than a heartbeat, Bannock's demeanor changed. He was a gunfighter once again. This is what he'd been waiting for. A cold fire danced in his eyes. Killing Cole Creed would be a deed people remembered. They'd tell of the dashing pistoleer Wade Bannock and how he bested Creed's hand.

The young gunman's lust for fame was greater than his want of flesh. There would be other women, but only one Cole Creed.

Without warning his iron fist shot out striking Molly on the chin, then, grabbing her by the hair before she could fall, he took off in long strides dragging her across the ground, leaving her to find her feet. She struggled up with enough presence of mind to catch the blue satin dress as they went.

Clutching it to her body, Molly stumbled along on her bare feet next to Bannock almost running trying to keep pace. Suddenly they stopped. She followed the men's eyes to the rider not more than fifty yards away. It was Cole and her heart sank. Why had he come alone? Wade Bannock's wicked fast gun was known to him better than anyone. In her heart Molly knew the answer, but even now she struggled to deny it.

So many years she'd spent hating Cole, painting him as evil, but in this moment hanging naked in Wade Bannock's ruthless grip, she understood what Cole was fighting for. Her cruelty had been unjust. He didn't deserve to die this way.

Almost giddy with joy, Bannock danced like a schoolboy. "It's him Molly. It's him. It's Cole, I'll be go to hell Creed. Come to see me, Wade Bannock. Tell me I ain't important."

The hollow droning of hooves falling on the hard earth came to a stop. With the sun behind him, Cole sat tall with both hands pressed against the pummel of his saddle as he calmly took in the scene. Death could wait one moment more.

Bannock bounced on the ball of his feet unable to contain his excitement. "What the hell is he waiting for Molly?"
Wade spoke to her as if she shared his joy. "You are going to see who's the better man now Molly. I'll prove it to you. You'll see."

With Bannock chewing on a short fuse, Cole finally swung his long leg over the roan and dropped to the ground. There was something in the way he moved that said he was a different kind of man. He let go of the reins, then took the time to pat Brazo on the neck before calmly strolling towards the grotesque scene.

Everyone, friend and foe, was stunned that a man would ride in so boldly to his death. One by one each member of the unlikely troupe stepped up to an imaginary line waiting for the infamous Cole Creed.

Timidly, coming out of the shadow of the trees where his horse was saddled and ready to ride, Bobby Maxwell took his place to the far left holding Jean's hand tightly as she tugged him forward eager to see her uncle. If there was any hope for rescuing her mother, it was in this man she so desperately longed to know, yet after their night of hell she feared even he was not enough to stand against the heinous cruelty of Wade Bannock.

Still nursing his wounds, Pete Briscolm stood the middle ground no longer afraid of the tall man who humiliated him in the cemetery. He knew Bannock's fast hand and had no doubt who would win. When Cole lay dead on the ground, he'd would empty his gun into him just for spite.

To the left of the surly foreman stood Buck Taggard, a cowboy of no renown who followed orders without conscience. When the gunplay started, he would pull on Cole like the others; a jackal against a lion.

Standing confidently apart from the rest, Wade Bannock held Molly in his left hand. This was the moment he'd been waiting for since childhood. His days were spent honing his fast draw, dreaming of meeting Cole Creed in gallant battle. While most youths grew up wanting to be like their heroes; not so for Wade. In his injured mind, he had to kill Cole to become him.

Impatient, the gunfighter laughed hysterically dragging Molly forward by her hair. "Cole!"
Reaching across her, he ripped the satin dress from Molly's grasp and threw it aside. "Look what I done to your family."

Molly cried and tried to cover herself, but Bannock shook her violently making her dance on her toes. He laughed at her misery. "See what I done?"

To Bannock's dismay, Cole showed no reaction. Instead he coolly stared down the line at the other men.

Outdrawing Bannock was unlikely. Beating them all was impossible, yet Cole Creed was a dangerous man. That was the fear that unnerved them all.

Cole paused, admiring little Jean, standing bravely in a flimsy dancehall dress with a runny nose, and tears streaming down her cold cheeks. His heart went out to her, but she'd have to be brave a little longer.

At length he turned his eyes to Molly. Her hands hung limply by her side. She had nothing left to hide. With blood smeared across her face, a torn lip, her slender body stained by dirt and scratches, only a heart of stone could not be moved by her plight.

Weary beyond all measure, Molly slowly lifted her head and stared blankly through her tangled hair into Cole's piercing blue eyes. He nodded. "Mornin' Molly. You sure are pretty."
She held his gaze a moment longer, then dropped her head, no longer fearing what was to come.

Bannock opened his mouth to speak, but Cole cut him off addressing Pete instead. "I'm guessing your name isn't really Bob Wilson?"

The foreman sneered. "No it ain't, I'm Pete Briscolm, the judge's foreman, and I come to watch you die."

Nodding politely Cole allowed the man his contempt. "Well Mr. Briscolm we don't always get what we want. Perhaps your last minute here on earth would be better spent regretting how you treated my little Jean. If you have any remorse in your heart, you might find some comfort in telling her you are sorry before I put my bullet through your brain."

The foreman shuddered. Cole's matter-of-fact decree left him speechless. Bannock however thrilled at the talk of gunplay. "Bold boast...for a dead man."

Cole turned his steely eyes on the gunfighter. Bannock took a stepped backwards, then cursed. "Hell! You won't ever clear leather old man. You Creeds are all high n' mighty. This whore laughin' at me, well I ain't dirt."

He shook Molly for effect. "You stroll in here. Gunna' save your precious family when ya' know ya' ain't got no chance. That's just Creed stupid."

Cole shrugged. "Always a chance."

The gunman's irritation was visible. He had come to kill Cole and he'd wait no longer. "Say your piece old man and be done. I'll show you, show everyone there ain't no chance. I'm Wade Bannock the man who killed Cole Creed."

Unimpressed Cole slowly shook his head. "You're fast Bannock. Faster than me for what that's worth...but you are a lousy shot. Never had the discipline. Always in a hurry."

Bannock jolted, injured by Cole's contempt for his skill. In spite of Wade's murderous intent, Cole's opinion mattered to the young man. He sneered. "Yea! Yea...well there's a lot of dead men who'd say different." He hesitated, then boasted. "...one of 'em's your brother."

Molly opened her eyes. A painful question that had haunted her was finally answered, yet she would not waste her breath cursing this man. He wasn't worth it.

Cole showed no emotion either. "I always wondered. You ran away and hid about that time like the frightened kid you were. I'm guessing the Judge had you back-shoot old Paz and Miguel too."

Showing his arrogance, the gunman boasted. I killed that young greaser for myself, but I'm done back shootin' for the judge. After I kill you, everyone will know I can shoot, so you can go to hell if you think I'm a bad shot."

With cold confident Cole mocked the young man. "...there are plenty of men you missed."

Bannock took the bait. "Who?"

Cole took another step forward. "You emptied your gun into Carlos and only winged him. Was embarrassed for you myself, …you had Jimmy Webb dead to rights, and you missed his heart by a full three inches. Like I said, son you're a lousy shot."

Rising on her toes, Jean's voice squeaked. "Jimmy is alive?"

The tall man smiled at his teary-eyed niece and tipped his hat affirming her deepest hope. No one else noticed what Cole had done, but Bannock did.

The gunfighter tensed like a cat on hot coals. Cole had done more than tip his hat. He had lifted it off his head in a manner not normal for tipping a lady let alone a niece. More telling, Cole used his left hand.

Wade Bannock processed it all in less than the blink of an eye. Before Cole's hat was returned to his head, Bannock shoved Molly to the ground and went for his gun. Cole answered the challenge, but neither man had cleared leather when a round hole appeared in Wade Bannock's forehead. He teetered for a moment then collapsed as if his legs were chopped out from under him. A half second later a distant crack echoed through the valley proclaiming the gunfighter's death by another's hand.

Pete and Buck never saw Cole draw. Their own guns hung useless by their sides as Cole fanned his black .44 sending both men to hell. True to his words, he drilled Pete Briscolm through his brain. Before the foreman hit the ground Cole's sights were on Bobby Maxwell, but Jean jumped in front of the boy screaming. "No Uncle Cole."

Cole raised his sights above her and drew a steady bead. "Throw your gun away boy or I'll kill you where you stand."

Terrified, Bobby froze unable to move, but Jean took quick action. Pulling Bobby's pistol from his holster she threw it to the ground then stepped in front of the boy. Cole lowered his gun. "Brave as your mama."

Turning, he didn't bother looking down as he stepped over the dead body of Wade Bannock, giving a wasted life no merit. There were men faster than Cole Creed, but few deadlier. Playing fair doesn't count in a gunfight, a rule Bannock never learned. There was no glory in killing for Cole, never had been, it was his promise to protect. He'd come to save his family, that was all that ever mattered.

Calmly Cole holstered his pistol. His steady blue eyes gave up nothing, yet inside, his heart was aching. Before him huddling on the ground was the reason he'd rode out of Mexico.

Kneeling, he brushed the tangled hair from Molly's sweet face. A weak smile let him know she was okay. She struggled for a breath of air. "I knew you'd win Cole. Saw it in your eyes. It's who you are." He touched a knuckle to her cheek. "Nobody won, not here. Sorry for ruining your chance to see me die."

Her eyes darkening, Molly leaned against him. "I guess I deserved that."

Standing, Cole helped Molly to her feet. He held her in his arms for a moment and he breathed in her scent assuring him she was real. Her warmth, her softness, errant strands of hair touching his face, her heart beating against his chest; she was real.

At length he released her, then reaching down, picked up the blue satin dress. "You better put this on. Will is coming."

Molly shuddered. She looked off into the distance. Will was riding Brownie out of the trees with his back to the sun. Cole had planned everything down to the last detail. He knew exactly how it would end before he even rode in.

 She looked at the dead gunfighter, a sob for her son caught in her throat. "Oh Will."
Molly almost cried.

Though her son didn't know it, he had avenged his father's death. The irony was, John had given Will the gun the boy used to killed his own assassin. A day might come when she'd find some justice in it. For now, her family had survived was all that mattered.

Cole slipped his arm around her waist. "He's okay Molly. Like you n' me, he did what he had to for our family. Will's a Creed too."

Burdened with a mother's concern, Molly watched her son. When Brownie turned a little sideways, she saw baby Polly sitting before him. Shaking her head, Molly thought to herself. 'What an unlikely pair to come to a gunfight. Bannock never stood a chance.'
She looked out of the corner of her eye at Cole. "Surprised you didn't give her a gun too."
The big man grinned. "Who says I didn't?"

Leaning her hand on Cole's shoulder, Molly took the satin dress. "Help me. I need to be presentable. Looks like we got another hero in the family."

Bad Water
Chapter 29
The Long Ride

"Polly!" Jean reached up and took the smiling baby from her brother. This time it was tears of joy that streamed down the young girl's face. She bounced the baby and held her to her breast. "I missed you."

His rifle in hand, Will dropped down from the saddle. Taking his time, he looked at the dead man, then to his uncle. Cole knelt by the boy and mussed his hair. "You figure out what's important here and let the rest go."

Will nodded. "Yes sir. I already know. It's family."

"Will!" The boy turned to his mother, his eyes shining. "Hi Mama. Pretty dress."

Molly threw her arms around her son sobbing. "Will, you're talking."

He wrapped his arms around his mother's neck. "The bad men are dead. I don't have to be..."

Will went silent not wanting to upset her. Cupping her son's face, Molly smiled and finished his sentence. "...Bad Water." She kissed him. "It's alright. There's water that gives life too. You did what you had to."

"I know." The boy stared intently at his mother. "...like Uncle Cole." Molly lowered her head regretting the wasted years. Slowly she lifted her teary eyes to her son. "Yes Will. Just like your Uncle Cole."

Bobby and Will helped Cole tie the dead men over their horses, and then they rode off. Cole intended to dig their graves next to the main trail; a message to men like the Judge that no one should be so arrogant as to treat common folk like they don't matter.

When they were gone, Molly and Jean returned to the warm spring. Slipping off their satin dresses, they bathed and helped each other do their hair while baby Polly collected pine cones from the soft bed of needles beneath a tall spruce.

The girls found a bar of soap in the provisions sack which they immediately put to good use. Jean sat on a smooth rock in the stream soaping her slender legs while delightful thoughts played in her head. She suddenly spoke out-loud. "Will told me that Uncle Cole had him fetch Doc Hein to the farm to patch up Carlos and Jimmy. He said Carlos is taking care of both of them with his good arm, but Jimmy is confined to bed. Poor Jimmy. That's why Uncle Cole had to bring Polly with them; nobody to watch her."

Bending her knee to her chin, Jean scrubbed her leg. "Funny a man like Uncle Cole taking a baby to gunfight."

Molly laid back in the water and soaked her hair. "Your Uncle Cole is full of surprises."

Shifting to the other leg, Jean scrunched her shoulders and giggled. "Will said Jimmy told him that if they found us to tell me that he loves me."

She grinned. "It was hard for Will. He said mush."

Jean stopped soaping and stared forward. "Been so much hate...makes love all the more precious. Guess it's the most important thing."

Setting the soap down, Jean turned to her mother. "Mama. I... well… what you did for me. I love you Mama."

Reaching up from the water, Molly patted her daughter's knee but remained quiet. In two of the longest days of their lives they went through hell together. There were no words that could say it all. Filling with emotion, Molly silently rose to her feet and stepped out of the water. A pleasant midday breeze softly dried her skin while overhead brilliant white clouds floated in a serene blue sky.

Jean came to her side. "What Mama?"

Offering a soft smile, Molly took her daughter's hand. "Just noticing how different this little valley looks compared to a few hours ago. I think I could actually live here."

Jean leaned her head on her mother's shoulder. "We grew strong here Mama."

"We sure as hell did baby."

"Mama!" Jean reproached. "Uncle Cole will get mad if you swear."

Molly laughed. "Come on. Let's get dress. They will be coming back and I think enough people have seen me naked for one day."

Taking the blue satin dress in her hands Molly held it high. "You know they really are quite pretty."

Her eyes dancing, she looked at Jean and they both laughed shamefully. This time when they put the dresses on it would be their choice.

Holding the red dress at arm's length, Jean watched it sparkle in the sun. "Mama, do you ever get tired of cotton, I mean isn't being forced to live only one way...well we should belong to ourselves, and no one should lay a brand on us. We aren't whores, are we Mama?"

Molly stroked her daughter's cheek. "No baby we are not. What you are is inside of you. The dress doesn't make you beautiful; it's you who makes the dress beautiful."

Jean hugged the dainty garment to her and twirled. "I wish Jimmy was here to see me."

Enjoying a moment where they could finally be carefree, the girls played and modeled for each other. Jean beamed as her mother spun full around. "I think Uncle Cole will drool like a lovesick hound when he sees you all dolled up."

"Jean!" Molly tried to scold her but they both burst into giggles that wouldn't stop.

Jean snickered. "Well he will."

Beneath the pine, little Polly suddenly laughed with excited gibberish. When the ladies turned, Polly was standing, offering a pinecone to a squirrel, which to the child's dismay, snatched it and quickly ran away.

Laughing herself, Jean hurried to Polly's side. She stooped and picked the child up. "Mean ol' squirrel."

Jean tucked Polly under her chin and rocked her in her arms. She cooed while smoothing her short blond curls. "She needs a bath too!"

Molly smirked. "Could you see Cole or Will bathing a baby?"

Jean walked away with little Polly cuddled to her breast only to return. She grew serious. "Mama. Do you think I'm grown up? I mean I'm not a child any more. My body has changed...you know."

Coming to her daughter's side, Molly put an arm around her. "I know. You have grown into a beautiful young lady."

Lifting her eyes Jean searched her mother's face. "I mean I do my chores and cook and work right alongside you and everything."

Molly smiled patiently. "What are you trying to say Jean."

The girl suddenly blurted it out. "I want Polly. I want to raise her as if she was my own."

Her daughter's desire did not come as a surprise. Jean had always babysat for Annie. Every Sunday she happily tended Polly in church, and after services she was always reluctant to let her go.

Jean looked up pleading. "I've known her since the day she was born. Please Mama. I want her so bad."

Molly brushed her daughter's hair. "Raising a child is a big responsibility, and you will have Jimmy to take care of for a while."

Jean's eager face glowed with radiance. "Oh Mama, it will be so wonderful." She poured her heart out. "Will has kept food on the table and taken on the responsibilities of a man, protecting us and all. No one ever expects anything of me other than to be pretty, but I'm much more Mama. I'm as strong as Will and I'll be a good mother to Polly."

"I know you will darling. It's...it's just seeing my baby all grown up." Tearing, Molly wrapped her arms around Jean. "If I had any doubts about how strong you are, these last few days have wiped them away. You don't need my blessing. Polly has always been yours. It's what Tom and Annie would want. I'm proud of you."

"Oh Mama."

It was a short time later when Cole and the boys came riding down the grassy trail leading the rider-less horses, their empty saddles a silent footnote on this journey out of darkness.

Molly and Jean shyly stepped from under the shadow of the trees. Their hair was neatly combed and tied in shiny ribbons that matched their tightly cinched low-cut dresses. Black stockings and high-heeled shoes completed their risqué attire.

Eyeing the mischievous pair, Cole swung from the saddle. Molly folded her dainty hands in front of her and sashayed forward.

Gripping the reins, Cole felt his heart stir. He had not seen her like this. Something about Molly had changed and it was more than just the dress.

Coming closer she kept her head down hiding the blush on her cheeks. When she was nearly toe-to-toe she burst into a broad grin.

"Don't know what you're staring at cowboy, you already seen everything I got." She turned a shade redder.

Cole dropped the reins and took Molly's hand. "Can we walk?" Without saying anything Molly stepped to his side and leaned against him. He tried to not look down, but he knew she was smiling.

Pointing her toes as she strolled down the path, Molly adopted a feminine stride amused at seeing her own legs. Out of the corner of her eye she caught Cole admiring them too. She laughed and he quickly looked away.

The warm spring air under the midday sun was pleasant. In no hurry, they wandered beneath the scented pines getting comfortable with each other. So much needed to be said but Cole could not find the right words.

On this fateful morning when he had ridden down the hill to rescue her, he'd expected to find Molly angry as usual. Now a radiant smile on her face caught him off balance.

The wall he couldn't penetrate was gone, and there he was standing beside her. It was like wanting something your whole life, but knowing it would never happen, then one day it did.

Cole struggled to sort it out. There had been so much killing and sorrow, yet in this moment with Molly's soft warm hand in his, he couldn't think of anything else but her.

They walked a little further, then after a long silence, Cole suddenly realized Molly was waiting for him to speak. His breathing quickened. She was giving him a second chance.

Digging deep for courage he cleared his throat. "I buried a feller up there I didn't kill. Bobby said he was poisoned."

Molly took several steps ahead of Cole then turned and faced him. "Maybe I had a change of heart."

A perceptible smile danced on her red lips. She stepped closer resting her fingertips on his belt. "Having to protect someone you love will do that to you."

Edging nearer Molly leaned her forehead on his chest and went silent again.

Cole's hands felt large and clumsy as he took her by the waist. He hesitated still struggling to find the right words, then he filled his lungs. "Do you think you could have a change of heart about me?"

Lifting her head, Molly burrowed her chin against him and flashed a teasing smile. "Are you asking if I could stop hating you...or are you asking if I could love you?"

She felt his breath lock in his chest. Molly giggled. "You know you can put your arms around me if you like."

Moving in slow motion Cole pulled her to him. For the first time in Molly's life, she felt this brave man tremble. "Why Mr. Creed! Are you cold, or are you looking down my skimpy low-cut dress?" Cole grinned. "Ain't cold."

Molly lifted on her toes and coquettishly slipped her bare arms around his neck. "Well just to be safe, maybe you better warm yourself on my lips."

For a brief moment Cole stood frozen in time wondering if he'd heard her right, but as he looked down into her beautiful questioning eyes he lost all doubt. Wrapping Molly tightly in a warm embrace, he lifted her off the ground, and pressed his lips to hers in a slow tender kiss that confessed a love long hidden.

Since the first day he saw her in ponytails so many years ago he had loved her. Even in his denial, his heart beat the truth. He had stepped aside for his brother and watched silently pretending he didn't care, but now with her soft lips touching his, a love that was lost returned as gentle as a butterfly on an early spring breeze.

Leaning back, Cole exhaled. "I think that dress has made you shameless."

Molly slapped his chest. "No dress will ever change me." She grinned. "If you don't believe me you can take it off me and kiss me again."

A thin smile tugged at the corners of Cole's mouth. "You know it's not over yet."

Molly softly laid her head against his chest and closed her eyes. "For me it is."

She nuzzled closer. "You can fight for justice, that's what men do, but I've got what is important; my family. Nothing else matters."

Cole brushed the hair from her forehead and placed a kiss. "There's a lot to talk about."

She shook her head. "No there isn't. I'm a big girl Cole. Stop protecting me and think about what you got in your arms."

Cole hugged her tightly. "I've been thinking about what's in my arms most of my life."

His voice grew doubtful. "That family you are talking about... is there room in it for me?"

Molly's eyes sparkled. "Guess it's always been your family...kids are crazy about you, though I think they are looking for a father an' not an uncle."

For a long while he stared over her head coming to grips with what it all meant, then slowly he lifted her chin capturing her eyes. "What are you looking for Molly?"

Her face hungering in tense silence, Molly whispered. "A second chance."

Struggling with emotions she hid her head, then bravely looked up. "A second chance Cole, for me...for us...for love."

Cole kissed her fingertips. "Everybody deserves a second chance." He smiled softly. "...Love was always there waiting for you, but if you need to hear the words; I love you Molly. I never stopped loving you."

Taking her hand in his, he stepped beside her. "Molly let's go home."

About the Author

Duane Vadron Evans learned about life in a two room school near the family farm. His early years were spent on the edge of the Utah desert. The forgotten trails and lonely mountain held secrets of the past. As a young boy he often played hooky exploring the ghost towns and abandoned mines in search of their history. He formed a deep love of the land and the people who carved their homes in the wilderness.

Duane's father taught him about hunting and guns. In his youth, he could be found wandering in sagebrush or deep pines with a six gun strapped to his side. A favorite uncle fostered in Duane a keen understanding of mining and how to read the land's history from a rusty nail, a broken bottle or length of barbed wire. A mere handful of dirt could tell the story of the old west.

As a grown man, Duane moved to the deep South, making his home in a stone and log cabin on Black Warrior Mountain at the edge of the Sipsy Wilderness with his sweet Alice. They call their home Ravenwood. Here on the Cherokee Trail, he continues writing his stories with an authenticity that comes from having lived with his heart in the past.

Ravenwood was built by a Cherokee Chief from log cabins dating back to the 1700's. Duane and Alice have added a guest cottage and several gardens making it the perfect writer's retreat.

Made in the USA
Monee, IL
17 September 2021